Lulu's Café

Lulu's Café

T. I. LOWE

Tyndale House Publishers, Inc.
Carol Stream, Illinois

Visit Tyndale online at www.tyndale.com.

Visit T. I. Lowe at www.tilowe.com.

TYNDALE and Tyndale's quill logo are registered trademarks of Tyndale House Publishers, Inc.

Lulu's Café

Previously published in 2014 by CreateSpace Independent Publishing Platform under ISBN 978-1-4959-7475-5. First printing by Tyndale House Publishers, Inc., in 2019.

Designed by Julie Chen

Edited by Kathryn S. Olson

Published in association with the literary agency of Browne & Miller Literary Associates, LLC, 52 Village Place, Hinsdale, IL 60521

Scripture quotations are taken from the Holy Bible, *New International Version,*® *NIV.*® Copyright © 1973, 1978, 1984, 2011 by Biblica, Inc.® Used by permission. All rights reserved worldwide.

For information about special discounts for bulk purchases, please contact Tyndale House Publishers at csresponse@tyndale.com, or call 1-800-323-9400.

ISBN 978-1-4964-3950-5

Printed in the United States of America

25	24	23	22		
7	6	5	4	3	2

For any woman who has had to slay
a demon spawned by an abusive past.

In memory of Momma, Debbie Hardee.
I kept my promise.

Prologue

MOONLIGHT WASHED OVER the couple as they swayed in each other's arms in the cool water of the lavish pool. The humid country night air enveloped them in their own intimate world.

He gently kissed behind her right ear and then traced his fingertips along the thin scar tucked there. "I want to know about this," he whispered as he skimmed his lips over the scar.

Saying nothing, she shook her head.

He surprised her then by tapping the jagged scar she thought was hidden on her hip. "I want to know about this," he murmured into her ear.

How had he learned about that one? He looked up and gazed at her intensely. She detected a deep sadness in his ocean-colored eyes. She didn't want him to carry any part of the burden of her pain, but he had obviously taken it on anyway.

He pressed his lips to the faint scar tucked in her left eyebrow. "I want to know about this." He worked his way to the scar barely visible on her chin, which had been in the process of healing when she had arrived in town last fall. "I want to know about this."

He remembered.

He looked into her eyes as they swayed. He released her hip and pulled her scarred palm to his lips and brushed kisses over it. "I want to know about this." He pressed it to his pounding heart. "I *need* to know about this." The deep timbre of his voice was strained with emotion. Her body trembled from the longing in his voice.

Lastly, he traced the long scar across her bottom lip with his thumb. "I need to know about this," he said again.

Her breath hitched at the passion in his voice. Tears pricked her eyes. He was too observant and too persuasive. She laid her head on his shoulder to hide the tears. "Why do you need to know about some old ugly scars?" she mumbled against his shoulder.

He dipped into slightly deeper water so that she would have to raise her head and meet his eyes. "I need to know so I can help them heal." He brushed his hand over her cheek to wipe away her tears.

"Some scars don't ever heal," she whispered. "No matter how awfully bad you want them to. They're just too deep." She let him dance her to a gentle rhythm in the water for a while longer as she buried her face in the comforting crook of his neck.

As she held tight to him, his words began to resonate. It was time to take care of the past, even if it meant losing the future she would do anything to have.

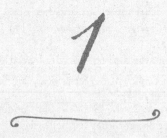

DONUTS . . . Donuts make everything better!

"It's a perfect morning for a perfect donut. Welcome to the Donut Diner. May I take your order?" asked the perky drive-thru attendant.

"Yes, I would like one dozen donuts and two small cappuccinos."

"That'll be $15.76. Please drive around."

Gabriella Sadler had been buying donuts from Shayna every week for the past year, ever since Shayna's parents had added the drive-thru to their shop. By now the young woman knew Gabby's favorites: Bavarian cream filled with chocolate ganache icing, lemon curd–filled powdered, and apple fritters.

"Oh . . . ," Shayna said on a gasp as she opened the window. "Wow, those are some really hot wheels you're sporting, Gabby." The young woman couldn't stop gawking at the shiny new Range Rover.

"Thank you." Nervous, Gabriella tried to hand the girl the money.

Instead of taking the cash, the young woman studied Gabriella as if seeing something she wasn't supposed to.

"Hmm, I get it. This is one of those make-up gifts, isn't it?"

"I guess you could call it that," Gabriella said. She gathered her scarf closer around her neck. *Stop asking questions and just give me the donuts.* "I'm in a bit of a hurry, Shayna."

"I knew it was a make-up gift. I need to find me a honey who can afford a new Range Rover. You are *so* lucky." Shayna giggled.

"You have *no* idea," Gabriella said under her breath and tried once again to pay for her order.

Shayna finally took the money and handed over the fresh treats and coffees. "I hope you and Mr. Sadler enjoy breakfast."

"Okay. Thanks." Gabriella carefully set the box on the luxurious leather passenger seat. After placing the coffees in the cup holders, she steered the SUV away without another word. All she wanted was to be alone to enjoy her donuts.

As she pulled out of the lot, she fished out a Bavarian cream. She scarfed down the fresh fried dough in three bites and washed it down with some of the sweet coffee. Feeling a bit better, she headed toward the market. Today was Thursday, and Thursday was designated as grocery shopping day.

As she parked at the far end of the lot, her phone rang. She reluctantly pulled the phone from her purse and cringed at the name on the display.

"Hello?"

"Where are you?" Brent asked in his cool, controlling voice.

"I'm almost at the market." Her stomach knotted as she sat there staring at the building in question. Her mouth watered as her fingers worked the donut box lid off. One of the apple fritters screamed her name. It was all she could do not to dig in at that moment, but he would know what she was doing. She didn't feel up to the tongue-lashing that would surely follow.

"You have one hour to be back home." Brent hung up.

"I hate you," she whispered into the phone before throwing it back in her purse.

She moved her seat back to make room for the donut box on her lap and then indulged in the remaining treats. She loved the privacy of the tinted windows on the silver Range Rover. It made her feel like she was in her own bubble. She refrained from inhaling the apple fritter in three bites. She savored each bite and then continued on to the homemade strawberry jam–filled one. It practically melted in her mouth. She washed the lemon curd–filled donut down with the rest of the first cup of coffee. Trying to fill the void in her life, she moved through the donuts until the box was empty and both coffees were drained. Then the dread of what she had just done pointed its disapproving finger at her.

After taking a few difficult breaths, Gabriella checked for donut crumbs and reapplied her lip gloss. Easing out of her vehicle, she gathered her trash and placed it in the receptacle she had purposely parked beside.

Just as she entered the sliding doors of the market, a wave of nausea and dizziness from the donut binge rushed over her. As she worked to regain her composure, she glanced at her surroundings. Standing at the produce area near the entrance was a group of local hens, clucking away. She couldn't avoid them. They had already spotted her, and there was no escape.

"Look who just waddled through the door." The tall brunette named Junie smirked.

"What in the world does Brent see in Gabby? I mean— really. Look at her." Sara wrinkled her nose.

"What?" asked their clueless friend, Hannah. "I think

she looks like a porcelain doll with that creamy skin and beautiful hair." She shrugged as the other two laughed.

"More like a fat porcelain doll," Junie said.

"Hello, Gabby. Honey, I just love that scarf. It really makes that big ole trench coat pop," Junie said in her sweetest voice as she watched Gabriella grab a cart.

Gabriella barely glanced at them as she walked over to the tomato section. She tried to force the tears to stay at bay. "Thank you," she mumbled. She wasn't stupid, but she didn't feel up to being sassy back. She heard them snicker as she moved on to the fruit section. Sweat beaded on her top lip and the wooziness grew more intense. She knew better than to eat all those donuts in one sitting, but she just couldn't bring herself to toss any of them. Next time, she would only order a half dozen.

The hens moved to the checkout line, so Gabriella tried to focus on the task at hand. A wave of nausea slammed into her so forcefully she had to abandon her cart and rush to the restroom. She barely made it into a stall before vomiting up the donuts and cappuccinos. Severe pain radiated from her sore neck, causing another sudden bout of retching. She braced both sides of her neck and held her hair back at the same time. After the heaving passed, she flushed the toilet. *What a waste.*

Snapping out of the fuzz of the sugar overdose, Gabriella slowly moved to the sink to wash out her mouth. She glanced at herself in the mirror with disgust. She knew this qualified as an eating disorder. She gingerly rubbed her throbbing neck, feeling hopeless as to how to escape any of it.

Knowing that time was rapidly ticking away, she made her way back to the produce section to retrieve her cart. She placed everything on the list—yogurt, fresh fish, lean steak, fruits and vegetables, gourmet coffee, and skim milk—in the buggy. Brent was very specific as to what brands Gabriella could purchase and was adamant she keep to his precise list. She also gathered items on a mental list consisting of Oreos, Fudge Rounds, Snickers bars, Twinkies, and canned soda.

Trying to pick a new cashier, Gabriella made her way to the cash register. She separated the two orders, paying with a credit card for the things on Brent's list and paying cash for her own. As the cashier bagged the junk food, Gabby looked around; she was relieved not to recognize any faces. Taking a deep breath, she made her way to the Range Rover, loaded the groceries, and headed home.

Home was an ultra-sleek loft in downtown Olympia, Washington. It probably had once been a nice rustic space with exposed brick and worn wood floors, but there was no evidence of that now. Everything was modern with crisp, straight lines and a monochromatic color scheme of grays and whites. The only other color that was sparsely placed throughout the loft was a deep orange. To Gabriella, nothing looked inviting. The furniture was more for design than function; there was no give to the surface when you sat on the couch or on the linear chairs. It was a space that rarely had any visitors.

As Gabriella pushed through the doorway, her phone began to ring. Sheer terror shot through her, knowing it was only rings away from going to voice mail, so she dropped the bags and rummaged through her purse for the phone. Fumbling to hit Answer, she spoke before the phone was even to her ear. "I'm here."

"You're late."

"No!" She rushed to explain, "I was in the bathroom."

"What's wrong with your voice?" Brent's voice rose with impatience.

Well, let's see . . . you nearly choked me to death this week, you sick monster. I tried to forget it by downing a dozen donuts and two cappuccinos. I got violently sick, and now I'm worse for the wear because of it. Gabriella pulled herself together.

"My throat and neck are pretty sore," she said quietly. "Brent, I think I need to go to the doctor." She knew he wouldn't allow it, but she hoped this would get him off her back.

"Just give it a few days. You'll be fine." He almost sounded remorseful. *Almost.* "Did you pick up the fish like I asked?"

Gabriella rolled her eyes. "Yes."

"Good. My flight is scheduled to land a little after five. I want fish and sautéed vegetables served at seven."

"Okay," she said, but he had already hung up. "I hate you," she whispered into the phone as she stared at her reflection in the shiny black-lacquered cabinet in the kitchen.

Gabriella considered how her life had been a nightmare from the very beginning. *After surviving the foster care system, aren't I due some goodness in my life? Instead, I've moved out of hell and taken up residence with the devil himself in his fancy loft.*

After putting away the regular groceries, she grabbed her junk food bags and headed for the guest bedroom closet that served as a storage closet. It was also Gabriella's holding cell when Brent couldn't take the sight of her anymore. She poured the individually wrapped snack cakes into empty shoe boxes and hid the other treats and soda in the far corner where extra water bottles were stashed. She gathered all of the packaging, carried it outside, and stuffed it into her neighbor's trash bin.

Once she made her way back inside, she glanced at

the clock. She had about seven hours before beginning supper. She popped a couple of Tylenol PMs and headed to bed, hoping to escape the world for a while. She set her alarm clock and wiped away a tear. Her neck ached and her soul felt broken. She slipped off the scarf that concealed the deep-purple bruises and gently rubbed her neck as she stretched out on the bed. She mentally began to sing her theme song, "Fly Away" by Lenny Kravitz, as she waited for the medicine to kick in.

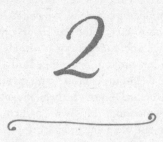

A groggy Gabriella turned the alarm off and made her way to the shower. Making herself presentable was the first task before starting supper. After allowing the scorching water to massage her tender neck, she stepped out and dried off. She plugged in the flat iron, another one of Brent's demands—*Your hair is to stay a deep, dark red and as straight as possible. No curls, ever.* Once she finished that task, Gabriella moved to the large master closet to find suitable attire for Brent's return home. She chose a high-neck sweater, then thought twice about it and selected a scoop-neck blouse that would remind him of the bruises. She didn't want to provoke Brent, but she hoped he would keep his hands to himself. After sliding on black lounging pants and touching up her makeup, she headed for the kitchen to prepare supper.

She glanced at her watch. There was time for a short detour to the guest room closet. Her anxiety over Brent's return was overwhelming. She opened the closet door and sat cross-legged on the floor. With shaky hands, she dug out a few snack cakes, hoping the treats would give her the courage to get through the night. She ate two and then stared at the empty wrappers. Pangs of guilt and loneliness returned. She fished out a candy bar. Surely the chocolate would do the trick. By the last bite the usual remorse showed up.

Defeated and ashamed of herself, Gabriella left the closet and headed to the unreceptive kitchen to mindlessly begin the tasks at hand.

Supper awaited on the modern dining table as Brent entered the front door. He dropped his luggage and briefcase onto the floor and faced Gabriella. She plastered on her best smile and hid her trembling hands behind her back as he assessed her appearance. His eyes lingered on her neck for one brief moment before he turned his attention to the meal.

"Go change that top." Brent took his place at the table without another glance in her direction.

Gabriella quickly slipped into the bedroom and traded it for the sweater. She was glad this was the only response she had received. Her neck throbbed, and she hoped that the other top had accomplished its purpose of keeping him at bay for the night.

She returned to the dining table to discover Brent had almost completed his meal. She took her seat beside him and tried to be pleasantly silent, as he preferred. When she reached for her fork, she noticed the tremor of her hand and tried to calm it before he noticed.

"You need to get the kitchen cleaned," Brent said.

Gabriella was about to take her first bite of fish. She hesitated and then decided to take the bite. Before she could blink, Brent backhanded her, sending her flying out of her chair. She lay there, one hand caressing her throbbing cheek while the other one held her sore neck.

She held the bite of fish in her mouth and didn't know whether to spit it out or swallow. With her neck freshly jostled, she didn't know if she *could* swallow. The fish seemed to be growing in her mouth, but she felt like she had no other choice.

Gabriella managed to get herself upright and began to clear the table as Brent made his way to their room to shower. She hoped it would sober him some. He was always harder on her when he was drinking, and tonight he smelled like a bar. She didn't need to guess where he had gone until it was time for supper.

She spit the fish back on her plate, and without eating anything, she meticulously cleaned the kitchen and dining area before Brent returned for his nightcap.

She had already poured his usual, bourbon on the rocks, when he strode back into the room. His dark hair was still damp from his shower, and he was wearing only a pair of black night pants.

Brent was a good-looking man who found great satisfaction in keeping himself in impeccable shape. If only that were enough. It was in the beginning. She couldn't believe how shallow she had been with her choice of him, looking no further than the handsome shell and dollar signs.

Looking back, Gabriella tried blaming it on her circumstances. After spending a childhood shuffling between foster homes and children's group homes, she found herself living on the streets of Chicago at only age eighteen. It didn't take long before she hooked up with some girls heading to Vegas to begin their careers as dancers. Gabriella had no desire to be in any spotlight, but she fell into waitressing pretty easily. That only lasted four months before she jumped on the Brent Sadler ride to hell.

He had sauntered into the casino with confidence and charm that night and couldn't keep his eyes off Gabriella. After a few hours passed, he finally motioned her over. He stood to greet her as she reached him in the congested place.

"It's entirely your fault," Brent had said as his dark eyes took in every inch of Gabriella. She could tell he appreciated the way the casino uniform of hot pants and a skintight, glittery tank top emphasized her shape.

"I'm sorry. I don't understand." Although he sounded seductive, the statement had confused her.

"I've lost every bet I've made tonight because of you distracting me with those mile-long legs," he whispered into her ear as he ran his hand up her thigh.

Gabriella playfully slapped his hand away. "Sounds like your fault, sweetheart. Not mine." She intentionally sashayed in the direction of the bar, knowing he was following her closely.

Once they reached the bar, he put his arms around her waist and gently turned her to face him. "No. It's absolutely your fault, and I think you need to make it up to me," Brent said. "What time do you finish your shift?"

"Midnight." Gabriella could barely breathe. The cool confidence this gorgeous man emitted had hypnotized her. With the cut of his white dress shirt, unbuttoned at the collar, and expensive black dress slacks, he looked like a promising companion for the evening.

By the end of the night, Gabriella found herself in his penthouse suite. And by the next morning, Brent had talked her into marrying him and going back to Washington, where he promised to take care of her for the rest of his life. The man had worshiped her in the short time they had been together. He was older by fifteen years, and Gabriella found him and his promises absolutely irresistible.

Before making the trip to her new home and life, Brent had an agenda for them to complete. They shopped for an entirely new wardrobe, which he handpicked for Gabriella with the assistance of the salesladies, in expensive boutiques. The salesladies and Brent showered her with compliments on how everything fit so well on her long, lean body. He would slip into the dressing room and run kisses down her neck and stare at them both in the mirror. Their opposite appearances—her with pale-blonde hair and ice-blue eyes and him with a shock of dark-brown hair and brown eyes—contrasted each other beautifully.

"We even look like we belong together, baby. You're perfect for me." He intoxicated Gabriella with the lavish attention. She had never felt loved until meeting this stunning man.

After the shopping spree, a complete spa pampering followed. She had her nails and toes professionally done for the first time and also experienced her first massage. She was eager for this gift of a new life, so Gabriella gladly agreed to have her hair dyed to a deep red after Brent and the stylist insisted that it was the perfect color to bring out the color of her eyes.

Once her entire body was polished and her new dark-red hair had been perfectly straightened, Brent whisked Gabriella away to the closest wedding chapel to officially make her his property—as he called her. In those few short days, he completely erased who she was and made her exactly what he wanted. Being only eighteen and neglected for so long, Gabriella had welcomed the change. It all felt like a fantasy come true. A Prince Charming rode into town in his fancy sports car and rescued the poor damsel stuck in a casino tower.

Brent had paid the wedding officiant a hefty bonus to omit certain details about her on the marriage certificate. Although her full name was Leah Gabriella Allen, the marriage certificate stated that Gabriella Allen had wed Brent Donavan Sadler. Brent told her he was a very powerful businessman, and he did this to protect her privacy. He would put up with no one bothering his bride in any way whatsoever. She agreed to it all and never asked a single question.

If she'd only known then what she knew now. As she watched him retrieve the glass from the counter and take a gulp, Gabriella thought of how easy it would be to simply poison the jerk and be freed of her prison life. Disgusted with herself, she quickly dismissed the absurd thought. No matter how rough this situation was, he was her husband.

He quickly finished his drink and then met her gaze. His glassy eyes bored into hers. "You like what you see, baby?" His lips curled into the familiar sneer.

Uh-oh. She hadn't meant to stare as she tried dissolving the ugly thought of killing him.

Before she could answer, Brent sauntered over and pulled her close. He gave her a deep kiss that stung her tongue with the sharp taste of the alcohol that was still so fresh in his mouth. He grabbed her by the back of her head to deepen the kiss even more, making Gabriella wince and cry out from the pain in her neck.

It had been four days since the incident, and her neck felt no better. He had shaken her violently for forgetting to pick up the dry cleaning that afternoon. Then he had lost his cool because supper was five minutes late due to his act of rage. It was her fault, always her fault. When she bent slightly beside him to place his plate on the table, Brent had grabbed her by the neck and choked her until she passed out.

When she came to, Gabriella had been horrified to find Brent still sitting at the table, finishing his supper, as she lay on the floor next to his chair. She continued to lie there, not knowing if she could manage to move with her neck in pain, until he demanded that she get up and take care of the mess.

Pushing the memory away, she tried to focus on the new threat before her. "Please, Brent. My neck is hurt badly. I'll do whatever you want. Just *please* be easy—"

He grabbed her jaw to shut her up. "Maybe you should spend a few days in the closet so you can let your neck recover!" In a drunken rage, he began pulling her toward the guest bedroom.

"But the New Hope Children's Home benefit supper is tomorrow night." It was a hopeless plea. She knew he wouldn't let her help with the one thing dear to her heart.

Brent sneered. "Guess you'll think twice next time before you talk back to me. Those brats will have to make it without you, my dear."

Gabriella ended her appeal. There was no point in it. "Please, Brent. Please let me use the bathroom first. I won't give you any more trouble. I promise."

To her surprise, he gave in and let her go. "You have one minute."

She hustled inside to do her business. While she was washing her hands, she eased the medicine cabinet open and fished out the Tylenol PM bottle from the back. She stuffed it in her bra and made her way back to Brent, who was waiting in the hallway. She willingly walked into the closet and turned to look at him. His chocolate-brown eyes were rimmed red and had an evil glare to them. He leaned on the doorjamb and watched her for a few moments. She made a step in his direction, wanting to close the distance and make him love her. He slowly shook his head at her advance, so she stood still.

"You could prevent all of this if you would just do as

you should," he said in a tired voice. "You always make everything so difficult." He closed the closet door in her face.

Gabriella's shoulders automatically sagged when she heard the all-too-familiar click of the closet door locks. She stood numbly in the middle of the narrow closet until she heard Brent close the bedroom door. She knew he wouldn't return anytime soon. The pain pulsing from her neck, all the way down her back, was reaching an excruciating crescendo. She tried adjusting to being in total darkness and felt around the top shelf for a U-shaped pillow she had placed there a few years ago. Someone from Brent's office had given it to him as a Christmas present, thinking it was a reasonable gift for someone who flew frequently. Of course, Brent would never be caught using the silky pillow. Gabriella had held on to it and now was relieved to have a makeshift neck brace. She slid it off the shelf and wrapped the soft, cool pillow around her angry neck.

Exhausted, Gabriella tossed extra pillows and blankets onto the floor. She rummaged around the edge of the closet for a bottle of water. She kept more than she needed hidden in the closet at all times. Not doing so was a mistake she had made only once, a few years back. By the time Brent had released her, she was so severely dehydrated that he had no choice but to take her to the emergency room. That was only the second time he had allowed such a trip. He blamed the dehydration on a nasty bout of stomach flu, and Gabriella had weakly agreed with him.

The other visit to the ER happened about two years into their marriage. Gabriella was to meet up with Brent after work for a gala. She had worn an exquisite emerald gown with gold stilettos. Brent, equal to her normal height of five foot eleven, was horrified to discover the shoes made her tower over him. He made her stand at the opposite side of the room from him for the whole evening. Once they returned to their loft later that night, a drunken Brent argued with Gabriella about how she had embarrassed him. As she walked up the stairs in front of him, trying to get away from his rage, he grabbed her by the hair and slung her back down the stairs. The fall resulted in a broken ankle that required surgery. Gabriella was on the couch for six weeks, and so began her humiliating weight gain.

Sitting in the dark closet now, Gabriella pulled the pills out of her bra. It was almost a full bottle. After shouldering so much unbearable physical, mental, and emotional pain, she weighed the decision to finish off the pills and just be done with it. It was so tempting to go to sleep and never have to wake up in her nightmare again. Brent hated her. She hated her. She had no one.

She shook three pills out into her palm and popped them in her mouth. She washed them down with a drink of water and shook three more pills into her palm. Tears streamed down her face as she caressed the pills in her hand. She wanted this so badly, but she couldn't bring herself to do it.

"You are such a coward. I hate you," Gabriella whispered in the dark as she put the pills back into the bottle.

She repositioned the neck pillow and tried to settle in for the undetermined length of her sentence. As she waited for the medicine to take effect, Gabriella continued her verbal assault on herself, naming all the reasons why she was a loser and why she deserved the life she was living. No one hated Gabriella Sadler more than Gabriella herself.

Her first visit to the closet came to mind as she tried

to get comfortable. She had only been married to Brent for about five months when she decided to change her hair color back to blonde as a surprise for him. When he had come home, she received her first beating and was thrown into the closet. He said he couldn't stand to look at her. A shocked Gabriella was trapped in the closet for two days with no food or water. Shamefully, she ended up soiling her clothes. Once he let her out, Brent had begged for her forgiveness, saying that he didn't know what came over him. He had promised to never do such a thing again. He bought her a new diamond bracelet to make up for his wrongdoing. A young and naive Gabriella believed him.

The next stay came as a punishment for a guy speaking to her at the gym. Along with the closet stay, Brent canceled her gym membership. As she lay in a ball on the floor of the closet with wet pants, all she could think of was the saying "Fool me once, shame on you. Fool me twice, shame on me."

Gabriella thought Brent was just going through a difficult time and that it would all pass. This was what she told herself, even as she focused on the closet doorknob. A lock had been purposely placed on the outside of the door. A wave of confusion, followed by understanding, had sliced through her at the realization of the premeditation. She had hoped she was the first to endure the closet.

After Brent released her the second time, Gabriella began hiding items in the closet for her stays. As she was hiding a coffee can with a lid for a makeshift portable potty, she slumped to the floor, confused by her own actions. Her instincts were telling her to run and never look back, but then where on earth would she go? She had no one and nothing. She felt trapped and helpless.

So instead of running, she tried to make the situation as comfortable as she could.

Gabriella woke hours later with her entire body throbbing. She was so tired of hurting. She lay there for a few moments, trying to force her weary body to move. She felt around for the watch. She found it and hit the button on the side to illuminate the face. It was nine in the morning. Relieved that Brent was gone for the day, she fished out the large flashlight and moved herself to a sitting position. After a wave of dizziness passed, she reached over to check the lock on the closet door. Not surprisingly, the door remained locked. Every morning in the closet began with the torturous hope of being released. Brent never unlocked the door while Gabriella was awake. She guessed it was his way of not having to face the *elephant* he locked up, so to speak.

Her next order of business was to take care of business. After that she pulled out a toothbrush, toothpaste, and a bottle of water. The closet routine had become second nature after ten years. Once she had her teeth clean, she wiped her body off as best she could with a few baby wipes. She checked the watch and found that only twenty minutes had crept by. As if knowing she needed something to do, her stomach growled. She gave in and dug out a bag of Oreos.

"Breakfast of champions," she murmured before popping a cookie into her mouth. She indulged in about half the bag before putting them away. A Twinkie was next, followed by two candy bars. She washed it all down with a can of warm soda. Ashamed, Gabriella put the junk food away. She rechecked the time, only to find that breakfast had taken all of ten minutes. She decided on two more Tylenol PMs and settled once more on the makeshift bed.

The next two days passed in a foggy routine of checking the lock, eating junk food, crying, more pills, and restless sleep. By the third day, all of the Tylenol PM and water were gone. Feeling grimy and slightly panicked, Gabriella dug out a hidden screwdriver and picked the lock. After hearing the familiar release of the catch, she breathed a quick prayer of thanks at being able to get out, only to discover that Brent had fastened the child safety latch above the door.

Nothing could describe the relief Gabriella felt when, on the fifth morning, she found the closet door unlocked. She swung the door open and drank in the cool, fresh air of the open room. Slowly, she stood and headed to the sink faucet in the guest bath, where she drank greedily from it. After several gulps, she splashed her face with the refreshing water. As she stood up to stretch her aching back, she caught a glimpse of a tangled, redheaded monster, with hideous black rings under its eyes, reflecting from the mirror. She studied herself for a minute, realizing that her light-blonde hair was beginning to peek through again. At least the bruises had finally disappeared enough that she could go to the salon.

Gabriella headed to the master bedroom to retrieve her phone. She needed to figure out what day it was and what appointments she had to reschedule. As she grabbed it out of her purse, her hand came upon her packet of birth control pills. She pulled it out and popped one in her mouth. Missing the daily pill for the past four days had led to a poorly timed period. At least it wasn't a heavy one, or so she tried to reassure herself while imprisoned. After plugging her phone into the charger, she rescheduled her hair appointment for first thing the following

morning. She knew her less-than-perfect hair would set
Brent off.

She retrieved a garbage bag and took care of the closet.
Once she had it cleaned out, she added an entire case of
water she previously had stored in the pantry and a newly
emptied coffee can. She placed the garbage by the front
door to take out later. Fatigue was already trying to set
in, so she headed to the kitchen for some real sustenance.
Bypassing the enormous bouquet of white roses and the
large, beautifully wrapped gift box—Brent's token apology—that were on the kitchen island, Gabriella went
straight to the coffeepot. The apology would have to wait
until later. After starting the coffee, Gabriella popped two
slices of bread in the toaster and began heating a skillet.
While she cooked six eggs, she munched on buttered toast
and gulped down a cup of coffee. She feasted on more
toast and coffee with the eggs.

After starting in on a third cup of coffee, Gabriella got
some wits about her. She made quick work of cleaning the
kitchen and living room, as well as the bathrooms. As she
straightened the master bedroom, she noticed a spread of
several one-hundred-dollar bills and a book of matches
from Vegas on top of Brent's dresser. The evidence lay
before her that he'd not only locked her up but also left
her alone. Sadly, it didn't even surprise her. Shaking her
head, she swiped four of the hundred dollar bills and
added them to her stash behind her dressing table. Brent
was terrible at keeping up with his money, which worked
to Gabriella's advantage. He would give her large sums of
cash to deposit in their banking account, without count-
ing it himself. She had no idea how he came up with
such cash, and she had a nagging feeling that she really
didn't want to know. It was nothing for her to swipe a few
thousand dollars with no detection from him. Over the

past few years, Gabriella had been able to hide a nice bit. Although she knew it was enough to take off with, she was terrified to actually go through with it.

Unable to stand her own stench any longer, Gabriella headed for a long, hot shower. She stopped by the washing machine and tossed her top and bra inside. She knew the bloodstains on her panties and pants would be next to impossible to remove, so she added them to the garbage bag.

As Gabriella numbly went through the routine of straightening her curly hair and applying makeup, the ringing phone broke the silence and startled her. Silence had become a constant companion. She went days without hearing one single word from anyone.

"Hello?"

"Yes, Mrs. Sadler? This is Mr. Sadler's secretary. He asked me to inform you that he will have supper delivered tonight so that you can have the night off." The secretary seemed pleased to relay the pleasant message.

"Okay. Thank you." This was another part of the making-up ritual. At least it wasn't a new vehicle this time. Gabriella had adored the gifts in the beginning, but as she'd matured over the past ten years, this act only made her feel cheap.

After hanging up the phone, Gabriella decided to explore the gift box waiting for her attention in the kitchen. She took the luxuriously wrapped box back to the bedroom and sat down on the only comfortable surface in the loft, the bed. Once the silver paper was removed, Gabriella pulled an emerald-colored silk nightgown and matching robe out of the box. The gown was long and elegant, with a built-in bodice. She cringed when she discovered that the size, 18, was correct. Embarrassment coursed through her as she realized Brent had to take such a large piece of lingerie to a counter to be purchased. How dreadful it must have been for him to have a slim, young salesclerk ring up his purchase in none other than a lingerie store. Gabriella was sure the saleslady pitied such a fine-looking man for being stuck with a plus-size wife.

As she looked at the gown, she believed that Brent had to love her. Why else would anyone choose to be with a fat nobody? What possible reason could he have but *love*? She re-dressed in the gown and robe, and then she touched up her makeup. Staring at her reflection, she vowed to do her best to please Brent. Surely she could never find a better man than him. Gabriella was in love with Brent, and she needed him. These thoughts, along with other tangled thoughts of trying to stay alive, played through her head in loops.

She glanced at the clock and realized it was nearly time for Brent to arrive home, so she made her way to the liquor cabinet to prepare his drink. Needing some encouragement, she took two shots of the bourbon and plastered a smile on her face. Soon after, the door opened and Brent sauntered in. She handed him his drink, but he declined it with a rueful shake of his head.

"I'm trying to cut back." He wrapped his arms around her softly and nuzzled her neck. "I've missed you, baby."

Gabriella drank in his affection. She could happily spend a week wrapped in his comforting arms. "I've missed you more," she said against his shoulder.

"I love this color with your hair." He held her at arm's length long enough to inspect her attire before pulling her back into his embrace.

"Thank you. It's beautiful."

"Only the best for my baby," he whispered in her ear, sending goose bumps down her body. This man, the one who could beat her down to nothing, could also make her feel like the most important woman in the world. This was the man she fell madly in love with. Although he didn't visit much, it was more than worth it when he did. He could spellbind her with one look or turn that same face into pure terror.

Brent pulled Gabriella's face close and gently kissed her. Tasting the unexpected bourbon on her lips, he pulled away and grinned at her. "You started our party without me? I guess I could have one drink with you." He smiled wickedly as he reached for the glass.

Gabriella wished she had not indulged in the alcohol now. She was not a drinker. From her time waitressing in Vegas, as well as witnessing Brent's drunken rages, she was totally against it. Now, in one weak moment, she was afraid she might have ruined the evening and would have to deal with drunken Brent and not her sweet Brent. He was rarely able to stop with one drink.

But she was lucky tonight. After his third bourbon, Brent pulled Gabriella toward their bed, where they spent the rest of the night making up for the closet visit. Supper was delivered and later thrown away, untouched.

Brent took these apology nights seriously. It was as if he thought he could wipe her memory completely clean of his crimes against her. She knew she should stand up to him and demand that they talk about getting him some help. She knew she should file a report against him. She knew it had to stop, but when he loved her, she couldn't turn the affection away. To feel significant on nights like that was irresistible. She thought this was true love. It *felt* like true love . . .

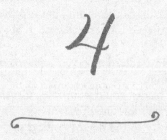

DONUTS . . . Donuts make everything better!

"It's a perfect morning for a perfect donut. Welcome to the Donut Diner. May I take your order?" Shayna asked from the drive-thru speaker.

"You took the words right out of my mouth," Gabriella responded.

"Hey, Gabby. The usual?"

"Yes. But could I change one coffee to a milk?"

"Sure. Drive around."

Gabriella had hoped the large sunglasses would sufficiently hide the bruises and her swollen nose. But apparently not.

"Oh . . . ," Shayna muttered after she opened the window. "Wow, Gabby. What happened to you?"

Gabriella nervously laughed it off as she tried to shield her face with her hair. "I tripped into a stupid table and nearly took my face off in the process."

"You're the clumsiest woman I have ever met. Is your nose broken?" Shayna asked, suspicion creeping into her voice.

"I don't think so." Gabriella handed over the money.

Shayna passed the box of warm donuts and the coffee

through the window. Once Gabriella set those down, Shayna passed the bottle of milk but kept her grip on it. As Gabriella tugged for her to release it, Shayna gave her a knowing look.

"Does Mr. Sadler know yet?" Shayna asked as she released the milk.

Before Shayna could continue, Gabriella quickly rolled up the window and drove off.

On the way to the doctor's office, she enjoyed half the box of donuts and saved the rest for the way home. She was already nervous, and now she was a bit frazzled with Shayna figuring it out so easily. Gabriella hadn't had a period since that last extended stay in the closet, a little over two months ago. Her body felt all out of sorts, and she was pretty certain she was pregnant.

Brent had been relatively good lately, so Gabriella had been starting to feel confident about telling him the news. He had made it very clear from the start there was no room for children in his life plan. She tried to broach the subject three days ago. That led to her busted face and a one-night stay in the closet.

After her release, Gabriella secretly made the doctor's appointment. She was too worried to wait for her face to heal before getting checked out. She would have to start her relationship with her new obstetrician with lies. Shayna was good practice, but even she hadn't bought it. The makeup seemed to be enhancing the swelling and bruising instead of camouflaging it. Gabriella decided she would go Hollywood-style and keep her sunglasses on until she was tucked into an exam room.

Since it was Thursday, she used her grocery-shopping time for the appointment. Before leaving that morning, she'd made arrangements to have groceries delivered to the loft around one. She'd used the delivery service before when she was down with her ankle. She also set up a post office box before hitting up the donut shop so she could have an address for the medical forms. After her appointment, Gabriella was determined to put together a solid plan to escape Brent. She had to, for the baby's sake.

As she pulled up to the medical office, her phone rang at the designated time. "Hello?"

"Hey, baby. Have you made it to the market yet?" Brent asked.

"Just pulled up." She hoped the quiver in her voice didn't reveal the lie as she stared at the medical plaza. "Is there anything else you need?"

"No. Just checking on you. Are you wearing your new earrings?"

Gabriella glanced in the rearview mirror and studied the one-carat diamond earrings sparkling on her earlobes.

"Yes. They're beautiful. Thank you again." She tried to sound genuine but knew she fell flat.

"Have supper ready at seven." Brent hung up.

"I hate you," she whispered into the phone before placing it in her purse.

Taking a deep breath, Gabriella exited the Range Rover and made her way into the medical suite identified as the office of Dr. Clara A. Simmons, ob-gyn. Ignoring the receptionist's stare, Gabriella prepared to tackle the medical history forms. Before she could sit down, a nurse ushered her into an available exam room. She was impressed at how fast the place operated. By the time she removed her sunglasses, a tall woman with coffee-colored skin and a funky yet neatly kept Afro entered. The embroidered name on her white coat identified her as the doctor. She met Gabriella's gaze.

"I was told we have an emergency. I'm Dr. Simmons."

Her caramel eyes studied Gabriella as she waited for an answer.

Gabriella, struck by the Southern accent that accompanied the doctor's words, was momentarily speechless. "No. No emergency. This is just a regular visit."

"No?" the doctor asked, her brow puckered. "You sure?"

"This?" Gabriella indicated her face. "I tripped into a coffee table and nearly took my face off." She laughed. By the doctor's expression, she wasn't buying it any more than Shayna did. "I think I'm pregnant," she blurted, hoping to get the focus off of her lie.

"Okay." Dr. Simmons stepped into the hallway to beckon the nurse. "This is Julie. I believe you already met briefly. Julie, will you please get a blood and urine sample from Mrs. Sadler? Once you get a pregnancy confirmation, set her up in the ultrasound room."

"Yes, Dr. Simmons."

The nurse led Gabriella to the lab area. Gabriella took a deep breath before she stepped onto the scales and nearly cried when the needle rested on 237 pounds. How had she let herself go that badly?

After checking her height, temperature, and blood pressure and collecting the necessary samples, the nurse led Gabriella to the ultrasound room, where she instructed her to put on an exam gown and lie down on the table. She offered Gabriella a reassuring smile before she left the room.

Ten minutes passed in complete quietness before the doctor entered the room. "Congratulations, Mrs. Sadler. You're pregnant." She patted Gabriella on the shoulder. While the doctor put on her gloves, she instructed her patient to place her feet in the stirrups and to try to relax.

"I'm going to do a vaginal ultrasound since you are in the early stage of your pregnancy."

Great. Gabriella shimmied down the table to reach the stirrups. *More fun stuff . . .*

Once the dreadful exam was completed and Gabriella had re-dressed, she met the doctor in her office. Seated across the desk from Gabriella, Dr. Simmons began going over all the information.

"By my calculations, you are approximately ten weeks pregnant. The ultrasound and blood work shows that everything is on a healthy course." The doctor handed Gabriella the ultrasound pictures and pointed to the white, oddly-shaped spot peeping out of the dark abyss of her uterus. "That small peanut is your little treasure." The doctor flashed a warm smile.

Tears trickled down Gabriella's face as she returned Dr. Simmons's smile. She could finally celebrate this intimate news with someone, even if it was with a stranger.

Gabriella allowed herself to briefly pretend . . .

This newly acquainted woman was actually her lifelong friend. They'd even attended the same college and had been roommates. They were meeting for lunch to plan a backyard barbecue, where they would announce to a yard full of family and friends about their joyful bundles on the way. Of course, they both had doting husbands who were over the moon about the pregnancies and had made it a competition to see who could pamper their pregnant wife the best. This life was perfect, and it was filled with love and family and lots of laughter . . .

"Gabriella?" Dr. Simmons spoke after she cleared her throat to get Gabriella's attention.

As the daydream faded, the reality of sitting in a doctor's office with a bruised face and an unexpected pregnancy, which she had to keep secret, sank in. Fear and nerves suddenly wiped the smile off her face.

"Are you okay, Gabriella?"

"How far along do you have to be when you can no longer get an abortion?" Gabriella asked as she openly wept.

Her question took the doctor by surprise, but she quickly recovered and pulled a business card from her desk drawer. "If you want to terminate your pregnancy, I can refer you to another doctor." She tried to pass the card to Gabriella. "I do not perform abortions, but I will respect your choice," she stated in a very clinical voice.

Gabriella refused the business card. "No . . . you don't understand." She paused before she wrestled with the decision to confide in Dr. Simmons. She focused on her hands folded in her lap. "Is what I share with you confidential?"

"Absolutely. Patient privacy is a big deal." The doctor waited patiently for Gabriella to continue.

"My husband says absolutely no children, so it's very important for me to keep this a secret until he can no longer do anything about it." She continued to weep as she fiddled with her wedding ring.

"Your husband has no right over your body, Gabriella." Dr. Simmons hesitated and then added, "He also has no right to do that to your face."

"I fell into a table. It's my fault. If I would just learn to do better, these accidents wouldn't keep happening." She slumped in her chair, stunned that she had totally screwed up her excuse. She sounded pathetic. She started to retract the statement, but the doctor interrupted her.

"Look at me, Gabriella," Dr. Simmons said in a steady voice and waited to continue until Gabriella finally looked up. "No *table* has the right to do that to you. You can blame it on being clumsy, but you have a baby that you are responsible for now. You have to protect your baby from the *table*."

The only thing Gabriella could do was nod her head in agreement.

"I'm going to be praying for you."

"Oh . . . okay," Gabriella mumbled.

"Don't you believe in God?"

Gabriella looked away from the doctor's questioning eyes. "Yes. I've just never gotten to know him very well. I bounced around between group and foster homes all of my childhood." She shrugged. "Mostly the homes didn't seem to have much faith in him. I've only been to church a handful of times." She clamped her mouth shut, surprised at sharing so much with this stranger.

The sound of a drawer opening brought Gabriella's attention back to the doctor. "Well, how about you get to know him." She produced a Bible and handed it over. "Start with Romans. Jeremiah is one of my favorite books too. My favorite verses are highlighted."

"I can't take your Bible." Gabriella tried to give it back, but the doctor raised her hands and shook her head.

"No. It's yours. Now, tell me, what are you taking for the pain?" Dr. Simmons asked as she studied Gabriella's face.

"Regular strength Tylenol. I called a pharmacy to make sure it was okay for the baby."

"Very good. The nurse is putting together a packet for you to take home. It will include all the pregnancy dos and don'ts, as well as a book that shows the weekly stages of your growing baby. There is also a month's worth of prenatal vitamins. If those agree with you, I'll write you a prescription at your next appointment."

Gabriella nodded as she tried to pull herself together.

"Watch your diet closely. Remember, your baby eats what you eat. If you eat half a dozen donuts, then so will your baby."

Gabriella flinched. She wondered if the doctor could smell the donuts on her.

"Try to stick with lean meats, fresh fruits, and veggies. Also low-fat dairy and whole grains are needed. Let's try to be mindful of your weight gain throughout the pregnancy. With you already being overweight, we need to be cautious and try to avoid unwanted risks to you and your baby."

Gabriella hung her head and fell completely to pieces. Dr. Simmons moved to the vacant chair beside Gabriella and held her hand.

"Honey, most of my patients are a little overweight. Don't be embarrassed." The doctor squeezed her hand. "I wouldn't be doing my job if I didn't try to encourage proper health for my mommas and their babies. Right?"

"Yes. I'm sorry. I'm just having an emotional day," Gabriella whispered as a headache nudged its way to the surface.

"Welcome to pregnancy hormones, sweetheart." Dr. Simmons smiled. "Julie also grabbed you a splint for your broken nose from the plastic surgeon's office next door. And I'm going to have her give you a dose of Tylenol before you leave. Okay?"

Gabriella nodded as she watched the doctor stand. "Can I ask you a personal question, Dr. Simmons?" She knew she had taken way too much of the doctor's time already.

"Honey, you've had to shine me all of your glory God gave you and confide in me about your peculiar troubles with tables. I think you are due a personal question." Dr. Simmons laughed warmly.

"Where did your beautiful accent come from?" Gabriella had fallen in love with the rich Southern dialect of the doctor's words as soon as she first spoke. It sounded like home to her, warm and soothing.

"Good ole Georgia," the doctor answered with a grin. "I thought I sounded like a Southern hick."

"How did a Southern belle make her way to Washington?"

"That's two questions, but I think you earned it. I followed the love of my life here. My husband was offered a job proposal he couldn't refuse, and so here I am." She glanced at her watch.

Taking this as her cue, Gabriella slid her sunglasses back into place and followed the doctor to the nurses' station, where Julie awaited them. Dr. Simmons asked the nurse to give Gabriella a dose of Tylenol. Before heading to her next appointment, Dr. Simmons turned and took Gabriella's hand in hers.

"Gabriella, it was very nice to meet you. My number is in the information packet. Call me if you need *anything*."

"Thank you, Dr. Simmons. It was really nice to have found you."

The doctor smiled, then headed to exam room three and slipped inside.

After Gabriella took the pain medicine, the nurse went over everything in the packet, which included her next appointment card. She thanked the nurse and headed out to the Range Rover. As she opened her door, she spotted the half-eaten box of donuts. Determined to make better choices, she gathered the box and dumped it into the closest trash bin.

Once she climbed in and buckled her seat belt, she dried her tears and made a few resolutions. First thing was to form and execute an escape plan. In the meantime, she would steer clear of Brent, at all costs, to protect her baby.

After sending a stunned grocery delivery boy away with all the junk food she'd ordered for delivery, along with a thirty-dollar tip and a new order of healthy foods, Gabriella spent most of the afternoon cleaning the house of her former lifestyle. The hidden junk food was boxed up, and a worker from the children's home stopped by to pick it up. She restocked the closet with the new delivery of healthy snacks of granola bars, dried fruit, almonds, and juice boxes. She also hid her prenatal vitamins in an empty Midol bottle and tucked her pregnancy packet in the guest room closet. Oddly enough, her prison cell had become a personal sanctuary of secrets.

OCTOBER HAD SWOOPED IN on Olympia, Washington, with a chilly breeze and had taken its lovely paintbrush to the landscape. Rich oranges, warm burgundies, and deep yellows accented trees and bushes that lined the downtown streets. It was hands down Gabriella's favorite season. She snuggled into her sweater as she took her morning walk.

Ever since the first doctor's visit, she'd been taking much better care of herself for the baby's sake and had actually lost some weight. At six and a half months pregnant, Gabriella was down fifteen pounds due to eating healthier—and an extensive bout of morning sickness. Thankfully, that had finally passed. With no more nausea and the cool crispness of autumn in the air, Gabriella felt invigorated and hopeful. She was even getting to know God better by reading the Bible the doctor gave her. Yes. She was most definitely feeling hopeful.

With the exception of last night's punch to her eye, Brent had been fairly good at keeping his fists to himself lately. She'd caught him giving her odd looks in the last month and that worried her. He would comment on not understanding why every part of her body seemed to be shrinking except for her midsection and breasts. Gabriella didn't know if Brent was in denial of the obvious fact that she was pregnant or simply that clueless.

After her walk, she grabbed her purse and headed to the doctor's office for her monthly exam. She also wanted to tell the doctor good-bye. If everything went as planned, Gabriella would be on the East Coast by the following week. Brent had a business trip scheduled in California, so she felt it would be the perfect opportunity.

Walking into the doctor's office, Gabriella felt excited and a bit apprehensive at her unknown future. After being ushered into the room, Gabriella settled on top of the exam table and waited only a few minutes before Dr. Simmons strolled in.

"Gabriella?" Her knowing gaze lingered on the black eye.

Gabriella touched it lightly with her fingertips. "It's just this."

"Oh . . . I'm relieved you *only* have a black eye," Dr. Simmons said sarcastically as she examined it. "Did you encounter a fall?"

"No. Just one punch."

"Okay. Lie back and lift your blouse so we can get a measurement of that beautiful bump." The doctor pulled a small tape measure from her coat pocket and measured Gabriella's rounding belly. "Twenty-six and a half centimeters. Right on target," the doctor noted. She picked up the Doppler fetal monitor from the cart and pressed it against Gabriella's abdomen. She quickly found the healthy heartbeat of the baby. "Sounds good. Did you want to try another ultrasound today to see if that stinker will finally turn around and let us find out the gender?

"No thanks. I'm beginning to like the idea of keeping it a surprise," Gabriella said as the doctor helped her get into a sitting position.

"I guess we are done then. Unless you have any questions."

"I reckon I should let you know, you ain't gonna be seein' me no more 'cause I'm scootin' on down South to fetch me one of them there fine Southern twangs."

Understanding registered on the doctor's face. "I'm really going to miss you." She gave Gabriella a big hug.

"I'm really going to miss you too." Gabriella hugged her back tightly.

Dr. Simmons pulled back from the hug and gave Gabriella a pointed look. "Promise me two things."

"Anything."

"You are nearing your third trimester. It's very important to find a new doctor as quickly as possible so that you can get your birthing plan in order."

"Okay. What else?"

"For pete's sake, work on that awful excuse of a Southern accent." Both women laughed and hugged once more. "Please promise you will call me if I can help you in any way."

"That's three things, but I guess you deserve that." Gabriella smiled. Without another word, she made her way to the front desk to settle her bill. Feeling brave, she headed back to the loft.

Gabriella's bravado evaporated once she arrived back home to discover Brent's Mercedes sitting in its parking spot in the garage. Panicked, she almost put the Range Rover in reverse to take her leave early, but then that would mean leaving behind her few belongings, the money, and her only shot at pulling it off successfully.

Reluctantly, Gabriella parked beside the Mercedes and tried to form some plan. Before she could get a grip on the situation, her driver's door flew open. In an instant, she was being dragged out by her hair.

With a vicious grip on her hair, Brent dragged Gabriella up the stairs while spitting out a long string of vulgar expletives at her. The pain in her scalp and the attack of words barely registered. All she could think about was protecting the baby at all costs.

Once inside, Brent slammed the door shut, spun Gabriella around, and shoved her against it. "You think I'm so stupid, don't you?"

She could smell the alcohol heavy on his breath. "I don't know what you're talk—"

Brent punched her, causing the skin over her left eye to split. "Don't lie to me, you worthless cow!"

"Lie about what?"

He clenched her jaw in his hand and drew her close to his face, his breath hot and repulsive against her cheek. "You've been stealing from me, you thief."

"No—"

Brent released his grasp on her jaw and landed another punch. This time to her chin. The skin gave way and sent the wet warmth of blood down her neck.

Brent gripped Gabriella by the shoulders and shook her. "I give you everything, and this is how you repay me. My account books are off, and you know it's your fault." He released her and snatched a bottle of bourbon from the liquor cabinet. He tilted his head back, drinking straight from the bottle.

As Gabriella watched, she scolded herself for increasing her cut of the bank deposits. He had finally caught on to the glitch in the balances. She knew she had been taking a risk in the last few months, but she hoped she would be long gone before he figured it out. Of course, she should have known better than to think it would be that simple. She realized she was going to pay a hefty price for her sin.

Brent turned back to Gabriella, who was still standing by the front door. She instinctively cradled her protruding belly. His eyes registered her action and he nearly choked on the bourbon.

"How could you?"

"Just let me leave and you'll never have to worry about this." She began to cautiously open the door, but Brent was there before she could turn the doorknob. He landed a punch square on her mouth, splitting her lip and causing another excruciating point of pain. Brent grabbed her once again by the hair and dragged her to the guest bedroom closet. Once he opened the door, he pushed her up against the back wall.

"Where did you hide my money? I know it's in here along with your junk food and other crap." Outraged, he began pulling stuff off the shelf. Every time he stumbled upon a package of food or a water bottle, he would hurl it at Gabriella, who tried to deflect the assaults away from her belly.

After relinquishing the idea of the money being in the closet, Brent pulled her toward their bedroom, grabbing his half-empty bottle of bourbon on the way. "Where is it, Gabriella?" He shoved her into the master closet and began the same assault he had given in the guest room closet. "You're hiding it somewhere! I know you haven't spent it!"

She couldn't believe she was witnessing Brent fall apart so dramatically over a mere hundred grand, when he had spent nearly that much on her luxury Range Rover.

"What's this *really* about, Brent?"

Brent gave her a measured look and drained the remainder of the bottle. He then turned it upside down and gripped it by the neck, raising it as if to strike her.

"'What's this *really* about?'" he asked, mocking her. "First off, it's about thousands of dollars disappearing from deposit slips in the past couple of months. You've become quite greedy." He tapped the bottle against Gabriella's upper arm, almost in a tease.

"I'll give it to you," she offered, but he was too far gone in his rage to acknowledge it.

"Secondly, you've been keeping secrets. Nosy old Mrs. Harper from across the street stopped me this morning to see if you were okay. Said she's noticed that the market has been delivering our groceries lately!" He swung the bottle at Gabriella's head.

She shot her arm up to block the blow, causing the bottle to strike close to her wrist. Pain ricocheted up her arm and then down the entire length of her body, triggering bile to rise up her throat. While her arm was still raised, Brent delivered one more blow—into her side. At the impact, Gabriella felt several pinching sensations in her rib cage, and she could no longer take deep breaths. Brent lost his grip on the liquor bottle, and it shattered all over the closet floor.

He stumbled out of the closet and sat on the edge of the bed, his gaze never leaving a weeping Gabriella. "Why?" he asked.

"I *n-needed* to *g-go* to the doctor, *s-so* I *h-have g-groceries d-delivered.*" She shuddered.

"You're really pregnant?" Brent stared at her rounding midsection as he beckoned her forward, but she stayed rooted in the closet.

"Come here, Gabriella."

"*P-please* don't *h-h-hurt* us." She cradled her belly while watching him sway. Brent had drunk way past his limit. She hoped that all she had to do was tread lightly until he passed out. She promised the baby they would take off as soon as Brent blacked out and that they would never come back.

"Gabriella," Brent said her name as a warning.

She slowly moved out of the closet, barely noticing the glass shards stabbing the bottoms of her feet. She was already spinning in a haze of pain.

Gabriella cautiously stood in front of her husband. His hair was mussed in all directions and his face was flushed with sweat beading along his forehead. He gently laid his hands over her bulging belly and placed a kiss near her belly button. She almost sighed in relief, but the pain in her side took her breath.

"What did I tell you about this?" Brent asked as he continued to stare at the baby bump.

"I know, but it happened after you locked me up for that entire week this past spring. I couldn't take my birth control . . ." She hushed as soon as his hands stopped moving. Gabriella knew she had messed up. *So much for treading lightly,* she scolded herself.

"Don't blame this—" he slurred as he poked her harshly in the belly, causing Gabriella to take a protective step away from him—"on me." He shot to his feet and backhanded her across her right cheek. A flash of numbness, followed by an instant throb, mimicked the pain of the left side of her swollen face.

Gabriella worried that she would pass out before Brent did. "Please, Brent," she said. "I'll do anything. Just please stop." Her entire body trembled.

"You have a lot of making up to do," he murmured as he ripped off her thin cotton blouse, exposing her bare belly. He clawed and pulled and tore at her remaining clothes until she was completely naked before him. He slung her around and shoved her onto the bed.

Things became a blur for Gabriella at that point. She blinked and tried to clear her vision. She remembered trying to push him away from her belly, but this enraged him more. She kept pleading with her eyes to adjust. She couldn't keep Brent in focus. The rough assault went on and on. At one point, he rose up and violently punched her directly in the belly.

She screamed as the piercing pain in her side protested. "No!"

Brent clamped his hand over her mouth and continued to brutally rape her. Time felt like it was at a standstill and yet simultaneously passing at an unfathomable speed. Gabriella could no longer see out of her left eye, which was nearly swollen shut, and she couldn't focus with her right eye, so she surrendered and waited for blackness to take her.

She lost consciousness briefly before being brought back to the surface by her inability to breathe. She forced her right eye open and discovered Brent's hands locked around her neck, strangling her.

Gabriella was resigned to the fate finally being played out in front of her. *This is what you get for staying.* Her vision became spotty as she ineffectually clawed at Brent's face. He was in a rage that she couldn't snap him out of.

She was jerking her head back and forth, trying to loosen his grip, when she spotted a crystal vase on the nightstand. It still held the roses she had received for her now-forgotten black eye. Gabriella grabbed it and—with all the might she could muster—cracked Brent over the head. He moaned and then collapsed on top of her. It took all of her strength to push him off so she could wiggle from beneath him. She lay, totally spent, beside him and blacked out.

As she regained consciousness, not knowing how much time had passed, reality awakened her completely. Looking over, she was relieved to find that Brent was still knocked out. She took stock of herself and was horrified to find herself covered in blood.

With great effort, she crawled out of the bed and stumbled toward the bathroom, falling twice on the way. Her equilibrium seemed out of sorts. Gabriella locked the door behind her and stepped into the shower, turning it on full blast. A wave of nausea slammed into her as she watched large amounts of bloody water pool around the drain. Before she could think of exiting, she vomited violently in the shower. She pulled down the handheld showerhead and rinsed the mess down the drain. She began washing the gore off her body and tried picking the shards of glass out of her feet.

Gabriella washed sufficiently and wasted little time drying off. She knew her window of opportunity to escape was limited. She fished around in the sink cabinet for a pad and placed it in her panties to catch the blood that seemed to be slowing down. She then bandaged her face as best as she could. Her left eye was swollen completely shut, and she felt extremely light-headed. Her mind was foggy and disoriented. She had to constantly remind herself to concentrate.

After gathering extra pads and toiletries, Gabriella listened at the door. She could only hear stillness, so she emerged from the bathroom as quietly as she could. Out of the corner of her right eye, she could see that Brent was still in the bed. She went directly to the dressing table and retrieved the money that was stashed behind it. She scooted into the closet, trying to avoid the shards of glass scattered all over the floor. Gabriella dressed and then packed as quickly as her mangled body would allow. Not really paying close attention, she tugged a drawer out and dumped all of her underclothes into a duffel bag. Without replacing the drawer, she scooped several pairs of shoes into the duffel bag as well. She then pulled handfuls of tops and pants off the hangers and into her suitcase. She grabbed a baseball cap off a hook and crammed it on her head.

She pulled both pieces of luggage back into the bedroom as quietly as possible, stopping to catch her breath at the bedroom door. The pain was unbearable, and her vision was in a constant haze. Gabriella stole one more look at Brent before she went into the hall. She found him slumped awkwardly on his side, staring past her vacantly. She grabbed a fistful of the long coat she was carrying and held it to her mouth to muffle her scream, causing her lip to split further. Tremors rocked her body, wave after wave, as the realization hit her.

Brent was dead, and she was the one who killed him.

Without another glance, Gabriella stumbled across the loft. She wrenched the front door open and shoved her luggage down the front steps, stumbling behind it. She pushed it over to the Range Rover and tried to lift it inside, just as a taxicab pulled up across the street. She abandoned the fruitless effort and waved the cabdriver down. He loaded Gabriella and her luggage into the cab and asked if he could take her to the hospital. She replied no but asked him to take her to the closest bus station. She needed to get far away from Brent as quickly as possible.

Once at the bus station, she found a lady who took pity on her and agreed to go to the ticket counter to purchase Gabriella's ticket to Georgia. She thanked the lady and offered her fifty dollars, but the lady refused it.

She settled into her uncomfortable seat as the bus pulled out of the station. The last two things she remembered were profound—relief when the baby started kicking, and Lenny Kravitz's hypnotic voice crooning from another passenger's handheld radio. As she listened to Lenny sing about flying away, the lights dimmed and complete darkness took over.

TIME HAD COMPLETELY FALLEN OFF its track, and Gabriella felt oddly suspended in it. Somehow, she ended up in a hospital in Lincoln, Nebraska, with absolutely no memory of how or when she arrived there. Countless days passed as she lay helplessly in a hospital bed, hooked to an IV and monitors. The only constant she could recall was a dark-haired nurse with a warm smile. She seemed to always be there when Gabriella regained consciousness.

Resurfacing from another spell of darkness, Gabriella felt the already-familiar small hand holding hers. After a few failed attempts at focusing, she was finally able to hold a steady gaze on the comforting nurse. Gabriella licked her brittle lips and winced. The effort to swallow was agonizing and sent a growing panic throughout her.

"Here, sweetie," the nurse said softly as she held a cup with a straw near Gabriella's mouth.

Sipping cautiously at first and then greedily sucking the delicious ice water, Gabriella drained the cup completely. The cool liquid soothed her parched throat, and she couldn't get it down fast enough.

"Slowly," the nurse encouraged. "You don't want to pull too much on the stitches in your lip."

After draining another cup offered generously by the nurse, Gabriella lay back on the bed. Reality gradually teased at her consciousness. Her hands moved of their own accord before her foggy brain could comprehend. She grazed her fingers along her deflated belly in confusion. A part of her—the most important part—was absent. And in that moment, her heart plummeted.

The nurse seemed to know what Gabriella was thinking. "You don't remember, do you, sweetheart?"

Wisps of memories gathered around the edges of Gabriella's brain, but she couldn't make sense of them. Brent beating her, someone holding her, pain and more pain, someone ripping her baby out of her arms, terror at losing the most precious part of her, pleading for someone to take care of her baby, more pain . . . always, the pain.

Gabriella's world abruptly closed in on itself again, the darkness overtaking her. The next glimpse of awareness was of a middle-aged doctor standing by her bed, alongside the nurse. Concern and empathy riddled their features and did nothing to soothe her aching heart.

Gabriella cleared her throat. Barely able to voice her fears, she mumbled, "My baby." She didn't need to form it into a question. She already knew. She felt it was what she deserved. She had failed at her promise.

"Mrs. Sadler, I'm Dr. Daniels. Your nurse tells me you are starting to remember what happened." He paused as if unsure how to proceed. "I'm sorry to have to tell you, but your placenta detached and caused a severe hemorrhage. . . . We were barely able to save you. . . . I'm sorry to say . . . the baby didn't make it."

A thick silence stifled the room until sharp gasps of agony escaped from Gabriella. The hurt clamped down on her in a stinging vise.

The doctor spoke over the gasps, trying to be reassuring, but failing monumentally. "The good news is there is no permanent damage. You'll be able to have more children with a very low possibility of complication." He nodded his head, clearly hoping to have delivered some comfort.

All of the abuse from the past decade, the abandonment issues, failures after failures, and most importantly, the cruel impact of losing her child, slammed into Gabriella in one brutal blow. Years of unacknowledged, unvented pain erupted in a scream that ripped through her body, directed at the doctor. Fresh blood trickled from the newly torn lip wound, causing the doctor to take a step closer, but Gabriella rendered him motionless as she slashed him with her tongue.

Clutching her throbbing side, Gabriella spit out through gritted teeth, "You act as though losing my baby—my very own flesh and soul—was nothing more than losing an earring that I can simply replace. My. Baby. Is. Not. Replaceable." Her voice, low and menacing, struck out full of venom.

"Mrs. Sadler—"

"Don't call me that!"

Gabriella noticed that other staff members had arrived to inquire about the disturbance but were dismissed immediately by the nurse. She offered a small nod to the nurse in appreciation.

"Gabriella," the doctor said, his hands raised in surrender.

She turned on her side, with her back to the doctor. She would not waste one more word on this man. She shut him out completely after his insensitive statement. She hated him in that moment and couldn't care less that he saved her own life. She hated him for that, too.

"Gabriella," Dr. Daniels whispered. "I'm going to let the nurse explain to you about your injuries and take care of your lip." His defeated voice trailed away as he exited the somber hospital room.

She refused to acknowledge him as she continued to lie on her side, staring at the mint-colored wall until the nurse filled her vision. She knelt, a sympathetic smile tugging at her lips as she gently pressed a wet cloth to Gabriella's bloody lip.

Leaning close, the kind nurse whispered, "You had a beautiful baby girl." The last word was almost inaudible as the nurse's emotions overtook her. "And she looked like an angel. I promised you I would take care of her, and I did."

The news of the baby being a girl beckoned another wave of intense, violent grief. Gabriella's body trembled as she cried a sob so forceful no sound could escape her. Pain, both physical and emotional, engulfed her and she welcomed it—wanting nothing more than to drown in it. She had failed at taking care of her baby. She deserved every second of pain she withered in.

Hours of grief passed before Gabriella calmed enough that the nurse could explain the extent of her injuries. She was told that she had suffered two cracked ribs and a cracked collarbone, all of which were taped up tightly. She'd also received twelve stitches to her bottom lip and nine above her left eye. Her fractured wrist was uncomfortably set in a plaster cast. She had no recollection of those treatments taking place.

After consoling Gabriella as much as she could, the nurse administered a sedative through an IV. As Gabriella was losing consciousness, she heard a whispered prayer for her healing. She wanted to beg the compassionate woman to pray for her death, but her numb lips couldn't form the words. For death was the only way Gabriella thought life could ever be acceptable again.

•   •   •

With the help of a morphine pump and an occasional sedative, another week passed in numbing agony for Gabriella. She refused to communicate to anyone the events that had taken place. She refused to eat. She refused to give the hospital any personal information about herself. She suspected that they had rummaged through her bag and found her ID since they knew her name. When she wasn't sleeping, Gabriella would just stare off into no particular place. She had erected walls and shut the world out as she let her pain hold her captive.

When the weekend arrived, Gabriella began to resurface from her haze. Panic replaced the numbness as she realized the danger of staying in one spot for too long. The hospital knew her name and where she had come from. Surely they would soon know that she had abandoned a dead husband.

Late Sunday night, Gabriella finally mustered enough bravado to leave. The first few attempts to get into a sitting position without any support were a nightmare. It took four tries before she could stop the room from spinning. Sitting on the edge of the bed, she began trying to remove her IV as the door opened.

"I had a feeling this was coming." The nurse didn't reprimand her. Instead, she removed the IV and bandaged the prick site before walking Gabriella to the bathroom to get cleaned up and dressed. Once that was done, she made Gabriella sit in the guest chair and drink several cartons of juice and eat a few crackers.

"I know you don't feel like eating, but I can't let you go

if I don't get anything in you," she said, coercing Gabriella when she refused to take the graham crackers.

After Gabriella successfully ate a few more crackers and drank another carton of juice, the nurse helped her walk a few laps around the room to work out the rubbery feeling in her legs. Gabriella was in a rush to leave, but the nurse wouldn't have it.

"Let me do my job so we can get you out of here, okay?" The nurse brushed out Gabriella's knotted hair before pulling it up under a cap.

For the next two hours, the nurse came in and out, helping Gabriella with preparations for leaving. Finally, at one in the morning, she ushered Gabriella out the back hospital entrance. As they waited for the cab to arrive, the nurse pulled two prescription bottles out of her coat pocket.

"I had Dr. Daniels prescribe these for you, and the hospital pharmacy filled them," she said as she handed them over to Gabriella. "One is Percocet. It's for pain. Just follow the directions for dosage and time. The other is an antibiotic. You are to start taking it immediately at the first sign of any fever. With so many wounds and with you traveling, your risk for infection is going to be quite high. It's very important for you to remember this, okay?"

Tears escaped from the corners of Gabriella's eyes as she nodded. She thanked the nurse and was surprised when the nurse offered up a tender hug. This woman had been so compassionate that it almost overwhelmed Gabriella. The cabdriver pulled up, and the nurse helped him load the bags into the trunk and Gabriella into the backseat.

"Remember what I said about the medicines. And I took care of everything, just as I promised you. *She* will always be taken care of." The nurse smiled sadly at

Gabriella and gave her hand a parting squeeze before closing the cab's door.

Gabriella quietly cried as the cab took her to yet another bus station. Her only choice was to disappear, so she decided to keep heading east for the time being. The sympathetic cabdriver stayed with Gabriella, helping her with her luggage, until she successfully boarded her designated bus headed to Tennessee.

The bus ride was another numb haze for Gabriella. She only took half of a Percocet, trying to keep some wits about her. She was hurting too badly not to take anything. She tried to sleep but only managed a restless doze. The bus rocked too much and the engine was too loud.

As the day emerged and stretched on, Gabriella thought of the caring nurse and tried without luck to recall her name. This woman had gone above and beyond for Gabriella during the nightmarish past weeks, and she was dumbfounded that she couldn't remember her name. She thought she could almost make out the typing on the nurse's name tag. *Was it Kelly? No. Her name was Carrie. No, it was Terrie. No . . .* Gabriella played the name-the-nurse game almost all the way to Tennessee, giving herself a nasty headache. It was driving her mad not being able to remember it.

Focus, Leah. In that moment, she decided to leave Gabriella Sadler back in Nebraska, and Leah Allen would be starting her new life today. As she sat in the uncomfortable seat trying to form a plan, she absentmindedly scratched at her eye, wincing when she snagged a stitch. She knew the itching was a sign of healing, but it was about to drive her mad. Her bottom lip pricked into her upper one when she tried to deepen her frown. She attempted to let out a sigh from the aggravation of not being able to successfully frown at her misery. Her tender side pinched in pain with the huff. Anxiety caused her hands to tremble, and the fear of falling completely apart on the cramped bus worried her.

Before the panic overwhelmed her too much, Leah gathered her purse and slid into the small bathroom on the bus.

Focus, Leah. Pull it together. She retrieved a moist towelette from the little bag the nurse had filled with pads, lip ointment, and other supplies she said Leah would need. "What is your name?" she whispered to the absent nurse as she unwrapped the towelette and gently wiped it over her face. She then applied some ointment to her mangled lip, realizing it would probably never look right again. But then again, nothing would ever be just right again.

While she was replacing the bag in her purse, her phone caught her eye. She fished it out, dropped it into the toilet, and flushed. She pulled off her wedding rings and did the same with them. She then pulled out all of her identification cards, along with a clean pad. She unwrapped the pad, placed her driver's license, credit card, and library card inside, and rewrapped it before tossing it into the waste receptacle. With all that done, she made her way back to her seat. She felt productive and calm. From the back of her wallet, Leah pulled her old expired driver's license from Nevada and placed it in the designated license spot. She studied the picture of the naive young girl, and she cringed at her distorted reflection in the bus window. Leah looked back down at the photo of her old self and whispered, "I lost you."

Leah shook off her despair the best she could and focused on getting her red hair back under the ball cap, which was no easy task with her arm in a cast. She decided that her first priority would be to find a salon that could get rid of her red hair. She knew she should do it herself, but that would be nearly impossible with all of her injuries.

As Leah exited the bus in the mountains of Chattanooga, Tennessee, she spotted a hair salon in a strip mall right beside the bus station. She gathered her luggage and made her way over to it, only to be disappointed. The salon was filled with only black women. As she turned to leave, someone called out to her.

"Whatcha need, honey?"

Leah slowly turned around to find the entire salon staring at her. She knew she looked hideous and very *white*.

"Umm . . . I need a haircut and color, but . . ."

"Well, sit your white butt down in that empty chair and we'll get started."

Leah turned once more and found a woman nearly a foot shorter than her, with intricately braided hair, speaking to her.

"Umm . . . can you do my kind of hair?"

"Sure. Why not?" The cute lady laughed as she tied her apron on.

Leah placed her belongings by the lady's workstation and eased down into the salon chair. She winced a bit when her tender side brushed against the chair's armrest. The beautician carefully pulled the cap off of Leah's head.

"Ouch!" she snapped, as though the full sight of Leah's face caused her pain. "Honey, you got any, umm, *boo-boos* on your scalp?" she asked as she gently looked Leah's head over.

Leah felt her cheeks grow warm. "No."

"Don't you worry 'bout a thang, honey. Good ole Gina gonna hook you right up."

"Okay."

And Gina held to her promise too. She expertly cut away about seven inches of red hair, making it shoulder length. She also matched the rest of Leah's hair precisely to her blonde roots. The beautician took great care in being gentle with Leah when she rinsed out the color. She then added some curl serum and dried Leah's hair with a diffuser. The natural blonde curls felt so heavenly that Leah purchased a bottle of the curl serum when she paid her bill. She was surprised when the bill only came to forty-eight dollars. The same services would have cost at least two hundred dollars at her fancy salon back in Washington. Leah was so grateful that she tipped the beautician a hundred dollars.

Gina called a cab and, in the fading light of day, sat on a bench outside the salon with Leah as she waited. Leah reluctantly put the cap back on her head to conceal some of the carnage of her face. She sat quietly, waiting, sensing the beautician wanted to say something.

As a white minivan taxi pulled up, Gina lightly placed her hand on Leah's arm before she could stand. "Honey, you don't need to be lettin' no good-for-nothin' man beat on you like that ever again."

Leah lifted her head to meet Gina's eyes. "I promise. Thank you for taking such good care of me this afternoon." She tried to give the sweet woman a reassuring smile, but her split lip and swollen eye protested. *Humph, I can't frown or smile. How peculiar.*

Leah boarded the taxicab and asked the driver to take her to the nearest nice hotel. She so badly needed a shower and bed.

After paying a sympathetic hotel clerk in cash and signing in under the name *Gina Honey*, Leah managed to get into her well-appointed suite before completely falling apart. Sobbing, she pulled out some clean clothes from her suitcase and made her way to the bathroom. She set the water to scalding. While she waited for it to heat up, Leah peeled her clothes away and was taken aback by the sickly, rank odor that came from her body. It had been almost a week since she had sufficiently washed. She glanced in the mirror at her broken body as she fumbled to wrap an unused plastic ice-bucket liner around her cast.

She stayed in the shower for forty minutes, trying to scrub away the dried blood that seemed to be hiding everywhere. She felt so revolting that she thought she might need a gallon of bleach to get the nastiness off. She washed, rinsed, and repeated until the pink water finally became clear. After dressing and scrubbing her teeth, Leah washed down two pain pills with a couple of glasses of water. She then climbed into bed and waited for the medicine to take effect. Every part of her body throbbed, especially her heart.

After holding it together for the last few days, Leah finally let the walls back down and allowed the grief to overtake her. For all she had endured in the past ten years, the baby had made it all worth it. Her own flesh and blood. Something she knew nothing about but wanted so badly.

And yet, Leah lay there in a hopeless heap, with no understanding and no escaping the debilitating pain of her broken heart. Her baby was dead, and she took full blame.

"Please, God," she cried out. "Please help me." She lay in the darkness, sobbing. "I'm so lost. Please help me." She desperately tried to remember some of the Bible verses she had recently memorized. Her mind could only recall part of Jeremiah 17:14, so she began to pray the partial verse. "'Heal me, Lord, and I will be healed; save me and I will be saved.'" Leah repeated her prayer until the pain medicine finally took her under.

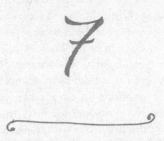

7

THE BUTTERY SUNLIGHT cascaded down, lightly caressing Leah's face and warming her. She closed her eyes and leaned back onto the worn quilt to take it in. As she lay in the meadow, sweet giggles tickled her ears, rousing her back out of her peaceful dozing. Smiling, she opened her eyes and watched the beautiful little girl skip toward her. She stopped at the edge of the quilt and stared at her mom with a mischievous grin. Leah watched as the warm afternoon breeze danced through the little girl's golden-brown curls. Her light-blue eyes glittered as she jumped into Leah's waiting lap and wrapped her soft arms around her neck. She playfully kissed Leah on her eyelids and cheeks and nose before whispering, "I love you, Mommy."

Leah giggled and returned her daughter's kisses in the same manner. "I love you too."

"Will you braid my hair real pretty, Mommy?" she asked, scooting around in Leah's lap.

"I'll try." Leah laughed as she tried to weave the curls into a braid, but the curls kept escaping. Her daughter's curls were much tighter than Leah's and had a mind of their own. Leah had to restart twice.

"Mommy, you have to hurry up."

"There's no hurry." Leah continued to lazily play in her daughter's hair.

"You have to hurry," the little girl urged Leah once more.

"Why, baby girl?" Leah asked as she planted a kiss on top of her daughter's head. She smelled of a perfumed mix of honeysuckle and freshly cut grass. Leah wanted nothing more than to spend the day snuggled up to her daughter and taking in the sweet smell of her.

"It's almost time for me to go."

"Go where, baby girl?"

"Back to Daddy." Upon her reply, the little girl began to slowly fade away.

"No. Stay with me, and I'll protect you from him." Leah tried to pull the child closer to her chest, only to find that she could no longer hold on to her. "Please stay. I promise to take better care of you this time. Please, baby girl." Tears seeped down Leah's face.

"Silly Mommy. You're too late." With that, she kissed Leah's cheek one last time and skipped to the edge of the field. She placed her tiny hand in Brent's waiting one. Leah had not realized that he had been standing there, watching, the entire time. She watched helplessly as her daughter and husband walked away from her, giggling.

Leah woke up sobbing from the heart-wrenching dream. She had somehow ended up at the foot of the hotel bed with no blanket. She tried to right herself in the bed and was suddenly struck with a new ache from deep inside her pelvis. The odd heat coming off her body was a fever, just as the nurse had predicted.

It was her second night in the hotel. She had spent the entire time barely moving from the bed. She had been trying to rest so that her body could heal, but it seemed that she was getting worse.

She dragged herself out of bed and dug out the bottle of antibiotics from her purse. She also pulled out a pain pill and a pack of graham crackers the nurse had loaded her down with. It was the only sustenance she had eaten since leaving the hospital. Leah stared at the package of crackers. She wasn't hungry. She weighed eating the unwanted crackers against the side effects of taking medicine on an empty stomach. She didn't think she could manage any other form of sickness. She washed the pills and crackers down with a couple glasses of water before heading back to bed.

She repeated the routine of medicine, water, crackers, and restless sleep for the remainder of the next two days before the fever crept away for good. Leah knew she had to get moving, but she just couldn't get it together enough to act on it. She knew she needed to eat to regain some strength and she needed to purchase a car. She needed . . . There was just too much to figure out and it left her completely overwhelmed.

After another day or so passed, Leah demanded her body get up and head out to take care of those tasks. After finishing the complicated task of washing and dressing, she called the front desk and requested a cab. She pulled her cap down over her eyes and grabbed her purse before heading to the lobby, where she got a much-needed cup of coffee, a muffin, and a banana from the continental breakfast buffet. She ate slowly and waited outside as her eyes tried to readjust to sunlight.

Leah was relieved that the driver knew where a pretty good car dealership was and gladly took her there. She thanked him and exited the cab to begin her automobile hunt. The car lot was a sea full of silvers, blacks, and shiny whites. Her eyes skimmed over them and landed on a beauty at the back of the lot. She fell in love instantly. It was a vivid teal-blue with a white stripe down the side.

She had never owned a vehicle of any color and perked up at the possibility.

By the time she made her way to the back of the lot to get a better look, an eager car salesman greeted her. Noticing her injuries right away, he tried to act as though he didn't.

"Good morning, ma'am. I'm Jim. Looking for a car today?" He enthusiastically stretched out his hand.

"Yes. I want that one," Leah said, ignoring his handshake attempt. She pointed to the 1978 Jeep Wagoneer.

"You don't want that bulky thing. It's considered a collector's car. Let's me and you go check out one of those sweet little sedans up front with all the bells and whistles," he said.

"Sir, I'm not sweet and I'm not little. I'm bulky. I need something with some room." Leah walked around the Jeep, giving it a good looking over. It had been fully remodeled, with tinted windows and new tires with shiny chrome rims. Jim reluctantly unlocked it so she could inspect the inside. It had custom tan leather seats and a new radio with a CD player. It seemed quite retro with a few updated touches. She knew she had to have it.

"Can you pop the hood, please?"

Jim did as he was told. "Everything has been restored. It has a brand-new V8 motor and a newly upgraded transmission." He droned on for a few minutes about the other upgrades.

Leah nodded as though she understood exactly what he was saying. He could have told her it had a new space engine and she wouldn't have known any better. She continued the act for a few more minutes before asking about the price.

"This beauty will run you forty-five thousand dollars," the salesman said without hesitation.

"That's ridiculous."

"I agree. This is intended for old geezers with more money than sense, who just want something to add to their car collection." The salesman motioned back to the front of the lot. "I can put you in a brand-new car for half that, and it would be a lot better on gas too."

Leah motioned to the Jeep. "You can do better than that, and you know it."

"My boss is going to kill me if I go any lower than forty." He shrugged.

"I'll pay you thirty thousand, cash." Leah couldn't care less about the cost. It just felt good to stand up to a man and not worry about being punched in the face for it.

Jim stood there, shaking his head, while looking at the vehicle in question. Leah removed her hat so that he could get a good look at her. "Sir, excuse me for saying this, but I have literally been living through a hell you wouldn't be able to fathom. I don't have the strength to stand in this lot all day. Now accept my offer, or I'm leaving." She turned to leave.

"Okay. Thirty thousand, cash, and you have yourself a deal."

Within thirty minutes, Leah had paid the man. In return, he handed over two sets of keys and signed over the title for the Jeep Wagoneer.

"I would have paid forty-five." She smiled slightly as she climbed into her very own vehicle.

"Figures." Jim laughed.

Leah celebrated her successful purchase with a stop at a donut shop. Before returning to the hotel to pack, she stopped to fill the gas tank and grabbed a road map of the East Coast. It was time to pick a new beginning, and Southern coastal living sounded like a good enough place to start. A few hours after sunset, Leah struck out on her road trip to the unknown.

She had no clue interstate driving would take such a toll on her broken body. She stopped every so often to stretch her cramping legs and aching neck and shoulders. She couldn't take her prescribed pain medicine and drive, so plain Tylenol had to substitute during the trip. Close to dawn, the pain became nearly unbearable. She spent the next hour driving through tears.

She begged her throbbing body to just hold out until she could make it to the Atlantic Ocean. The more she begged, the more the pain and fatigue increased. She finally gave in and took the next exit off the interstate. She knew she was less than an hour from the coast, but making even that short distance would not be happening.

THE SIGN WELCOMED HER to Rivertown, South Carolina. The quaint town skirted a wide river that was lined with well-kept homes and shops. Leah noticed Mother Nature had not divvied out her fall gifts yet. Lawns were still lush and green with summer color, and most of the trees were holding on to their shaggy green coats. This didn't seem to bother the townspeople, for they had spread their own autumn decor throughout the area. Various scarecrows leaned against the black lampposts that lined the sidewalks, and with their mischievous grins and button eyes, they watched over the town.

An array of wreaths adorned each and every door for as far as Leah could see. A clothing boutique's door was almost hidden behind the voluptuous wreath made out of fat mesh ribbon in orange and brown with gold cording woven throughout. It was odd to describe but very appealing to look at.

Various sizes and styles of pumpkins and gourds, along with fall leaf garlands, were visible on each porch. A brick town house had a scarecrow sitting in a rocking chair on the front porch, making Leah do a double take. At first glance, it looked like a farmer wearing his overalls and straw hat, sitting lazily.

As Leah slowed the Jeep to a crawl, she spotted a café on the corner, facing the dark, enchanting water and a cozy park. She parked at the curb and tried to pull herself together before climbing out. She grabbed her scarf out of her bag and wrapped it around her neck to cover the healing bruises. She pulled the sun visor down to inspect her face in the mirror. Not happy with what she saw, Leah grudgingly shoved her black cap back on her head. As she eyed the sickly yellow-and-green palette of her skin, she wished that she'd grabbed her makeup during her hasty escape from the loft. Some concealer would really come in handy. Nothing could help the mess on her bottom lip. The jagged split was puffy and resembled leather with tiny barbs sticking out. Leah wished she had something she could use to extract the gross-looking stitches. Adding that to her mental to-do list, she stiffly maneuvered out of her Jeep and walked to the café entrance.

The building was a two-story redbrick structure with expansive windows along the first floor's front and sides. Each set of massive windows was shaded with sprawling royal-blue awnings, which were decorated with vibrantly painted sunflowers and whimsical white letters spelling out *Lulu's Café* across the remaining space. It looked inviting from the outside. Peering into the window, Leah could see that the café was bustling with customers. Outside the café, the sidewalk was lined with wrought-iron tables and chairs. Every table was occupied with customers chatting as they sipped steaming mugs of coffee.

The sign for the store hours indicated that, Monday through Saturday, the café opened at six each morning and closed at two each afternoon, and it was closed on Sundays. Leah found the hours a bit odd. Most restaurants served dinner and were open on Sundays too, or so she thought. She reminded herself that she was in a new environment and that the customs from the West Coast probably wouldn't apply here.

The café had its fall decorations on display as well. Large planter boxes overflowed with giant yellow and orange mums. One had a wooden sign sticking out from the middle declaring, *Happy Fall, Y'all.*

Leah was beginning to think the place was too happy and, more importantly, too busy for her liking, when she spotted a vacant four-person table right inside the door. She made her way in and slipped into the chair closest to the window. She deliberately faced away from the entrance, hoping not to draw much attention. Once she was situated, she noticed that the back of the café was made up of a large butcher-block counter that housed a bakery case full of treats on the right. The remainder of the counter was lined with half a dozen stools, with customers perched on each one. Leah noted approvingly that the tables and chairs were a variety of mismatched shapes and sizes stained in the same mahogany tint. She liked the relaxed, unpretentious atmosphere.

Leah watched a petite lady behind the counter serving up coffee and laughs. Her stomach began to rumble at the fragrant smells whirling around her, so she turned her attention to the menu resting on the table. Turkey sausage, turkey bacon, egg-white omelets, whole grain breads and cereal, fresh fruit . . .

Leah blinked at the odd menu. She gazed around at the customers enjoying their healthy meals. Her heart had been set on a stack of pancakes and greasy bacon. She studied the bakery case but found no donuts hiding.

"Humph." She went back to studying the menu.

"I didn't keep you waiting too long, did I?" A Southern drawl interrupted Leah's thoughts.

Leah looked up to find the petite lady with a perfectly

coiffed silver bob smiling at her. She was so short that she was nearly eye level with a seated Leah. Her clear gray eyes seemed to bubble with hospitality. Leah instantly liked the woman and gave her a slight smile, being careful not to stretch her bottom lip.

"Well, you gonna keep giving me that sweet smile or are you gonna order something?" the lady asked in a teasing voice.

Leah pointed at the bright-orange cursive *L* embroidered thickly on one of the lady's apron pockets. "Please tell me you're Lulu."

"Of course I'm Lulu. Why do you ask?" Lulu smoothed her ruffled apron, which swam in a variety of rich-blue swirls.

"You match the happiness of the place perfectly," Leah said.

"Well, that's the nicest thing someone has said to me today. What can I get you?"

"Coffee and whatever you recommend."

Lulu gave her a wink and strolled back to the kitchen. Almost immediately, a young lady carried back a mug and a carafe full of coffee. While Leah waited for her breakfast, she retrieved a halved pain pill and washed it down with some hot coffee.

Her hands trembled from the unrelenting pain in her neck and shoulders. Other body parts, still suffering from the beating and miscarriage, screamed for relief as well. Tears threatened at the acknowledgment of those pains. Leah tried to make a quick escape to the restroom. Wincing in pain from standing too quickly, she inhaled a shaky breath to ward off the dizzying pain. Once secured in the restroom, she pulled the hat off and splashed cold water onto her puffy face. Leah took several deep breaths before looking at her reflection in the mirror. Oh, how she hated the mirror. She dug out the curl serum and a comb to fix the rat's nest on her head. She worked the serum through her hair and tried to smooth the curls. The task helped to calm her down.

After composing herself, Leah headed back to the table and discovered a bounty of breakfast waiting for her. A royal-blue plate held an egg-white omelet filled with tomatoes, onions, and spinach, and topped with a sprinkling of white cheese and fresh herbs. Resting beside the plate was a steaming bowl of oatmeal covered with dried fruits and nuts. A jar of honey and small cup of cream had been placed beside the bowl. She sampled the omelet and was pleasantly surprised at how flavorful it was. Once she devoured the omelet, she turned her sights on the oatmeal. *At least it's not the mushy kind I had to eat in the group homes.* She pulled the bowl closer and carefully added some honey and cream. She gave it a good stir, then took a cautious bite. Once again, the flavorful dish surprised her. The combination of the creamy oatmeal mixed with the tangy fruit bits and crunchy nuts was perfect. With the bowl empty, Leah felt completely satisfied and nourished. She was astonished that a meal could have such an effect. She sipped her coffee and thought it was no wonder the place was crowded.

The pill was finally easing the pain, so Leah decided to stay and enjoy the coffee for a little while. She needed to find a hotel, but she couldn't muster the motivation to leave.

"You get enough to eat, sweetheart?" Lulu asked as she strolled over and deposited another carafe of coffee. She gathered the dishes and empty carafe.

Leah smiled at the lady's endearment at the end of her question. "More than enough. That was delicious." She fished out her wallet.

"No need in rushing off. Have some more coffee." Lulu grabbed a newspaper off the neighboring table and handed it to Leah. "And enjoy this boring newspaper." She didn't wait on a reply from Leah before rushing back off with the energy of a teenager. The lady's face held very few wrinkles, making it hard to accurately gauge her age, but Leah thought she was somewhere in her sixties.

Leah did as she was told. An hour later, the carafe was empty and the newspaper had been thoroughly read, twice. She found nothing boring about the local paper. It was unexpectedly upbeat with very little in way of the negative stories that normally dominated her paper back in Washington. This paper was dotted with celebratory news of weddings and births and new business openings. The entertainment section, filled with details on upcoming festivals, dominated a good portion of the paper. There was a date change announcement for an upcoming community class on how to prepare perfect jars of fruit preserves. The selected book for the upcoming book club meeting at the Rivertown Library was *Chasing Fireflies* by Charles Martin. Leah jotted the book title down on a scrap piece of paper so that she could remember to read it sometime. The paper also held a registration page for a youth fishing tournament at the Big Oaks Plantation. And on the back page was a large advertisement for the annual fall fair coming to town the following week. The paper was filled with refreshing articles. Leah decided in that moment that her fantasy of Southern charm was not a myth, but a lovely reality.

Leah figured it was time to settle her bill and find a hotel for a night or two. She neatly folded the paper and left it on the table. After paying the young lady at the counter, she made a stop at the restroom. When she came back, she spotted Lulu, with a large basket of potatoes and carrots, sitting at her table. She approached the table to gather her coat and say good-bye.

"Do you mind keeping me company while I work on this stuff for today's soup?" Lulu asked as she continued to peel the first potato.

Leah glanced at the door before easing back down in her chair. "Only if I can help."

* * *

Lulu had watched the poor girl all morning and hated to guess at what could have happened to her to cause so much visible damage. She seemed so fragile and tightly bound by grief. Lulu would have never expected the young lady's willingness to help out.

"What's your name, sweetheart?"

"Leah."

"An *L* name. This is fate." Lulu smiled as she got up to fetch another knife from the kitchen. She grabbed the onions and garlic for peeling also, trying to prolong Leah's company. As she sat back down, she noticed the cast that was nearly undetectable under the long-sleeved shirt.

"Can you manage with a broken arm?" she asked as she held up the knife.

"I'm right-handed, and I can use my fingers on my left hand." Leah raised her left hand and waved the fingers that were peeking from the cast.

Lulu handed the knife over to a slightly shaky Leah, and both women set out on the task at hand. Lulu observed that Leah worked quickly and efficiently for someone far from being up to par. She commented on Leah's neat knife skills and asked if she had much practice. This question only got her a slight shrug, but the action seemed to cause the young woman pain. Lulu chatted about a special singing at her church next week and discussed how she would try to manage judging a pie contest and make it in time to listen to the singing group. She went over the day's menu as Leah politely listened and worked in silence. Lulu tried engaging Leah in conversation.

"I've lived here all my life. It's a great town. How about you? Where are you from?"

"Up North," Leah said.

"So, what brings you down South?"

"Relocating." Leah finished up her last potato and reached for the carrots.

"Where are you relocating to?"

"Down South," Leah said with a slight smile.

Lulu roared with laughter. "Spoken like a true smart-mouth!" She gave up after that. Once they completed prepping the vegetables, Lulu gathered everything up into the basket. "I need to get these in the pot. I'll be back in a few minutes."

* * *

Leah watched the petite lady disappear into the kitchen. She slipped out of the chair and wandered around the dining area to stretch her legs and get a better look at the paintings on the wall. One painting was of a rooster with a burnt-orange head, which gradually blended into a rainbow of brightly colored feathers that fanned through to his tail. Another was of a large sunflower with deep-golden petals that appeared to be dancing in a breeze. One canvas was decorated in blues and greens that swirled in brilliant patterns. It reminded Leah of ocean waves in an abstract way. Her absolute favorite piece of artwork was the beach sunrise. The glowing oranges and yellows seem to seep from the teal waters and burst into the sky.

"I need to see that for myself," she whispered as she

studied the breathtaking artwork. After admiring the picture for a while, Leah made her way back into the restroom, splashed some cold water on her face, and rewashed her hands. When she returned to try for another good-bye, a large basket of luscious red apples sat on the table along with two paring knives, two round cutting boards, an apple corer, and a large bowl. She decided to sit back down and wait for further instructions. She glanced at her watch and was surprised that it was only ten thirty in the morning. Lulu joined her at the table with two glasses of ice water.

"Would you mind helping me prepare these apples for tartlets?" Lulu handed Leah one of the water glasses and took a long sip from her own.

"Sure." Leah took a sip from her glass and thought how energetic Lulu appeared when compared to her own slothful movements.

"Drinking water can help reduce swelling," Lulu said matter-of-factly. Without waiting for a response, Lulu dove into apple slicing. "I like to leave the skin on, so just core it and cut it into thin slices," she said as she demonstrated.

After they sliced all the apples, Lulu squeezed some fresh lemon juice over the slices and gave them a good toss.

"I'm trying out a new recipe for vegetable soup today. Would you mind sticking around a little while longer and giving me your opinion on it?" Lulu asked. "Sometimes I don't know if these locals really like something or if they are just trying to appease me."

Leah glanced at her watch. She had already been in the café for over three hours. Although she really had no desire to leave the oddly cozy place, she knew she needed to locate a hotel soon.

Lulu seemed to pick up on her hesitation. She hurried to the counter, where she grabbed two magazines and a freshly baked pumpkin muffin that her helper had just pulled from the oven. "Here." Lulu handed Leah the treat along with the magazines. "This will hold you over until the soup is done."

Leah accepted the offer and sat back down. After every morsel of the muffin was consumed and she finished her glass of water, Leah opened one of the magazines and began skimming through it. Out of the corner of her eye, she noticed another apron-clad young woman come in the café and join the other two ladies in the kitchen.

The waitress bustled back into the dining area and wiped down the tables. She refreshed napkin holders and replaced the breakfast menus with lunch menus. As she placed one on Leah's table, she introduced herself as Alice and asked if she could get her anything.

"Do you have a Diet Pepsi?"

"No, ma'am," Alice said.

"How about a Diet Coke?"

"No, ma'am. We don't serve any type of soda. Lulu says they are bad for you. We serve iced tea, juices, coffee, flavored seltzer waters, and plain water."

"Wow. This has to be the first restaurant I have ever been to that doesn't serve soda."

"Yeah. Me too." Alice laughed. "I make sure to get my soda fix before my shift."

"I guess I'll just take some more water, please."

Alice brought back a small pitcher of ice water. She filled Leah's glass, then set the pitcher on the table. "Lulu said to leave it with you." She smiled politely and then headed back to the counter. She pulled out a small chalkboard and wrote out the day's specials. Harvest vegetable was declared the soup of the day and apple ginger tartlets were the dessert of the day.

It was well after eleven, and the tables began to refill

quickly. Leah enjoyed the sweet and savory aromas drifting from the kitchen. Her mouth started to water, so she picked up the menu and studied it. The selection consisted of interesting salads with homemade dressings, turkey burgers, various healthy sandwich choices, and vegetable sides. A note reminded customers that the menu changed seasonally or whenever Lulu got a wild hair to do so.

Several minutes later, Alice dropped off a generous bowl of vegetable soup and an apple tartlet.

"I didn't order yet," Leah said as the waitress started to walk away.

Alice turned around. "Lulu said to bring you that, on the house. Around here, you do as Lulu says, no questions asked." She then scooted over to another table to take an older couple's order.

Leah glanced around to find a packed house. She waved Alice over and asked her what day it was.

"It's Saturday," Alice said and gently patted Leah's hand before heading to the kitchen.

That explains why the café is so busy. Wait . . . Saturday? How long has it been since the accident? Almost two weeks? She couldn't do the math. The frustration and unsuccessful attempt at concentration brought on a headache. She dismissed the trivia and studied the bountiful meal before her.

Just looking at the steaming bowl, filled with every vegetable imaginable, was instantly soothing. After scraping the bowl clean, Leah moved on to the dainty apple tartlet. The thin, crisp apples, combined with an equally thin crust, were quite enjoyable. The subtle hints of cinnamon and ginger didn't overpower the delicate flavor of the apples. Her only disappointment was when it was all gone.

With the dishes now empty and the pitcher of water completely drained, Leah sat back and marveled at how well she had eaten. She had no doubt she was well over the recommended servings of fruits and vegetables for the day. Ignoring what the waitress said about being on the house, Leah paid and left a hefty tip. She was gathering her things when Lulu strolled out of the kitchen with two cups of freshly brewed coffee.

"Will you keep me company for a while longer?" Lulu asked as she sat at Leah's table.

"I really should go, but one more cup of coffee does sound good." Leah accepted the coffee, thinking it would perk her up some before searching for a hotel.

The two ladies sat chatting about the beautiful paintings, the unique menu, and the breathtaking view of the park and river from the café. Before Leah realized it, her watch indicated it was approaching two in the afternoon.

She absently picked at the itchy stitches in her lip while trying to figure out how to get away from the sweet lady.

"Those look like they are about overdue to be removed," Lulu said.

"I think so too. I haven't figured out what to do with them yet." Leah stared down at the empty coffee cup. "Could you direct me to a hotel? I've been up for over twenty-four hours . . . I think."

"Can you hold out for a few more minutes?"

Leah nodded and wondered what the woman was up to.

"I think I have the perfect place for you to stay."

"Okay. As long as it's near, I guess I can hold out a little longer," Leah said.

"It's in walking distance. Trust me." Lulu patted her new friend's arm before heading back to the counter.

Leah tried to stretch her sore back, causing her left side to pinch in sharp pain. She was contemplating taking some pain medicine when she noticed a tall, blond-haired guy stroll through the door and head straight to the counter. In a flash, a short brunette came up on his heels. They placed their orders, and the tall guy paid. Leah watched as they chatted with the others at the counter.

Leah gave a quiet snort as she noticed the guy was wearing ratty cargo shorts, a T-shirt, and flip-flops. Where she came from, the shorts were put away long before October. She pondered for a minute and was pretty sure it was already November now. Leah thought the warm-skinned woman, looking all fancy in her designer jeans and sequined tank top, resembled an exotic Barbie doll. She looked down at her own attire of a long-sleeved black shirt, black stretch pants, and a long, bulky coat. The only color came from the multicolored scarf that she now self-consciously gathered closer around her neck.

The woman at the counter grabbed her take-out bag and was turning to leave when she caught Leah's eye. She spun back around to face the tall guy and stretched way up to plant a kiss on his lips. As she did this, his gaze landed on Leah and remained there for the duration of the kiss. Leah was unable to free herself from the snare of his gaze. The beautiful brunette eventually let go of him and sashayed out of the café, leaving the guy frozen in his tracks. He gave Leah a measured look before following the young woman out the door.

• • •

Crowley Mason looked down at the brunette bombshell beside him.

"Why did you kiss me?" He and Ana were lifelong friends, but they both knew they'd never be anything more than that.

"You did kiss me back," she said, raising a perfectly plucked eyebrow.

"I'm a gentleman. It would have been rude not to. Now answer my question."

Ana dropped the sweet girlie act. "Jenna stopped by and informed me that a strange woman had been hanging around Lulu's all day. You are the most eligible bachelor around, and I didn't want some gold digger messing in your life." Ana placed her well-manicured hand on her hip. "I was trying to do you a favor, *sir*."

Crowley's mouth twitched to refrain from laughing. "Ana, strangers pass through this town all the time on their way to the beach. Lulu's is a famous stop for tourists, you know."

"This woman ain't just passing through, Crowley. She's been sitting in that café since way early this morning. Why on earth would anyone sit there that long? It's just plain weird." Ana frowned.

"You didn't get a good look at that woman, did you?"

"No, but I guess you did!" Ana said, unable to hide the obvious jealousy.

Crowley chose to ignore her jab. "She was riddled with nasty bruises and stitched-up cuts. There was a cast on her arm. I'm guessing she is recovering from some awful accident. Wouldn't you be moving a little slow too?"

It was evident from Ana's expression that she felt foolish, and Crowley knew he had made his point. Reluctantly, he still had one more problem to discuss. He placed her in a fierce bear hug and mussed her hair. "Ana, you know I love you. As a sister. Your friendship is priceless to me."

"I think you've explained that already to my stubborn butt about a hundred times. I obviously don't know how to take a hint." She leaned her forehead against his taut abdomen. "Can't blame a girl for trying." Full of sass, Ana tried to push the tension away even further. "Besides, I could never be with a man who actually makes me go fishing." She wrinkled her nose and looked up at him. "Gross!"

Crowley chuckled with relief. "I see your point. You're a lucky woman to figure that out before it was too late. You should see the giant catfish I caught this morning. I'm going to have Lulu make a stew out of the monster."

"You need to wear sunblock and a hat." Ana's eyes lit up in a teasing smile. "Those crow's-feet around your eyes are going to get worse." She pushed away from him and pulled her salad out of the bag.

Crowley watched her for a few minutes. He had tried to make a go of the dating relationship and really had wanted it to work, but he couldn't get past the feeling of dating his sister. He also knew that Ana loved and respected him too much to deny his wishes of remaining good friends.

"You know I love you too," she said as he walked away.

He raised his hand without turning around. "I know." He made his way over to a bench where the stranger's vehicle was parked and sat down to enjoy his lunch. Crowley was about to take the first bite of his chicken club wrap when he noticed Jessup Barns shuffling by.

"Some weather we having. Here it is November and it still feels like August," Jessup commented without slurring, which was surprising.

Crowley shrugged. "I don't mind. Winter will show up eventually." He tore his wrap in half and offered a portion of it to Jessup as the little man sat beside him.

"True." Jessup accepted the food and took a big bite. Crowley did the same and regarded him out of the corner of his eye, relieved to see he was dressed in semi-clean clothes and having a lucid day. Jessup was a decent man deep down. Sadly, he fell into a bottle when he couldn't deal with circumstances and his whole life went to pot.

Jessup let out a low whistle. "Now that's a nice set of wheels right there. Don't you think?" He nodded his head toward the Jeep Wagoneer.

"I sure do. I could use a set just like them for beach trips." Crowley took another bite of his wrap.

"Now that you mention it, I think that would be a perfect beach cruiser."

Crowley chuckled at the idea of Jessup cruising the beach in anything, especially since the little man didn't even have a driver's license or enough wits to earn the privilege back.

"You have a good one," Jessup mumbled once he finished his part of Crowley's lunch.

"You too," Crowley said as he watched the man cross the street to the riverside park.

Crowley polished off the rest of his wrap and devoured the apple tartlet in three bites. He had lost track of time earlier while he was fishing and had not eaten all day. Once he was finished, he tossed his trash into a metal bin and slowly walked around the Jeep to give it a good looking over.

His phone had beeped nonstop all morning with texts and calls about a strange woman, who looked like death warmed over, in town. Hearing that she was hanging around Lulu's had raised a red flag with Crowley. Lulu was considered his longtime guardian, but Crowley actually felt obligated to take care of her. So, of course, he ended his fishing trip early and came over to check on her.

Nothing could have prepared him for what he found

sitting in the café. It wasn't just the obvious evidence of
the young woman's broken body. It was the haunted look
in her eyes. He knew instantly that this wasn't a typical
tourist heading to the beach, but a woman on the run.

The vehicle gave away very few clues. Crowley spotted
a large suitcase and duffel bag, along with several empty
coffee cups, in the backseat. The teal-colored Jeep had a
temporary tag that gave no indication as to where it had
been purchased.

After circling once more, Crowley sat back on the
bench to sip his tea and wait for the departure of the lady.
He contemplated going inside and getting something else
to eat when he heard Lulu at the door with the young
woman. He slid his sunglasses down to mask his con-
cerned eyes and struck a casual pose, resting his arms over
the back of the bench. He watched her out of the corner
of his eye as she stiffly walked to her vehicle. Just walking
seemed to be causing her a great deal of pain.

"Nice day we're having," Crowley said.

Leah jumped a bit at the sound of his deep voice.
She opened the passenger door and placed her purse
on the seat before replying to him. "Isn't it November?"
She raised her right palm up to the sky as if gauging the
temperature.

He knew instantly that this woman was in the wrong
parts by her northern accent. "Ma'am, you're in the
South, and the South refuses to play by the seasons' typical rules." Crowley studied her all-black wardrobe, noting
the black ball cap pushed low over her blonde locks. He
could see fading bruises peeking out around the edges of
her scarf. "So we just have to play along with the South's
rules." He lifted his legs slightly and flapped the bottoms
of his flip-flops to make his point.

He continued to study her through the sunglasses.

She looks like she should be in a hospital bed somewhere. She had gathered the scarf closer around her neck before she walked to the driver's side, and Crowley wondered if she caught him staring at her.

"You have a good one," Crowley said before she closed the door behind her.

She paid him no attention as she cranked the engine and drove forward a little before taking the alley street between the café and Ana's boutique. She parked and began easing out of the vehicle.

Crowley jumped up and jogged after the Jeep. "Excuse me, ma'am. You can't park there. This is a private lot."

Lulu was at the back door of the café by then. "It's okay, boy. I told her to park there."

"Unbelievable," he said to himself as he jogged over to question Lulu. *"Why?"* he asked in an exaggerated tone as he reached her.

"We are doing each other a favor. I need someone to help me run the café, and she needs a place to stay."

Crowley gestured toward the wounded woman standing beside her Jeep. "She doesn't look like she's going to be much help. I just don't think this is a good idea, Lulu."

"Your opinion has been duly noted. Now, help her unload her stuff."

Crowley reluctantly followed Lulu back to the young woman. As they approached, she turned to face them.

"Crowley Mason, this is Leah Allen," Lulu said. "Leah, this here is my most favorite young man in Rivertown. Crowley watches out for me and I watch out for him."

Crowley tipped his head at Leah, not wanting to be rude as he slipped his shades off and crammed them in one of the cargo shorts pockets.

"If you need anything, you let me or Crowley know." Before Crowley could protest, Lulu said, "Now, let's grab your stuff and get out of this heat. I'm starting to melt."

Crowley reached in the backseat and swooped up the suitcase and duffel bag before grabbing up Leah's oversize purse. He turned to make his way inside to the second-floor apartment without another word. It was pointless to try to reason with Lulu. He bounded upstairs, taking two steps at a time, and deposited the luggage in the small bedroom. He was back down the stairs by the time the two women made it through the back door.

"Go on up and get yourself situated. I'll check on you in a little while, sweetheart." Lulu smiled at Leah. Without another word, the exhausted-looking woman trudged up the stairs. Once she closed the door behind her, Crowley turned his attention to Lulu.

"You want to explain to me what in the world you are thinking?" Crowley whispered. "She could be a mass murderer or career thief, and you are just going to let her loose in your life?"

Lulu stood with her hands on her hips. "Is that really what your instincts are telling you?"

"No, but they are telling me that this woman is in some kind of trouble."

"Well, she may be, but my instincts are telling me that this young lady needs to grow a sit for a while," Lulu said as she moved to the café's counter, where she started jotting down a list. "I've called some things in already to the drugstore, but here are a few more things I need you to pick up." She handed the list to Crowley.

He accepted it and turned to head out. "I don't like you very much right now," he said as he pushed through the front door.

Lulu laughed. "That's okay, as long as you still love me."

• • •

Crowley hurried through the door at the Rivertown Pharmacy, grabbed a shopping basket, and made quick work of tackling Lulu's extensive list. He rechecked the list against the items in his cart—antibiotic ointment, Epsom salt, assorted vitamins, and bandages. Once the supplies were rounded up, Crowley headed to the checkout, where more supplies were waiting.

"Hey, Nancy. Is this stuff for Lulu too?" Crowley scanned over everything, which included a large box of maxi pads, stool softener pills, medicated lip ointment, small scissors, and tweezers. He was a bit relieved that Lulu hadn't left it up to him to pick out women's personal products. He shook his head and mumbled, "I left my boat for this?"

"What's all this stuff for?" Nancy asked while she rang up and bagged the supplies.

"Looks like Lulu is taking on another pet project." Crowley shrugged. He knew Lulu all too well. Once that stubborn woman set her mind to something, there was no changing it. All Crowley could do was try to protect her. As he gathered all the bags, he contemplated how to get some information on the new woman in town. He was fairly certain she would not be freely sharing her life story with him, but he had to figure out what exactly Lulu was getting herself into.

Crowley's phone began to play "Dirt Road Anthem," pulling him out of his train of thought. He pulled the phone out of his pocket and saw Lulu's name flash on the screen. "What did you forget?" he asked, instead of a proper hello.

"Nothing. I've been so wrapped up in welcoming Leah today that I completely forgot I was supposed to babysit the Oliver twins this evening. Just drop the stuff off to Leah and lock up behind you, okay?"

"Yes, ma'am," Crowley said.

"Listen, Leah has taken some pain medicine, so she is probably already out for the rest of the day. Try to be quiet, please."

"Yes, ma'am." Crowley hit End and pocketed his phone.

He reentered through the front door of the silent café, pausing long enough to lock it behind him before heading upstairs to the apartment. He was surprised to find the young woman passed out on the oversize floral sofa and not the bed.

Crowley placed the bags on the small dining table and turned his attention back to the woman. Her long-sleeved shirt and scarf were discarded on the floor, leaving her wearing a black tank top that exposed even more damage. He noticed her hair was damp from sweat, so he checked the thermostat and bumped it down to sixty-five to quickly cool the apartment.

As the air kicked on and sent a hushed hum throughout the apartment, Crowley quietly walked over to the sitting area and noticed that most of Leah's purse contents were spilled out onto the coffee table. Her license lay exposed, so he took out his phone and snapped a picture of it. That would be a start at finding some information. He calculated her age at only twenty-nine years old. Crowley thought that was mighty young to have already lived a complicated life.

Leah hadn't moved an inch the entire time Crowley had been there, so he took a moment to make sure she was still breathing before inspecting the numerous wounds riddling her body. The edge of her tank top had ridden up some, revealing an Ace bandage wrapped haphazardly around her midsection, but he wasn't sure what it was supposed to be protecting. His eyes moved to Leah's right hand where it cradled her broken left wrist and noticed surgical tape residue from where an IV had been inserted. With her hat removed, he could now see a nasty line of stitches over her left eye. Stitches also etched her bottom lip, and her bruised chin was scabbed over thickly. He had to resist the strong urge to inspect her swollen and bruised upper left arm and shoulder with the tips of his fingers. Crowley figured whatever had happened did most of its damage to her left side. The battered woman looked like she had come close to death.

Shaking his head, Crowley crossed the room and checked out the fridge. He found it empty with the temperature bumped up. He adjusted the temperature on both the fridge and freezer before slipping downstairs to the café. He filled a take-out bag with bottled waters, a few leftover sandwiches, and fruit salads. He stepped into the kitchen and pulled out some Gatorades he kept stashed in the back refrigerator and added them to the bag.

Crowley quietly reentered the much-cooler apartment and found Leah still sleeping soundly. He put everything away in the fridge except for one bottle of water, which he placed on the coffee table with a scribbled note—*Food in fridge.* He readjusted the thermostat, pulled a light quilt out of the linen closet, draped it over Leah, and headed down to lock up the café for Lulu.

LEAH WOKE WITH A START, feeling disoriented and absolutely parched. She was slowly righting herself to a seated
position on the couch when her eyes fell on the bottle of
water. She grabbed it up and drained the entire bottle.

She sat for a few moments, trying to get her bearings.
She'd had the recurring dream of being in the meadow
again. Although it was incredibly painful, Leah welcomed
it. The brief unconscious moment of pure peace with her
daughter was worth the tears of grief that always followed
waking up.

As the tears and grief subsided, Leah shuffled to the
bathroom. When she reentered the living room, she saw
shopping bags on the dining room table, a note on the
coffee table letting her know there was food in the fridge,
and a quilt draped from the sofa to the floor.

"How did I sleep through all of this? How long have
I been asleep?" Leah moved to the kitchen to check out
the contents of the fridge. She immediately pulled out
an orange Gatorade and gulped it greedily. As she raised
her arm to take another long drink, she caught a whiff
of herself. She tried to figure out how many days had
passed since her last shower, but the fogginess of her
brain refused to clear enough to allow it. Frustrated, she

gave up and was about to go grab some clean clothes and head for an overdue shower when there was a knock at the door.

"It's Lulu."

"Come in." Leah opened the door and moved out of the way, hoping Lulu didn't smell her.

Lulu hurried off to the kitchen with a plate of food covered in foil. "I brought you some Sunday dinner. Chicken bog with some butter beans, okra, and a baked sweet potato."

Leah had no idea what chicken bog could be but thanked the little lady anyway.

"It'll keep for a while. I thought you might like to get those stitches out and get cleaned up a bit first." Lulu rummaged through the bags and pulled out a pair of small scissors and tweezers. She pointed to one of the dining chairs and instructed Leah to sit down.

"You're a little overdressed for stitch removal," Leah said as she took in Lulu's light-blue linen dress and tan pumps.

"Oh, this is what I wore to church. I've just not had a chance to change yet, but I can manage stitches just fine in high heels."

Leah happily let the determined woman free her from the itchy things. Lulu started with the stitches over Leah's left eye, then removed the ones in her lip. Leah couldn't help but run her tongue over the smoother surface of her bottom lip, knowing it would never be completely smooth again.

"Thank you. That feels amazing." Leah worked her tongue over her lip again.

"You're welcome," Lulu said as she pointed to the bags. "In one of those is some medicated lip ointment and a tube of antibiotic cream for any other wounds."

"Okay," Leah said as Lulu fished the ointments out and then went over the rest of the contents, explaining how Leah was to use it all.

"Be sure to take the vitamins daily with food. They will help your body heal as well."

"How much do I owe you for all of this stuff?" Leah asked as she took it all in.

"You owe me getting better so you can start helping me run the café. Remember that was our deal," Lulu said.

"Yes, but that didn't include you buying me things. I have mon—"

"Don't argue with me. It's pointless." Lulu laughed. "Just use all of this like I said. Don't let my efforts go to waste." She looked Leah over. "How long has it been since your . . . um . . . accident?"

Leah hesitated. "I think it's been about two weeks. It's hard to remember exactly." She was beginning to think something was wrong with her jumbled brain.

"Sweetheart, that's understandable. Let's give you another week to heal before I start acquainting you with the café," Lulu said.

"I can start tomorrow."

Lulu lightly tugged at the edge of the Ace bandage that was unraveling around Leah's midsection. "What's going on under there?"

"A few cracked ribs." Leah pulled the bottom of her shirt down.

Lulu then pointed to the cast. "And how about this?" She gently touched Leah's puffy collarbone next. "And this?"

"They're both just fractures."

"Take another week to rest and heal. I promise to work you good and hard once you're better." Lulu looked around. "Where's the sling for your shoulder?"

Leah had just about forgotten about that thing. She had barely worn it. "In my bag."

"Put it on after your shower and leave it on," Lulu said and gave Leah a warm smile.

Leah was beginning to think the little woman didn't know how to frown nor take no for an answer. "Why are you doing all of this for me?"

"Why not?" Lulu began gathering the pharmacy purchases and putting them away in the appropriate places. "I'll check on you tomorrow. If you need anything, my number is by the phone. I only live a few blocks from here, so don't hesitate."

"Thank you, Lulu, for everything."

"No problem, sweetheart." Lulu walked out the door but spun around as if she forgot something. "By the way, welcome to Rivertown." She gave Leah another warm smile before disappearing down the stairs.

Leah headed to the shower and spent a good part of the afternoon grooming her neglected body. She was thankful that all the supplies she needed, which included soap, shampoo, and a much-needed razor, were waiting for her in the bathroom. Lulu forgot nothing. After applying the antibiotic cream to the various wounds and slathering the ointment on her lip, she secured a new Ace bandage around her tender abdomen. She dressed in yoga pants and an oversize T-shirt and then strapped her left arm into the sling.

Once Leah had painstakingly completed all of that, she was famished. She pulled a red Gatorade out of the fridge and stood at the small kitchen counter to eat. She was getting tired of all the sitting and lying down. She pulled the foil off the plate to inspect the chicken bog. She had no idea what a bog of any kind could possibly be, and she didn't find the word *bog* very appealing. She was relieved to find rice cooked with chunks of chicken breast and what she suspected to be smoked turkey sausage. It smelled heavenly. She dug into it, as well as the butter beans and okra, with gusto. Once Leah finished all of that, she unwrapped the sweet potato that had been split and seasoned with a heavy sprinkling of cinnamon. It tasted like candy to her. She was amazed at how sweet the potato was without tons of added sugar.

After rinsing the plate and taking her vitamins as directed, Leah set out to take a good look around her new home. It was a cozy apartment with soft buttercup-yellow walls and worn wooden floors. Nothing matched but somehow it all went together quite well. She had already fallen in love with the oversize sofa. A charming rocking chair and a golden-yellow wingback chair accompanied the sofa to form a quaint sitting area. The cream-colored lace curtains let the sun peek through, casting a warm hue over the apartment. The living room also shared the space with a round dinette table and four chairs, all stained red. Leah inspected a small cabinet that reminded her of Brent's liquor cabinet in the loft back in Washington. She was pleasantly surprised when she opened it and discovered a small flat-screen television.

The living room was separated from the kitchen by a small counter. The off-white appliances were outdated but immaculately clean and surrounded by handcrafted oak cabinets. Leah was absolutely falling in love with the charming apartment that she could now, somehow, call home. Only a day before, she was homeless and hopeless. Now she had a place of her own and an appealing job awaiting her.

Three doors lined the left wall of the apartment. Leah knew the first was the bedroom and the second was the bathroom. She crossed the room to inspect what was behind door number three. She found a large walk-in utility closet that housed a full-size washer and dryer. On the shelf above, a new box of washing powder, a jug of bleach, and fabric softener sat ready to be used. Leah gladly gathered her dirty laundry and began washing. Once that task was under way, Leah grabbed the rest of her Gatorade and finished it as she tried out the rocking chair.

The evening passed quietly. Feeling a bit hesitant on unpacking just yet, Leah decided to place the fresh laundry back into her suitcase for the time being. She then enjoyed one of the chicken salad sandwiches with a fruit salad for supper. Her appetite was coming back with a vengeance, and she was half-tempted to venture out for something sweet and fattening. She was uncomfortable leaving the apartment, so she settled for the other fruit salad.

To get her mind off her sweet tooth, Leah filled the claw-foot bathtub with steaming-hot water and Epsom salt that was infused with eucalyptus oil. She soaked her achy body until all of the heat had seeped away from the bath. After dressing in a loose cotton gown and taking a pain pill, Leah crawled underneath the soft chenille bedspread that adorned the antique brass bed. As she drifted off, her mind lingered on the peaceful thought that she felt at home for the first time in her entire life.

●　　●　　●

The week dragged by as the fog finally began to clear away from Leah's mind. She spent her mornings attending to her wounds and the rest of the day enjoying her cozy apartment or napping. She began taking over-the-counter pain medicines, hoping her mind would finish clearing.

Unfortunately, with the fog lifting, the memory of her dead husband came back with clarity. She was not remorseful about the devil being dead, but she was scared of going to jail because of it. Were the officials hunting her down? Had she been careful enough to leave no trail? Would they be able to recognize her if they did somehow catch up with her? All of these questions played over and over in the back of her mind, followed by repeated reassurances. The officials probably thought she was dead somewhere too, considering all the blood she had left behind. She had been careful not to leave any clue of herself in Tennessee. She had lost at least twenty pounds since anyone from Washington had seen her, and she was now back to her natural blonde hair color. All of the new scars helped too. Surely she was safe in this small, unknown town.

Lulu visited every day with three prepared meals, one hot and two cold. The meals always included spinach, blueberries, and something citrusy. Lulu explained these food items were said to promote healing, so she continuously forced them on Leah. She would also send up a freshly baked treat and a fruit smoothie once a day. Leah was astonished at how quickly she began feeling stronger, and the debilitating aches considerably receded.

Leah grew restless by midweek, so Lulu tried to talk her into going to the town's fall fair with her and Crowley. Leah, remembering how Crowley had unpleasantly reacted to her arrival, declined. She knew he wasn't thrilled with her presence, so she decided to avoid him. She enjoyed hearing all about Lulu's night out the next afternoon. Lulu went on and on about the pie contest and how she selected a coconut custard pie as the winner. She also talked about how Crowley tried eating his weight in pie and declared all the pies winners, to the delight of the contestants. Twenty blue ribbons were ordered and paid for by Crowley himself.

Lulu laughed her way through telling Leah how the fool got sick and nearly returned all the pie he devoured at the fair when he agreed to a marathon of rides with a few of the local teenage boys. Leah had to hold her side as she tried to subdue her own laughter at Lulu's telling of the story. She could sit and listen to the little lady for hours. The soft yet strong Southern twang of Lulu's voice was pure comfort.

•   •   •

Lulu tried to give Leah her space, but still enough attention to not let the young lady get lonely. She tried talking Ana and Crowley into visiting Leah, too, but both were hesitant.

"You'll warm up to her eventually. I don't see why you don't go ahead and get started with it now." Leah needed some younger company.

With Sunday approaching, Lulu put together a plan of introducing Leah. She invited her to attend church and then have a Sunday feast at her home. Leah finally agreed after the fourth time Lulu hounded her about it on Friday afternoon.

"I need some makeup or a brown bag to go over my head before I completely agree."

"I'm fresh out of paper bags, but the drugstore has a great makeup counter with all kinds of brands. Get ready and we'll go," Lulu said.

As they made their way past Ana's boutique, Ana was locking up. Lulu stopped so that she could introduce the two women.

"Ana, this is my new friend Leah." Lulu gestured toward the incredibly tall Leah before gesturing to the incredibly short Ana. "This is Ana, and she owns this fine boutique. She is an absolute expert when it comes to all things fashion."

Leah studied the building and noticed it to be quite similar to the café—two stories of red brick. She looked at the building's owner. "You're perfectly styled. It's evident you know what you're doing," Leah said. "Fashion doesn't come easy to me."

Lulu smiled, knowing the compliments would boost the tiny brunette's confidence.

Ana struck a pose and stood a little straighter. "It's nice to meet you, Leah. What are you two ladies up to?" Ana hitched her designer bag onto her shoulder.

"Heading over to the drugstore to pick out some cosmetics for Leah," Lulu said.

"I told her a brown bag over my head would work better," Leah said while staring at her shoes.

Lulu knew how much Ana hated to hear any woman demean herself. She smiled proudly as she watched Ana hook her arm through Leah's.

"Come on. Let's go get you fixed up. I won't have any more of that self-degrading mess. It's not very ladylike. If you are going to be living in the South, you need to learn how to hold your head up and be proud of what God blessed you with," Ana said, full of prissy sass.

Lulu walked behind the two young ladies and whispered, "Thank you, Lord." She had a feeling that things were going to be just fine. If she could only get Crowley on board, that is. The stubborn boy had kept to himself all week.

Lulu watched as Ana pampered Leah for a good two hours at the cosmetics counter. Ana took her time picking out the right shade of concealer and foundation, and then she showed Leah how to properly apply it. Leah didn't seem to mind letting Ana take charge. Lulu's only contribution was to the conversation. She thought it probably felt good to Leah to be social after acting like a hermit for the past week.

After Leah purchased all of Ana's recommendations, which included a full line of facial care products, Lulu suggested that they swing into the bookstore to pick up a copy of the book club read. Leah was excited to discover that the small bookstore also housed a coffee bar. Lulu and Ana purchased small nonfat lattes with low sugar, and Leah reluctantly followed suit. The trio sat outside at a small table and enjoyed their coffee.

As they sat in the fading sun, Ana chatted away about some jackets she was busy designing for a company in Atlanta and how excited she was about the handbag sketches she was working on. Lulu was glad to see Leah listening with apparent interest.

"The entire top floor of my building houses my studio. You have to come up and check out what I'm working on," Ana said to Leah.

Lulu seconded the idea. Then she told Ana, "Leah is going to church with me on Sunday. Do you want to join us for dinner afterward?"

"Sure," said Ana.

"Won't you be going to church too?" Leah asked.

"No. I go to Mass with my parents," Ana said.

Lulu took a sip of her latte. "They're Catholic."

"What are you?" Leah looked to Lulu, but Ana answered instead.

"She's Baptist, which she thinks is the only fitting religion," Ana said.

"I told you before that being Catholic is better than nothing." Lulu and Ana laughed together. "But being Baptist *is* the best," Lulu said.

"What religion are you, Leah?" Ana asked.

"Surviving." The young woman looked as if she wished she could bite back the brutally honest answer. "I mean . . . I guess I don't belong to one."

"I wonder if I could talk Crowley into converting to Catholicism if he ever decided to marry me," Ana wondered aloud.

"You would have to convert on over to good old Baptist, honey. You know that stubborn boy ain't changing his mind," Lulu said. She caught on to Ana trying to discreetly lay claim to Crowley in front of Leah. *Ana knows quite well that ship done sailed.* Lulu was beginning to worry that Crowley would never settle down. That boy was thirty-five and seemed to have no desire to move past bachelorhood.

"Is Crowley joining us for dinner too?" Ana took the last sip of her latte.

Lulu was hesitant to answer. "I don't think he is going to be able to make it. Looks like it's going to be just us girls. Do you have any meal requests?"

"Crowley eats Sunday dinner with you almost religiously," Ana said.

"Not every Sunday. You know sometimes he sneaks off to go fishing."

"I think fishing is his religion," Ana said. "Some of your shrimp and grits sure would be good."

"That would be a perfect Southern welcome dinner for Leah. Good suggestion, Ana." Lulu was already making a mental grocery list as they tossed their empty coffee cups.

"Sounds different." Leah's expression caused the other two women to laugh.

They gathered their books and cosmetics bags and headed up to Ana's studio to see what she was working on. By the time they finished going through it all, the sun had clocked out for the day and the moon's shift had peacefully begun.

Sunday came and went, with the women growing quickly in their new friendships, without an appearance from Crowley. *That boy sure can be stubborn,* Lulu thought. She had asked him to please be kind enough to join them, but he had refused. "I'm just not comfortable jumping on the welcoming bandwagon yet."

Crowley had been keeping busy with his project of finding out some information on their new neighbor, which had been quite frustrating. With help from some connections he had, Crowley was able to find out that she was an orphan from Chicago who spent her childhood in the foster care system. She received a Nevada driver's license at age eighteen and had drawn a paycheck from a casino in Las Vegas for four months. That was where he had hit a wall. It was like she had dropped off the face of the earth and just returned, beaten and bruised, a few weeks ago, he told Lulu. She could tell he was warning her about the mysterious young woman, but she told him everyone had a past and it wasn't polite for him to be nosing around in Leah's. "Fruitless . . . the search was fruitless," he had said.

10

THE WEEKS BEFORE THANKSGIVING had rolled along at a pleasant pace. Leah started out slowly at the café by helping Lulu with food prep, and then Lulu gradually trained her to work out front. The town folks seemed to take to her pretty easily, except for Crowley. He came in every day at closing and checked in on Lulu, or so he said. Leah wasn't dumb. She knew he was there to make sure she was doing right by Lulu and not taking advantage of the kind lady. Leah couldn't blame him. She was already developing a protective nature over Lulu herself.

Leah had grown more agitated with his presence and almost came unglued one afternoon while he sat at the counter after closing, watching her like a hawk, as she counted the day's earnings and made out the deposit slip. She had a hard time keeping a stern look due to his appearance, but it seemed not to bother him at all to sit there with speckles of dried mud all over him. His tattered hat, worn backward, gave him the appearance of a filthy little boy. Leah rolled her eyes as she listened to him tell Lulu all about spending the day mud bogging with a group of his buddies on four-wheelers.

"I have a pie to make," Lulu stated and wandered into the kitchen to start gathering ingredients.

"Looks like Lulu had a prosperous day," Crowley said as he scraped a dried splatter of mud off his earlobe.

Leah kept at her task. "Yep."

"How much did she make today?" he asked.

Leah frowned. "I don't think that is any of your business." She stomped off to the kitchen to hand Lulu the completed deposit slip with the money. Loud enough for Crowley to hear, Leah asked, "Doesn't he ever have anything better to do?"

Lulu laughed. "Apparently not." She looked over at Crowley, who was giving her a huge grin from his perch at the counter. Lulu shook her head and set the deposit to the side.

Crowley quickly wiped the grin off his face when Leah turned back to him. He kept his eyes on her as he asked Lulu, "Don't you think it ain't very wise to allow new help to handle your money, Lulu?" He dislodged another drop of dried mud from above his eyebrow.

"I think it ain't wise for you to keep running off at the mouth like you're doing," Lulu said, causing Leah to turn her attention back to her and the grin to return to Crowley's face. "And you gonna find yourself cleaning these floors if you don't keep that mud to yourself, young man."

• • •

The following week welcomed Thanksgiving, and the café was congested with customers. Leah was amazed at how many cake and pie orders Lulu prepared in addition to the usual demands. The pace helped Leah keep her mind off things and had been great at aiding her to sleep soundly at night.

Lulu had insisted on Leah joining her for Thanksgiving, but Leah politely declined. She knew if she agreed, then Crowley wouldn't show up. She had no desire to put a kink in any of their holiday traditions. The Wednesday before, Leah made a point to wish both Lulu and Crowley a happy Thanksgiving. Before heading upstairs, she told Lulu she would see her bright and early Friday morning. She wanted to reassure Crowley she would not be barging in on his holiday.

Late Thanksgiving afternoon, Lulu showed up at Leah's door with two generous plates of leftovers, and the two new friends had their very own Thanksgiving holiday.

"It's tradition to share something you are thankful for before we eat," Lulu said. "I'm thankful that God sent you to me." She smiled warmly as she squeezed Leah's hand.

Leah's throat tightened with emotion. She wondered how this woman could really feel this way about such a mess as herself. "That's the nicest thing anyone has ever said to me, Lulu," Leah whispered. She wiped away a tear. "I'm thankful you took me in."

The ladies enjoyed their meal, and Leah admitted to Lulu that it had been the best Thanksgiving she'd ever had.

"Good. You can walk me home and help do all the dishes I abandoned earlier to come see you, since you declined to come see me." Lulu winked. Leah gladly walked her home.

Leah believed Lulu's cozy river cottage was just as charming as Lulu herself. It was a two-story house, painted in pale yellow, with an inviting wraparound porch. Entering the front door, Leah admired the homey den that was anchored by a large brick fireplace that seemed to warm the room even when it wasn't lit.

After the dishes were cleaned, the two ladies lingered

over a cup of coffee and a slice of pumpkin pie on Lulu's
back deck, which faced the river.

As Leah readied to walk back home before dark, Lulu
tried handing her an uncut pecan pie. "Drop this off to
Crowley, please. He forgot it earlier."

"I don't even know where he lives." Uncomfortable
with this request, Leah rubbed the side of her neck.

"No? Well, I guess you wouldn't, would you? You'll
find him at the first brick town house across the street
from the café, to the left of the park."

"Maybe you should just call him to come get it." Leah
wanted nothing to do with the task of delivering anything
to that man.

"I'm pooped, and I don't feel like any more company
today. Do me this favor, please." Lulu pushed the pie into
Leah's hands.

Feeling as though she had no other choice, Leah
walked the three blocks to the town house. A small sign,
which advertised Mason Law Office, hung from the
porch. Leah paused to study it. *Surely that bum isn't a
lawyer. Must be his dad.*

Taking a deep breath, Leah climbed the brick steps
and rang the doorbell. She waited only a few seconds
before deciding to place the pie on the welcome mat and
make a run for it. As she bent down, the door sprang
open suddenly and her eyes landed on bare feet. She stood
slowly, her gaze traveling up long tanned legs, clad in the
usual ratty cargo shorts, and continuing upward until it
landed on Crowley's questioning gaze. He looked surprised to find her standing there.

Leah felt her cheeks grow warm at being caught staring. Unable to look away, she shoved the pie into his
hands. "Lulu said to give you this."

"Lulu pie! Yum!" Leah heard Ana shout from

somewhere inside, as other guests laughed at her enthusiasm. From the sound of it, they were watching football.

Crowley rolled his eyes, which were nearly hidden
under the brim of his tattered ball cap. "Great, now
I guess I have to share *my* pie."

His oddly colored eyes held Leah's captive for a few
seconds before she lowered her head. They stood in
silence until she couldn't bear the tension any longer.

●   ●   ●

The young woman turned on her heel and left without
another word. Crowley let her. He knew, without any
doubt, Lulu would have hit him over the head with that
pie, if she knew how rude he had been. He was a Southern
gentleman by nature, but something came over him when
Leah was around. He didn't trust her, and he couldn't let
his guard down.

11

It was the first Saturday after Thanksgiving, and the café was packed. Leah was refilling Ana's glass of tea when she glanced out the window and noticed a grungy little man pedaling what looked like a giant child's tricycle. A misshapen trucker hat sat lopsided on top of his greasy brown hair. He pedaled up on the sidewalk and nearly took out one of the round planter boxes.

"What in the world is that?" Leah pointed at him.

"That is Jessup Barns. He's our little town's drunk," Ana said.

Leah fidgeted at the word *drunk*.

Ana sensed the change in Leah's demeanor. "Don't worry 'bout ole Jessup, honey. He's harmless. Well . . . to everyone but himself, that is."

They watched as Jessup struggled to dismount the bike. His leg got caught on the seat, making him face-plant into a container of mums.

Ana let out a terse laugh. "That contraption he rode up on, which seems to be beating him up at the moment, is his liquor-cycle."

"His what?" Leah continued to watch the train wreck on the sidewalk. She just couldn't look away.

"Jessup can't have a driver's license on account he

can't keep from getting DUIs. The sheriff permanently suspended it. Jessup tried to get around on a regular bike but had a pretty hard time keeping it upright. So one night he raided Crowley's barn and came strolling up on that thing the next day. You have to give it to him, it's fairly creative." They watched him finally get up from the sidewalk.

"He's got a cooler strapped on the back, and the metal basket mounted on the front is for whatever he sees fit," Ana pointed out as Jessup began pulling beer cans out of it into Lulu's sidewalk trash bin. "At the moment, it's his trash can. But after visiting Lulu, it will become his grocery cart. He's a pet project of Lulu's. She thinks she can save him. I hate to break her heart, but that poor thing is just too far gone." Ana concluded her commentary on Jessup and returned her attention to her salad.

Leah moved back to the counter and mumbled to herself, "Aren't we all a Lulu pet project?"

Moments later, Jessup stumbled through the door, bringing along with him a stench of body odor and stale beer. Before Leah could figure out what to do about him, Lulu rushed out of the kitchen and made a beeline over to him.

"Good afternoon, Jessup. I got your food right here." Lulu handed him the white bag as she moved him in the direction of the exit.

He mumbled a thank-you and handed her a crumpled dollar bill.

"Jessup, the drugstore had a huge buy-one-get-one-free sale. Now I'm stuck with all this free mess that I don't need. You think you could help me out by taking it off my hands?"

"I guess I could help you out, Miss Lulu." Jessup swayed in place when he nodded.

Lulu grabbed a large grocery bag full of toiletries that was stashed behind the counter and hurried to give it to him.

He peeped inside. "That's mighty kind of you."

"Now don't go wasting my kindness, Jessup." She waved him out the door.

"No, ma'am." He placed both bags into his rectangular basket and haphazardly climbed onto his big tricycle. From the front window of the café, the ladies watched as he slowly made his way over to a bench by the river to eat lunch and inspect his free loot from Lulu.

That afternoon at closing time, Lulu and Leah were cleaning up when Crowley ambled in, laughing.

"What's so blame funny, boy?" Lulu asked as she continued to wipe down the counter.

Crowley stood by the front windows. "Looks like Jessup is trying to turn the river into one gigantic bubble bath."

This got the two women's attention, and they quickly made it over to the windows. They saw Jessup, waist-deep in the river, with a thick ring of foam encircling him. His hair stuck straight out all over his head, covered in more white foam.

"No. That fool is wasting my kindness, is what he's doing." Lulu slapped her palm on the counter, making both Crowley and Leah laugh harder. "He is supposed to get his nasty butt cleaned up with that stuff."

"Looks like he's washing to me, Lulu," Crowley said, causing Leah to laugh more as he joined in.

"The two of you laugh it up." Lulu clutched at the ruffles of her frilly apron. "You think fishy river water is gonna help get the stench off his hide?"

Crowley shrugged. "It's got to be better than nothing."

"Yes. Then he's gonna climb out and put back on those beer-stained, sour-smelling clothes. Yes, Crowley Mason, that's got to be better than nothing," Lulu said.

Crowley bolted out the door and ran across the street to the riverbank. The six-foot, four-inch giant was comically trying to look inconspicuous. The two ladies watched as he gathered up the filthy clothes Jessup had left by the liquor-cycle. Jessup had his back to the riverbank, so Crowley was able to grab the clothing undetected. He held the clothes out at arm's length and jogged about three storefronts down, dumping them into a garbage bin. He turned and jogged back to Lulu's and headed straight to the kitchen, still holding his hands out.

Hands on her hips, Lulu shook her head when he blazed past her. "What are you doing now?"

"Bleaching my hands!"

A few minutes later, Crowley came back into the dining area, smelling like bleach and grinning. "You're welcome," he said to Lulu.

"Yes, Crowley. Thank you for going and getting that drunk arrested again for streaking through town."

The *again* caught Leah's attention. She wondered if this was a recurring problem.

"Getting arrested ain't a bad deal for Jessup. He gets a clean bed and three square meals a day." Crowley reached out and pretended to punch Lulu's shoulder.

The feisty lady slapped his hand away and pointed at a stool. "Sit down and behave yourself."

"Yes, ma'am." Crowley did as he was told and shot Lulu an exaggerated grin. She answered with a stern frown.

Leah was amused at how the tiny Lulu was giving Crowley a run for his money. She detected that Crowley found it amusing too. Leah was relieved that the little woman did know how to frown, as she caught Lulu shooting Crowley a look that Leah hoped she'd never encounter for something she did.

"He'll be okay. He's got his tighty-whities on. . . ." Crowley paused. They glanced back out the window and watched as Jessup, dripping wet, pedaled away from the river. He seemed to give no thought to the disappearance of his clothes.

"Well, tighty-tans are more like it." Crowley laughed and looked at Lulu. "Some airing out will do him good." He jumped up from the stool and popped his head out the side door as Jessup passed by. "Be sure to put some deodorant on!" Crowley yelled.

Jessup raised a hand in acknowledgment and continued to pedal down the street.

As she headed into the kitchen, Lulu muttered, "Putting perfume on a pig."

LEAH WAS SICK and tired and aggravated and couldn't stand it any longer. She truly hated to ask Lulu to help her out with it, considering she'd already asked so much of the generous woman. But by closing time a week after Thanksgiving, she saw no other choice.

"Lulu, I can't take this another second or I think I may have to scream." Leah raised her casted arm.

Lulu laughed. "I'll see what I can do about that." She went back to reheating a large bowl of her famous tomato herb soup and grilling two cheese sandwiches.

"Who is that for? It's closing time." Leah paused before heading up the stairs.

"Crowley. He had a long day. He should be here soon."

Before Leah could ask why, a tall man dressed in an expensive dark-blue suit sauntered through the door and relocked it behind him. She was taken aback to realize it was none other than Crowley Mason.

"Someone die?" Leah asked Lulu.

Crowley said, "No, but I'm sure the defense lawyer is going to wish he had, by the time his client gets done cussing him out."

"I take it the judge ruled in your favor," Lulu said.

"Yes, ma'am."

"Well, congratulations, young man," Lulu said as she served him his late lunch.

"Thank you. I'm starving." Crowley loosened his designer tie and quickly tucked into his meal. Leah just stood there, shocked that he actually had shoes on that covered his toes. His unruly locks had been styled with gel.

She had noticed his unusual greenish-blue eyes before, but they seemed especially striking without his trademark ball cap pulled low over them. She had to admit that he had a certain rugged handsomeness. His sandy-blond hair was several shades lighter at the tips, due, she supposed, to sun exposure at the beach. His square jaw, usually accented with a touch of beard stubble, was clean-shaven. She stared for a moment and then made her way upstairs, thinking her cast could wait. She had felt slightly intimidated by Crowley from the get-go, but now she felt completely overwhelmed by him.

Leah headed straight for her after-work shower. Forty minutes later, she was freshly dressed in a favorite pair of yoga pants and a wide-sleeved black tunic. She was about to cozy up on the sofa to read when she heard a knock. She opened the door to find Crowley leaning on the doorframe. He was holding a mini Dremel rotary tool and a pair of scissors.

"Someone order a cast removal?" he asked as he waved the tools in front of her.

Leah held her hand out to take the tools. "Thank you."

He ignored her and walked on into the apartment. He pointed to one of the chairs at the dining room table and told her to have a seat. Crowley set the tools on the table before removing his suit coat and neatly placing it across the rocking chair. He removed his tie and tucked it into one of the coat pockets.

Leah noticed the Hugo Boss label and tried not to be impressed. "You're a little overdressed for a cast removal."

"I can manage a cast removal just fine in a suit." Crowley rolled his shirtsleeves up.

"You and Lulu are a lot alike."

"From spending too much time together." He pulled his seat closer to her left arm and sat down. He tried to lay her arm on the table so that he could get a good look at the cast, but she was hesitant at letting him.

"It's okay. I'm an expert. I once removed my own cast the very same way," Crowley reassured her with a slight smile that reached nowhere near his vivid eyes.

"How'd you break your arm?" She reluctantly placed her casted arm on the table.

"Skateboarding accident. I was trying to be like Tony Hawk and pull off this epic stunt," he said. "Lesson learned." He nodded meaningfully as he turned on the battery-operated tool, which whined like a dental drill.

"What lesson was that?" Leah cautiously eyed the little saw closing in on her arm.

"I'm not Tony Hawk."

"So you broke yours when you were a teenager?" she asked, a little worried that it had been a long time since he performed his cast removal. The saw blade looked dangerously sharp. She was no wimp but had no desire for unnecessary pain. She felt she had already endured enough of that mess to last a lifetime.

"Nope. Just last year," he said. "And no, I'm not too old to skateboard." Crowley flashed a mouth full of perfectly white, straight teeth, causing Leah to hold her breath without realizing it. "How'd you break your arm?" he asked with a look that revealed he knew he wouldn't receive a proper answer.

Leah answered him as honestly as she could afford. "Stupid accident."

"How 'bout we get rid of this stupid reminder then." Crowley pushed the little saw blade into the cast. Once the saw passed over the length of the cast, he used the scissors to snip through the protective gauze wrapping between the hard outer shell and Leah's arm.

With the cast removed, Leah sighed and satisfyingly scratched over her itchy arm. "Thank you, thank you, thank you."

Before Leah could pull her arm off the table, Crowley caught a glimpse of the burn scar on the palm of her hand that had been hidden under the cast. It covered a good portion of her palm. He gathered her hand, palm side up, into his hand to inspect it. Running his index finger along it, he asked, "What on earth caused that?"

Leah tugged her hand free from Crowley's hold. "Another accident. Happened over four years ago. It's all healed up now, but I just can't get rid of its reminder." Unable to meet his intense gaze, she tried to laugh, but it fell miserably flat.

After a long moment passed in silence, Crowley shook his head and stood.

"Thank you again, Crowley. I know you've been working all day and have to be tired, so it was kind of you to do this for me."

"No big deal." He picked up the cast and threw it away in the kitchen trash.

"How long have you been a lawyer?"

He paused by the table to gather up his tools. "I was *born* a lawyer, but I've been licensed for ten years. I battled my way through being a criminal prosecutor for nearly six years before I hit a complete burnout. Being surrounded by scumbags day in and day out is for the birds. I just handle your run-of-the-mill law stuff now like divorces, wills, and estate settlements. Sometimes my lawyer buddies upstate talk me into taking second chair on a big case they are tackling." He scooped up his jacket and draped it neatly across his arm.

"Is that what you did today?" Leah asked. The guy had totally surprised her. A skateboarding lawyer . . .

He opened his mouth to answer but stopped. "What's this, twenty questions? Is my turn next?"

She shut up quickly. "Thank you again," she said.

Crowley took this as his dismissal and headed out the door. "No problem." He waved without turning back and was gone.

• • •

The following week, it hit without warning in a pretty remarkable way. The full-blown Christmas season had entwined its way into every nook and cranny of Rivertown. The entire town was full of tradition and festivity. The paper devoted an entire section to reporting all the coming events. There would be a cookie swap at the bookstore with free coffee served to the participants, a live Nativity scene would be on display each Thursday and Friday night at the First Baptist Church, and the annual floating Christmas parade on the river would be the night of the Christmas Jubilee. The festivities list was endless.

The town was all abuzz about the traditional Christmas decorating contest. Leah discovered that Lulu took the contest very seriously. Lulu even hired a few part-time holiday helpers. She had Leah and the helpers drape twinkly white lights from every surface, inside and out. The dining tables were covered in beautiful patchwork tablecloths, made up with various deep reds, olive greens, creams, and golden tones. The café staff wore matching aprons with rows of color-coordinating ruffles at the bottom and *Merry Christmas, Y'all* embroidered across the front. Elegant salt and pepper shakers, shaped like Christmas trees, sat on top of each table. Lulu also ordered Crowley to shuffle the tables around a bit to make room for an enormous tree to be placed up front. It took several days to cover with lights and ornaments and ribbons. Old-fashioned Christmas carols spilled from the café's speakers from the day after Thanksgiving until New Year's Eve.

Leah was astonished at the town's transition. Lulu went the traditional route with her decor, and Ana went completely in the other direction. Her main color scheme was hot pink and lime green with accents of zebra print and silver. She had incorporated brightly colored feathers and beads in the same color scheme in her artificial white tree and wreaths. Leah loved it and had secretly cast her vote for Ana. A large voting booth had been set up by the bank, where security cameras could keep an eye on it. Yep, the town took their decorating contest *very* seriously.

The bookstore was another one of Leah's favorites. Nick, the owner, decorated several three foot trees in various book themes. Leah's favorite was the apple tree, with lots of different herbs tucked along the branches, created to honor *Garden Spells* by Sarah Addison Allen. Leah had fallen in love with her magical stories. There were many more book-themed trees on display, and people enjoyed grabbing a cup of coffee and walking around, admiring the trees like they were pieces of artwork, which Leah considered them to be.

The drugstore, bank, church, and library went with the simple tradition of green garlands and white lights. Not a storefront—or home, for that matter—went bare.

Crowley jumped on board too. Multicolored icicle lights hung from the roof and porch of the brick town house. Green garland, with more multicolored lights, neatly draped from the porch banisters and around the doorframe. In the small yard off to the side, he had placed three Christmas trees in a staggered triangle—one twelve-footer, an eight-footer, and a four-footer. He had the local teens decorate them in different themes. The girls covered the eight-foot-tall tree in all glitter and gold. Crowley commented that it could be used as the disco ball at the holiday dance, causing the girls to giggle. The boys tackled the smallest tree quite literally with sports-themed decorations Crowley had personally ordered at their request. They also wanted blue twinkle lights on their tree. The grandest tree was a group effort covered with multicolored lights and all types of toys. Leah and Lulu watched in amusement as the kids, resembling a bunch of elves, surrounded the giant tree with stepladders of various heights. Each tree had a sign posted in front identifying it, to the kids' delight. The girls' tree was "The Disco Tree," the boys' tree was named "The Sports Fan Tree," and the group tree was called "Santa's Workshop Tree." The project took an entire Saturday to complete. After the youth revealed their creations at sunset, Lulu and Leah treated them to homemade popcorn balls and warm mulled apple cider.

Leah tried to isolate herself from all of the holiday cheer to no avail. Lulu would have none of that and dragged her out into the midst of it all. Leah gladly stayed after closing to help prepare the treats for the youth but insisted on not helping deliver. Of course, she ended up doing as Lulu said and stood in Crowley's yard for several hours getting to know some pretty great kids. One of the kids cranked up some music at one point, and everyone broke out in dance around the trees. Once that began, Leah snuck back to her apartment.

Her heart weighed heavily throughout that holiday season. Although the town merrily twinkled, the only things twinkling in Leah's apartment were the endless tears shed each night. Leah was haunted by the never-ending, tormenting thoughts of how different this time could have been.

Her belly should have been protruding impressively out with the ripening of her healthy baby, but instead it was sadly deflated. She should have been tucking presents under her tree for her soon-to-be-born daughter. She would have had the nursery ready by now, stocked full of diapers, wipes, and frilly outfits . . . if only she had lived in a different world than the one she had unbearably gotten stuck in. She should have been gazing at a Christmas tree as she rocked, happily placing her hand on her belly to feel her baby bumping and kicking. Instead, Leah was wrapped in a tight ball of withering despair, in a dark, lonely bed with her head on a damp pillow.

●　　●　　●

On Christmas Eve, the town's youth, children and teens alike, participated in the traditional Christmas Carol Hayride. Piled into the back of a long trailer filled with hay bales, the youth were pulled by a decorated antique red Farmall tractor, driven by none other than Crowley Mason.

Lulu had roped a very unwilling Leah into participating in the event. Lulu always provided refreshments, which included every cookie you could imagine and rich hot chocolate, in the riverside park for the carolers.

Both women had spent the better part of the day baking cookies and prepping large silver urns full of Lulu's secret recipe for hot chocolate, which she gladly shared with Leah. Lulu also did her best to make the cookie recipes as healthy as possible, but she admitted to Leah that there was just so much you could do.

"It's the holidays, so some splurging won't hurt," Lulu said as she arranged the treats on beautiful silver platters.

They loaded two large urns on top of a rolling cart and placed the platters underneath. Then they pushed it over to the park, having to make two trips for all of the cookies and urns, to where they had earlier draped fold-out tables with patchwork tablecloths.

The two ladies tied on their decorative aprons and manned their stations. Leah gladly volunteered to serve the hot chocolate. She was sick of looking at cookies. Leah had splurged a bit too much when Lulu wasn't looking and had earned herself a minor bellyache. Lulu handed her a small basket of Christmas-themed ceramic coffee mugs to place on the hot chocolate table.

"We may need more mugs than this, don't you think?" Leah looked down at the mere half-dozen mugs.

"Oh . . . no, dear. Everyone knows to bring their own. These are just in case someone forgets theirs."

Leah heard the tractor and carolers singing in the distance for a good five minutes before spotting them. As the tractor pulling the group rounded the corner, Leah caught herself before laughing out loud at the sight of Crowley. Perched atop the tractor, he was wearing a frumpy knit beanie cap and a matching bulky scarf that was knit in a variety of Christmas colors. *Boy, someone sure is in the holiday spirit.* Seeing that he had replaced his flip-flops for a pair of well-worn work boots, she thought he would make a fitting model for country boy Christmas attire.

The youth eagerly filed out the back of the trailer and headed to the cookie table. They stood in front of the two ladies and serenaded them with "We Wish You a Merry Christmas." As they sang sweetly, Leah noticed people coming out from everywhere, coffee mugs in hand. *So much for a short and sweet event.* She plastered a friendly smile on her face and filled mugs for the next hour.

Crowley made his way up to the hot chocolate as Leah set out the third urn.

"Merry Christmas, Leah," he said as he handed over an enormous travel mug.

"Merry Christmas to you too. You wouldn't happen to like hot chocolate, would you?" She grinned as she held up his mug.

"It's one of the very few times of the year that Lulu lets this town enjoy sugar, so I like to take full advantage of that," Crowley said. He took several sips from his mug and then had Leah top it off. He leaned over the table and whispered, "I even sneak into the café after I return the tractor every Christmas Eve and swipe the leftover cookies. So if you hear someone later on tonight downstairs, it ain't Santa."

As Leah handed him the mug for the second time, her eyes focused on the slouchy cap and scarf. "Nice getup you're wearing tonight."

A huge grin lit up Crowley's face as he mockingly straightened his cap. "Yeah? I was hoping you'd like it." A group of teenage boys called for Crowley to join them over at the cookies. He held up his mug to Leah and said, "Thank you" before sauntering off.

Leah couldn't stop watching him walk away. His broad shoulders seemed so relaxed as he stood over the crowd.

"Hmm . . . Yum, yum. Looks like pure hotness walking," Ana whispered at Leah's side as she admired the view. Leah blushed at being caught and turned to offer Ana some hot chocolate.

"Dang, Ana. Talk about hotness." Leah stepped back to take in Ana's Christmas attire. Her shimmering white bodice, which pushed her best assets forward, peeked out from underneath a fitted red jacket that had a white fur collar and cuffs. Dark designer skinny jeans and black knee-length stiletto boots rounded out the outfit. Ana's ensemble was completed with a silver sequined headband shimmering in her wavy brunette locks. Leah glanced down at her own black tunic that bulked out around the holiday apron and tugged at it self-consciously. She looked back at Ana and noted that even the girl's makeup was flawless.

"You like it?" Ana asked as she did a little twirl.

Leah giggled. "You are *so* girlie."

"I have a Christmas party to attend at my parents' beach house," she said.

"Now you're making me even more jealous."

"Sorry, honey, but I'm going to have to make you a little more jealous." Ana laughed and pulled out a small bundle of mistletoe. "Really, I don't mean to . . . Maybe you should just look away." She laughed some more, with Leah joining in.

Leah watched as Ana sashayed over to the group that Crowley was towering over and playfully demanded kisses from all of the young boys. She accepted each kiss on her cheek and planted one on theirs in return. It didn't slip Leah's attention that Ana deliberately left Crowley for last. Leah *was* jealous of how confident and sure Ana always seemed to be about herself.

Leah watched as Crowley bent to place a kiss on Ana's

cheek, but she strategically turned her head at the right moment, and their lips locked. The crowd responded with whoops and hollers. Ana delivered a slow, dramatic kiss to Crowley. The males stared at Ana's backside as she strutted away toward her car. Leah could hear the group hound Crowley about Ana, and his good-natured attempts to laugh it off.

The festivities were torturous. The people in Rivertown just seemed too darn happy for Leah's taste. Ten abusive years with Brent had left her bitter and lonely, and all the cheer left her feeling like an outsider. Her loneliness intensified as she stood in the midst of the park that night. During the event, the thought that maybe it was time to move on nagged at her.

Leah was relieved when the kids started climbing back into the trailer. She insisted that Lulu should finish out the hayride with the carolers, while she cleaned up. Lulu hesitated, but Leah could tell the older lady really wanted to go.

"Go ahead, Lulu. Let me clean up as a Christmas gift to you," Leah said.

"Only if you're sure . . ." Lulu lit up like a Christmas tree as a teenage boy helped her climb into the back of the trailer, with the youth cheering. The singing started before the tractor was even cranked.

Crowley stood on top of the tractor and let out an earsplitting whistle to get the crowd's attention. "Being that we have ourselves a special guest that most of you know has never had the opportunity of accompanying us on our hayride . . ." He paused and cut his eyes over to Leah, who was cleaning but listening. "Thanks to Miss Leah Allen . . ." He paused again as the crowd applauded. "I do believe we need to welcome Miss Lulu with a special song." Crowley cleared his throat dramatically and began belting out "Grandma Got Run Over by a Reindeer." After the roars of laughter ebbed, the crowd joined in with the silliest rendition of the song. Leah laughed so hard she had to hold her side.

Appearing quite satisfied with himself, Crowley hopped down into the seat, tipped his cap mockingly in Leah's direction, and drove the carolers off into the night.

It took Leah a little over an hour to move everything back inside and wash out the empty urns. She placed the few leftover cookies in a plastic container and set them on the counter, with a note saying *Merry Christmas*, for Crowley to pick up later. After she locked the café, she headed upstairs, contemplating whether she was ready to pack up.

She opened her apartment door and suddenly stopped. In the living room corner stood a Christmas tree, fully decorated, that lit up the entire space and filled the room with an inviting scent of spicy forest. Presents were tucked underneath. She made her way over slowly and stood before the beautiful tree as tears spilled down her cheeks.

"My very own Christmas tree," she whispered as she admired the tree. Hundreds of multicolored lights twinkled amid Christmas ornaments as the tree shimmered with a light layer of silver tinsel. It was perfect. Leah had never had a tree to call her own. The group homes where she was raised would have artificial trees put out on display. Usually some organization would donate a tree, adorned with large plaques announcing the name of the sponsor. Some of the foster homes she had briefly lived in wouldn't even bother putting one up, claiming Christmas wasn't part of their culture. Leah had been troubled that the child service system would even allow people to be foster parents if they didn't celebrate the holiday that all children held so dear. Of course, Brent refused to have such tackiness, as he put it, cluttering up his personal space.

Leah wondered who had pulled off sneaking a tree and presents into her apartment without her knowing about it. She slowly knelt in front of the tree and studied the mystery gifts underneath. Each tag stated it was from Santa Claus. Curiosity finally won out, so she picked up the smallest one, wrapped in lime-green paper with a hot-pink bow on top, and carefully unwrapped it. To her delight, the gift was two beautiful fabric headbands, one black with white swirls and the other turquoise. "Thank you, Ana," Leah whispered as she slid the black-and-white swirly one in her hair. She then pulled a rectangular package out and peeled the candy cane–striped wrapping away to reveal the first three books from the Stephanie Plum series. Leah smiled and whispered a thank you to Nick from the bookstore. He was a jolly old man who resembled Santa a bit. The next gift was in a green gingham bag. She pulled it into her lap and peered inside. To her joy, it held her very own Lulu's apron. She took off her Christmas apron and replaced it with the whimsical black-and-white floral-patterned apron, complete with a hot-pink cursive *L* embroidered on one of the pockets. Black, white, and hot-pink tulle ruffles adorned the bottom, resembling a tutu. Leah adored it. She did a girlie twirl so she could admire the apron fully.

The wrapping on the last present depicted swimming fish wearing Santa hats. The silly paper and the gift inside made it obvious who it was from. It was a floppy knit beanie hat and scarf that were identical to the ones worn by Crowley earlier. Laughing out loud, Leah placed the cap on her head and wrapped the scarf loosely around her neck.

She stood up and scooted the rocking chair over to

the tree. She sat down to rock and to enjoy her gifts in the glow of the luminous Christmas tree lights. The gifts were the most special she had ever received, for they were from the heart.

After rocking for a while Leah became drowsy, but a noise downstairs followed by a "Ho, ho, ho" roused her enough for one more chuckle. She contemplated going downstairs to thank Crowley but figured he wouldn't want to be bothered by her at that late hour. Instead, she grabbed several quilts and pillows and made a makeshift bed beside the Christmas tree. After placing all her gifts back under the tree, where she could continue to admire them, Leah snuggled into her blankets and allowed the twinkling lights to lure her into a peaceful sleep.

• • •

Leah had been invited to Lulu's house for a Christmas brunch. She awoke early and prepared an apple cinnamon French toast casserole to contribute to the meal. While that was baking, she wrapped Lulu's gift, a specialty cookbook full of healthy recipes. Nick had ordered it last week when Leah was unable to find one among his selections. She was excited to see Lulu's reaction to it. Lulu always had Leah look up healthy recipes on the computer, and Leah couldn't wait to do the same task with the cookbook. It was a thick volume, and she was sure they'd both be content for a while. As she thought about this, Leah discovered she had already grown some roots here without realizing it.

Leah dug around in her luggage and found a burgundy tunic top and a pair of dress pants. She thought the scarf and hat would go pretty well with her outfit. The pants were a little on the baggy side, but she didn't mind.

After dressing, Leah headed out the café front door and veered to the right. She took a few deep breaths and was thankful that the pain in her side was finally gone.

"Nice getup you're wearing there, young lady," Crowley said as he walked up behind her.

"Yeah? I thought you might like it," Leah said in her best Southern accent. She noticed he was wearing his silly beanie hat and scarf too.

"Merry Christmas, Leah."

"Merry Christmas to you, Crowley. And thank you for my gift."

"What gift?" He winked. "Let me carry that for you." He pulled the covered casserole dish and gift out of her hand.

"Thank you, sir. That's mighty gentlemanly of you." Leah smiled.

The two neighbors walked on over to Lulu's house, where they feasted on a Southern Christmas brunch spread of sweet potato biscuits with ham, French toast casserole, spinach quiche, and cinnamon rolls with plenty of fresh-brewed coffee to wash it all down. The trio enjoyed a lazy morning of eating and visiting. Leah observed Lulu and Crowley together; it was like watching an adoring son with his very wise and loving mother. Leah was content to just sit, smiling and observing them, without adding much to the conversation. It felt like she was seeing what a true family was meant to be like.

NEW YEAR'S EVE brought with it a new, purposeful air. Change came in on a brutally frosty wind, and the day seemed to curiously attack Leah.

Lulu and Leah sat at one of the outdoor tables in front of the café after closing. Bundled in warm coats and sipping cups of hot tea, the pair tried to relax as they aired out the café and Leah's apartment.

"The business of collard cooking is stinky," Leah said, repeating what she'd stated earlier in the day when she had been stirring a massive pot full of the greens.

Lulu had to explain the Southern tradition of eating collard greens and black-eyed peas on New Year's Day if you hoped for a prosperous year ahead. Leah tried making the point that they were a day early. Lulu then had to explain that *this* town's tradition was to have her cook it a day ahead since she didn't open on New Year's Day. Most of the customers took their plates of prosperity home to be eaten the following day.

By the time the last plate was out the door, the strong smell had attached itself to every surface, including the women. Lulu and Leah spent a good chunk of the rest of the afternoon cleaning, and then they decided to take a break and sit outside for some fresh cool air. This idea sounded wonderful to Leah, who wasn't feeling so well. She sat with her feet propped on the chair in front of her. Every so often she would give her collar a sniff and grumble about stinking.

As the women sipped their hot tea, Crowley strolled up with Ana on his arm. They were carrying four champagne flutes and a fancy bottle.

"Wow. If it isn't Ken and Barbie," Leah said, bringing a chuckle from Lulu.

Ana was dazzling in a gold-sequined strapless mini and matching gold stilettos. Her hair was swept up in a flirty updo that showed off her bare shoulders. Crowley was laid-back chic, wearing a white dress shirt, untucked, with dark designer jeans and a tailored black sports jacket. Leah noticed his normal flip-flops were replaced with black leather loafers. He even had his unruly locks tamed down a bit.

"We just wanted to share a toast with my two favorite ladies before Crowley escorts me to the New Year's celebration at the beach club," Ana said as she handed out the flutes for Crowley to fill.

"I don't drink," Leah said.

"Good thing for you it's just sparkling cider." Ana smiled and raised her glass. "Okay, New Year's resolution time. I'll go first. Let's see . . . Oh yeah. I want to start a website to sell my clothing line."

Everyone agreed she could succeed with no problem.

Lulu went next. "This year, I want to commit more of my time to charity work."

Leah raised her groggy eyebrows at that. "Seems to me you commit a good bit of time to me and ole Jessup already." Everyone shot her a surprised look.

Crowley cleared his throat. "This year, I promise to spend more time fishing and being lazy."

The group laughed again.

"It's your turn, Leah," Ana said.

"I resolve to avoid any more stupid accidents," Leah mumbled, causing Crowley to give Lulu an I-told-you-so look.

"That's a mighty fine resolution." Lulu patted Leah's leg before taking a sip of sparkling cider.

"I agree," Crowley said. He tilted his head and gave Leah a once-over. "What's up with you today?"

"Everything hurts." Leah rubbed her neck and grumbled.

"Why are you ladies outside in this chilly air, anyway?" Ana asked.

"We *stink*," Leah said. "Collards *stink*."

"But they sure do taste good." Crowley looked at Leah. "You have to eat collards on New Year's if you want to prosper financially."

"Didn't your preacher say last Sunday that money is the root of all evil?" Leah asked.

"No. The *love* of money is the root of all evil," Lulu clarified.

"Either way. I would rather stay away from anything that might lead to evil. Been there, done that." Leah pulled her knees up and rested her forehead on them.

"You're not acting like yourself, Leah." Ana reached over and rubbed Leah's shoulder.

"I guess this sudden weather change has me achy all over." She raised her head and shrugged.

"Speaking of weather, I'm about to freeze my little behind off." Ana set her flute on the table and touched Crowley's arm. "I'm gonna pick out a jacket and a purse to go with my outfit. It won't take but a few minutes."

As Ana entered her boutique, Crowley grouched,

"More like a half hour." He ran his hand through his hair and plopped down in a chair.

"Problems in paradise?" Leah blinked several times without it helping to soothe the burning sensation.

"What gives with her?" Crowley asked Lulu.

"She was hurting so bad earlier, I told her to take one of her leftover pain pills. She didn't want to because they knock her out, and then she would miss the fireworks later tonight," Lulu said as she lightly rubbed Leah's back. "The poor thing seemed to get worse as the day went on, so I finally talked her into taking a half. I didn't realize she hadn't eaten until it was too late."

Crowley's face lit up as he chuckled. "Oh . . . so she's tipsy."

"*She's* sitting right here listening to you." Leah raised her head long enough to glare at him before resting her head back against her palm.

Crowley turned his attention to Lulu. "Why did you volunteer me for this tonight?"

"You know you'll feel better knowing Ana is taken care of," Lulu said.

"Yes, but this feels like I'm leading her on."

Lulu gave his hand a gentle pat. "Ana knows better than that."

Crowley glanced over his shoulder to make sure Ana was still tucked away inside her shop. "Her kissing me every time I turn around lately leads me to believe she doesn't."

"Poor, *poor* Crowley. Having to put up with a gorgeous woman kissing on him." Leah tsked and poked out her bottom lip for effect.

"This is none of your business, so stay out of it." His teal eyes narrowed in a glare.

Leah raised her arms in surrender and got a whiff of her sleeve. "Ugh . . . I stink."

Crowley let out a quiet snort. "I don't know whether to be agitated or amused at you, Leah. Why don't you just go wash?"

"It doesn't make much sense to go wash until we air the place out." Lulu finished off her cider. "Leah, dear, why don't you just come on home with me? We might get some of that ice storm tomorrow and I'd feel better if you were with me."

"Boy, the South likes to show off its rebellion over the seasons, doesn't it? Just yesterday Crowley was strutting around in shorts and flip-flops. Now we're talking about an ice storm for tomorrow." Leah shook her head.

"I'll be right back." Crowley stood and gathered up the champagne flutes before jogging across the street to his town house.

A few minutes later, he pulled out of his garage around back, driving a powder-blue late-model truck that was decked out in chrome. He parked in front of the café and rejoined the two ladies. He pulled his phone out and hit a button. "Hurry up." He hung up without waiting for a reply.

"Oh. Not that, Crowley." Lulu flicked a wrist at the truck.

Leah snickered. "Ana will be pissed if you make her go partying in a pickup truck."

"Leah, your language." Lulu clucked her tongue.

"What?" Leah raised an eyebrow. "Is *p* . . . is that considered a cussword?"

"No, but it doesn't sound very nice," Lulu said. "Why not say *ticked off* instead?"

Leah shrugged. "Sure. I guess."

Crowley laughed. "Lee, I'd love to sit you down sometime with one of those pills in you and let's have ourselves a conversation. This is as loose as I've ever heard your tongue get."

"Lee?" both women commented simultaneously.

"Yep. I think it's gonna be her nickname," Crowley said, seemingly proud of himself for ruffling her feathers.

Leah shrugged again. "Okay, *Crow.* Two can play that game."

"Crow?" Crowley laughed. "I've never been called that. I like it, *Lee.*"

"I like your truck, Crow," Leah said as she checked out the fully restored truck.

"Thanks. It's an antique Ford F-100. My dad gave it to me on my sixteenth birthday. The model year is the same year I was born. He told me it was in honor of the best day of his life."

"Wow. Sounds like you are one blessed man. I'd like to meet him sometime," Leah said and noticed Crowley and Lulu exchanging looks.

Crowley redirected his attention to Lulu. "I really need to put some distance between Ana and me."

"Just take her out tonight. Then, yes, I think that would be wise of you."

As if on cue, Ana shimmied back up to them, wearing a cropped black leather jacket and carrying a matching leather clutch. She glanced around, her gaze stopping on the truck. "*Nooo,* Crowley. No." She stomped her foot.

"*Yes,* Ana. Yes." Crowley stood and playfully stomped his foot back at her. "It's either the truck or I stay home."

Defeated, Ana climbed into the truck with Crowley's assistance. Before he climbed in the driver's side, he turned and waved. "Happy New Year, ladies."

"Happy New Year to you too," Lulu replied while Leah gave a small wave.

Lulu finally talked Leah into going home with her. While Lulu closed all the windows, Leah went upstairs and dumped everything out of her duffel bag, then repacked it with a few days' worth of outfits and toiletries. By the time the ladies made it to the river house, Leah was feeling pretty sick. It would end up being a very long night.

• • •

The next day around noon, Crowley made his way through Lulu's door to find her working on building a fire.

"Here, let me do that," he said as he took the kindling wood out of her hand. "Why isn't Leah helping you with this?" He knelt before the fireplace hearth.

"The weather wasn't attacking her yesterday. It was the flu."

He grimaced. "That woman's luck seems pretty crummy."

Lulu nodded. "By the time we got home last night, she was burning up with a fever. Dr. Lindy came by and diagnosed it as the flu. The poor girl was so beaten by the fever she just lay there staring at him. She even missed the fireworks."

"Sorry to hear that." Crowley continued to build the fire but paused long enough to shuck off his coat and scarf. "You know it's starting to sleet?"

"Yes. You just getting out of bed?"

"No, ma'am. I've been pretty productive. I rode out to check on Jessup. I delivered him a load of firewood and a box of canned goods to get him through for a few days. I also got you another load in the truck." He added a few good-size logs to the fire and stood up, wiping his hands on his jeans and brushing off some wood chips from his dark-green thermal shirt.

"How was Jessup?" Lulu asked.

Crowley shook his head. "You don't want to know." Lulu stared at him, waiting for an answer. "I found him buck naked and passed out in a lawn chair." He raised his eyebrows.

"Good heavens. You're absolutely right. I could have lived without knowing about that." Lulu wrinkled her nose and shuddered.

"Don't worry. I pulled the lawn chair into his living room, and that sucker just kept snoring away. I called Preacher Davis, and he agreed to go check on Jessup later on."

"I hope you warned him."

"Nah. Now what would be the fun in that?" Crowley laughed.

Lulu tried to be disapproving but gave up and laughed along with him. "How 'bout some lunch, funny guy?" Lulu smiled.

"Sure. I'm gonna unload the truck first." He bundled back up in his coat and scarf before heading out.

• • •

Lulu reheated two plates of collards, black-eyed peas, grilled pork chops, and corn bread. She cracked the back door and turned the fans on so that the scent wouldn't reach Leah upstairs. Leah had refused to eat. The doctor told Lulu to just worry about keeping fluids in her, so she had diligently encouraged the poor girl to drink water, hot tea, and juice. Thinking about that reminded her of a request, so she slipped her coat and shoes on to go find Crowley. He was stacking a large pile of wood onto her deck.

She was surprised that a small layer of ice had already formed on the surface of the deck. The sleet, coming down in a steady stream, made a hushed pinging sound. "Wow. This is happening fast. I hate to ask you, but I have a favor."

Crowley looked up as he unloaded his arms. Without hesitation, he asked, "What's that?"

"Could you go get some of your bottles of Gatorade?" Lulu pulled her coat up over her head to shield from the sleet. "Leah kept saying she thought she could manage drinking some. Said I left her some in her fridge while she was healing from her accident. It wasn't me, so my guess is it was you."

"Anything else? 'Cause this will probably be your last chance for the next day or two."

"That should do it. Just grab a bunch."

"Yes, ma'am." Crowley jumped down the steps.

Lulu was glad to see he was wearing work boots. That boy despised all forms of footwear except for flip-flops, but he had good enough sense to wear appropriate attire when it was called for.

She made her way inside to watch the weather updates while she waited for Crowley to return. The reports weren't very favorable. Broadcasters warned that the inevitable power outages were already being reported. Lulu was glad she heated with gas and had a gas-powered water heater and stove. Ice storms weren't as common as hurricanes in her neck of the woods, but she was glad to be prepared.

Crowley returned within twenty minutes with a case of Gatorade and another box that he stashed in the hall closet for later. The two ate lunch, exchanging their happy New Year wishes, and then hunkered down for the storm.

Lulu coerced Leah into swallowing some of the sports drink while Crowley made a large stack of wood by the fireplace to keep it dry. He then brought in his overnight bag and briefcase.

Later in the evening, the power went out as expected. Lulu carried a battery-operated lantern as she went to Leah's room upstairs, along with another Gatorade and a dose of NyQuil. As she reached the door, she heard muffled sobs. She quietly stepped into the room and saw Leah lying on her side, curled up in a ball.

Lulu heard soft sniffling as she placed the lantern on the nightstand. "What's the matter, sweetheart? Are you hurting?"

"I just can't win," Leah whispered as the tears spilled in a steady stream.

Lulu helped her sit up before handing Leah the medicine. She uncapped the Gatorade and gave it to Leah after she had downed the medicine. As Leah lay back down, Lulu climbed onto the wooden four-poster bed and ran her hand over Leah's back to offer the poor girl some comfort.

"Just cry it on out. It'll make you feel better," Lulu encouraged.

"No, it doesn't. The more I cry, the more it hurts. I never get any relief."

"You know some seasons really stink," Lulu stated.

"The ice is getting worse?" Leah asked between sobs.

"I mean the seasons of our life, dear," Lulu said as she continued to rub Leah's back. "You know our lives and the weather do have a lot in common. Change is constant. Just like spring, we are continuously renewed in some form or the other. Summer can be an exciting season, full of fun and adventure. Fall can be a slow time for us to just reflect and take life in. Winter sometimes can bring things into very crisp focus." Neither spoke while Leah continued to sob.

"Take this ice storm." Lulu motioned to the window, where icicles were forming. "It's not a welcomed event. Storms come in and make a mess, and when you are in the midst of one, you can see no end in sight."

They listened to the pelting of the sleet for a few moments before Lulu continued. "I know it doesn't feel like it right now, but this season of your life, just as all other seasons, will pass in due time."

"It's been twenty-nine years of a very long season," Leah said, her tears finally slowing.

"Here." Lulu handed Leah the bottle of orange sports drink. "Sit up and drink some more of this before you go back to sleep and listen up for a few minutes."

Leah propped up her body and took small sips as Lulu continued.

"We can look at the wrongs all day long, but we should be thanking God for all the rights—"

"There are no rights in mine." Leah's words began to slur from the effects of the cold medicine.

"That's nonsense." Lulu took the bottle out of a groggy Leah's hand, worried it was going to be spilled. "Maybe not before I met you, but since you've been here, I've witnessed plenty of good happening in your life." She patted Leah on her left arm. "I witnessed your broken body heal completely. I've seen many good people befriend you. And your greatest blessing, of course, is meeting me." Lulu smiled, trying to lighten Leah's mood. She could see she was failing.

Leah scooted back down on the bed, resting on her side to face Lulu. Lulu tucked the quilt around her fevered body and brushed a few curls off Leah's forehead.

"You know I prayed for you before I knew you. I

asked God to send you to me and he did. I know this was meant to be. Just look at how well Rivertown suits you." Lulu smiled. "Will you do me a favor, Leah?"

"I'll try," Leah said between sniffles.

"I know the bad can't be ignored. It's everywhere, and I have no doubt that you have survived something horribly bad, but don't overlook the good. Please remember good is like treasure. You have to seek it out. And remember how rewarding it is when you find it."

"Lulu, I love you." Leah's words were but a breath as she closed her eyes.

"I love you too, dear," Lulu said through a tightened throat full of emotion and made her way to the door. She spotted Crowley holding a blanket and pillow he had obviously swiped from the linen closet.

"You're my treasure," Leah mumbled and then began snoring lightly.

Lulu smiled at the eavesdropping man, who was shaking his head at her.

"What?" she whispered as they went downstairs.

"She's here to stay, isn't she?" Crowley asked.

"Yes, and it's time you accept this."

"Yes, ma'am." He offered her a small smile and began making his bed on the long couch. He'd bought Lulu the couch for Christmas several years back, declaring he was too tall for one of those small girlie couches. This one was sage-green, ultra-soft suede that he didn't mind sleeping on. He had always preferred it instead of the guest room, saying that room felt like it belonged to someone else.

Lulu now thought *that* person had finally made her way home.

Leah woke up, unsure of how long she'd been sleeping. She peeked out the window and saw that it was dark. Fighting grogginess, she mustered enough energy to take an overdue shower. As she finished her shower, a wave of dizziness struck her with such force that she sat on the tub's edge. Taking several fortifying breaths, she looked down at her withered body and guessed she had lost around forty or fifty pounds in the past few months.

After she gathered a little strength, Leah climbed from the tub and scrubbed her fuzzy teeth, twice. She wrapped a towel tightly around her body and crossed the hall to her room. Exhausted from the energy used for the shower, Leah sat on the bed, waiting for strength to return.

Leah woke up freezing. She had no idea how long she'd been napping—she'd only meant to rest for a few moments. She dragged her weary body back out of bed and dressed in a pair of jogging pants and a hoodie. She ran some curl serum through her still-damp hair and headed downstairs.

Leah reached the bottom of the stairs and found Crowley sitting on the couch. His head was bent down as he studied a case folder. She turned around to head back upstairs.

"Where you going?"

Leah took two steps up. "Just going to go back to my room. I don't want to disturb you."

"I could use some company. Lulu goes to bed way too early. You've got to be feeling claustrophobic in that room by now." Crowley glanced away from the file and met her eyes. He held her gaze until she looked away.

Leah wished Crowley wouldn't look at her that way, like he was determined to discover her secrets. Secrets she had no desire to share. But some company did sound appealing, so she crossed over to the fireplace and stood with her back to it for a while to warm up. She watched as Crowley made some notations on a yellow legal pad. A few minutes passed in silence until her belly disrupted it by releasing a rude growl. She'd not eaten in three days but didn't have the strength to make something.

Crowley glanced up from his folder and gave her a thorough looking over, causing her to fidget. "You look a little puny, Lee," he commented. "And you're too pale."

"I feel a lot puny, Crow." Leah walked over to the couch and sat at the opposite end from Crowley, where two bed pillows were piled. She rested her head on them, and Crowley went back to jotting notes for a while. "Working on anything interesting?" she eventually asked.

"I'm working out negotiations for a high-profile divorce. They're some bigwigs who own an island off the coast of South Carolina. The sad part is that they've been married thirty-eight years and are now divorcing after investing all that time." Crowley shook his head.

"That's one heck of a way to start the New Year off." Leah propped her feet on the couch and shifted around to face Crowley as he spoke.

"Yeah. They didn't want to ruin their family's holidays, so I agreed to have the paperwork ready by the end of the month." He grabbed hold of Leah's bare feet, which were freezing. "Where's your socks?" He shot her a disapproving look as he rubbed her feet.

Leah didn't pull away, finding the heat and contact of his hand comforting, which surprised her immensely. It took a moment to find her voice. "At the apartment. I forgot to pack some."

Crowley released her feet and sat up so that he could pull out the quilt he was resting on. He placed it over Leah and tucked it firmly around her feet. The quilt was warm from his body heat, and she gladly snuggled into it.

"How do you feel?" He placed his hand on her forehead and looked at her with concern.

"The fever is finally gone." Leah was astounded by the comfort she took in his attention. "I'm just weak. I'm feeling pretty hungry, actually."

Crowley removed his hand from her forehead. "What sounds appealing?"

She gave a guilty smile. "Something chocolate, but I'm guessing I won't find that in this house."

Crowley made a show of looking over his shoulder before fishing out a king-size Snickers bar from his briefcase. "I'll share it with you, if you promise not to tell Lulu," he whispered as he opened it and gave Leah half. His eyes held a hint of mischievousness.

"Promise," she whispered back as she took her first bite. "Hmm. It's been too long. You wouldn't happen to have a Diet Mountain Dew hiding in there too?" She pointed at his briefcase.

"Nope, but I can get you a cup of hot coffee." Crowley shoved the last of the candy bar in his mouth and headed into the kitchen. He returned a few minutes later, carrying two steaming cups and handed Leah one. "Instant will have to do until the electricity is restored."

"I don't mind. I actually like the taste. It was all I could afford starting out." Leah took a sip. "Even though I've drunk my share of gourmet coffee since then, I still enjoy a cup of instant every now and then."

"I like it pretty well myself." Crowley sipped from his cup and gazed at the fire.

"Hey. Thanks for sharing your chocolate with me." Leah smiled.

"I don't take sharing my chocolate lightly either. Most people don't know this, but I have an overgrown sweet tooth," he said, causing Leah to snort in amusement.

"You don't have anyone fooled on that one, Crow. I heard all about your pie contest binge, and I've seen you in action, with my own two eyes, with all of those Christmas cookies."

As Crowley grinned at her, she took a good look at him and quietly giggled. His unruly hair was sticking up in every direction and his long-sleeved T-shirt and plaid night pants were pretty wrinkly.

"Why are you camped out on Lulu's sofa instead of your bed at home? You scared of a little storm?"

He gave her a sidelong glance and shrugged. "I've always stayed to help her out during any storm for as long as I can remember."

"But why?"

"For one thing, it was actually stated in my parents' will to always take care of her." Before she could say anything, he added, "Both my parents have passed away. Can we just leave it at that?" He looked away with a bit of uneasiness.

"I'm sorry to hear that."

"It just hurts too much to talk about it." They sat in silence for a few moments, studying the fire, before Crowley continued. "I genuinely love Lulu. I'm a blessed man that God saw fit to give me two mommas. My momma and Lulu were best friends. Lulu had no children of her own, so Momma always shared me. I see it as an honor to fulfill my parents' wish, but I would have done it regardless." Crowley smiled somberly and met Leah's gaze as she shook her head. "What?"

"How can you be born so *good* when some men are born so *bad*?"

"I have my moments, Lee." He stood and stretched before tossing a few more logs onto the fire.

"Not evil ones," Leah said quietly.

Crowley looked over his shoulder at her for a moment and then went back to tending to the fire. "I guess it comes down to the choices you make." He shrugged. "I've worked on some criminal cases where I thought I was fighting the devil himself. All I know is that drugs, alcohol, or childhood abuse typically plays a big factor in crime. A lot of consequences can come from one bad choice." He rejoined her on the couch, propped his socked feet up on the coffee table, and leaned his head against the couch.

"Tell me about your New Year's Eve date." Leah wanted to change the subject, and she just couldn't resist teasing him with this topic.

Crowley closed his eyes and shook his head. "Next subject."

"Oh, come on. It couldn't have been that bad." Leah nudged him in the side with her foot. "I guarantee I had a worse New Year's than you."

Crowley turned his head and opened his eyes to meet Leah's. "I would have rather been burning up with fever."

"You're full of it."

"Look, I love Ana as a sister. Sometimes she takes my brotherly love and tries to make it into something more."

He ran his fingers through his hair and let out a long sigh. "And the party was a total bust. I spent the entire night keeping idiots in line as she showed off in front of them all. Instead of looking like the protective brother, I looked like the super-jealous boyfriend."

"Why not love her more?" Leah asked.

"I tried for a while, but it just felt wrong. You can't help who you fall in love with, or not."

"You're right." Images of Brent flashed through Leah's head, with the last one being him motionless on their bloody bed. She shivered.

"Next subject?" Crowley arched an eyebrow and smiled when Leah nodded in agreement.

The next few hours passed by with them rambling through various topics, steering clear of any serious ones. They debated what soup they would beg Lulu to make the next day. Crowley wanted chili, but Leah thought vegetable soup would be better. They teased each other about who Lulu liked the most between them.

A little after midnight, Crowley's eyes shut as he dozed off midsentence. He had been telling her all about his ideas for the next youth fishing tournament. She watched him for a while, wondering if he would rouse back up and finish his sentence. But his bottom lip puckered out, making him look like a youth himself, so she decided he was out for the count. Leah eventually dozed off too.

● ● ●

Lulu came downstairs at sunrise and found her two guests snuggled in quilts on opposite ends of her couch. She didn't know if she was supposed to like that or not, but chose to like it. She was relieved Crowley was finally warming up to Leah.

A hot breakfast of grits, eggs, and turkey sausage encouraged the sleepyheads off the couch by mid-morning. After eating and helping Lulu clean, the trio spent most of the day playing board games and snuggling up in quilts by the fire. Lulu was amused at how the two "young'uns," as she referred to Crowley and Leah, teased and bickered like siblings would.

They both had different requests for supper, saying Lulu would fix her favorite person's request, and she did just that. Lulu began prepping the ingredients for chili, making Crowley whoop in victory over Leah, until Lulu started a second pot for the vegetable soup. Leah doubled over in laughter and stated that Crowley was no longer the only favorite Lulu had. Lulu loved her house filled with young banter and laughter. This was how her house was always meant to be, and she was happy that it was finally happening.

Later that night, Crowley bundled up and said he was going to check things out. He stopped by the closet and pulled out the box he had tucked away and took it with him. The two ladies were in the kitchen, heating water for coffee, when the first set of booms sliced through the silent night. They rushed to the back door just in time to see the night sky burst into a rainbow of sparkles. They spotted Crowley, crouched down by the deck, lighting fireworks and aiming them up over the river.

Lulu pulled the door open to holler at him. "Are you crazy?"

He stood with a mischievous grin on his face. "No, ma'am. Lee missed her fireworks show, and I'm just being the gentleman you raised me to be, trying to make it up to her." He crouched down to get back to work. "Now close that door before she gets sick again," he ordered.

Lulu huffed at being told what to do but listened.

The two ladies grabbed dining chairs and planted themselves in front of the French doors in the living room to enjoy the show. Crowley lit the sky up in a continuous procession of flamboyant bursts for the better part of the next hour, before coming in and placing a light icy kiss on Lulu's cheek. He then did the same to Leah, causing her to shiver at his cold yet soft lips. "Happy New Year, Lee," he whispered before planting himself in front of the fireplace to unthaw.

"Thank you." She smiled after regaining her composure.

Trying to hide her grin, Lulu didn't miss how the young woman had become flustered, or the lingering kiss that caused it.

The following day, the ice melted, the electricity was restored, and Leah and Crowley moved back to their own homes. Even though Lulu's house emptied of her family, her home stayed warm and cozy with the memories made and the ones to come. She was quite hopeful about it and went ahead and whispered a prayer of thanks.

15

Mid-January crept up on Leah at an unforgiving rate. She did everything to repress it, to avoid it, to forget it, but nothing could wash away the knowing from her mind. Her expected due date showed up on a frustrated Saturday, empty-handed.

She asked Lulu after closing on Friday if she could spend her Saturday shift on kitchen duty.

"What for?" Lulu asked, distracted by slicing fruit. When Leah didn't answer right away, Lulu put the knife down and turned to give Leah her full attention. "You need tomorrow off?"

Leah cleared her throat. "No. I need the distraction of work. I just don't think I'll be up for customers."

Lulu nodded. "Tomorrow is very significant," she guessed.

Leah batted away an escaped tear and whispered, "It was supposed to be."

"The kitchen it is." Lulu wiped her hands on her apron as she crossed the kitchen and gave Leah a much-needed hug. Moments later the tumbling of the door locks had both women glancing that way. She patted Leah's back and released her. "Crowley's here. Why don't you head on upstairs?"

Nodding, Leah mumbled as she walked to the stairs, "Why'd you let him have a key?"

"I didn't really have a choice." Lulu chuckled.

Leah took the stairs two at a time, without replying to Lulu's comment. She had no desire to let Crowley see her in another hot mess. She had not seen him but in passing since the ice storm. Lulu mentioned that the high-profile divorce case had kept him quite busy. He even had to spend a few days locked up on the island, negotiating with the other spouse's lawyer on the final details.

Leah had actually been relieved not to have him around. He was genuinely a nice guy, but she couldn't take being pitied by him. Crowley kept referring to it as being gentlemanly, but Leah knew it was pity. She didn't want to be painted as some pathetic damsel in distress, and she had no desire to be rescued by some knight in shiny flip-flops.

As Leah tried losing herself in work on Saturday, she had to constantly fight the lump in her throat. Even though Lulu kept her extremely busy, Leah barely held it together.

Lulu also had Leah research two different healthy versions of brownie recipes online. Leah prepared both versions so they could be tested the next afternoon at a community picnic. She typed and printed out voting comment cards, which were placed in fifty bags containing bite-size samples of the two versions. She made fifty bags with plenty of brownies to spare.

All the busyness did the trick. Before Leah knew it, the café was closed for the day. She stayed for several hours after work to organize the kitchen and storage room. After that task was complete, she tackled cleaning out the refrigerators. Leah eventually ran out of chores in the café to occupy her time, so she moved upstairs to give the apartment an early spring cleaning. Baseboards were scrubbed, curtains taken down, washed, and rehung. Windows were washed until they glittered . . . the tasks continued at an almost-obsessive rate.

Her thoughts continued in a looping pattern. *If I can get through this day—if I can not think about what could have been—if I can not think about how sweet-smelling my baby would be—if I can just not wonder how soft my baby's delicate skin would feel . . .*

After trying so hard, Leah found herself in a heap of despair in the middle of the living room floor, holding a dust rag to her cheek imagining . . . A wave of grief slammed into her so hard it left her gasping for air.

As night fell, Leah deteriorated even more. She tried a scalding-hot shower to wash away some of the anxiety, to no avail. She went to bed, but sleep would not find her. She sat in the living room with her latest book but ended up reading the same page over and over with no focus.

Leah felt completely gutted, hollow, with a part of her missing and the realization that she would never be able to get it back. Not able to handle it any longer, Leah grabbed some money from her wallet and headed out to find something to stuff in the void. She needed the pain numbed.

She got no farther than the bakery display in the café before she found an old standby. She placed the money by the register and loaded a bakery bag full of brownies. She turned to head back upstairs and almost plowed over Lulu. The two stared at one another for a few moments.

Leah asked hoarsely, "What are you doing here?" She eyed Lulu's outfit, which consisted of blue polka-dot night pants and a matching shirt. Her feet were crammed in rain boots, of all things. Leah peeked out the window and found no rain in sight.

"*Hello. I'm Lulu.* I think I'm welcome at Lulu's any time I see fit."

"Sorry. I didn't mean—"

"I know. Besides, you're not the only one around here who likes a late-night snack. Well, I'm having a snack." She eyed Leah's large bag full of brownies. "Looks like you are having a feast."

"I paid for them," Leah said.

"Yeah, and you'll still be paying for them after you eat all that." Lulu grabbed the bag away from Leah and reached inside to pull out three brownie bites. She placed the treats on a small plate. "Here you go."

Leah refused the plate. "But I want the whole bag, please. I paid for them."

Lulu walked over to retrieve Leah's money and handed it back. "It's on the house." She grabbed Leah's hand and waited for Leah to meet her gaze. "Sweetheart, food is intended to be used as fuel for our bodies. You use it for something else, and it's just going to end up fueling your pains even more."

Lulu guided Leah over to a table. "Come on, and let's enjoy our treats together. Nothing better than good company to go with late-night snacking."

Leah sat while Lulu filled two glasses of milk and rejoined her at the table with her own plate of brownies. "We need to figure out which recipe we like the best." Lulu was clearly trying to distract Leah, but she just stared at her hands in her lap.

Leah had no desire for company. She only wanted to take the bag upstairs and indulge in private as she always did. With no witnesses.

"So . . . would you like to talk about it?" Lulu asked between sips of milk.

"I don't think I can, yet," Leah said.

Lulu was silent for a moment. Then, "Can I share a secret with you?"

Leah shrugged as she continued staring at her hands. "Sure. I guess."

"I was madly in love with a movie star," Lulu said.

Intrigued, Leah looked up. "A movie star?" It was hard to picture this tiny, old-fashioned country lady loving someone *famous*. "Did he . . . umm . . . love you back?"

"Oh yes. Most definitely. He was shooting a movie down along the coast and tried to escape all of the publicity between filming by staying out here in the very same house I live in now." Lulu took a bite of her brownie and chewed attentively. "Not this one." She made note of the recipe. "The texture is a bit gritty."

"I thought so too." Leah waited for more of the love story.

"We met at this café and couldn't unglue our eyes from one another. We spent the entire summer sneaking here, there, and yonder to be together. I'd meet him on one of the secluded river bluffs where we would spend the day tangled in each other's arms trying to figure out a future together. Or I'd meet him in the top of my daddy's barn. When I got home, I would have to explain why there was straw all tangled up in my hair." Lulu paused to laugh. "We had a passionate love affair that summer. One I will always treasure. We were engaged to be married that following fall. We had no desire to wait to begin our lives together." Lulu sighed.

Leah couldn't help but ask, "What was his name? Do I know him?" She mentally reviewed all of the leading men during the golden age of Hollywood.

"Oh, I doubt it. He was just starting out when we met. His name was Gabriel Banks. Oh, and how he was such a catch," Lulu reminisced.

"What happened?" Leah hated to ask but knew it was coming—the unhappy ending.

"A stupid war is what happened. The nonsense took him away to some foreign country and never gave him back."

"I'm so sorry, Lulu," Leah whispered, unsure of what to say or do.

"All I wanted was to die too. I didn't know how sharp pain really was till then. Most people know pain, but some of us have been pulled into a much deeper darkness of it. I wish that pain on no one. I'm sorry you know all about it too." The two women looked at their hands in silence for a while.

"No glass of liquor . . . no extra dose of pills . . . *nothing* could take the pain away in those dark days of my life. I learned quickly that the pain always grew a bit worse afterward."

"So what did you do?" Leah asked, hoping for a great secret on how to cope.

"I decided to take the pain fully on and endure it. Sometimes you just have to surrender to the nightmare and live in it for a while. Trying to fight against it is useless," Lulu said before finishing the last of her milk.

"Gee, that sounds like such a fun idea."

"Honey, there's nothing fun about pain, but you have to face it in order to heal from it. It wouldn't hurt you to ask God for some help. It wouldn't hurt you to trust me or one of your other friends around here enough to confide in."

Leah shook her head.

"You think it's easy for me to confide in you about losing the best thing I ever had in such a barbaric manner? No, ma'am, but I trust you. I want you to figure out how to trust me too." Lulu gathered her plate and glass and carried the dishes into the kitchen. She left, just as quietly as she had entered, without another word to Leah.

Leah sat awhile longer. She knew Lulu was right. She needed to face it and she needed to confide in someone, but she just wasn't ready to take on the challenge. Feeling rebellious, she snatched the bag of brownies and stomped up the stairs. By the time she reached her apartment door, she had inhaled at least a half-dozen brownie bites, trying to fill the void.

Leah headed straight to her bedroom to prepare her suitcases for escape. She reached for another brownie while packing and made the mistake of looking in the full-length mirror by the window. She was at midbite and was disgusted at the mirror's unrelenting tale. It reflected a bloated, red-faced mess of a woman. A ghost of what she could potentially be. She despised what the mirror shared with her and desperately needed it to tell her a new story.

"This has to stop," she whispered to the reflection staring back at her, still holding the brownie. She repeated to herself more sternly, "This has got to stop."

After taking the bakery bag back to the café, Leah crawled under the covers, where she cried until the sun announced the arrival of a new day. Instead of feeling better, she felt achy all over. Her nose was congested, her eyes swollen and bloodshot. Trying to be roommates with pain was unbearable.

Needing some fresh air, Leah pulled on a pair of sneakers and headed out the door into the still-sleeping town. She walked for long stretches that morning, and when the pain of memories or thoughts would surface, she would strike out in a sprint. She ruthlessly refused to slow her pace until the only thought was about the burning in her lungs or the screaming in her calf muscles. She kept it up for an hour before limping back to her apartment and collapsing on the sofa out of pure exhaustion for the remainder of the day.

The exercise soon became part of Leah's daily routine after work. During that hour of exercise, she was freed completely from the captive chains of her nightmares. The feeling at the end of each session was a reward of rejuvenation and peace.

She was sick of feeling weak and incapable. "Strong," she would repeat. "I will be strong."

By mid-March, Leah felt truly strong, physically. Her walk/run routine evolved into a steady hour-long jog. The beautiful Southern countryside was filled with boundless treasures to be discovered. Her chosen route took her by the exquisite gated entrance to the Big Oaks Plantation. Leah always slowed her stride a bit so that she could check out the stone archway and the grand oak trees towering overhead. She held the hope that one day the gate would be left open so she could peer further into the plantation's mystery.

*　*　*

Just as she was finally building some confidence, fear struck Leah out of the blue one spring night. She had already gone to bed when she was jolted awake by sirens blaring through the hushed town streets. With her heart in her throat, Leah bolted to the living room window and peeped out as the flashing blue lights of three county cop cars zoomed by. She sprinted over to the kitchen window in hopes of seeing them continue on past, which—thankfully—they did.

"No, no, no," she whispered into the dark as panic settled in. She grabbed a glass of water and waited for the walls of protection she had been hiding behind for the past five months to come crashing down. Twenty minutes later, a state trooper followed in the path of the other police cars. Leah knew this wasn't good. Not good at all.

Knowing that too many officials were crawling all over town, Leah couldn't just leave. Her only choice was to stay and wait it out. Scared beyond belief, she did the only thing that came to mind. Leah hid in the closet.

She felt sure someone would be there knocking the door down eventually, so she sat in the cramped space and waited while trying to slow her racing heartbeat. Hours later, Leah unfolded herself from the closet and stood staring at the open door. Months had passed, and she naively thought the remnants of abuse had crept away with time. One night showed her just how wrong she had been in her thinking. Shaking her head, she closed the closet door behind her and got in the shower to try undoing all of the pointless knots.

By four thirty, Leah was down in the café with the coffee brewing and the ovens heating up for the morning's muffins. Lulu joined her shortly after, and the two women fell into their daily routine as if they had done it for several years together. They were a very efficient team, and Lulu took pride in that fact.

Crowley made his way through the door around nine that morning, looking worse for wear. He had on his lawyer getup of a designer suit and silk necktie, though the tie hung loosely around his neck, undone. His hair was still wet from a shower and his eyes were beyond exhausted. He sat on a stool and rested his head on the counter.

"Wow . . . wild night?" Leah asked as she poured him a cup of coffee.

"You have no idea," he mumbled before taking a sip.

Lulu delivered some plates of breakfast to a table and

then headed over to give Crowley an inspection. "What's ailing you, boy?"

"Jessup Barns," he replied before taking another sip of coffee, which Leah immediately refilled. She worried about him appearing in court that tired and figured it would require a large quantity of caffeine for him to pull it off.

The two women waited for him to elaborate, but he seemed to doze off with his eyes open.

Lulu banged her knuckles on the counter with several rapid taps. "Wake up and tell us what's going on."

Crowley rubbed his eyes and tried to explain. "That blatant drunk crashed through a couple of Old Man Stevens's fences and then proceeded to take out about a half a field's worth of strawberry plants."

"With his *tricycle*?" both women asked at once.

Crowley propped his elbow on the counter and cupped his face with his hand. "No. A *car*. Old Man Stevens's car. And he ended up flipping it."

"Oh, mercy!" Surprise registered on Lulu's face. "Did he get hurt?"

Crowley shrugged. "Who knows?"

"What do you mean by that?"

"Me and half a dozen cops spent all night looking for the punk. We searched every barn and field at the Stevens farm. Then we searched the patch of woods beside where he wrecked. Twice. I guarantee that scoundrel was up in one of the trees watching us the entire time."

"When did you call the search off?" Lulu asked.

Crowley checked his watch. "About three hours ago."

Leah hated the ordeal for Crowley's sake, but she was mighty relieved those blue lights weren't for her after all. She relaxed and began putting Crowley's breakfast together. He rarely ordered anything specifically, so Leah took cues from Lulu as to what to fix him. Normally, she would slide him an extra portion without Lulu seeing it.

Crowley noticed her working away at preparing him some food. "Leah, can I get that to go, please? I'm due in court soon." His voice was husky from exhaustion.

"Sure thing," she said as she cooked a couple of egg whites.

Crowley placed his head on the counter and immediately began snoring. Ten minutes later, Leah had Crowley's breakfast sandwiches assembled and was about to slide them into the bag, when she spotted him.

Jessup pulled his liquor-cycle close to the front door and slowly climbed off it. He limped inside and went straight over to the counter, where he had the audacity to sit right next to Crowley.

Crowley lifted his head and stared at Jessup with a deadpan expression. "You have got to be kidding me."

Lulu made her way back to the counter, where she looked the grungy little man over. "What in Sam Hill happened to you, Jessup?"

Leah tried to not to breathe in his harsh odor. He was quite dirty with cuts of various depths and lengths all over his exposed skin. One of his wrists looked pretty banged up, and he was sitting in a way that revealed he was starting to feel the hurt of the wreck.

"I fell off my bike," Jessup said.

"More like a *car*," Crowley muttered as he shook his head and exchanged a knowing look with Leah.

"What you doing out this early?" Lulu continued.

"I just got up early and thought some of your coffee sure would hit the spot." Jessup's smile wobbled, and he fisted his trembling hands.

Leah suspected he was trying to make an appearance, thinking it would prove him innocent in the whole fiasco.

"You better give Jessup my breakfast, Leah," Crowley said in a tired voice. "It might be a while before he has something fitting to eat again."

"Wh-what y-you mean b-by that, C-Crowley?" Jessup began squirming on his stool.

Crowley didn't answer him. He just sat up and started knotting his tie. Leah took this as his cue that he was about to leave, so she poured a tall to-go cup of coffee and placed a freshly baked blueberry muffin in his bag. She then put a stale muffin in another bag and handed it to Jessup. She had been intending to feed it to the ducks at the park later. There was no way she was going to hand Crowley's breakfast over to that drunk.

"Thank you, Miss Leah," Jessup said as he slowly slid off the stool. He looked at Crowley, with the apparent intention of apologizing. He seemed to change his mind when the tall man glared down at him. Instead, Jessup just quietly limped out the front door, climbed back on his man-size tricycle, and pedaled down the side street.

Crowley walked over to the window to watch Jessup go by. He pulled out his phone and dialed the sheriff. "Hey, Danny. You're not going to believe who is about to pedal his drunk self right past the police station." He paused and listened for a moment. "I know. After all that, the idiot is practically turning himself in. Look, do me a favor and get a doctor to look him over before you arrest him." Crowley nodded as he listened to Danny. "Thanks, man," Crowley said before ending the call and pocketing his phone. He walked back to the counter to collect his food and then headed out the front door to where his truck was parked at the curb.

Leah hollered at him right before the café door closed behind him. "Hey, Crow!" He turned back with a disoriented expression as she pointed at his feet. "You might want to change those before going into the court-room."

Crowley glanced down at his feet and found that he had put his flip-flops on instead of dress shoes. "Good call, Lee. Thanks." He rushed over to place his break-fast in the truck before jogging to his town house. A few moments later, he hurried back to his truck. Spotting Leah through the window, he waved his briefcase, shak-ing his head about forgetting that too. She laughed and gave him an encouraging wave.

Lulu came to stand by Leah at the counter. "I saw what you gave Jessup for breakfast."

Leah shrugged because she really didn't care. "At least I didn't spit on it." Leah huffed and headed to the kitchen.

Lulu chuckled. "We're a lot alike, you know."

"That a good or bad thing?" Leah fired back with a little snark.

"Definitely good." Lulu winked at her and started humming as she started a fresh pot of coffee.

Leah watched the little lady for a few beats, a smile on her face, before getting back to work.

ANA CAME BY THE CAFÉ a few days later, demanding the full scoop from Lulu and Leah about the Jessup fiasco. Leah filled her in on the dreadful mess. The police had arrested him after a doctor patched him up. Since it was a repeated offense, the court decided it was in Jessup's best interest to spend some time in prison.

"Well, ladies, we are about to have all kinds of excitement in this little town," Ana said as she eyed Leah's outfit. "We've got to get you some new outfits for the big event."

Leah felt her cheeks grow warm as she tugged at her bulky top. "What are you carrying on about, Ana?"

"Spring break!" Ana bounced up and down on her stool like a giddy child.

"I thought you were telling us *news*." Lulu laughed. "Spring break happens every year." Unimpressed with the subject, Lulu strolled over to catch up with some of her customers.

"What's so great about that?" Leah asked as she handed her friend a glass of iced tea.

Ana took a long sip. "Thank you, honey. Crowley's herding in his college fraternity brothers for a weeklong spring vacation. I'm talking about prime real estate here.

Single, successful guys our age who are ripe for the pick-ing." She eyed Leah's attire once more. "Honey, we have to get you some prime picking outfits."

An hour later, Ana was still harassing Leah about her wardrobe while Leah continued to prep for the lunch crowd. Leah kept complaining that Ana needed to go do something more productive, but Ana had one of her helpers covering the boutique for the day. She said she had nothing better to do than to advise Leah about her awful wardrobe.

"What's wrong with the clothes I already have?" Leah asked.

"They all look like they are swallowing you whole. I mean, seriously, are you safety-pinning the waistband of your pants to hold them up?" Ana leaned over the counter and tried to yank on Leah's pants.

Leah scooted out of the way. "Hey! Cut that out!" Leah *was* using safety pins to hold her pants up but had no intentions of admitting that to anyone.

Ana kept trying to grab at her giggling friend. "I'm gonna sneak upstairs and steal all of your clothes and burn them suckers. Then you'll have no choice but to get new ones that actually fit."

Leah kept batting Ana's hand away. "Really, Ana, I don't see what's so appealing about entertaining a bunch of guys with you."

"Come on. That has to interest you. Unless . . ." Ana left the question in the air, and when Leah didn't respond, Ana tried again. "Unless men don't *interest* you."

Leah raised her hands and laughed. "Ana, you're really cute and all, but I prefer men."

"Well, that makes two of us." She got up and helped herself to some more tea and returned to her stool. "You know . . . I have noticed how you check out Crowley."

"Girl, how can you not appreciate that view!" Leah teased and was relieved when Ana returned her grin.

Crowley strolled through the door as if on cue, causing the two women to laugh harder. "Why were my ears just burning?" He perched on the stool next to Ana and playfully elbowed her.

"Oh, Crowley. I do appreciate those sweet ears on that gorgeous head," Ana said in full Scarlett O'Hara imitation. "Don't you just appreciate those ears, Leah, darling?"

Leah, trying to mock Ana's Southern drawl, replied, "Honey, how can you not appreciate the view of those sweet ears?" Both women burst into a fit of giggles.

Crowley swiped two of the oatmeal bars that Leah was cutting into rectangles. "I missed the joke, didn't I?" he asked before cramming half of one in his mouth.

"Yep." Leah smiled and handed him an iced tea.

"I was just telling Leah here that you are bringing in a whole panel of available bachelors for her and me to choose from." Ana winked at him.

"I don't know about all that. Some of them are married. Besides, they're *my* company, not a potential dating game for you girls." He shot them a pointed look.

"We'll see about that, won't we, Leah?" Ana sassed.

Leah ignored her and asked Crowley while brewing another pot of tea, "What are you guys going to be up to?"

"We're gonna hang out at the beach for a couple of days to surf."

"No epic skateboarding?" Leah caught his eye and grinned at him.

"Nope. The skateboard is still in temporary retirement." Crowley laughed as he drained his glass.

"I bet they're going to be doing some of that nasty ole fishing." Ana wrinkled her nose.

"We've got a few fishing trips planned," Crowley said, swiping another oatmeal bar.

"I've never been fishing," Leah commented as she wrapped the bars in parchment paper and placed them in a basket for display.

"No way." Crowley shook his head. "We're just gonna have to correct that injustice after the guys head back home."

Ana rolled her eyes and flicked her wrist. "Leah, honey, you are not missing a thing. Trust me."

"I wouldn't mind trying it." Leah shrugged.

"Cool. It's a date. We'll introduce you to Old Man River sometime soon," Crowley said as Leah refilled his glass. "Thank you, ma'am."

"You're welcome." Leah smiled.

Crowley scanned the café. "Say, where's Lulu?"

"She's already headed out for the rest of the day," Leah answered.

"What?" Crowley didn't sound like he believed her.

Ana snickered. "Leah practically shoved her out the door earlier."

"A bunch of her lady friends came in and begged her to go to some flea market with them, and I insisted she go. That stubborn woman is always turning them down. I told her to quit being so rude to her friends, so she really had no choice but to go," Leah said.

Crowley let out a low whistle. "Lulu got told what to do! Man, what I would have given to have seen that!" He gestured around the café. "You got all of this covered, Lee?"

"Yes, *Crow*. I can manage just fine. The soup is already done. The salad and sandwich prep is finished. You can go check if you don't trust me," Leah challenged, and Crowley shook his head no. "Also Kara and Alice will be here soon to help finish out the day."

"Just asking." He raised his hands in surrender.

"What's with this *Lee* and *Crow* business?" Ana asked.

Leah pointed at Crowley with the knife she was about to take to the kitchen sink. "He started it. As a matter of fact, Crow started it the very night of your big New Year's date," Leah said as she walked to the kitchen. She hoped it made Ana as uncomfortable as she had made Leah all day.

It did the trick too. Before Leah could return to the counter, Ana had slid off her stool and headed to the door. "I've got something more important to do than to entertain the likes of you two." She stopped at the door and looked at Leah. "Come see me after work today so we can get started on you with a proper dating wardrobe. I've got a few hot dresses with your name written all over them." Ana did a little finger wave and sashayed next door.

"Finally," Leah muttered after Ana was gone. She turned and caught Crowley helping himself to another oatmeal bar. "You keep it up and I'm gonna have to make another batch." Leah batted at his hand.

He talked around a mouthful of oatmeal. "Sorry. I missed breakfast." He washed it down with the last of his tea. "Don't worry, Lee. You're free from me the rest of the day, too." He handed her a ten-dollar bill and headed for the door. "I've got some shopping to do before my company arrives."

"I don't mind your company so much, Crow." Leah grinned.

Crowley turned and held Leah's gaze for a long moment, wearing an odd expression that she couldn't decipher, before heading to his truck.

"What was that about?" Leah whispered to the empty café.

● ● ●

Two days later, Crowley came in with a herd of guys. Each was on the tall side, but none meeting Crowley's impressive stature. They were all nicely tanned and gave off that outdoorsy vibe. They went straight to rearranging a few tables together to form a large rectangular one in the left corner of the café.

"Good grief. Did Crowley attend the Tall, Dark, and Handsome University?" Leah quietly asked Lulu as they both stood behind the counter taking in the view.

From the men's bulky forms came booming laughter and steady conversation. They all seemed to have limitless issues to catch up on with one another. The group of guys was such an anomaly to Leah. She wondered how it would feel to have such a bond formed from years of friendship.

Lulu shoved an order pad in Leah's hand, snapping her out of the staring. "Good luck."

"What? I think you should handle them." Leah tried to give the order pad back to Lulu, but Lulu had already moved to the other end of the counter to take an elderly man's order.

Leah gave a haughty huff in Lulu's direction, but of course it went ignored. She walked over to the boisterous table and stood by Crowley, who was seated at the head of the table. She nudged him on the shoulder to interrupt him in midsentence.

He looked at her and smiled politely. "Guys, I'd like you to meet Lulu's number one sidekick, Leah." Crowley commenced introducing the large group as if Leah would be able to remember their names. "Leah, this is Todd, Josh, Ben, Greg, Brad, Rob, Matt, Than, Jake, and Will."

Leah tried to stifle a laugh at how each guy had a one-syllable name. She thought Crow was perfect for Crowley and wondered why no one else called him that.

"You guys ready to order, or are you going to let me do what I do with Crowley and just bring you whatever I see fit?" She smirked.

"No. We're big boys and can make our own decisions, unlike our buddy Crowley," answered the tall, dark, and bright-blue-eyed guy, who Leah thought was Matt.

"Hey now. I just try to be easygoing on these ladies, but you creeps always have to be complicated." Crowley laughed.

Each guy rambled off his massive order quicker than Leah could write.

"I want two spinach omelets and an order of French toast," said tall, dark, and chocolate-brown eyes.

"I'll take two sausage and egg sandwiches on English muffins and oatmeal," ordered the tall, fair-skinned, strawberry blond.

"I want . . ." continued until Leah had three pages full of orders.

She was about to head off to the kitchen when Crowley stopped her. "What about me?"

"You'll eat whatever I bring you, big boy," she said, earning a roar of laughter from his friends.

Leah quickly went to work on the massive order. While the breakfast meats cooked and the oatmeal boiled, Leah delivered the drink orders, along with a basketful of freshly baked banana-nut muffins to hold the guys over until she had their orders finished.

The group gave her a round of applause after she successfully delivered each order correctly to its owner. She served Crowley a huge, overfilled Western omelet with wheat toast and a side of fruit and yogurt.

"Not bad, Lee," Crowley commented.

"Lee?" a few guys asked.

"It's Leah if you want me to answer." She poked Crowley in the side. "Poor Crow has a hard time pronouncing *Le-ah*." This got a few whoops and hollers from the group.

"Crow?" Jake asked, laughing. "I like it, Leah." Leah remembered his name. He was intriguing to look at. There was something about his caramel skin tone and bright-green eyes.

Leah gave him a smile and headed back to the kitchen, where Lulu stood, pulling more muffins out of the pan. "Good grief, Lulu." She clucked her tongue, feeling right exasperated, and took a much-needed drink of water from her glass. "I hope you ordered extra food for this week."

"Sure did, don't worry," Lulu said and continued her task. "They'll be heading to their beach house this evening for the next two days, so we'll get a small break." Lulu playfully bumped into Leah on her way to the display case with the muffins. "Besides, those boys will tip you more than you make in two regular weeks. It'll be worth the extra work."

Lulu was right about the tip. Lying on the table after the guys left was an extra hundred-dollar bill for her. The same happened after they inhaled a massive lunch of two turkey burgers each, extra-large orders of potato wedges, and side salads.

Leah was relieved when they announced their departure for the beach. She helped Lulu load them up with an assortment of goodies for their trip.

The next two days were considerably quieter, but a bit lonely. By the time the guys returned to their claimed corner of the café with deeper tans and more tales to share during a late lunch of soup and sub sandwiches, Leah was actually glad to see them.

While the guys finished up their meal, Crowley made his way to the counter to speak with Leah before he headed out for an evening of fishing. "You missed us, didn't you?" he teased.

She pretended not to hear him as she refilled some glasses and returned them to customers at the counter.

"You go shopping yet?" he asked.

"I think *you* missed me, Crow." She smirked. "Yes, I went shopping in your absence and found something super sexy that I think your friends will find interesting." She raised her eyebrows and leaned close to whisper, "But I want to show you first. Come on."

Leah led him out the back door and pointed to a teal-blue beach bicycle that almost matched her Jeep's color. The retro-style bike was decked out with chrome finish and whitewall tires. The bike was complete with a black wicker basket.

"Great bike, Lee." Crowley huffed out a laugh.

"Found this beauty at a yard sale yesterday at the park. Only paid thirty bucks for it," Leah bragged as Crowley sat on it to try it out.

The back door banged open with Ana staring the two down. "Whatcha doing hiding back here together?"

"Showing Crowley my big find from the yard sale yesterday," Leah answered.

"Oh, that's a sweet bike, Leah," Ana said in approval. "I got me a bike too. Let's load them up and spend the day at the beach tomorrow."

"Sure, but after church. I already promised Lulu I would go," Leah said.

Ana rolled her eyes but nodded in agreement.

"You two ladies have a good time," Crowley said as he climbed off the bike and walked back into the café.

"He didn't seem too sincere," Ana sassed after the

door was closed. She waved her hand as if to dismiss the thought. "I've got a huge surprise for you, my friend."

"What?" Leah eyed her.

"Oh, you'll see . . . real soon." Ana smiled.

THE FRATERNITY BROTHERS' VISIT ended up stretching for over a two-week period. The married friends kept the original departure time, which left six guys behind. Leah enjoyed getting to know the guys but craved some alone time as well. She and Ana struck out a couple of times to the beach with their bikes loaded in the back of Leah's Jeep.

After work on the following Friday, Leah hid herself behind the back shelves of the bookstore. Her long legs were draped over the armrest of an oversize stuffed chair she had dubbed her favorite, her bare feet resting on the chair beside hers. She was enjoying a new mystery suspense novel she had just purchased, along with an iced coffee.

Leah's mind wandered midpage. The week had been filled to the brim with excitement and chaos. Ana went and fell head over heels for Crowley's friend Jake and had worried Leah to death about it—wanting her opinion on what to wear, should she call him or wait on his call, if it was wise to date a friend of Crowley's . . . After the stunt Ana pulled on Leah, the Southern belle better be glad Leah was still talking to her, Leah thought. She huffed at the memory.

"The book that bad?" Crowley asked quietly as he lifted her feet and sat beside her.

"No. Trying to decide on whether I want to pinch Ana's cute little nose right off her face," Leah said as she put the book down and looked at her unexpected company.

"What'd she do now?"

"She did exactly what she's been threatening to do. Yesterday she snuck into my apartment and stole every stitch of clothing she could find."

Crowley chuckled and patted Leah's feet, which were now draped lazily in his lap. "Did she at least replace them with new clothes?"

"Yes."

"Then I don't believe that merits pinching her nose off."

"No? Well, I rummaged through my new wardrobe at four thirty this morning for something to wear to work. I threw this T-shirt on with these jeans and went on to work." She pointed to the chocolate-brown and teal T-shirt with some Southern girl logo at the top left.

Crowley shrugged his broad shoulders while studying her outfit. "What's so bad about that?"

"Your buddies came in for breakfast without you this morning and enjoyed pointing out what the back says." Leah stood up and turned so Crowley could read the back: *Once You Go Southern, You Ain't Gonna Want No Othern.*

His laughter was so rich it seemed to fill the entire bookstore. "I bet the guys got a kick out of that. Hate I missed it. You know that's a true statement." He tapped his finger on the back of her shirt.

"I can't believe you weren't hospitable this morning to your guests," Leah said in mock disapproval, turning around to face him.

"Had business to tend to, Miss Leah." He swiped her

iced coffee and took a sip. "Yuck, Lee. You know Nick has sugar behind the counter. All you gotta do is ask for it." Nose wrinkled, he handed the coffee over to her.

She shrugged and took a sip. "I've finally gotten used to it without."

"Tomorrow night is the last night before the guys head home. They want you to join us for supper at the town house tomorrow."

"You mean that massive pot of chili Lulu and I started working on today?" Leah asked as she gathered her stuff.

"Yes, ma'am. Hey, don't let me run you off here. I'll get going so you can enjoy your peace and quiet." Crowley stood and motioned for her to sit back down.

Leah slipped on her new flip-flops. "No, I've got to go put up with Ana for a little while. Miss Busy Bee forgot some important wardrobe needs."

"You finally got some flip-flops, Lee. I'm impressed."

"Yeah, they work better at the beach than my tennis shoes. I've sort of fallen in love with them, actually." She smiled, and Crowley's tanned face responded with a smile of his own. Leah noticed his hair had lightened up even more from all of the recent outdoor excursions.

"What did Ana forget to give you?" Crowley asked.

"Umm . . . What do Southern women say? *Unmentionables*?"

Crowley snorted. "You just sounded like such a granny."

Leah playfully popped him in the stomach. "You're pushing it today." She waved bye to Nick as Crowley held the door open for her.

"See you kids later," Nick said.

Crowley waved and said to Leah as they reached the sidewalk, "You never gave me an answer about supper tomorrow night."

"Oh . . . the privilege of being invited to the great Crowley's humble abode. How could I possibly refuse such an invitation?" Leah said in her fake Southern accent.

Crowley laughed. "Great. I'll leave you to your 'unmentionable' chore."

•   •   •

The next afternoon, Crowley drove up to the café about an hour after closing. He unlocked the front door and caught a glimpse of Lulu and Leah in the kitchen, finishing up his meal. They were working quietly as he sauntered into the kitchen. The first thing he did was pop a corn muffin in his mouth as Leah was boxing them up.

"Wow, Lulu. These are the best muffins you ever made," he mumbled around a mouthful of muffin.

"She made those." Lulu nodded at Leah.

Crowley looked in Leah's direction and was surprised to see her in a hot-pink T-shirt and jeans that hugged her body instead of her usual baggy black garments. Her hair was down, and a black-and-white swirly headband was secured neatly in her pale-blonde curls.

"Wow, Lee. You look good."

"Thanks," she whispered. "Ana thought I might catch one of your buddies tonight, but I don't think I'm going to be able to make it." She looked up at him with squinted eyes.

"What's the matter?" he asked.

"She's had a migraine headache all afternoon," Lulu said as she stirred the large pot of chili.

"Then why didn't send her home?" Crowley asked in a bossy tone. He walked behind Leah and gently massaged her neck, slowly working his way up to her temples. Leah closed the lid of the muffin box and leaned into his hands.

Lulu put her hands on her hips and looked Crowley dead in the eye. "Because she refused to go until we finished your supper." She turned to Leah. "Everything is done now. Crowley can load this by *himself.*"

"Okay," Leah whispered. She gave Crowley and Lulu a weak smile and slowly made her way upstairs.

Once the door shut, Lulu whispered, "Two investigators came in today flashing a photo of a woman they were looking for. Leah avoided them like the plague, but they finally cornered her to show her the picture. The girl looked like she was about to faint."

"Did you see who was in the picture?" Crowley crossed his arms and leaned a hip against the counter.

"Yeah. It was some woman I had never seen before."

"Did Leah seem to recognize her?"

"No. She looked right relieved with the fact of it too." Lulu pulled Crowley's strawberry cream pies out of the refrigerator. "Shortly after the investigators left, she started rubbing her neck. I could actually see the headache come upon her."

Crowley pushed off the counter, scooped up the large pot of chili, and started for the door. "You think she's ever going to tell us what happened to her?"

"When she's ready. I don't think she can keep right on carrying that load all on her own." Lulu followed behind him with the pies.

After Crowley loaded everything, he went up to check on Leah before he left. He knocked softy on the door but didn't get any answer. He didn't linger long, figuring she was resting, so he headed on out.

Throughout the night, the town house was loud and alive with laughter and fun. Crowley played his part as a fun-loving host but kept sneaking to the porch to see if any light had come on in Leah's apartment. Disappointingly, it never did. He gave up around nine, finally accepting that she wouldn't be joining them.

• • •

The next afternoon Leah went on an extended jog. After yesterday's debacle, she was having a hard time shaking her ever-nagging anxiety. She was beginning to think God was sending her warning signs that it was time to come clean with the business of Brent.

She slowed down and walked over to a park bench at the river and sat to catch her breath. She licked the scar on her lip as she wondered how difficult it would be to prove self-defense. She wished desperately that she had agreed with the doctor in Nebraska and filed a report. Then she would have proof. She was pretty sure it was too late now, but she knew a really good lawyer who would know the answers if she could ever gather enough courage to ask him.

"I was beginning to think you took off on that jog never to return," Crowley spoke as he walked up to her.

She shook her head, thinking the man had a way of popping up unexpectedly. "I was just thinking about you, Crow." She wiped her sweaty face with her collar. The curls that had escaped her ponytail now clung to her damp neck, and she tried to wipe them dry too.

Crowley sat beside her and offered one of the red Gatorades he was carrying. "I hope it was good thoughts."

After taking a substantial gulp of the cold sports drink, she held the bottle up. "Thanks. Did your company make it off all right?"

"Yep. Everyone was disappointed you couldn't make it last night." Crowley produced a pout as he unscrewed the lid off his bottle.

"Me too. I feel bad about missing it. How'd it go?"

"*Terrible,*" he grumbled. "The dating game wasn't much fun with Ana and her little boutique girls."

Leah scoffed. "*Please.* Those women are walking models. I bet you all managed just fine."

Crowley nudged her with his elbow. "I think Greg was the most disappointed you didn't show. He spent the entire night pining away over your absence."

"I'm sure the boutique beauties were good distractions." Leah laughed.

"The guy has really got the hots for you, Lee. He spent the night looking outside, hoping to see your lights on and hoping you'd feel well enough to come spend some quality time with him." Crowley slipped another mocking pout on his face.

"*Please,* Crow." Leah shook her head and stared out over the dark water, watching it slowly glide by. The sun was starting to droop a bit in the late-afternoon sky.

"I can give you his number, if you'd like."

"No thanks." Leah leaned over and unlaced her running shoes.

"Why not?"

Leah wondered why he sounded genuinely curious but chose not to say anything about it. Instead, she slid her shoes off and tucked the damp socks inside them before rolling her capri running pants up over her knees. Leah had to admit that Ana did do a great job in choosing exercise outfits. She loved how the fitted material moved with her strides and didn't feel binding.

"In case you haven't noticed, I'm not into the dating scene." She got up from the bench and made her way down to the water's edge.

Crowley slipped his flip-flops off and followed. "Well, that's not true."

"How so?" Leah asked as she stood ankle-deep in the refreshing water.

"You agreed to a date next weekend." He lightly kicked some water over the backs of her legs.

She squinted at him. "I don't know what you're talking about."

"Yes, you do. Our fishing trip." He tilted his head to the side and looked rather smug for no apparent reason.

"A fishing trip is not a date, Crow." Leah took a few watery steps and stopped. "When exactly are we going anyway?"

"Next Sunday," he answered slowly while watching her closely.

Leah angled her body slightly away from him and stared at the water without answering. She knew what next Sunday was, but there was no way he knew. Or so she thought . . .

"What's the matter, Lee? That day's not suitable, or do you already have a hot date planned?" he teased. He shoved his hands inside his loose pockets and studied her.

"Lulu won't like us skipping church to go fishing." She mumbled the excuse without meeting his scrutiny.

"You just leave Lulu to me. It's her fault anyway that you never have any other day off besides Sundays." He began leading her in a lazy stroll along the water's edge.

"It's my choice to not have any other day off. Lulu has offered me more, so don't go harassing her."

Crowley raised his hands defensively. "Yes, ma'am."

Leah turned quickly and splashed water at him but realized too late that she'd kicked up mud. "Oops." Eyes wide, she raised her hands. "I didn't mean to do that." She gave up being sincere and laughed when the mud speckling his cheeks caught her attention.

Crowley stood almost completely still with his hands resting on his lean hips, as if contemplating how to react. Leah understood too late that he was working the mud with his toes.

"I didn't mean it!" Leah swore and turned to make a run for it, but the excuse was too late. The mud slapped against her from the back of her calves all the way up to the crown of her head. She stopped dead in her tracks and started digging in the mud with her toes again. She launched a good splatter up Crowley's side as he turned to retreat a little too late.

"You are so going to get it now, Lee," Crowley said too calmly for Leah's likings.

She didn't wait for the retaliation. She gave up the whole toe method and bent down to grab two fistfuls of mud and flung it at his midsection. Crowley responded with a slimy chunk aimed at her chest. It landed perfectly, then slid beneath her tank top as she screamed and giggled. Both ended up covered head to toe in mud.

Crowley had gathered another handful of mud and was about to launch it when he froze, midthrow.

"Leah, stop moving."

She ignored him and pulled her arm back to launch another mud grenade.

Crowley dropped the mud and held his palms up in surrender. "I. Said. Stop." The stern look on his face and his sharp tone made Leah automatically obey in confusion. Before she could figure it out, Crowley slung her over his shoulder and in an instant they were on dry land.

He placed Leah back on her feet and quickly grabbed up a broken tree limb. He sprinted back to the river's edge and began beating the water with all his might. Leah stood stunned at the man's strength. He broke the limb and had to grab another to finish his job. Shock hit her when Crowley pulled a dead five-foot-long water moccasin out of the water. The monster hung limply in his powerful fist. His face was still set in a stern manner. Clasping the snake, Crowley started up the shore, and that was the last thing Leah remembered.

"Leah?"

She pried her eyes open and saw that he was crouched beside her. When she couldn't form a reply, he lightly shook her shoulders.

"Are you okay? It didn't bite you, did it?" Crowley asked in a rushed tone as he started running his hands over her legs to check for any marks.

"I'm fine. . . . It was beside me . . . in the water . . . wasn't it?" Leah asked though the answer was already clear, even in her hazy state.

Crowley helped her sit up. "Yep. Maybe you'll listen to me a little quicker next time."

"Was it poisonous?" Leah leaned forward, resting her forehead on her muddy knees.

"In a big way." He patted her back. "You think you can stand?"

"Sure." She slowly stood with Crowley's help.

"Let's go hose off." He draped his arm around Leah's lower back for support.

"I really hope no one just saw that," she said. She allowed Crowley to pull her toward the back of his town house while she tried to untangle her jumbled thoughts.

"You actually *fainted*." He laughed as he lightly tickled her side. "You wimp."

Leah popped him in the gut with the back of her hand in response. He released her as they made it to the hose. He turned it on full blast and sprayed her.

"Ladies first," he declared as she let out a yelp, hopping around under the cool shower.

"You're trouble, Crow." Leah yanked the hose out of his hand, sprayed him in the face, and then turned the water back on herself. She pulled her tank top away from her body and aimed the hose underneath it to wash out the sticky mud.

"I can help you with that." A muddy Crowley grinned as he reached his hand out.

Leah shook her head. "Trouble," she said as she refused to give him the hose and aimed the spray at the top edge of her pants. After a few moments, she handed the hose back to him. "I think that's about as good as it's gonna get."

Crowley turned the hose on himself and tried unsuccessfully to work the mud off. He gave up and put the hose away.

Knowing the only solution was a shower, Leah left him fiddling with the hose and went to retrieve her shoes by the bench.

"What? No 'Thank you for the great time' or 'Thank you for saving your life'?"

"Thank you for the great time. Thank you for saving my life. Blah, blah, blah."

She turned as he strode toward her. She picked up his flip-flops and tossed them at him.

Crowley caught them with ease and tried eliminating the space between them, but Leah was already moving away. "You just gonna take off on me?"

Leah laughed. "Look, buddy, I've got mud in places where mud is not welcome." She crossed the street and waved at him. "I'll catch you later."

Leah flew through the door and raced up to her apartment, going straight to the bathroom and turning on the shower. She stripped and jumped in before the water had time to warm completely. As she washed away the mud, the idea of her playing in the mud with a grown man had her giggling uncontrollably.

Leah stepped into her bedroom to retrieve some clothes after de-mudding. As she pulled a shirt over her head, there was a knock at the door. She hustled to put on a pair of pants and dashed to the door, grinning.

As she opened the door, Leah had to readjust her eye level—way down. "Who are you? Aerobics Barbie?"

Ana stood before her wearing a pink tank top bejeweled with silver rhinestones and matching yoga pants. She whipped her flirty ponytail off her shoulder. "Please. My legs will never be long enough to pull off being Barbie. You, on the other hand, can be." She looked at Leah's long legs.

"Whatever," Leah said as she stared down at her petite friend before glancing down the stairs.

"What? Are you expecting someone else?" Ana asked, raising her perfectly plucked eyebrows.

"No. There's only a few who can get up to my apartment. I didn't know you were one of them."

"Let me in," Ana said as she raised her full arms. "I brought pizza and Diet Mountain Dew."

"Oh. I'm sorry." Leah stepped aside and motioned for her to come in.

Ana headed straight to the dinette table and began unloading supper. "Lulu gave me a key for emergencies."

"This is an emergency?" Leah asked, gesturing toward the pizza and soda.

"Yes. Jake went home, and now I'm lonely." Ana pouted.

Leah went a few steps to the kitchen to grab two plates and some napkins. "I can't believe you would actually bring such contraband into Lulu's."

"The pizza is Lulu-approved with super thin crust

loaded with veggies only and very little cheese. And the sauce is even organic." Ana slid a piece onto each plate.

"Regardless, you're bringing the trash home with you," Leah said around a mouthful of pizza.

"Fine." Ana shrugged and dug in, too.

"By the way, thank you for supper." Leah smiled.

"You're welcome, honey." Ana smiled back.

They enjoyed their pizza in silence for a short bit until Ana asked, "Why do you have a pile of muddy clothes?" She pointed to the soiled clothes near the bathroom door.

Leah served them both another slice of pizza. "Crowley saw me down by the river earlier and thought it would be fun to mud bomb me," she said, trying to sound annoyed.

"Jerk," Ana said between bites.

Leah nodded as she chewed. Changing the subject, she asked, "When's Jake coming back?"

"Next Thursday. He and Crowley were talking about him moving his office down here. He handles all of Crowley's financial stuff anyway. It would be more convenient for us all." She took her last bite before asking, "So, what do you think of Jake?"

"Good grief, Ana, he is just the dreamiest thing."

"What do you think about us together?"

"You're dreamy. He's dreamy. I think you make a perfect match."

"I agree." Ana slid a can of soda over to Leah and opened one for herself. They took large guzzles of the cold fizz to help wash the pizza down. Ana put her can down and released a man-size burp.

"*Eww.* Gross, Miss Priss." Leah laughed and burped in the process, causing both friends to be overtaken by a giggling fit. After they settled down, they moved over and stretched out on the comfy sofa.

"We missed you last night," Ana said, resting her head on the back of the sofa.

"Yeah?"

"Yeah. After you called to tell me you weren't going, I brought two of my friends so I wouldn't be the only female around all of that testosterone."

"Oh, come on, you wouldn't have minded *that*." Leah grinned. "Did any of your friends make a love match?" Leah began flipping through the TV channels for a movie.

"My friend Marla didn't mind flirting with the whole bunch of them." Ana shook her head in disapproval. "But my friend Jenny seemed to really hit it off with Greg."

Leah stopped flipping and looked at Ana. "Really?"

"Yeah. Why?"

"Crowley was taunting me today about Greg having the hots for me, but I figured he was just giving me a hard time." Leah shrugged.

"*Puh-lease.* Crowley barely hung out with us last night long enough to know anything that was going on. He kept going out onto the front porch." Ana shook her head and eyed Leah.

Leah shrugged and went back to surfing through the channels. "Maybe that spicy chili gave him gas." Both women laughed at the idea. Leah found a chick flick playing, and the two settled in to watch it.

Two hours later, they gathered the pizza garbage for Ana to carry with her. Ana turned around at the door. "Let's go biking tomorrow."

"Okay. I'll let you use me to keep your mind off *Jake*," Leah agreed, knowing she could use a little help keeping her mind off a few things and perhaps a certain person.

18

"ARE YOU SURE we are allowed on the property?" Leah asked again as Crowley loaded her bike into the back of his truck. She couldn't believe how matter-of-fact he was about trespassing, especially for a lawyer.

"Absolutely. It's where I go to do all my fishing," he said. After he finished loading her bike, Crowley glanced at her black T-shirt and black capris. "Black isn't the best color for a fishing trip."

Leah looked down at her outfit. Dawn was breaking, and she wasn't awake enough yet to have given her wardrobe much thought. "What color is?"

"Lighter colors reflect the sun and heat," he said, and she headed back inside to change.

Five minutes later, she pulled the truck door open, startling Crowley. "Wow. That was fast." He nodded his approval of her choice of a light-blue T-shirt paired with tan cargo shorts.

She'd bought the baggy, well-worn shorts last week from a thrift store as a joke for Crowley and to annoy Ana. As she glanced his way, she felt as if the joke was on her, because there he sat, wearing nearly the exact same outfit. *How did I not notice earlier?*

"Funny, Lee." Crowley shook his head and pulled away from the curb. "Fishing twins."

She waved off his tease. "Are you sure we won't get in trouble for trespassing?"

"I'm sure."

"Well. Good." She smiled. "Ever since I've started jogging past that beautiful drive, I've been dying to get a glimpse past the gates."

Crowley hit a button on a remote control attached to the sun visor as they reached the wrought-iron gate a few minutes later. A massive stone archway outlining the gate announced they had arrived at Big Oaks Plantation. As the gate slid open, he looked at Leah. "Stop holding your breath, Lee. I don't want you passing out on me again." He pulled the truck into the drive.

Leah gasped in awe as the truck crept under the massive oak trees that lined the driveway. She'd never seen trees like this before. Long branches were dressed in a sweeping drapery of silver Spanish moss and reached out as if to greet the trees opposite them. The grand hostesses graciously beckoned their visitors forward toward the enormous white plantation house.

The three-story mansion was fitted with a deep porch that lined the entire front. The porch, with its inviting heavy rocking chairs, two hanging porch swings, and cushioned wicker chairs that were grouped around small tables, called to guests to come sit awhile. Voluptuous ferns swung on hooks across the front of the porch. Large black shutters and a shiny tin roof dressed the house with even more Southern charm.

Crowley nudged Leah as he steered the truck to the side drive at the left of the house. "I said breathe, Lee."

She did as he instructed and took several deep inhales. "It's absolutely breathtaking. Have you ever gotten to see the inside?" Leah asked, mesmerized. The plantation was an image straight from *North and South*.

Crowley's voice sounded a little funny when he said, "Yeah. I've been allowed in a few times."

As she admired the property, Leah noticed that the plantation seemed to be vacant, yet well maintained. "Do the owners live here?"

"No, the *owner* does not." Crowley pulled around back.

"Why on earth not?" Leah thought it an injustice to leave such a lovely place standing empty. She surveyed the back of the house, finding it dressed with an extravagant veranda towering over a swimming pool and Jacuzzi.

Crowley parked beside a two-story garage and glanced at the house. "Too large," he answered and he climbed out of the cab. "I just have to grab a tackle box."

"Okay," Leah said. She looked out at the majestic view. The wide river bordered the back of the property. There was an open field that looked to be about a half mile wide between the house and river. Lodged neatly on the bank near the water was a large cabin. The one-story building was partially shaded by thin river birch trees. A long deck jutted out into the river, much wider than the one in front of Lulu's. A dry dock housed a boat that Leah instantly knew belonged to Crowley. The custom paint job matched his Gator.

Crowley hopped back in and took off toward the water.

"Why would someone own such a large place if that's not what they wanted?" she mused out loud. "It's nice of them to let you store your boat out here." She pointed at the striking boat.

"How do you know it's mine?" he asked as he parked by the cabin.

"The flames," she said, eyebrows raised, making him chuckle.

Crowley pulled a khaki-colored fishing hat out of the glove box and placed it on Leah's head. "Here." He handed her a tube of sunblock before exiting the truck. He tugged a tattered gray baseball cap out of his back pocket and shoved it low onto his head, almost hiding his ocean-colored eyes from view. He took off down to the dock.

Leah slathered some sunblock on her exposed arms and neck. While she rubbed in the lotion, she watched him quickly lower the boat into the water and tie it off on the dock with an efficiency only attained by a lot of practice. There was no doubting Crowley Mason was well-versed in any and all things fishing related.

After she gathered her bag and tackle box, Leah moved down the small incline and onto the dock. "What should I do with my stuff?"

"Just set it on the dock for now while we get every-thing else hauled down here." Crowley led Leah back to the truck, where they scooped up the fishing poles and cooler.

"What's in the cooler?" Leah asked as they carried the supplies to the boat dock.

"It's a surprise for lunch." He set the cooler down and handed Leah one of the fishing poles. "Let's you and I have a quick casting lesson before we take off."

Crowley led Leah to the end of the dock, where he went over the simple mechanics of the fishing pole. He gave her pointers on how to hold the casting button and when to release it. He showed her the easiest way to flick her wrist to cast out the hook, which in Leah's opinion looked easier than it really was. Crowley also advised her on how not to hook herself—or him.

He demonstrated a few times with his pole and then watched her practice, letting her get a feel for the pole. The lesson wasn't rushed, and he answered all her questions as a patient teacher.

Before Leah was sure she had the knack of it, he asked, "You think you're ready?" When she hesitated, he encouraged her to practice some more. Eventually Leah declared she was ready, so they walked back to the boat, and Crowley loaded the fishing poles. He held out his hand to help Leah step onto the boat.

"I'm quite impressed, Crow," Leah said as she took the seat next to his and looked around, noting the dark-gray interior and lighter-gray seat cushions. The boat was fairly roomy. It had another row of seats behind theirs and additional seating at the front. "I've never been on a boat before."

"Never?" he asked.

"Never."

Crowley gave her a measured look. "Do you know how to swim?"

"Yes."

"Then you'll be just fine," Crowley reassured her. He turned the key, bringing the boat to life as the motor began to quietly gurgle. He eased the boat from the dock and headed away from town.

Leah sat back and enjoyed the new experience as Crowley navigated down the river for quite a ways. The river was busy with a variety of Sunday guests. An assortment of birds sat perched on overhanging tree limbs, waiting intently for their breakfast. Snapping turtles neatly lined floating logs to get a head start on their sunbathing.

Leah didn't spot any snakes, but she knew they were welcomed in the river as well. The memory of last week's snake wrangling flashed through her head, causing her to shiver.

A good-size bass breached out of the water as the boat cruised by. Leah reached over and slapped Crowley on the arm to get his attention. He leaned forward so he could hear her. She pointed behind the boat in the direction of where she had spotted the fish.

"There was a big one!" she yelled, trying to be heard over the roar of the motor.

"A big what?"

She rolled her eyes. "Fish."

"There's plenty more where that came from." He continued on down the river.

Minutes later, Leah leaned close to him and in a mock whine asked, "Are we there yet?"

Crowley shot her one of his signature grins. "Almost. Now sit back and enjoy the view."

Leah did as she was told and tried not to look at Crowley. The variety of wildlife drew her attention again. She wished she owned a camera to capture the stunning river landscape.

Crowley slowed the boat to a stop. "Look," he whispered. He pointed over to the riverbank.

Leah gasped at the sight of a giant alligator sunbathing on the shore, motionless. She watched intently for any movement from the ancient-looking creature and found none. "Is it real?"

"Oh yeah. Those suckers can hold considerably still. I've gone past some with my boat before and returned after several hours to find them in the same spot," Crowley said.

"The river is like a zoo without the barricades."

"It sure is," Crowley agreed.

He continued on down the river for about ten more

minutes. He then cut the motor and set the anchor. He looked at Leah and waved a hand in the air. "Welcome to my favorite fishing hole." He scooted to the back row of seats, where he began prepping the hooks.

Once he had both rods prepped, Crowley handed one to Leah. He cast his out from the back right side of the boat and instructed Leah to cast out from the left side, staying in her seat. That way they wouldn't get tangled.

They sat quietly for ten long minutes. "I don't think there are any fish here." Leah pulled the fishing hat off to wipe the dewy sweat from her face and then replaced it.

Crowley kept his focus on the river. "Patience, Lee. Fishing takes patience," he whispered as he concentrated. With one small flick of his wrist, he began reeling in his line. On the end was a good-size bass. He didn't hoot or holler as Leah expected he would. He just grinned.

"You've got to be kidding me." Leah shook her head. "That thing is huge." She set her pole down to get a better look at the fish while Crowley worked the hook out of its mouth.

"It's a bass." He seemed to judge the weight of it before holding it out to her. "About five pounds, I'm guessing. Here, check it out."

Leah cautiously took the fish. The top was a yellowy green with a fat white underbelly. "Great day. This thing is heavy." She handed it back to him and returned to her fishing pole. "It's my turn now." She recast her line, hoping for a better spot.

Crowley lightly chuckled as he placed the fish in the live well. He baited his hook and recast. He stretched out his long legs and prepared for another wait.

Leah let out an exaggerated sigh. "I must not be any good at this. I've not gotten a nibble in the half hour we've been here."

Crowley set his pole down and walked over to Leah. "Let's reset your line a little deeper, okay?" he asked. Leah reeled it in and handed it over to him. He pulled the orange bobber up a good ways and gave it back. "Now try this." He dug in the cooler and pulled out two bottles of water and handed one to Leah.

"Thanks." She took a refreshing pull from the cold bottle. "I'm surprised Lulu seemed okay with this Sunday trip."

"Why's that?" Crowley asked after taking a long sip.

"Playing hooky from church seems like a no-no in this town."

"We can and should worship God in all we do. People who limit that to only a designated time on Sunday mornings are missing out. I see him in everything." Crowley motioned out over the water. "Look at the splendor and wonder of this river—how it works perfectly balanced. Man didn't do a thing to be able to take any of that credit. God's miracles are all around us. It's such a shame to not take the time to witness it all." He gazed out, deep in thought.

"Wow. I think I just heard my sermon for the day." Leah had great respect for this statement coming from a man who very rarely missed a church service. She watched him as he slumped lower into his seat and slid his cap over his eyes before resting his hands behind his head.

"You know, Sunday is supposed to be set aside as a day of rest too," Crowley mused. "Now I'm gonna honor God's wishes for a little while."

A few minutes passed with Crowley napping and Leah intently watching her pole. She finally felt a small pull and excitedly reeled it in only to discover her bait had been stolen. She glanced back to see Crowley with his eyes still shut and then looked at the container of worms by his seat.

She cleared her throat and quietly called his name, but it didn't rouse him. She hesitantly pulled the worm container over and fished one out. Taking a deep breath, she studied the worm and quickly laced it onto the hook. It wasn't the most favorite thing she had ever done, but she managed okay—she thought.

Leah regarded Crowley's large, dozing form stretched out across the back of the boat. She liked having the opportunity to finally get a good look at him without worrying about someone seeing. His hair was a bit damp from the humidity and was curling up along the edge of his tattered hat. His bottom lip was pushing slightly forward, giving him that boyish look. She was pleased to finally spot an imperfection on this beautiful man—even if it was only a slight imperfection. Crowley's nose had a small bump that probably occurred from a busted nose at some point in his precarious life.

She tore her eyes away and went back to fishing. Leah had no sooner cast the line than it came alive with excitement. She began reeling it in with great effort. Whatever she had hooked was playing a mighty game of tug-of-war with her. "Crow!"

He hopped up to retrieve a hand net from a hatch and jumped over to her side. "You got it?"

She kept on reeling in the line as fast as she could while she danced around—or that's what it felt like with the force of the tension bouncing the pole all over. She must have hooked herself a pretty big monster. "Crow! Help!"

"Keep reeling it in. You almost got it," he assured her calmly as he leaned over and positioned the net for a quick retrieval.

Leah was shocked when the creature finally made its way to the surface, almost causing her to drop her pole.

The thing was slick, with skin that resembled a shark's, and had long whiskers protruding out from both sides of its mushed face. Crowley reached over the side with the net and scooped it up with considerable effort.

"What on earth is that ugly thing?" Leah wrinkled her nose and curled her top lip while trying to shake the tremble out of her arms.

"Lee, you just wrangled yourself about a twenty-pound blue catfish." He patted her on the shoulder. After getting it into the live well, he reached for her pole.

Leah placed her hand over his. "I need a break," she said as she gasped for air.

Crowley laughed and checked his watch. "I reckon I could feed you an early lunch now." He pulled out a pack of hand wipes from a compartment and offered Leah one, taking one for himself. "I can't believe you just wrangled that big ole river monster all by your girlie self."

"I'm not Ana," Leah said before she could stop herself. She felt her cheeks grow hot and looked away. She hated that she'd just sounded so negative about her friend.

"No. You definitely are not." Crowley nudged her with his bare foot. "But you're still a *girl*." He slid the cooler to the backseat with him and patted the seat beside his. "How 'bout you join me for some lunch?"

Leah took the seat as she cleaned her hands with the wipe. She watched as Crowley pulled out two glass bottles of Coke and opened them. He handed her one and placed his in the cup holder by his seat. He then produced two honey buns and placed them on the seat in front of him. "I'm baking us dessert," Crowley quipped, wiggling his eyebrows. Next came two small cans of Vienna sausages and two packs of cheese and peanut butter sandwich crackers.

Leah eyed the small can as he offered it to her. "What is this?"

"A true fisherman's lunch," he said, popping the lid off his can.

Leah wiggled a petite sausage free and took a bite. She was not expecting the super-soft texture of the salty fare. Crowley had already eaten his entire can and was working his way through the crackers by the time Leah had eaten two sausages. She decided she liked them, but not enough to eat any more, so she passed her half-empty can over to him.

"You didn't like 'em?" he asked, popping a sausage into his mouth.

Leah opened her crackers. "I liked them . . . in a strange way." She made a face that caused Crowley to laugh. She took a long pull from her bottle of soda, then held it up to examine the tiny shards of ice inside. "Wow. Now that's really good."

"It's the glass bottle. Cans and plastic don't hold a candle to it," Crowley said.

"Lulu would definitely not approve of this meal." Leah gestured with her soda bottle toward the honey buns that were heating in the warm sunshine.

"Eating like this every now and then won't do any harm." He brushed off her worry and handed her the warmed honey bun.

The super-sweet treat melted in her mouth, and the taste was incredible when she washed it down with the remaining soda. "You're a pretty good cook, Crow."

"You ain't seen nothing yet, Lee. Wait till you see what I'm serving you for supper."

"Supper?"

"Sure. With fishing, you get to eat your hobby." He grinned and cleared away their garbage into a small bin. He then baited the fishing hooks. "Okay, back to business."

The sun was starting to loom heavily above when the two decided they were fished out. The live well was brimming full of the day's catch, and Leah felt sun-kissed and pretty satisfied that she had caught the largest fish of the day.

After the boat was moored back in its designated spot and the truck was loaded, Crowley drove the short distance to the garage and cut the engine.

He climbed out of the cab and motioned for Leah to follow. "Come on, Lee."

"What are we doing?"

He was quiet as he walked her to the pool's edge. An intricate flagstone patio surrounded the oversize pool, keeping company with a large stone fireplace and outdoor kitchen.

"Do you really think we should be here?" she asked. The fishing trip had left her sticky and sweaty, and the glittery pool seemed to be luring her closer. She slid off her flip-flops and cautiously dipped her foot into the water. No surprise, it was incredibly refreshing.

"I keep an eye on things around here," Crowley said. "Don't worry. We aren't going inside." He walked into the pool house and returned with another cooler filled with ice. By now, Leah had crouched down and was swirling her hand in the water. She looked up as he stopped beside her.

"Nice pool." It had been over twelve years since she had been swimming.

"Go for a swim," he suggested.

"No suit." Leah shrugged as she continued to gaze over the inviting water.

"Just swim in your unmentionables. I won't mind." Crowley winked at her.

"No thanks."

"Okay." He started to walk past Leah and bumped into her just enough to send her headfirst into the pool.

She popped up immediately. "You jerk."

"You know you wanted to go swimming. Now you can. No need in calling me names, ma'am." Crowley grinned and started back toward the truck, lugging the cooler along with him.

"Wait. Shouldn't I help you?" she called out as she swam over to the steps to get out.

"You want to help me gut and scale fish?"

She released the rail and started swimming backward. "You can handle that." She then plunged deeper into the water. When she resurfaced minutes later, Crowley was still in the same spot watching her.

"This pool doesn't smell like bleach," she commented while swimming to the side where he stood watching.

"It's a saltwater pool," Crowley said as he turned to leave. Once his back was turned, Leah splashed his entire backside.

"Wow. That felt good, Lee." He laughed and left her to swim.

● ● ●

An hour later, Crowley rejoined Leah by the pool. He had washed his face and hands, tamed his hair, and put on his hat, backward. A clean shirt replaced his dirty one.

Leah was as wrinkled as a prune but refused to climb out. "You aren't going to join me for a swim, Crow?" she asked. She continued to do laps around the large diameter of the pool.

He smiled watching her swim around like a kid. No one had enjoyed the pool that much in quite a while. "Maybe another time. I'm going to start cooking you supper."

Leah swam over to the side.

"You can keep swimming if you want."

"I think I've swum myself out." She pulled at her soaked clothes. "I need to start drying out some."

"There's a small laundry room in the pool house. You can toss your clothes in the dryer."

"And be left with no clothes?" Leah crossed her arms.

"There are brand-new guest robes in the linen closet. Come on. I'll show you." He grabbed hold of Leah's hand and pulled her gently inside the pool house. "The bathroom is through that door. Go ahead and I'll grab you a robe." When he returned, the bathroom door had crept slightly open. Without intending to, he caught sight of a jagged scar on her hip. Another wound she had endured. With a heavy heart, he wondered if the trail was endless.

Clearing his throat, Crowley called out, "Throw your wet things into the hall and I'll get them into the dryer for you. The robe is hanging on the doorknob." The wet clothes slapped him across his shoulders, pushing away his concern. The woman always seemed ready to keep things lighthearted, and he liked that about her.

After getting the dryer going, Crowley headed to the outdoor kitchen, where he started up a deep fryer. Leah padded out to join him as he pulled out some potatoes and onions for slicing.

She stood beside him, wrapped in the white robe, watching. "Can I help?"

"You cook and wait on me almost every day of the week. You do a mighty fine job at it, I might add." He looked at her. "I'd like to wait on you for a change." Their eyes held each other's for a moment before he focused back on slicing the potatoes and onions.

Leah sat on one of the stools at the stone counter to

watch him. "Okay. But I'm telling you, this feels pretty weird."

Crowley reached into a small refrigerator under the counter. "Would you like some house wine of the South?"

Leah shifted around on the stool. "I don't drink alcohol."

He held up a pitcher. "Neither do I, but I love drinking iced tea." He poured two glasses and handed one to Leah. Once she accepted it, he raised his own. Before he could stop himself, he said, "Happy birthday."

Leah's eyes widened. "How'd you know?"

Crowley stood frozen for a moment and slowly set his glass down. "Don't look at me all suspicious." He played it down coolly. "When I brought the food and pharmacy stuff up to your apartment that first night, your license had fallen out of your bag. I checked it out." He shrugged. "You know you have to renew them things when they expire."

"You were the one who brought all that stuff to me?" she asked, looking embarrassed.

Crowley went back to slicing onions. "It's no big deal, so let's not make it one, okay?"

"Why didn't you tell me you knew it was my birthday?"

"I sort of hoped you would tell me, but when you didn't . . . there was no way I was going to let your day not be celebrated. I know you're a private person, so I thought I could celebrate it privately with you." He placed his hand over hers and waited for her to look up at him. "Please don't be upset with me."

She gave him a smile. "I've had the best birthday. Thank you."

He patted her hand and let go. "It ain't even over yet, ma'am." Crowley breathed a sigh of relief. *I'm a lawyer,*

for crying out loud, and I just gave away information. . . .
Stupid . . . stupid . . .

Crowley served up a country boy feast of fried catfish
nuggets with fried potatoes and onions, along with some
coleslaw and iced tea. They sat by the pool, happily eating
their meal as they watched the day fade into night and the
evening settle around the plantation.

"That was delicious," Leah said as she leaned back in
her chair, propping her feet on the opposite one.

"Glad you liked it," Crowley said while striking a
similar pose. "You know, Lulu is going to be upset with
you when she finds out today was your birthday."

"I know. It just felt sort of egotistical to announce to
her that my birthday was coming up like it was some holiday or something." Leah shook her head. "She would know
if she ever bothered making me fill out a work application."

Crowley let the subject go—glad it had resolved
so easily. They relaxed in quiet as crickets crooned out
their night serenade and fireflies sparkled gracefully over
the darkened field. Neither one seemed uncomfortable
with just sitting in the stillness of the silent conversation
between them. When they heard the dryer buzzer sound,
Leah followed Crowley inside the pool house to retrieve
her clothes.

Crowley reached down and opened the door to the
dryer. Leah's pink panties fell out onto the tile floor. Leah
quickly snatched them up.

He grinned. "I see you took care of your unmentionable problem."

Leah rolled her eyes and grabbed the rest of her
clothes before stomping off to dress.

By the time Leah made her way back out, Crowley
had all the food put away and the few dishes washed and
dried. "Wow. You work fast, Crow."

He shrugged and rejoined her at the table, where he'd left their glasses of tea. "I thought we could give Lulu the rest of your catfish so she can make us some fish stew one day next week."

Leah sat down. "Sure." She smiled when he referred to it as *her* fish. "This has been a day filled with firsts." Leah gazed at the pool.

"Yeah?"

"Yeah. First time on a plantation, first boat ride, first time fishing, first time swimming in a saltwater pool, and first time eating catfish nuggets."

"Wow, Leah. Where have you been all your life? Locked up in a closet or something?" Crowley laughed but stopped when he saw her expression.

Leah cleared her throat and stood up. "Thank you for this day, Crowley. I need to be heading home now." After a curt nod in his direction, she headed over to his truck and pulled her bike out from the back. She threw her bag into the basket and took off.

Crowley stood scratching his head. "Leah, wait a minute!" Shaking off the bafflement, he ran over to the garage and grabbed the first bike in reach. He had to make fast work of the pedals to catch up to her.

Once he reached her side, Crowley could see her damp cheeks illuminated by the streetlights.

"What are you doing, Crowley?" she asked, focusing on the road.

"I'm escorting you home. Lulu would whoop me good if I didn't."

"Always the gentleman," Leah muttered as she wiped the tears away.

"Always," Crowley agreed.

She slowed her pace and did a double take. "What's with the girlie bike?"

"You took off like a shot. I had to hurry to catch you, so I grabbed the first bike I came to." Never mind that it was a woman's hot-pink bicycle with a white basket covered with flower decals. "Leah, I don't know what I said wrong, but you have to believe me when I say I didn't mean it."

"I know," she whispered and left it at that.

Once they reached the café and parked their bikes, Crowley watched Leah fumble with her key. Before she could push through the door, he gently reached for her left hand and pressed a tender kiss onto her scarred palm. "Happy birthday, Leah." He released her hand with a slight bow, slipped back onto his bike, and left Leah standing there, speechless.

CROWLEY WAITED until the lunch crowd was gone for the day before he struck out to the café. He didn't like how he took a perfectly good day with Leah and ended it so poorly. After he left her last night, he stayed awake for a long time looking for clues as to what he said wrong but found nothing. Needing to check on her, he quietly entered the back door and followed the feminine chatter drifting from the kitchen. Instead of going in, he hovered in the darkness of the hallway and watched the two women working together like they'd done it for decades instead of mere months. The older one meant the world to him and the younger one was starting to do the same.

"You keep smiling like an old Cheshire cat today." Lulu laughed. "You don't smile enough in my opinion, and I'm enjoying seeing it."

Leah stood at the sink washing a pot as she looked at Lulu and widened her grin. "I wrangled a *twenty-pound* catfish."

"I think you're wrangling a 190-something-pound man too."

The pot clanged against another one, making a racket. "What'd you say?"

"A true Southern gal in the making," Lulu said instead, but Crowley had heard her and had to roll his lips inward to contain the chuckle.

Clearing his throat to draw their attention, he began limping into the kitchen. Leah caught sight of him and laughed.

"Last night really ended up being a pain in my backside, Lee." He groaned. "How about you?" He hobbled over to the sink and leaned on the counter beside Leah.

"No complaints." She kept washing dishes as a smile played over her lips.

Lulu walked over with a few glasses and handed them over to Leah to wash. "Obviously. All that girl can do is grin today."

"I wrangled a twenty-pound catfish," Leah repeated.

"Yep. We have ourselves a natural fisherman here, Lulu," Crowley said. "You'll have to go with us next time."

"Sounds like a plan." Lulu made her way to the counter to wipe it off, leaving Leah and Crowley alone.

He couldn't take his eyes off of Leah. That smile and the slight blush to her cheeks was his favorite look on her and he agreed with Lulu. Leah didn't smile enough. He was probably foolish in his thinking, but he wanted to be the reason for her happiness.

Leah glanced up at Crowley and caught him staring. Her eyes lingered on his lips as the blush of her cheeks deepened in color. He lightly traced along the heated side of her face with the tips of his fingers.

The moment stretched until Lulu let out a playful cough. "Enough of y'all mooning over each other. Us girls have work to do."

Crowley watched Lulu move over to the magazine rack and begin straightening them. He brought his attention back to Leah and picked up her wet hand and brushed a kiss on her damp palm. "I'll see you later." The only response she gave him was a nod, so he reluctantly left her by the sink and exaggerated his fake limp as he left the café, replacing the intimate moment with the lightness he wanted to bring into her life.

As he reached the street, out of Leah's view, Crowley straightened his stance and walked normally. Smiling to himself at catching her in a blush, he headed to his office to catch up on some work.

An hour later, as Crowley sat with his legs propped up on his desk and a file open in his lap, he heard a faint knock at the door. He put the file down and made his way to the front door. When he opened it, he found a white pharmacy bag tied to a yellow *Get Well Soon* helium balloon. He opened the bag and found a bottle of extra-strength Tylenol and ice packs. Laughing, he looked up just in time to see Leah slipping into Ana's boutique. He sat in a rocking chair on his porch and waited for her to come back out.

*   *   *

Leah walked into the boutique to look at the latest batch of sundresses that had just arrived. She spotted Ana, tucked among the racks, hanging up the new inventory.

Ana looked up at the sound of the bell over the door tinkling. Seeing Leah, she smiled and waved her over. "That run must have done you good," Ana said, taking in her friend's running clothes and large smile.

"I haven't been yet," Leah said. "I wanted to check out these sundresses before you swiped all of the good ones." Leah pulled an orange-and-gold one out of the shipment box and slid it on a hanger. "These colors would look gorgeous on you."

"You're too happy. I guess that means you *enjoyed* fishing yesterday." Ana wrinkled her nose.

Leah grinned and repeated her catfish speech for Ana, who wasn't impressed in the slightest.

"Here, try this one on." Ana tossed Leah a one-shouldered flowing sundress in several shades of teal and aqua blue.

Leah handed it back. "I will later. I want to get my run in and a shower first." She turned to leave, but Ana hopped in front of her.

"Oh no you don't. Not until you share every detail of yesterday." She walked over to the counter and placed the dress behind it for Leah. She turned back to Leah and waited.

Leah shrugged. "We went out to Big Oaks Plantation and went fishing. After that I went swimming in that massive pool while Crowley cooked me supper. That's it really."

"I'm amazed y'all hung out at his place. He hardly ever entertains company out there," Ana said as she walked back to the sundresses. She pulled out a black haltered one with an intricate pattern of aqua-blue-and-silver rhinestones along the top. "I'm holding this one back for you too." She placed it with the other one before noticing Leah's silence. "What?"

"Crowley owns Big Oaks Plantation?"

"Yes. Oh, he didn't tell you? Oops." Ana laughed.

Leah crossed her arms. "It's not funny. Why would he do that?"

"Honey, don't take it personal. He's very private. He wants people to just like him for who he is. You know . . . *love me for my body, not my money*," Ana said.

Leah's stomach knotted as if she'd just been punched. Without another word to Ana, she bolted out the door and took off running.

* * *

Crowley watched her take off from his front porch. "Hey, Lee!" When she didn't respond, he jumped off the porch and sprinted after her. He sensed something was wrong, *again*.

Leah pointedly looked at his smooth stride as he caught up to her. She turned her head toward him in brief acknowledgment. "You lied about the sore butt too? Humph."

Crowley saw the coldness in her eyes. "Lied about that too? What are you talking about?" Crowley asked as they continued running. For a few moments, the only sound between them was the *flap-flap-flap* from his flip-flops as they beat the sidewalk.

"Ana just informed me that you are the spoiled rich kid who *owns* Big Oaks Plantation. I feel like such a fool for not figuring it out yesterday." She took off toward the edge of the river. "Just leave me alone."

"You're one to insinuate me being spoiled as you walk around this modest town in enormous diamond stud earrings and sporting a Rolex watch."

Leah stopped dead in her tracks. She took the earrings out and slung them into the dark water. "Yes, Crowley. You have me figured out. Growing up in foster homes and orphanages really spoiled me rotten," she said, full of venom. She unfastened her watch and tossed it in after the earrings.

"Let me apologize." Crowley took a step in Leah's direction and reached for her arm.

She yanked out of his grasp and stomped off in the direction of her Jeep Wagoneer. "Forget this!"

"Where are you going?" Crowley asked.

"I need a donut."

Once she reached the Jeep, Leah retrieved the key from under the floor mat and climbed in. She checked the glove compartment and found the emergency cash she had stuffed under paperwork. She shoved a few twenties into her pant pocket. As she cranked the engine, Crowley pulled the passenger-side door open and climbed in.

"What do you think you're doing?"

Crowley shrugged. "I want a donut, too."

Leah just sat there while the engine idled and stared at him. She was fuming, and he looked like he didn't have a care in the world.

"Leah, you ain't driven anywhere since you arrived last fall. Do you really think you can find donuts and your way back here?" Crowley asked as he adjusted the air conditioner.

"I found my way to Rivertown all by myself the first time. I think I can do it again, if I want."

"True, but I know where the best donuts in the county are secretly located," he said as he raised an eyebrow for emphasis. He was trying to smooth things over with his charm, but it appeared that Leah wasn't letting him off that easy.

"Why did you feel like you had to hide stuff from me? I thought we were friends."

"'Why do you feel like you have to hide stuff from me?' Really, Leah? How are you any different?" he asked. "We *are* friends. We just need to start trusting each other some. Don't you agree?"

"Fine. I trust you to show me where the donuts are." She gave in and headed out of the lot.

"Take a right. You know this is a really sweet ride. A 1978 Jeep Wagoneer, right?" Crowley asked.

"Yep."

Crowley ignored the clipped tone of her response.

"Take a left at the light," he said. "This would make a really cool surf-mobile."

"A what?" Leah asked as she took the left turn.

"It's already got surfboard racks on the roof. All you need are a few boards." His eyes lit up like a kid's as he imagined it.

"First off, I have no surfboards. Secondly, I don't even know how to surf," Leah said and glanced in Crowley's direction.

"First off," Crowley said, "I have plenty of surfboards. And secondly, I can teach you."

Leah concentrated on driving. "Whatever."

Crowley sighed and fiddled with the radio, settling on a country station. He sat back in his seat and hummed along to the twangy song.

"No," Leah said.

"No?" Crowley asked as his head bobbed to the rhythm of the music.

"No."

"You can't live in the South and not like country music."

"I do live in the South, and just let me tell you . . . *no!*" Leah took over the radio controls and was glad to hear the Steve Miller Band serenading away about being a space cowboy.

Crowley lit up at the familiar tune and started singing.

Leah cranked the volume and joined in. She was belting out lyrics when Crowley turned the volume off. Startled at hearing only her voice all of a sudden, she shot him a scolding look.

He was staring behind them. "We just drove past the donuts."

"Good instructions, Space Cowboy," Leah said as she made a U-turn and parked where Crowley instructed.

"I wouldn't be doing illegal car maneuvers without a license, Lee."

"Don't give me a hard time, and I'll let you take me to the DMV next week."

"It's a date." Crowley smiled.

Leah shook her head. "No wonder you're single, Crow. You don't get what constitutes a *real* date." She took in the shop's appearance as they sat at the curb. It looked like a little red barn with a wooden sign. *Nate's Cakes.* "I thought we were going to a donut shop."

"Nate can bake up a mean cake, but he also serves these amazing gourmet donuts." Crowley climbed out and waited for her to join him on the sidewalk.

Maybe having Crowley along wasn't such a bad idea after all, Leah thought as they entered the quaint shop, decorated tastefully to resemble a barn. Leah closed her eyes and inhaled. The sweet aroma lingering in the air was heavenly.

"You're gonna love this place," Crowley whispered into Leah's ear as he led her to the display case.

A young woman wearing a red bandanna in her hair stood behind the counter. She gave Crowley a big smile in recognition. "Hey there, Crowley."

"Hey, Emma. Is Nate in?" Crowley asked as he casually draped his arm across Leah's shoulders.

"Sure. I'll go get him."

As they waited, Leah wrangled from beneath his arm and checked out the glass display case full of treats. Her mouth watered as she absentmindedly stroked the hand-carved wood trim.

"Not them," Crowley said.

"Why not?"

"Be patient," he said as a blond-haired guy walked in from the back. "Nate, my man, how's it going?"

Nate walked around and joined them on the other side of the counter. He shook Crowley's hand and gave him a slap on the back. "It's been a while, man. You haven't been able to sneak away from Lulu lately?" he asked, laughing.

"Something like that. I'd like to introduce you to my friend here, Leah."

Nate reached out to shake her hand. "I'm Nate, young lady." He smiled warmly and she responded in kind. He looked over to Crowley. "Hey, she's taller than me. You finally found you one with the right height."

"Yep. Leah's the perfect fishing partner," Crowley said, winking at Leah as if it were their inside joke or something.

"What can I get the two of you?" Nate asked.

"Whatcha got?" Crowley asked in an exaggerated tone as his eyes wandered over to the kitchen door.

"I just finished up two fresh batches. One batch is powdered donuts with a strawberry and fig preserve filling, and the other is a chocolate, hazelnut, and banana–stuffed batch. Some coffee-mocha ones will be done soon."

"Give me two of each," Crowley said. "What do you want, Leah?"

Leah's mouth watered even more at the donut choices. "The chocolate-hazelnut donut sounds good."

"And two bottles of water, please," Crowley said.

"Sure thing, buddy. Just give me about five minutes." Nate headed off into the kitchen as they took a seat by the front windows.

"How did you find this place?" Leah asked as they waited.

"The courthouse is right up the road. I go by here on my way to work. Nate delivered some special-order donuts to a litigation meeting a couple of years ago, and we became quick friends. He serves the best apple fritter you could ever find."

Leah thought of a place that could give him a run for his money and almost blurted it out. Crowley, sensing she was about to say something, asked, "What?"

She shook her head. "Nothing."

Leah almost purred when Nate carried out the treats and placed her donut in front of her. The massive donut filled the entire plate. It was sliced in half and brimming over with fresh sliced bananas and a chocolate-hazelnut filling oozing deliciously all over. She looked at the platter holding Crowley's large order. Two delicately powdered donuts she was sure were filled with the preserves and two coffee-mocha glazed donuts that resembled small cakes accompanied the chocolate, hazelnut, and banana–stuffed donuts.

"There's no way you can eat all that." She eyed the large platter apprehensively.

"I've seen him do it before." Nate laughed. He set the bottles of water on the table. "Y'all enjoy. I've got a delivery to make." He looked at Leah. "It was nice to meet you. Try to keep this one in line," Nate said, motioning toward Crowley.

Leah laughed. "I don't know if that's even possible. It was nice to meet you too."

Nate headed back into the kitchen, leaving them to eat.

"Why weren't these in the display case?"

"They were probably a special order," Crowley said as he dug into his first donut.

"So we just snatched a part of some person's order?"

"He always makes a few extras. You worry too much, Lee. Just enjoy your treat," he said around a mouth full of coffee donut. "Hmm . . . this is amazing." He offered Leah a pinch.

She took it and popped it into her mouth as she watched him dig into the next one. The chocolate-coffee goodness just melted in her mouth. "Please never bring me here again," she said before digging into her own donut.

"You don't like it?" he asked as he finished the second donut.

"That's the problem. I like it too much." She took another bite. "I'm a donutaholic."

"We have this problem in common," Crowley said as he moved to the preserve-filled powdered donuts.

"Yes, but you can eat a half-dozen donuts and walk away looking like that." She motioned to his body.

"I'm long. I've got a lot of space to fill."

"Well, if I eat that amount, I blow up to the size of a house." Leah sighed and pushed the remaining half of her donut over to Crowley, who gladly finished it off.

"Do you always eat this many?" She watched in amazement as he devoured his last donut.

"No. I usually just eat one or two with a cup of coffee." He shrugged. "Please don't tell Lulu. She would be spitting mad at me."

Leah took a swallow of her water. "Your secret is safe with me." She got up to go settle their bill, with Crowley following. She noticed as he started to pull his wallet out. "Don't even think about it."

Crowley slid the wallet back in his pocket with a shrug. "Emma, can I get another preserve-filled donut for the road?"

"Sure. Let me go grab it." She hurried into the kitchen.

Leah shook her head. "Really, Crow? That's your seventh donut."

Crowley shrugged.

After leaving Nate's Cakes, Leah drove in the direction of the courthouse.

"We're heading in the wrong direction," Crowley said as he slowly ate his donut.

"I want to see the courthouse. I see you in a suit sometimes, but you may be joshing me about that too." Truth was, she just wasn't in a hurry to head back yet. Crowley might have upset her earlier, but she genuinely enjoyed his company.

"I kid you not, Lee."

They rode in silence until they came upon the massive historical courthouse. Leah did another U-turn and headed home.

"Happy?" Crowley asked.

"Just peachy," Leah said as she turned the radio up a bit and sang along to Creedence Clearwater Revival's "Have You Ever Seen the Rain."

"How do you know all these old songs?" Crowley asked.

"I lived with a couple of hippies for about a year when I was a kid. They taught me all I needed to know about this music and all I needed to know about peace, man." Leah made a peace sign and directed it toward a smiling Crowley. She then focused back on the road. "They were cool and had great taste in music, but they were pretty forgetful on the whole parenting business. They had about five foster kids at once. We never had to wash regularly, and sometimes they would forget to feed us."

"That's terrible." Crowley's smile was gone.

"Not really. It was one of the best foster homes I ever stayed in. I got to attend lots of music festivals. When the school reported that me and the others had missed more school that year than we'd attended, we were removed from their custody." She shrugged. "I was twelve, so I thought it was a pretty cool year."

"What happened to your parents?"

"I don't know. They threw me away like I was garbage when I was a baby, so who cares?"

The song on the radio changed to Steppenwolf's "Magic Carpet Ride." Crowley started belting out a silly performance.

Leah fought a smile. "How do *you* know all of this music?"

"I'm cool like that, sweetheart." He continued singing as he played his air guitar.

Leah punched him in the arm to get his attention, and then she turned the radio down some. She was trying really hard to stay mad at him, but she was slipping. "Why are you always so darn happy?"

"Why not?" Crowley asked.

"I don't know if you're faking it or if it's genuine."

"You've seen me at less happy times. I know you recall I wasn't too happy the day you limped into Lulu's or the day after searching all night for Jessup," he said.

"But you plaster a smile on anyway." Leah turned in to the back lot of the café and parked.

"It feels better than a frown." They sat in silence for a moment before he spoke. "Look, Leah, I don't have a clue what life has put you through. I actually know very little about you—"

"You're one to talk, as you parade around like a poor country lawyer who trades his services for chickens."

Crowley raised his hands in defense. "Hey now! I've only done that once."

Leah rolled her eyes. "Can you ever be serious?"

"I am. Mrs. Jacobs gave me a roast chicken last year for notarizing some papers for her." He grinned.

"You really need a license to flash that thing," she said as she motioned to his grinning mouth.

"Lee, that's the second compliment you've paid me today. I think you're starting to like me *just* a little bit."

"Don't flatter yourself, Crow." She made the mistake of looking back to his stunning face. "Humph!" Leah opened her door to get out.

Crowley placed his hand lightly on her forearm. "Life's too short."

Leah pulled her arm free. "It feels too long to me." She slammed the door and headed to the back café entrance with her half-empty water bottle, trying not to look at him anymore.

"Thank you for the donuts, ma'am."

She couldn't resist turning around and looking at him, even as she told herself not to. Her frown quickly dissolved and was replaced with a smirk. "You saving some for later?" she asked, pointing to the corner of his mouth where a glob of strawberry and fig preserves sat.

Crowley leaned in close to her. "Why don't you get it off for me?" His alluring greenish-blue eyes gazed seductively into hers.

Leah grabbed the bottom hem of his white T-shirt and held it out while she took a gulp of water. She then spit the water into his shirt and yanked it up to his mouth, smearing the preserves all along the front of the shirt. "There," she said, pleased with herself.

He moved so quickly that she flinched, thinking he was about to strike her. He ripped his shirt off and tossed it at her. "I hope you're happy. Now I have to walk all the way home half-naked. I can't be seen with donut smears." He grinned at her.

Leah went from one shock to the next, taking in his perfectly toned chest and abdomen. "You. Have. Got to be kidding!" she said as she indicated his physique. "You just ate a pile of donuts, and that's what's hiding underneath your shirt. Unbelievable."

He raised his hands in surrender and pranced away, letting her take in his bare, broad shoulders that culminated nicely into a V shape near his low-riding shorts. She held her breath until he was out of sight. She stomped up the stairs and went straight to the laundry closet to retrieve a bottle of stain remover. She smirked at her bold actions. It felt good not to let a man get the best of her. He seemed so pleased to let her, too.

Her demeanor softened at the thought, and she couldn't resist holding the T-shirt up to her nose to take in the smell. The scent was masculine and clean with a touch of spice. She inhaled several deep breaths before she caught her reflection in a mirror. Feeling foolish, Leah doused the stain and put the shirt in the washing machine.

* * *

The next morning when Crowley opened his front door, he found a plastic bag dangling from his doorknob. Inside was his shirt, freshly laundered, with a note.

> *Sorry about yesterday. You have a right to your privacy.* —*Leah*

He was glad she sounded over it. He thought back to her flinching at his quick movement as though she expected him to hurt her. He stared down at the note. "Who has hurt you, Leah?" he whispered and returned into the house.

Crowley itched to go over to Lulu's to see Leah, but he felt she needed a break from him. He made his own meals for the day and kept himself busy with some paperwork he had to catch up on. Crowley didn't have a secretary or a paralegal. His dad had ingrained in him to never have someone do something for you that you can do yourself.

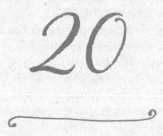

CROWLEY LET HIMSELF into the café the following day well after closing. Leah was in the process of mopping.

"You still full from all those donuts?" She glanced at him while wringing out the mop. After one more pass, the floor was finished, so she rolled the mop bucket behind the counter as he came up beside her.

"Where's Lulu?" He swiped an extra cold sandwich from the small display fridge. He laid into it at his normal speed.

"I made her go on another play date with her old ladies' group." Leah focused on scrubbing a stubborn spot.

"You've been really good for her," he said between bites. "You managed to succeed in something that I've been trying to do for the past fifteen years." He smiled in appreciation.

"She's been really good to me," she said as she mopped behind the counter.

Crowley took the last bite of the sandwich and tossed the wrapper. He placed his hand gently on her shoulder to get her attention. She stopped mopping and looked at him. "Leah, would you take a ride with me?"

"I guess. . . . Just let me finish up here first." She began to mop again.

Crowley pulled the mop from her hand. "Here. Let me finish and you can get washed up."

"It's my job. It won't take too long. A customer shouldn't do the mopping." She held her hand out and wiggled her fingers, but he started mopping anyway.

"I'm not a customer. I'm the owner of Lulu's, so it won't hurt me to mop my own floors," he confessed sheepishly without looking up.

Leah blinked a few times, trying to make sense of what he'd just admitted. "What? I thought Lulu was the owner."

"I own the café but never confuse the fact that she is still the boss." He chuckled as Leah stared at him. "I purchased the café from Lulu to try to get her to slow down and smell the roses. Once she didn't have to worry about the books anymore, it freed her up to consume her time with just running the business. So technically, my idea totally backfired on me. I wanted her to retire comfortably and not have all these worries." Crowley held the mop in one hand and motioned around the dining room with his other.

"Why do you always pay for your food, if you own this place?"

"It's no one's business to know I'm legally the owner."

"Then why admit it to me?" Leah untied the apron and pulled it off.

"Because you and I are going to be friends for a long time, and I think we need to start trusting each other. Don't you agree?"

Leah nodded, then turned toward the stairs. "I'm going to get a shower real quick."

"I could help you out with that too," he teased as he started mopping again.

"Knock it off, Crow," she said before shutting the door. She thought about locking it but figured he had a key for that door too.

Fifteen minutes later, Leah, wearing a pink cotton shirt that hung off one shoulder and a pair of black leggings, met Crowley at the foot of the stairs. Her hair was still wet from the shower.

"You look as fresh as a spring flower, ma'am," Crowley said, full of his Southern charm. He pulled her close and nuzzled his nose along her neck to the tip of her bare shoulder, taking her scent in and causing goose bumps to rise on her skin. "You smell as fresh as a flower too."

"Stop getting *fresh* with me, and tell me where we're going," she said but didn't pull away from him.

Crowley breathed in her scent one more time before lifting his head to meet her eyes. "I want to show you my farmhouse."

"You have a farmhouse, too?"

Crowley's smile widened. "Yes," he said as he pulled her out the back door where his Gator sat.

"*Ooooh* . . . can I drive it?" Leah lit up and hopped into the driver's seat.

"Can you drive a stick shift?" Crowley asked. He climbed into the passenger seat, looking skeptical.

"No, but the *ole wise one*, Crow, shall teach me." She smiled.

He quickly went over the mechanics. "You think you've got it?"

"Sure. Now which direction?" She pushed in the clutch and brake and cranked the manly machine.

"To the plantation. You know the way." Crowley fastened his seat belt and reached around Leah to fasten hers as well.

"That is *not* a farmhouse, sir."

"*Plantation* is just a fancy word for farmhouse. Besides, it's what my family has always called it."

Leah took off slowly, making the engine stall. She tried again and got it on the second try. She followed his directions and had no trouble dropping into the right gears.

"Not bad, Lee."

"Being street smart requires picking up on things easily." She met his gaze, which didn't appear too happy with her comment. She wished she could take it back. *If he only knew . . .*

The gate was already open when they arrived at the plantation. Leah looked at him questioningly.

"I came out earlier today. Head up and park by the front porch," he instructed. After she parked, Crowley led her along the driveway.

"I'd like to show you one of my favorite spots before we go inside, if that's okay with you."

"Sure. We're in no hurry, right?" she asked.

He smiled. "No hurry at all." They walked halfway back down the drive, and Crowley went to sit underneath one of the giant oak trees.

Leah followed him. She rested her back against the trunk and looked at the perfect view of the house. It looked like a breathtaking painting, with the silver moss gently blowing from the tree branches, framing the mansion.

Crowley stretched out on his side in front of Leah to take in the view of her. She was a view he had become quite fond of.

"How does such a young man as you acquire a place like this?" Leah asked and continued taking in the scenery.

"It's been in my family for generations. My dad's parents lived here when I was growing up. Grandpa Mason was a real estate tycoon. He gave my parents the town house as a wedding gift with the orders to fill the place with children. They tried for years with no success. They eventually gave up and just started spoiling all of the town's kids rotten."

Crowley paused to sit up and propped one of his legs on a thick, exposed root. "I gave my parents an unexpected surprise on my momma's forty-fifth birthday. She thought she was going through menopause, but she turned out to be pregnant instead." He smiled at the memory of her sharing this story with him many times during his childhood.

"After I turned sixteen, my grandparents decided to retire to Europe and signed all of their properties over to *me* at my parents' request. I also got a fat trust fund to go along with that gift. That day was the first time I realized how wealthy my family actually was. We didn't live the way the rich do. My parents taught me to stand as a strong man without having the materials of this world propping me up."

"I'm speechless," Leah whispered.

"Well, soon after the paperwork was complete, my momma and I started a full-scale renovation project with the plantation. Before we got too far, the old structure caught fire. So we ended up having to start from scratch—researching the original floor plans and recovering as many pieces of furniture as we could."

Crowley picked at a few twigs as he resolved to finish his family's story. Without looking at Leah, he continued. "The summer after my high school graduation, the house had been completely rebuilt. The only thing left was to paint and dress it up. Me and Momma's summer project was to hustle at getting it completed before I headed off to college." He shook his head. "She was so excited to do this with me. We had it all planned out. Then she went to the doctor with a persistent chest cold, and two weeks after that she was diagnosed with lung cancer."

"That's awful," Leah whispered. She reached over to hold his hand as he regained his composure.

"The worst part is she never smoked a cigarette in her entire life. I see people smoking away their health and I just want to scream at them. Why her and not them?"

Leah noticed his normal casualness had slipped away with his brutal honesty.

"They fought it the best they could . . . surgery, chemotherapy, and radiation. It just didn't respond well to treatment." Crowley sat silent for a few moments before continuing. "My momma was a woman full of life. She could bring a room to life with her laughter. She loved laughing and joking around. She said you weren't truly living if you weren't laughing."

"So that's where you get it. That grin of yours is magic," Leah said.

Crowley shrugged. "It was torture to watch the disease just suck the life out of her. My parents rented an apartment near Duke while she participated in some experimental treatments. I wanted to go with them, but they insisted I start college on schedule. I spent every weekend with them, though." He paused to clear his throat and Leah patiently waited until he seemed ready to continue.

"She didn't quite make it a year, and my dad followed her by winter. The doctor said he died of a heart attack, but I know it was from a broken heart. They adored each other and were always saying they couldn't live without the other. I guess they truly meant it."

Crowley steadied himself for a minute before he looked up. When he finally glanced at Leah, a jolt of tenderness washed over him. Leah sat staring at him with a steady stream of quiet tears washing down her cheeks. He reached over and wiped her face gently with his fingertips.

"You're an orphan too," she whispered in the hushed breeze.

Crowley slowly shook his head. "No. Never. I've been blessed with a lifetime of love, memories, *and* Lulu." He scooted over to cradle her into his side and leaned back against the tree trunk. "You have her too."

Eventually, after her tears dried, Leah drifted to sleep in the lull of Crowley's comfort. She was roused awake an hour later with the scent of grass and honeysuckle, the scents that engulfed her repeated dream of her daughter. She opened her eyes and found Crowley studying her.

"Sorry I fell asleep." She rubbed her eyes. "I didn't sleep well at all last night." The dream had played in a constant loop in her sleep for the past few nights. The closer she got to Crowley, the more her ordeal plagued her.

"It's okay. I haven't slept the best in the last few nights either," he said.

Leah sniffed the air. "I smell honeysuckle."

"They line just about the whole property. I love the sweet smell of them. I guess my nose has the sweet addiction too." Crowley tilted his head and met her eyes. "You don't like honeysuckle?"

"I do. I actually smell them in my dreams quite often," Leah said. She sat up and wiped the corners of her eyes. As she finger-combed her curls, Crowley leaned over to touch her hair. She enjoyed having his hands there more than she thought was possible.

"Your hair is getting really long."

"You don't like it?"

"You have one of the loveliest heads of hair, Miss Allen." He slowly ran his fingers through it. "I'm crazy about these curls." He winked.

"Enough with your flirting, sir. I want a tour of your *farmhouse*."

"Yes, ma'am."

They stood and stretched before heading to the front porch. As they stood at the door while Crowley unlocked it, Leah surveyed the deep porch. "One of these days I'm going to sneak over here and sit on this porch all day."

"Why's that?" Crowley asked as he scanned the porch.

"It just begs for company."

Crowley looked over at the grouping of chairs around a small table. "I played many a game of checkers with my grandpa at that table. By the time I was twelve, I could beat him every now and then." He glanced back at the steps. "Ana would set up tea parties on the steps and make me host them with her along with a few baby dolls. I made her swear on the Bible to never tell a soul that I played such girlie games, and she never did." When Leah giggled at that, he gave her a pointed look. "Do I need to make you swear on the Bible too?"

"No. Your secret is safe with me, Crowley." She thought him admitting that was right adorable and had to tamp down the urge to kiss him on the cheek. She followed his gaze over to the porch swing. "Another memory?"

"That was my and my momma's favorite spot. We'd swing while I laid my head in her lap. She loved to play with my hair." A small smile played along his lips. "She told me about every time we sat on this swing that I was a gift from God—her most precious treasure on this earth." He stared at the swing for a few more moments before pushing the heavy black door open and motioning for Leah to go ahead of him.

The cool air of the house rushed to greet Leah as she stepped into the vast foyer. A grand chandelier dripped with elegance from the high ceiling by the cascading staircase. The beautiful wide-planked floors, finished with a rich walnut stain, appeared as though a foot had never been placed on them. Leah hesitated.

"What?" Crowley shut the door behind them and placed his hand lightly on the small of Leah's back to beckon her forward.

"It's just . . ." She tried to take it all in. "Wow."

The foyer opened to a comfortable sitting room with large, thickly stuffed antique wingback chairs in rich burgundy, gold, and blue stripes. A wood-framed antique sofa in a deep-blue-and-cream paisley-printed fabric joined the chairs, with an intricately patterned Persian rug peeking from the edges of the seating area.

An oil painting sat on the mantel of the hefty brick fireplace. The scene was almost exactly the view Leah had taken in earlier of the plantation house framed by the curved oak trees.

Leah looked over her shoulder at the country boy in his signature tattered baseball hat, T-shirt, well-worn cargo shorts, and flip-flops. His ocean-colored eyes were studying her reaction. She glanced around at her exquisite surroundings and shook her head slightly.

Crowley stepped around Leah and faced her, his eyebrow raised. "Well?"

She was quite amused at how Crowley, who always exuded boundless confidence, was actually a bit unsure of himself at sharing his home with a girl.

"I would never have guessed this." She motioned around. "And you."

He scratched his stubbly chin as he gazed into the sitting area. "My momma designed this part. All of the salvaged pieces were restored and placed in here." Crowley shoved his hands in his pockets. "It's really not my style, but I left it this way in honor of her."

"I love how it's so open." Leah waved a hand in the air.

"We readjusted the floor plans by taking out several walls. We even had to add closets to all of the bedrooms."

"How many bedrooms?" she asked.

"Six. The one on the bottom floor was intended to be the office space, and all the rest are on the second floor. The entire third floor is now the office space. We turned the basement into a large game room with a full-size kitchen. There's also a fully equipped gym. I like to work out alone."

"Well, that's a relief," Leah quipped.

"What is?"

"You have to work out." Leah made a face, making him chuckle.

Crowley pulled one of his hands from his pocket and reached for Leah's. "Come on," he said as he led them upstairs.

At the top, Crowley pointed to the right. "There are four bedrooms and two full baths that way." He pulled Leah down the hall to the left and stopped in front of a pair of heavy doors. "This is the master suite." He pulled open the doors to reveal a breathtaking room. A massive four-poster rice bed dominated the tranquil space. It was dressed in lush sage green and cream–colored bedding. A charming wooden step stool waited to assist someone into the tall bed. A grand fireplace warmed the space even without being lit.

Crowley noticed Leah studying the oil painting hanging above the mantel. "This picture was painted by a local artist who stood on that very balcony to capture the river view." He pointed to a set of French doors.

Leah walked over and peered out to the cozy balcony, which held a sweeping view of the river flowing behind the property.

Crowley picked up a small remote from the nightstand. "Hey, watch this." He aimed the remote at the oil painting and pushed a button. The painting slid up and revealed a flat-screen TV.

Leah grinned. "Very cool, Crow."

She walked to the right of the bed and peeked into an alcove that housed an inviting sitting area and bookshelf. She turned back to Crowley. "This place is massive."

"We turned three bedrooms into one." Crowley placed the remote back on the nightstand. He made his way to an upholstered bench at the foot of the bed and sat down, propping his elbows on the soft bed behind him.

Leah pulled open another set of double doors and found the master bathroom. White marble floors with gray veining and an exquisite wrought-iron chandelier caught her eye instantly. The walls were divided, with the bottom dressed in white detailed wainscoting and the top painted in a shade of soft sage green. A huge claw-foot tub with a swooping back took up one whole wall.

"How hard was it to find such a tub to accommodate the gentle giant?" Leah called out to Crowley in the other room.

"Not an easy find. That's for sure."

The bathroom also housed a gigantic walk-in shower with a seamless glass surround that was designed as to not obstruct the view of the space. Leah stepped inside it. "This shower is larger than some bedrooms I've had," she yelled and turned to step out to find Crowley leaning on the doorframe, watching her.

"I'm a big man. I require a lot of space." He moved out of Leah's way so she could exit the bathroom.

The room had two more doors. Leah opened one to find an empty walk-in closet. She inspected the doorknob.

Crowley noticed her fascination. "What?"

Leah shrugged. "No locks."

Crowley looked at her, a bit confused. "A lock on a closet door makes no sense, Lee."

"I totally agree," she mumbled, not meeting his eyes. She checked the other door out of habit.

"That's another closet. And no, it doesn't have locks either." He reached for Leah's hand and began leading her out of the room. "Come on. I'm getting hungry."

Leah tugged Crowley's arm, making him stop. "You have a beautiful home, Crowley," she said sincerely.

"House," he corrected. "A family makes a home, and this one is lacking." He gave her a weak smile and descended the stairs.

Leah noticed the sad edge to his words. She wondered why such a wonderful man didn't already have this house filled with children. He didn't seem to enjoy the loneliness of his bachelorhood.

Crowley led Leah to the back of the house, where an enormous kitchen and den took up almost the entire space. The kitchen had a funky farmhouse vibe, and Leah could easily spot Crowley's hand in designing it.

Stainless steel appliances were softened by warm oak cabinetry, the upper cabinets adorned with detailed crown molding. A wood plank ceiling and exposed wooden beams added more character to the lively space, along with black granite countertops and a deep farmhouse apron sink.

A hefty island with a distressed white base and a walnut-stained butcher-block top took up the middle of the kitchen. On it was a three-foot-tall rooster figurine that looked as though it could have strutted right out of the painting at Lulu's and perched itself in Crowley's kitchen.

"I'm digging this kitchen," Leah said as she ran her hand along the smooth granite countertop. She inspected the contents of a set of antique white enamel canisters, finding each one empty.

Crowley reached up to cradle one of the pendant lights hanging over the island. "Me and my dad custom-made these." The light sconces were crafted from blue mason jars, which were held in place by curving wrought-iron details around the lids.

"Those are the neatest lights," Leah said as she studied them.

"We took our idea to a local metal artisan, and he helped us create them. I thought they were perfect for a farmhouse kitchen."

Leah smiled at his simpler term for the plantation. Her eyes moved over to a wall that housed a distressed olive-green hutch with chicken wire inserts on the cabinet doors. Beside the heavy furniture piece, the wall was dressed with a row of vintage tin signs. One of the signs showed a chicken sitting on top of a nest, with creamy writing that stated *Fresh Eggs for Sale*. Another advertised MoonPies with a yellow half-moon. Leah's favorite was a black sign with burgundy scripted lettering that declared *Life Is Unreliable . . . Eat Dessert First*.

"I know you handpicked that one," she said, pointing at the vintage sign.

Crowley eyed the sign in question with a smile. "Yep. That one definitely spoke to me." He walked over to the oven and adjusted the temperature knob.

"What are we eating?" Leah asked as she leaned on the counter near him.

"Steak, baked taters, and salad," he said as he popped two foil-wrapped potatoes into the oven.

"What can I do to help?"

"I made the salad earlier. So all you have to do is keep me company." Crowley flashed a crooked smile at her.

"Maybe I can handle that." She smiled back.

"We've got a little while on those taters. How 'bout we check out some more of the house?"

"I'd love to." Leah walked over to Crowley and reached for his hand for the first time, her heart racing in uncertainty. Her extended hand was a much-needed step forward, and with him accepting it, Leah was surprised at how right it felt.

They spent the next hour touring the den, the large washroom, and a hidden passageway behind the staircase. The tour ended in the grand formal dining room. A wood table, with twelve upholstered chairs surrounding it, shone as it sat on top of another richly toned Persian rug. The table was beautiful, but what Leah found intriguing was the large china cabinet.

"What in the world?" she asked, walking over to it.

Crowley followed behind her and let out a small chuckle. "Now that right there makes me miss my momma something awful." He opened the glass doors and pulled two dinner plates out. The china cabinet housed twenty fine china place settings—each piece in a pattern of its own. The plate in Crowley's right hand was white with a red-and-gold ring around the edge. The plate in his left hand was blue willow. Leah took them out of his hand delicately and studied the patterns.

"Momma and Lulu spent an entire day in a china shop selecting each mismatched piece. Momma knew she was blessed to live well financially, but she said she'd be darned if she would put up with the pretenses of it." Crowley chuckled lightly again.

Leah looked over all of the various patterns that seemed so whimsical. "Your mom sounded like my kind of woman."

Crowley gathered some flatware from the silverware

drawer and handed it to Leah. He then pulled two salad plates out, one with a bumblebee in the center with a kelly-green border and the other a lively magnolia flower pattern. He led Leah back to the kitchen and laid out the place settings on the island countertop.

After a hearty supper, Leah helped Crowley with the dishes. As they stood at the sink, Leah noticed how quiet he had become. She nudged him with her hip. "What's on your mind?" she asked as she handed him a soapy plate.

He shrugged. "This was the first meal eaten in this house since my parents died."

She felt his confession deep in her chest. "No . . . really?"

Crowley nodded.

Leah roughly did the math. "So this house has just been sitting out here for over ten years, all alone?" She pulled the plug in the sink and dried her hands on a kitchen towel before offering it to Crowley.

He focused on drying his hands. "Lulu kept on about throwing a house dedication party but finally agreed to hold it in the gardens. It was the spring after my parents' passing, and it seemed too personal . . . too intimate to have the entire world invited in."

Leah wrapped her arms around his waist and hugged him. "Thank you for inviting me in," she said with her head against his chest.

He lightly rubbed her back. "You think you could do the same?"

Leah looked up at him. "Same what?"

Crowley's hypnotic eyes bored into hers. "Invite me in, Leah," he whispered.

"I want to, but when I try, the words get stuck. . . ." She looked away.

"If this is going to work—" he gently squeezed her a

bit closer into his embrace—"then you are going to have to. Sharing all of this with you ain't easy for me either."

"You may not feel the same way about me once you get to *really* know me." She knew their relationship would surely be over once he found out she was a murderer.

"It's a bridge we are going to have to cross shortly," he warned her. He released her but gathered her hand in his. "You ready to go?"

"Sure," she reluctantly answered, wishing for more time.

Once outside, Leah headed to the driver's side of the tricked-out Gator, but Crowley beat her there. "I want to drive." She pressed her palms together in a pleading motion.

"Not this time, Lee." Crowley smirked as he slid his hat on backward and took on the air of pure mischievousness. "Buckle up. I'm going to show you how to really drive this thing."

As Leah snapped the seat belt into place, Crowley cranked the engine, dropped it into gear, and shot off toward a patch of woods beside the plantation. He made quick work of the gears and sent the Gator barreling down a bumpy path at lightning speed, making Leah grab ahold of the arm rails to steady herself.

Crowley reached a clearing, and with precision he took a sharp right and slammed on the brakes, causing the Gator to fishtail back the direction they had just come from. With the dust engulfing them, he dropped it back into gear and shot off again, causing Leah to whoop and holler in true country girl fashion.

In that thrilling moment, she resolved that she must have been born with dirt-road roots twining through her veins. Leah had never felt so alive until stepping foot on the Southern soil of Rivertown, South Carolina.

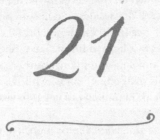

21

SPRING MOVED IN A RUSH toward summer with Leah taking on more café responsibilities and Lulu actually letting her. The two ladies enjoyed each other's company so much that they spent most Sundays after church attending flea markets and farmers' markets.

Leah continued her solitary jogs and her coffeehouse visits with Ana. Leah even helped organize campouts for the town's youth. Crowley camped out with the boys at the river cabin one weekend, complete with a day of fishing and supper by a bonfire. The next weekend, Leah and Ana chaperoned the girls at the pool house, which was more like a slumber party with manicures, dancing, and swimming. She liked the idea of bringing life around to keep the lonely plantation company.

May arrived with Leah and Crowley's friendship on constant pause. He seemed to be waiting for her to open up to him before moving any further in their relationship. Leah couldn't blame him. She was nearly content with them just staying friends as long as she got to keep him.

After the breakfast crowd dissipated one morning, Crowley strolled in wearing his lawyer's best—a tailored gray suit, white dress shirt, and a blue- and gray-striped necktie. Leah looked up and smiled at the handsome man grinning back at her. She checked to make sure he was wearing his black dress shoes, and he was. She thought he was absolutely beautiful, inside and out.

"Wearing your hero uniform, I see," she said.

"Yes, ma'am. I'm also taking your Jeep," he said as he grabbed his own cup of coffee while Leah made him a breakfast wrap. "I'm going to get it serviced after I get out of court."

"Okay. Thanks. There's some money in the glove box to cover it," Leah said.

Crowley sipped his coffee. "One sandwich will be enough for today," he whispered, making Leah scoff.

"Tell Nate I said hey."

"You want me to smuggle you something back?"

"No thanks." She assembled the egg whites and crumbled turkey sausage on the whole wheat tortilla, lightly sprinkled it with cheese, and wrapped it up neatly.

"One donut won't hurt you," he said.

"Hush before Lulu hears you. One won't, but one is never enough." She placed the sandwich in a bag and handed it over. "So . . . anything interesting on the court docket?"

"Freeing Jessup Barns," Crowley said as he gave her a ten-dollar bill and held up his bag. "Thank you, ma'am." He headed out the back door.

Leah followed behind him as she yelled out to Lulu, who was in the walk-in pantry. "I'll be right back, Lulu."

Crowley fished the key from under the floor mat and climbed in the driver's seat. He reached to adjust the seat farther back. As he did, Leah scooted on the edge of his lap and looked at him. He placed his hands on her hips and waited for the question he seemed to know was coming.

She straightened his necktie. "Why on earth would you want to help that drunk get out of prison?" Jessup had been locked up for a couple of months, and in Leah's opinion, that was where he should stay.

Crowley rubbed his thumbs in circles on her hips. "Jessup hasn't always struggled with alcoholism. He used to be a straight-up guy who was a true asset to this town. That man could figure out how to fix anything." He waited for Leah to look at him before he continued. "At least, until a car crash claimed the lives of his sweet wife and young son. His world crashed down and died along with his family that day. He never got over it and turned to the bottle to cope. I'm not supporting that choice, but I can sympathize."

"Why didn't you tell me?" Leah whispered.

"Jessup's story ain't mine to tell." Crowley tucked a curl that had escaped Leah's ponytail behind her ear.

"I hope you don't use *ain't* in the courtroom." She grinned as she tried to tickle his side, but he was too fast. He grabbed up her hands and tickled her.

"That's proper language in these here parts. *Ain't* no judge gonna hold it against this here country boy."

Leah placed a light kiss on Crowley's cheek and climbed out of his lap. As she neared the back door, she turned before he closed the Jeep door. "Crowley Mason, you are one fine lawyer."

"You mean my good looks or my mad lawyer skills?" he asked with a chuckle.

"Both. Always both." Leah waved and headed back to the café.

She found Lulu stirring a pot of strawberry preserves on the stove. It was her first batch of the season. She had shown Leah the recipe yesterday and told her by the end of strawberry season, Leah would have it memorized. The little lady made enough to last the entire year.

Leah leaned against the counter beside Lulu and

fiddled with her apron ruffle. "I'm such a hypocrite." She was right disgusted with herself for being so judgmental about Jessup.

"Ain't we all," Lulu commented as she turned the stove burner off. "It's ready." She stepped out of the way so Leah could move the molten liquid over to the large kitchen worktable.

"I'm no better than Jessup Barns. Here he is coping with a bottle of liquor as I point my finger at him in judgment, while I cram large amounts of junk food in my mouth to cope." Leah shook her head.

"It's easy to point out someone else's sin sometimes. But . . . hey . . ." Lulu patted Leah's hand to get her attention. "I think both of you are on the wagon at the present." She smiled.

Leah smiled slightly back at her. "I'll bake him a cake when Crowley gets him home."

"Crowley is asking the judge to place Jessup in a rehabilitation facility before allowing him to go home. So it may be a while." Lulu handed Leah a small ladle and took one herself so they could begin filling jars with the preserves.

"I just feel so bad for him. . . ." Leah filled another jar with the vibrant red jam.

"Jessup doesn't need pity. He needs support, yes, but not pity. Maybe you can go up on a visitation day and share with him how you struggle with your grief. Maybe the two of you can help one another move on from what you've endured," Lulu said.

"Yes, ma'am."

●   ●   ●

On her way home from her daily jog on a humid May afternoon, Leah stopped short at her Jeep Wagoneer.

Strapped onto the roof were two surfboards and placed on the back window was a surf logo sticker. Her eyes caught the card tucked under the windshield wiper. She pulled it out and read it.

Does a day at the beach count as a real date?
I sure hope so. I'll pick you up at nine in the morning.

Crowley

PS—I've already okayed it with the boss. Just sleep in and be ready to do some surfing.

Leah, excited for a new adventure, hopped into her Jeep and headed about five miles down the road to a surf shop, where she purchased a pair of board shorts and a rash guard top. She returned to the café to do some extra prep work to ease her conscience about taking the following day off. She precooked the chicken soup minus the whole wheat noodles, which would be added tomorrow. She also made up a few batches of her now-famous oatmeal bars and six dozen brownie bites so that Lulu wouldn't have to do any extra baking for lunch.

At five the next morning, Leah sat at her small dining table, unable to sleep in, smelling the aromas of freshly baked muffins and coffee escaping up from the café. The routine of the café was second nature to her now, and it was all she could do not to go help out. She resisted the urge and instead caught up on some laundry and housework.

Around eight, Lulu opened the door without a knock—it was her way, and Leah found it comforting. The petite lady carried a wicker picnic basket and had a grin on her face. Lulu absolutely loved witnessing the relationship of her two favorite people blossom right before her.

"I'm sorry for skipping out on you this morning." Leah looked remorseful, making Lulu laugh.

"Child, you deserve some time off every now and then too," Lulu said, placing the basket on the table. "Besides, you did so much prep yesterday that I had time to make you and Crowley lunch."

"That was sweet of you. Thank you." Leah bent slightly to give Lulu a hug.

"Have yourself a big time today." Lulu squeezed her close one last time before leaving.

By ten, Leah and Crowley were on the beach setting up. Crowley spread a large blanket out, and Leah placed her bag and picnic basket on top. He pulled off his T-shirt and tossed it on top of the blanket as he watched Leah pull her oversize T-shirt off to reveal her board shorts and rash-guard shirt.

"Are you kidding me, Lee?" He stood with his hands on his hips. "I got all excited yesterday when you came rushing home with a surf bag. I thought finally you were going to show off some of that lovely body to me." He winked.

"Dream on, Crow," Leah scolded him as she secretly admired his swim trunks, slung low on his lean hips.

They spent the better part of the day playing in the water. Leah got up on the surfboard successfully a few times before wiping out. Crowley seemed at home on his board and easily rode wave after wave. Famished, they returned to their picnic and devoured sandwiches, fresh vegetables, and homemade cookies. After the late lunch, the pair stretched out on the blanket to sunbathe.

Crowley reached over to tug at the bottom hem of Leah's board shorts. "You know you could have sent me off with a less covered-up picture," he said over the roar of the ocean.

"What are you talking about?" Leah lazily batted his hand away from her thigh.

"I've got to leave for a law conference in Atlanta tomorrow. Then I have to go straight to Columbia afterward to help Matt and his firm out with a high-profile case," Crowley said as his eyes drifted shut.

Leah's eyes opened wide. "How long are you going to be gone?" She worried she sounded desperate.

"I shouldn't be gone for more than two, maybe three weeks at the most. It depends on how the trial progresses."

They lay quietly for a long period as Crowley dozed. Leah felt uneasy about his abrupt departure tomorrow.

"Why didn't you tell me before now?"

Crowley opened his eyes and rolled to his side to face her. "Sweetheart, you don't tell me anything about yourself, but you are actually hurt when I don't. How's that make any sense?" He caressed her cheek, but she pulled away.

"I'm sorry. It's none of my business." She was disgusted with herself that he was so right about her.

"I only just agreed to it this week." He held her gaze as he ran his hand through her damp hair.

"Why did you decide to go?" She rolled onto her back and placed her left hand over her eyes.

Crowley pulled it away and placed a kiss on her scarred palm. "I want more, Leah. I worry we are going to make a mess of it, if you can't trust me. We play all the time—fishing, bike riding, raising Cain on the Gator— and that's all great. I've never enjoyed someone's company as much as yours . . . but it's not enough. I want to know you better." He ran his long index finger along the uneven scar before releasing her hand and rolling to his stomach.

"I thought it would be good to go on this trip to give you some space to decide if that's what you want too."

Leah replaced her hand over her eyes and gave the only part of her she could muster to confess. "Before I moved here, I had been living the past ten years in Olympia, Washington." She let the bit of truth resonate before continuing. "The only decent thing I did in all that time was to volunteer at a children's group home."

"That was generous of you." Crowley wiped some sand from her shoulder.

She dropped her hand and stared at him. "No. Not really. The only reason I did it was because I was lonely and living in some kind of hell on earth. I volunteered not for those poor kids, but for me. I was grasping for some thread of comfort your childhood home is supposed to provide you."

They stared at each other for a few moments, listening to the ocean waves crashing on the shore and the seagulls singing their song.

Leah shook her head. "You're not going to like the person I was before I arrived here."

"I *really* like the woman before me, Leah. Your past won't change that," he said confidently.

"I wouldn't be so sure." She took a deep breath. "It's easy for you to say that now, but . . ." Leah watched Crowley as she twirled a long curl anxiously through her fingers, wishing there was a way to end this conversation.

He reached over and cradled her nervous hand without another word. Thankfully, he let the conversation conclude.

He gazed at her sideways until his eyes drooped and then shut completely. His bottom lip pouted out slightly, and Leah knew he had dozed off. He seemed to always be so at peace with life. Here they were discussing their relationship—a relationship Crowley pursued at a snail's pace—and he was so confident with it that he could just doze off.

Not Leah. She lay there watching him and worrying. Crowley was a resourceful man. Her hope was that he would take it upon himself to investigate while on his trip—away from her so that she wouldn't have to see the sting of disappointment that would surely flood his enchanting eyes when he found out who she really was. She knew it would be there in volumes.

The rest of the day passed quietly between them as they sunbathed in uncomfortable silence. As the sun set, they packed up and headed back home with Leah in near tears over his imminent departure. She had grown quite attached to him over the past few months.

Crowley walked her in and stopped at the foot of the stairs as he always did. He pulled out a small piece of paper and a remote with a key hooked to it and placed them in Leah's hand. "I wrote my phone number down in case you need me for anything while I'm gone, and that's the remote to the gate. You're welcome to jog the property or go swimming if you'd like. I also wrote the alarm code down for the house." He pointed to the key. "And that's the house key."

Leah clutched the small gifts in her hand. "Thank you," she whispered. She felt herself slapping up a wall between them, and she wanted to rip it back down and blurt out a confession to him. Instead, she took a few steps away from him.

Crowley pulled her back to him for a long hug, making her ache all over. He was so strong compared to her weakness.

He whispered in her ear, "This isn't good-bye." He

drew back and waited for her to meet his gaze before producing a flirty grin. "You and Lulu and Ana are gonna be so busy planning the Summer Welcome Festival that you won't even miss the likes of this ole boy."

Leah knew he was trying to leave on a pleasant note, so she held the tears back and gave him the only gift she could. She tickled his side and teased him right back. "I see what you are doing, Crow. You're getting out of all the work." Lulu had already informed her that she would be helping organize the barbecue cook-off and the strawberry recipe contest.

"You caught me," he said with a weak smile. "I'm really going to miss you, you know." He pulled her in for another bittersweet hug.

"Me too." She forced herself to let go and head up the stairs to her apartment, leaving him standing at the bottom. She didn't wait as she normally did to hear him lock the back door. Instead, she went straight to the bathroom and turned on the shower as the tears spilled.

THE FIRST WEEK of Crowley's absence seemed to drag on at a miserable pace for Leah. Each day she had to talk herself out of calling him. He said to call if she needed him. She took that to mean some kind of an emergency, not just needing to hear his voice. Maybe he was right. Maybe the time apart would help her to see how important he had become to her—maybe enough to risk opening up to him. . . .

Leah fought agitation whenever Lulu or Ana would report about hearing from Crowley. She had hoped he would miss her too much not to call. She worried he wasn't missing her or that he'd squeezed in some investigation on her and knew the truth. Ana reported that the law conference was boring, but he got to catch up with some colleagues he hadn't seen in quite some time. Lulu mentioned that the case in Columbia had turned out to be more complicated than expected, and Crowley would be tied up until the weekend of the summer festival, to Leah's disappointment.

In the weeks since Crowley left, Leah had taken up jogging on the plantation property. Most days she would go for a swim afterward and then sunbathe until it was time to jog back home. A few times, she skipped the pool and opted for sitting on the welcoming porch, either in the swing or rocking chair. She never ventured inside, not feeling right about being in the house without Crowley.

The three-day summer festival kept Leah's mind off of Crowley's absence, almost. Lulu kept her busy with the barbecue cook-off and the recipe contest. She was tasked with organizing the booth locations and setup, phoning all of the contestants to confirm their participation and what their entries would be, picking the judges for the contests, and ordering the winner ribbons and trophies. It was a lot of work.

Ana sponsored a Southern belle night at her boutique the evening before the festivities kicked off. She roped Leah in to take care of the food preparations, which included light hors d'oeuvres of tomato tartlets, vegetable and fruit platters, mini strawberry shortcakes with fresh whipped cream, and strawberry punch. Leah even helped her friend host the evening.

They laughed through a silly purse game where the girls had to pull items out that started with the drawn letter. The well-dressed young debutantes had no problem pulling out tampons for the letter *T*, causing giggles to break out through the group. One young lady actually pulled out a bra for the letter *B*. This made Leah keel over in laughter.

After the games and food, Ana had a cosmetic representative demonstrate makeup application. Each young lady was presented a goody bag full of cosmetics. They were also delighted to receive a brightly colored beaded bracelet to wear during the festival, declaring them members of the Southern Belle League, as proclaimed by Ana.

After cleaning up from the party, Leah said her good-byes and headed to the door.

"Not so fast, young lady. I have two sundresses you've forgotten all about. You are going to need one for Saturday's dance," Ana said in her prissy tone.

The highlight of the three-day festival was the Dancing in the Streets event that fell on the last night of the celebration. It was all Ana and the teenage girls could talk about. Ana had sold out of all of her sundresses to the excited women in town, both young and old.

"I assumed you ended up having to sell them." Leah shrugged. She followed Ana to the dressing room, where her petite friend helped her try them on. She slipped the black halter dress on first and loved how it cascaded softly down to her ankles. Next, Leah tried on the shorter one-shoulder dress, with its vivid shades of blue and teal reminding her of a tropical ocean.

"This one will be better for dancing," Ana commented. She fetched a pair of gold wedge sandals and a gold cuffed bracelet for Leah to try on with the dress. Once Leah strapped the shoes on and stood straight, Ana stepped back to get a good look at her. "Twirl around."

Leah did as instructed, and the flowing skirt danced out like a soft umbrella.

Ana placed her hands on her hips. "Humph!"

"What?" Leah asked, looking down at her outfit to see what was wrong.

"I can't go to the dance."

"Why not?" Leah now stood with her hands on her hips.

"Because I won't be the hottest girl there this year." Ana playfully popped Leah on her butt. "Bend your tall self down." Ana pulled Leah's hair up and studied the result in the mirror. "What do you think?"

"You think I should wear my hair up?" Leah asked as Ana released her curls.

"Yep. Maybe Crowley would like it," she said, trying to provoke Leah.

Leah ignored her. "Is Jake going to be able to make it?" She slipped the sandals off her feet and began to re-dress.

"Yeah. He's driving up on Saturday morning. He said Crowley should be arriving sometime behind him." Ana eyed Leah. "Crowley told Jake he sure was missing you." Ana smiled when she finally got a reaction of relief from her friend.

Leah gathered her purchases and headed to the register to settle her bill. "How do you really feel about me and Crowley being friends?" The two women had danced around the conversation long enough. Leah knew they needed to clear the air.

"*Friends?*" Ana laughed. "Leah, the way that man looks at you was what I had desperately wanted from him for so long. I was selfish. I know that now. I love him and always will." She bagged Leah's purchases and grabbed a pair of gold chandelier earrings with teal stones to add to the bag.

"I don't want to hurt you," Leah said softly as she handed Ana the money.

"Then don't hurt him," Ana warned. "He will always be a brother to me."

"I know." Leah turned to leave.

"Don't forget your goody bag, Miss Allen. Be sure to wear your bracelet during the festival." Ana smiled.

Leah loved how everyone in this town always seemed to end a conversation on a good note. It was very charming.

"I wouldn't think of not wearing my *exclusive* Southern belle bracelet, Ana, dear." Leah blew her friend a farewell kiss as she scooped up her goody bag and headed next door.

* * *

The festival seemed to solidify Leah's town membership. Thursday and Friday afternoons were spent helping with the festival. To her amusement, Leah had a continuous shadow of teenage girls. People even asked for her recommendations as to what shows to attend or what booths to visit, making her feel accepted.

Lulu and Leah closed the café on Saturday for the festival but offered premade sandwiches and baked goods for sale at a booth near the contest tents. Lulu had a few part-time girls manning the booth while she and Leah occasionally popped in to help out.

Leah spent the morning setting up the strawberry recipe contest tent. A table was set up for preserves and jellies. Another was set up for pies and one for cakes. Baskets of lush berries dressed tables with red tablecloths. Leah had grabbed white tablecloths earlier, but Lulu advised against it—strawberry stains were a pain to get out.

Lulu, dressed in a white peasant blouse, denim capris, and her signature white Keds, swept in about midmorning to check on Leah. "How's it going, dear?" she asked as she tied a red bandanna in her silver locks.

"I'm not sure these things are safe with me." Leah inhaled the delectable berry aromas perfuming the air and shook her head.

Lulu chuckled. "You're a tough cookie. You can handle it." She scooted back out to check on the café's food booth. Leah pulled identification cards from her strawberry-patterned apron pocket and placed one by each submission.

The contest concluded late in the afternoon. Leah managed to only eat one slice of strawberry sour cream cake. She grabbed up a strawberry cream pie to present to Crowley, if she got to see him. She spent the day looking around, hoping to see the gentle giant hovering over the crowd. To her disappointment, he had not made an appearance.

After wrapping up her festival duties, Leah headed to her apartment. She placed the pie in the fridge and hopped in the shower to wash away her newly acquired strawberry perfume. She took her time washing, taking extra care to shave her legs smooth and to scrub her face in preparation for the new makeup she was given at the Southern belle party.

Once she dried off, Leah slathered her body with a scented lotion and spritzed the matching perfume, with notes of rose and crisp, clean citrus, all over. She wrapped the towel around her midsection and moved over to the mirror. After wiping the steam away, she inspected her eyebrows and plucked a few strays. Content with that, Leah stepped into her bedroom and admired the beautiful dress draped across her bed. She was determined to show off her new outfit with or without Crowley.

Leah spent the next hour applying her makeup and arranging her hair in a romantic updo. She finished off the look with a light dusting of bronzing powder on her exposed shoulder and arms to highlight her tan.

As she inspected herself one last time in the full-length mirror, Leah heard the town come to life outside with an explosion of festive music. The sound was followed shortly by a knock at her door. Relief and excitement flooded through her as she headed to answer it. The longing to reunite with Crowley made Leah antsy. She swung the door open to find a devastatingly handsome man leaning on her doorframe.

"Ana said for me to come up here and sweet-talk you into joining us at the dance." Jake smiled.

Leah's heart stung with disappointment at finding the wrong tall, dark, and handsome man outside her door. She tried to recover before Jake could pick up on it.

"You talked me right into it with that handsome smile." She smiled back at him as she wrapped her arm around his waiting one and allowed him to escort her outside into the crowded streets.

The music filled the air with loud vibrations full of excitement and spirit. Sundresses twirled in every direction, heads bobbed to the timing of the music, and raised hands clapped to the beat of the song. The rhythm of the dance music had cast its spell over the filled streets, causing the crowd to let loose and let the fun take over them.

She dropped her hold on Jake and started swaying to the vibrant melody. She gazed up to the clear evening sky, filled with glowing stars twinkling their approval down on the festival. Colorful paper lanterns, strung precariously over the streets, seemed to be dancing along to the music as well. The moonlight filtered through the trees and tickled the top of the joyful river. The energy in the air pricked at her skin and took over. With her eyes closed, Leah spun around, engulfed in the whimsy of it all.

When she opened her eyes, Crowley stood before her, only a few feet away. The sight of him, so handsome in his white linen shirt and jeans, took her breath away. His stare was hypnotic, and she was instantly caught in his trance. Her body continued to sway to the rhythm as he eliminated the space between them.

Without a word, Crowley pulled Leah to him and began to move to the music. The song crooned jubilantly about rocking in the dance hall. Crowley danced with grace and ease to the vivacious tones with Leah in his arms. He twirled her out and back as the song sent them flying away.

A quick pause in the music froze the crowded street for a split second. When the song continued, Crowley spun Leah as if choreographed, causing her to giggle. He spun her back in and tucked her against his chest as he serenaded her with words about needing to go away but coming back for his love.

Leah wrapped her arm around Crowley's neck and twined her fingers in his hair as the pair danced in sync to the punctuated beat of the music. The song came to a close and was quickly replaced by the next lively selection. Leah noticed no slow songs were included. Time sped by unannounced as she danced an unending dance with Crowley. Two hours passed as song after vivacious song played.

Crowley whispered in her ear, "Let's go," causing the unspoken emotional trance to end. He held firmly on to her hand as they wove through the congested street. They entered the back door of the silent café with their ears ringing.

The cool air felt invigorating on Leah's overheated body. She strode into the kitchen and poured a glass of water. She took a long pull from the glass, then offered it to Crowley. He drained the glass and set it on the counter.

He gathered Leah in his arms and gently swayed to the melody of their heartbeats. As they slow danced, Crowley worked the pins out of Leah's hair, causing the curls to cascade down her back. He ran his hands through her hair as they circled slowly around the kitchen until he gradually pulled her to the hallway. He danced her back up against the wall and stopped to admire her.

"You look lovely tonight," Crowley murmured, his eyes lingering on her bare shoulder. He ran his fingertips along her collarbone, sending shivers down her back.

Leah was unable to respond. She stood in his embrace, watching him watch her.

He placed his hand on her cheek and asked in a hoarse voice, "Leah, may I please kiss you?"

"Yes," she answered breathlessly, barely able to get the one word out.

Crowley ran his thumb along her bottom lip as he leaned down slightly and placed a soft kiss there. He looked back up at Leah for permission. She gave it by leaning forward until their lips met. It was a delicate kiss without rush, making her melt into the sweetness of it. They kissed until Leah had to pull away.

"What's wrong?" Crowley whispered.

She quietly chuckled and rubbed her neck. He sat on one of the steps of the staircase and pulled her to his lap.

"Better?" Crowley asked as he rubbed her neck. Leah nodded. "Good," he replied. "I'm not finished kissing you yet." With that, their lips met indulgently once again— soft and slow, then gradually building.

Crowley's lips were so tender and attentive, making Leah feel as though this was her first real kiss in her entire life. Each touch of his mouth sent an overwhelming longing through Leah that she had never experienced. Feelings of hope and compassion filtered all over her body.

The kiss lasted until both had to break away to catch their breath. Leah's pulse was racing and her lips felt swollen, giving her the overwhelming satisfaction of being thoroughly kissed. *That was amazing. Why on earth don't people spend more time kissing?*

Crowley noticed the smirk on Leah's face. "What?" His voice cracked as he spoke.

Too embarrassed to repeat her thoughts, Leah offered
up another confession instead. "I've missed you terribly."
She tried to stand, but Crowley clamped his hands firmly
around her waist.

"Please don't go yet."

Leah heard the strain in his husky voice. "Okay."

Crowley cradled her into his chest. She could feel his
heart hammering away inside.

Leah lay there as Crowley gently rubbed her back
until his heart rate settled into a more normal pace. She
snuggled into the crook of his warm neck, breathing in
the alluring scent of him until she dozed off.

•   •   •

Crowley was in no rush to leave her, so they sat for over
an hour as he soothingly rocked her. He felt like he could
spend the rest of his life perched right there on that stair-
well with her in his arms. He held her close while recalling
their first kiss. He knew it was the only first kiss he would
ever have with her, and he'd been determined to make it
count. Life served up only a small portion of firsts, and it
was up to the person to not take them for granted. There
were no do-overs with firsts.

Crowley picked up a sleeping Leah and carried her
into her apartment. He pulled the covers back and placed
his Sleeping Beauty in her bed. He slid her gold sandals
off and pulled the blanket over her. She woke to find him
staring down at her.

"I better go," Crowley whispered as he placed a kiss
on Leah's forehead. He went to stand, but she grabbed
hold of his arm, not wanting to be apart. "I have to hold
on to my gentlemanly reputation, Miss Leah." He leaned
in and placed a delicate kiss on her lips. "I might not be

able to if I stay much longer." He kissed her once more before slipping out of her apartment.

The music was long over by the time Crowley emerged from the café. He walked briskly around the corner and found Lulu sitting at one of the outdoor tables. The rest of the crowd had gathered down by the water's edge for the midnight fireworks display that was about to get under way. He pretended not to see her and kept beating a path home.

• • •

Lulu caught sight of Crowley strutting quickly in the direction of his town house. "Where you off to in such a hurry, boy?" she asked.

"I need a cold shower!" He raised a hand in a passing wave.

Lulu laughed. "TMI!" She settled into her chair as the first of the fireworks split through the sky and whispered, "Thank you, sweet heavenly Father, for the miracle of love." She enjoyed watching the young couple's relationship bloom. It made her feel hopeful that whatever Leah was holding on to would soon be let go.

23

Leah awoke Sunday morning with a renewed sense of life. She lay under the chenille blanket and watched the warm sunshine filter in as she thought back over last night's events. It felt like a dream. She might have even concluded it was, if her lips weren't pleasantly swollen and Crowley hadn't left a rash she could feel around her mouth from his beard stubble.

Leah ran her finger over her lips and smiled. He'd finally kissed her. She felt as giddy as a teenage girl after her first kiss. First kiss . . . that was exactly what she had received from Crowley last night, she thought as she looked at the alarm clock sitting on her nightstand. It read eight, which meant Leah had two hours before meeting Lulu at church.

Stretching her arms over her head, Leah reviewed the day's busy schedule and frowned. It would not be allowing her any alone time with Crowley. The church was hosting a community-wide picnic after services in hopes of luring the over-danced townsfolk to get out of bed. After that, Crowley and Jake were scheduled to play in a charity baseball game to benefit the new children's hospital in the next town over. Lulu had also asked Leah to accompany her on a visit to check on Jessup in the rehabilitation center, which was in the town in the opposite direction from the ball game. Yep. It was going to be a busy day.

After lazing in bed for another thirty minutes, Leah reluctantly swung her legs over the side to start her day. The moment she stood, a cramp clamped down on her right calf. Leah fell back on the bed and rubbed it away. The ache made her smile at the memory of swaying with Crowley. She had never danced so much. Shaking her head, she slowly stood and headed to grab a few Tylenols and a long bath.

She took special care to cover the pink rash around her mouth when she did her makeup. She left her curls casually down since Crowley liked her hair best that way.

Leah made it to church wearing the black sundress. She thought it was appropriate since the picnic immediately followed the service. Crowley greeted her at the door and escorted her to their normal pew. He sat close beside her and draped his arm around her shoulders.

He leaned in and whispered, "You're making my mouth water."

Leah met his gaze. Her face grew hot as she glimpsed his lips. With as much willpower as she could muster, she turned her attention to the preacher. Focusing was difficult with Crowley lightly rubbing his thumb in a meticulously slow circle on her bare shoulder.

The picnic tables filled quickly around the church courtyard, which was sheltered by ancient, moss-draped oak trees. By the time Leah helped set up the food tables and gathered her plate, she had to settle for sitting across from Crowley. Two teenage boys had claimed the places beside him and were discussing strategies for the highly anticipated baseball game.

Ana and Jake sat on Crowley's side of the bench as well. Leah's side was filled with a few more boys and a couple of Southern belles. Crowley, his legs intertwined with Leah's under the table, kept his eyes on her as he coolly conversed with the boys.

Leah could barely eat. All she wanted to do was grab her flip-flop–clad gentleman and run off with him. She saw Crowley lift his fork toward her to remind her to eat.

To Leah's horror, Ana homed in on her. "Leah, what in the world happened to your face?" she asked, causing Leah to blush deeply. "It looks like a rash around your mouth. . . . *Oh . . .*" She grinned.

The group erupted in laughter. The boys playfully punched Crowley in his arms in congratulations, and the teenage girls giggled. Leah placed her hand over her mouth and looked at Crowley, who didn't help matters. His eyes were smoldering from the memory, so she was on her own. She could see the prideful smugness in his expression. Leah guessed he was happy to let everyone know about them.

"It's probably . . . all of the strawberries . . . I ate yesterday . . ."

"I warned her they stain." Lulu came up behind Leah and defended the young woman. "Leah, are you about ready to head out?"

Thankful to have an excuse to flee, Leah nodded and quickly gathered her still-full plate.

Before she could stand, Crowley held her captive with his legs under the table. "Will we see you two ladies at the game later?"

"We should be able to make it to the last half," Lulu said.

The visit with Jessup went much smoother than Leah had thought. She had expected to find a filthy, drunken man; instead she found a humbled, clean man who was quite remorseful. She was glad to see he had put on a little weight. She brought him the strawberry cream pie that she had bought for Crowley. She wasn't much in the mood to give it to Crowley, not after he didn't rescue her in front of the group at the picnic earlier.

Jessup seemed tickled over the pie and insisted the two ladies share a slice with him. Leah had finally regained her appetite, so she gladly accepted. Lulu took the remaining pie to the nurses' station, leaving Leah alone with Jessup.

"That pie was delicious, Miss Leah," Jessup said.

"Yes, it was. It won second place in the pie category yesterday." She gathered their paper plates and tossed them. "I have to be very careful with sweets, though," Leah said. She was sorry about how she had treated him, and she needed to let him know. She sat down and fiddled with one of the turquoise rhinestones on her dress. "It's how I cope with pain."

"How's that?" Jessup asked.

"I . . . um . . . Before I came to Rivertown, I suffered . . . a terrible loss . . ." Tears filled her eyes, and she had to look away from his hollow ones. "I tried to make the pain go away with junk food binges," she admitted hoarsely. Leah swept the tears off her cheeks and looked back at him. "Lulu made me realize it wasn't working for me."

Jessup nodded as her words sank in. "You went to Lulu rehab, huh?"

Leah smiled at his understanding. "Yeah. I guess I'm in an extended program. I don't know if I will ever be cured, though."

Jessup placed his weathered hand on top of Leah's. "I guess we just have to keep on trying till we figure it out."

Leah nodded.

After promising Jessup another visit soon, Leah and

Lulu headed to the ball field. Leah was surprised to find the stands packed with onlookers. People also lined up along the fence with folding chairs. She had not realized the grandness of the charity baseball game.

Crowley's team was mostly made up of lawyers. To participate in the game, each player donated three hundred dollars to the charity. Crowley had secretly paid for two teenage boys, Jacob and Brandon, to play. They were the star players of the high school baseball team, and Crowley was bettering his team's chance to win the game with the two boys' help. Leah smiled as she realized all of the fraternity friends were scattered between the dugout and field.

The opposing team consisted of a few judges and nearly the entire local police force. At stake was mainly bragging rights for the winning team and a steak dinner bought by the losing team. Everyone was in good spirits and showed great sportsmanlike conduct.

Crowley looked up from the outfield and spotted Leah making her way over to the dugout. He jogged over to speak to her while the other players got into position for the fifth inning. He was wearing a dark-blue baseball jersey declaring *Lawyers Know Everything*.

"I might as well just go sit down with you," Crowley said to Leah as he neared.

"Why's that?" She rested against the fence.

He tucked his glove in the back of his ball pants and placed his hands over hers. "There's no way I'm going to be able to concentrate with you flaunting your lovely self in that pretty dress," Crowley said playfully into her ear, sending delightful tingles along her neck.

Crowley leaned over and placed a kiss on her cheek and started backtracking to the field, causing the entire dugout to come alive with whistles and catcalls. Crowley's buddies were having a heyday over him finally laying some claim to Leah publicly.

To egg his friends on even more, Crowley jogged back to the fence and used his tattered ball cap to block his and Leah's faces from the dugout as he kissed her thoroughly. With her looking so amazing, he didn't want his friends to have any doubt about his claim.

• • •

Leah was pretty impressed when Crowley hit a three-run homer in the fourth inning. It was a lively game, with the lead changing in each inning. The game concluded with Crowley's team winning by two runs. Everyone rushed onto the field to congratulate the winning team and to rag the losers in good spirit. In the excitement of the win, Crowley made a beeline to Leah and swept her up in his arms. She pulled his cap off so she could give him a celebratory kiss.

"The teams are heading to the steak house in a few," he said.

She smiled. "Have fun." Leah was disappointed at the small amount of time they could spend together in the long day, but she wanted him to enjoy his friends.

Before Crowley could reply, a group of players rushed him with a water cooler, and a free-for-all broke out. Leah and Lulu managed a quick getaway to dodge the shenanigans. On their way out, one of Lulu's friends mentioned that by the end of the game, with the player donations, concessions, and ticket sales, over ten thousand dollars had been raised to help fund an indoor playground for the patients at the children's hospital.

Several long hours later, Leah snuggled up on her sofa, trying to concentrate on the new mystery Nick dropped off a few days ago. At midnight, a faint knock on the door sent a thrill of anticipation through her. She had longed for Crowley to pop in but was about to give up hope and go to bed.

She tried tamping down the smile before opening the door, but the first glimpse of him did her in. "Hi."

He had both hands hidden behind his back and a grin on his face as wide as hers. "I want to go swimming."

"Well, you're dressed in a T-shirt and swim trunks. You also have a perfectly good pool. Go for it."

He pulled his right hand from behind his back and handed her a small gift bag. "I want you to go with me, Miss Smarty-Pants."

Leah reached inside the bag and plucked a skimpy black bikini from it. "No!"

Crowley placed his free hand on his hip. "Well, why not?"

"First off, it's a bikini. Secondly, it's a size small."

He shrugged. "Yeah . . . a small bikini seems 'bout right to me."

"No," she said firmly.

"Fine," he relented and offered the other bag that was hidden behind his back.

This time, Leah pulled out a baby-blue tankini halter top and bottoms. "Why didn't you just give me this one to begin with?"

"Hey, can't blame a guy for trying." Crowley stepped into the apartment and closed the door. Before she could go change, he gathered her in his arms and kissed her lightly on the lips. He then moved to delicately place kisses along her earlobe. "I'm glad you enjoyed the pool while I was gone," he murmured in her ear.

Leah backed away from him. "How do you know about that?"

Crowley pulled her back to him. "I had an attempted break-in a couple of years ago. After that, I had the alarm system installed along with some surveillance cameras around the property. The cameras are linked to my laptop."

Leah reared back the two gift bags gathered in her right hand and whacked him with them. "You *jerk*, you've been spying on me."

"Hey now . . . I didn't mean to. I should have warned you I'd be checking in now and then."

"If I would have known—"

"I'm sorry. I didn't mean to creep you out." He nuzzled her neck, his breaths tickling her. "It helped me to see you while I was gone. To know you were okay. It gave me the restraint not to call you up each day."

"What about me? I was miserable with you calling everyone else but me." She pouted as she laced her hands through his hair.

"I hoped it would make you miss me more." He grinned.

Leah extracted herself from his embrace and headed to the bathroom to change. "You succeeded, Crow."

Soon after, they hopped onto their bikes parked behind the café and pedaled off to the pool. The humid air blanketed them as they frolicked in the pool for the next few hours. The clear night sparkled with glowing moonlight and stars so bright that Crowley didn't have to turn the pool lights on. Leah felt as though the two of them were in their own private world.

As they tired of swimming, Crowley wrapped Leah's long legs around his waist and stood in the six-foot-deep water in the middle of the pool. He kissed her gently behind her right ear and then traced his fingertips along the thin scar tucked there. "I want to know about this," he whispered as he skimmed his lips over the scar.

Saying nothing, she shook her head.

He surprised her then by tapping the jagged scar she thought was hidden on her hip. "I want to know about this," he murmured into her ear.

How could he know about that? He looked up and gazed at her intensely. She detected a deep sadness in his ocean-blue eyes. She didn't want him to carry any part of the burden of her pain, but he had obviously taken it on anyway.

He pressed his lips to the faint scar tucked in her left eyebrow. "I want to know about this." He worked his way to the scar barely visible on her chin, which had been in the process of healing when she had arrived in town last fall. "I want to know about this."

He remembered.

Crowley looked into Leah's eyes as they swayed in the water. He released her hip and pulled her scarred palm to his lips and brushed kisses over it. "I want to know about this." He pressed it to his pounding heart. "I *need* to know about this." The deep timbre of his voice was strained with emotion. Her body trembled from the longing in his voice.

Lastly, he traced the long scar across her bottom lip with his thumb. "I need to know about this," he said again.

Her breath hitched at the passion in his voice. Tears pricked her eyes. He was too observant and too persuasive. She laid her head on his shoulder to hide the tears. "Why do you need to know about some old ugly scars?" she mumbled against his shoulder.

He dipped into slightly deeper water so that she would have to raise her head and meet his gaze. "I need to know so I can help them heal." He brushed his hand over her cheek to wipe away her tears.

"Some scars don't ever heal," she whispered. "No matter how awfully bad you want them to. They're just too deep." She let him dance her to a gentle rhythm in the water for a while longer as she buried her face in the comforting crook of his neck.

As she held tight to him, his words began to resonate. It was time to take care of the past, even if it meant losing the future she would do anything to have.

She pulled away from him and swam to the steps to exit the pool. "Fine. I'll meet you at your office after work tomorrow. I'll tell you everything then." She grabbed her towel and stomped over to her bike, trying to be mad at him but unable.

Crowley lifted himself over the side of the pool and reached out to stop her. "Please don't leave like this."

"It's late. I have to be at work in only a few hours." She climbed on her bike and tucked the towel around her.

"Don't you want to do this so we can make a good go of this relationship?" he asked, his voice pleading.

"After I tell you, there won't be any more relationship to worry about." She took off, hoping he wouldn't follow even though she knew he would.

Crowley didn't say another word as he escorted her to the back entrance of the café. For that, she was thankful. Seemed everything that needed to be said for the night had been. It was too late to go any further with it, anyway.

Leah knew it was time, though, so she turned before closing the door and said, "I'll meet you after work tomorrow."

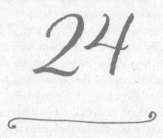

LEAH QUIETLY KNOCKED on Crowley's door a little after three the following afternoon. He opened the door and motioned her in. She stepped inside and noticed three doors, adorned with brass nameplates, lining a long hallway. She moved to the left and read the nameplate that stated *Crowley J. Mason III, Attorney-at-Law*. Then she moved over the right and read the nameplate on the door across from Crowley's dad's office. It stated, as she expected it would, *Crowley J. Mason IV, Attorney-at-Law*. Leah took the few steps to the last office and was surprised to find the nameplate inscribed, *Lydia C. Mason, Attorney-at-Law*.

Leah looked at Crowley. "Lydia?"

"Yeah. My grandmother. She followed in the footsteps of her dad, who was a lawyer as well," Crowley said as he ran his hand over the nameplate in question.

"That's a long line of lawyers." Leah admired the rich history of it.

"Yeah. It runs through my veins."

Leah decided to stop stalling and stood at bit straighter, trying to muster up some courage. "Good thing for me . . . because I'm in need of a lawyer."

Crowley nodded. If he'd changed his mind about

wanting to know her sordid past, he didn't let on. "Then I guess we need to go have a seat in my office."

Leah turned to Crowley J. Mason IV's office, but Crowley gestured toward the office of Crowley J. Mason III. "I moved into my dad's office after law school. Come on in." He opened the door and led the way.

The office was of a good size with a massive, intricately carved antique cherry desk in the middle of the room. Two wingback chairs sat in front of it, and a large leather chair that looked buttery soft stood grandly behind it. Leah sat in one of the wingback chairs as Crowley took his seat behind the desk and pulled out a legal pad. Even though he was casually dressed in a T-shirt and jeans, Leah was impressed at how quickly he took on the air of a professional lawyer.

He sat with a pen ready and patiently waited. When she remained quiet, Crowley tried to get the ball rolling by saying, "How may I be of service to you, Miss Allen?"

Leah took an unsteady breath and blurted, "I was married to the devil himself for the past ten years . . . Brent Sadler." Almost choking on his name, she looked down at her body. "He gave me all these scars."

"*Was.* So that means you're divorced?" Crowley asked as he jotted the information down. From the dark frown on his face, he was already forming a plan to find Brent and put a few scars on him.

"No. I killed him," Leah whispered. She couldn't believe she said it out loud. She watched a stunned Crowley drop his pen as his mouth fell open. She couldn't take it, so she stood abruptly and knocked the heavy chair over in the process. "I'm sorry." Leah bolted out of the town house.

● ● ●

Lulu stood in the kitchen, shocked to the point of being unable to move, after hanging up the phone. Crowley had explained in a rush what Leah confessed and asked her not to leave the upset woman. Before she could unglue her feet, the door banged open and produced a distraught Leah with tears streaming down her face.

Instead of going upstairs like Lulu expected, Leah headed over to the display case and snatched up a slice of chocolate cake.

"You know that won't fix anything," Lulu said quietly. She caught a glimpse of Crowley easing into the shadows of the back hall, visibly shaken. *Poor boy.*

"Can't I just eat this in peace?" Leah snapped. "Alone!"

Lulu placed her hand on Leah's trembling arm. "Honey, he can't hurt you ever again."

Leah yanked away from her grasp, threw the slice of cake down, and let out such a guttural screech her entire body shook from it.

At a loss as to what to do, Lulu could only stand there and witness Leah's walls crumble and spill everything that was locked inside.

Crowley began to move into view, but Lulu met his gaze and gave her head a slight shake to warn him to stay put. She knew this broken girl had to let it out.

After Leah's screams died down, Lulu repeated, "He can't hurt you anymore."

"Don't you dare say that to me." Leah gave her a warning look and began to pace like a caged animal reaching its breaking point. Abruptly, she whirled around and held her palm up for Lulu to view. "This scar was my punishment for burning his supper one night. He held it to the gas burner. It still tingles from the nerve damage—*still*!"

Lulu's stomach flipped, but she stood stoically and chose not to say anything. At the moment, the girl didn't need to listen. She needed to be heard.

She pulled her hair back so Lulu could see the long

scar behind her ear. "I have another burn. I earned this one with a flat iron for not having my hair perfectly straight when my husband arrived home early one day." She let her hair fall back down. "He got the iron as hot as it would get and branded me, saying he bet I would never forget to do my hair again. He was absolutely right."

Lulu's eyes moved to Leah's ankle when she lifted the leg of her pants to expose it.

"This aches every time it rains. Do you know why?" Leah asked, and Lulu slowly shook her head. "He slung me down a staircase for wearing heels that were too high. Broke it so bad it required surgery." Leah turned away from Lulu and yanked her yoga pants down to reveal another secret.

Lulu moved forward a step to get a better look at the jagged scar on her hip and barely contained a gasp.

"This beaut was acquired from a fire poker I was beaten with." Leah let out a derisive laugh. "He said he didn't mean to plunge it so deeply." She pulled her pants back over her thin hip and faced Lulu.

Lulu opened her mouth even though she had no idea what to say, but Leah moved on.

"You know why I can never turn my head but only so far to the right?" She cradled her neck with both hands.

Lulu just shook her head, thoroughly shell-shocked at all the scars riddling the young woman's body.

"He choked me one night until I passed out. This was after he shook me so hard that I heard something pop in my neck. But that didn't stop him from choking me again two more times after that. . . . You saw the bruises, didn't you?" Leah asked and Lulu nodded.

"And right now it throbs from me yelling, and I know I won't be able to even move it tomorrow." Leah batted the tears away from her red cheeks. "Ask me what the doctor says is wrong with my neck. Go ahead, ask."

"What's wrong with your neck?" Lulu asked cautiously.

"Who knows? He wouldn't let it be seen by a doctor." Leah raised her hands in the air. "Instead, I was locked in a closet for an entire week so Brent wouldn't have to be reminded of what he did to me."

There was no containing the gasp or her own tears from spilling as she moved forward only to have the skittish girl back away. "Oh, Leah . . ."

Leah was trembling uncontrollably as she spoke through gritted teeth. "So don't you dare tell me he can't ever hurt me again. He does it *every* day of my life!" She clenched her belly and nearly doubled over. "And it hurts so deep inside here that sometimes I can't even breathe," she whispered. "So how dare you tell me that cake won't make it better? It's the only way I can numb it."

Lulu gathered the courage to speak. "It seems to me that Crowley was numbing it pretty well."

Leah straightened and wiped her nose on the sleeve of her shirt. "Well . . . I told him I killed my husband, so I'm pretty darn sure that's over with. Right now all I want is that piece of cake!" Leah shouted, close to hysterics.

Lulu picked up the slice of cake and set it aside, causing Leah to raise her hands in defeat. Lulu pulled out two forks, handed one to Leah, and grabbed up the layer cake she'd just finished frosting. She set it on the nearest table and said resolutely, "We are going to eat all the cake we want."

The women sat down before the cake and dug their forks into the side of it. Still sobbing and hiccuping, Leah shoved an enormous bite into her mouth. Lulu, queasy from hearing about Leah's abuse, took a big bite of her own and dutifully chewed. She knew this would only make Leah feel worse, but Lulu was determined to share the burden with her even if it meant dealing with a belly-ache. She'd take on the pain of the poor girl's scars if she could.

Lulu looked over Leah's shivering shoulder at Crowley, who was shaking as well. She knew the best thing for him to do was go calm down, so she subtly waved him to leave. He hesitated briefly before slipping out the door.

●   ●   ●

Crowley stumbled over to the riverbank by his town house and plopped down in the tall grass. All the scars and all the reasons for them flashed through his head. "Stupid accident . . ." He huffed. It was how she described them. "Stupid accident," he repeated, shaking his head. Bile rose up in his throat as he tried to imagine the pain from having his hand held to a gas flame . . . or the pain from a fire poker piercing into his flesh . . . or how excruciating it had to be to have an iron branded into his skin . . .

He knew her news was going to be bad, but he never could have imagined how severe. Unable to hold the bile back, he rose to his knees and vomited.

Once the heaving passed, Crowley moved to sit by the bank and stared vacantly out over the water.

Lulu joined him sometime later. "She went to bed just before seven o'clock. The poor girl had to have been completely wiped out," she whispered.

"She eat that whole cake?" he asked hoarsely. His throat felt raw with emotion and from vomiting.

Lulu shook her head. "She barely ate enough to make up a slice. I think she realized it wasn't going to make her feel any better."

Something snapped inside Crowley as he shot to his

feet. "After everything that woman has been through . . . if she wants cake, then you let her eat cake!"

Lulu flinched. "Crowley Mason, you will never holler at me like that again, young man. I know you're devastated by all this. I am too, but cake won't fix what's broken in that poor girl." She paused to calm her voice before continuing. "You think putting about a hundred pounds back on is any good for her?"

"I don't care . . . if it makes her feel better," he said wearily. "I just want her happy. She deserves to be happy."

"Did she look like it was working for her when she arrived here last year?" Lulu asked.

Images of the broken woman flashed before Crowley's eyes. That man had to have beaten her within an inch of her life. He shook the painful images away and stormed off in the direction of his office. He was determined to fix whatever mess Leah was in—he just didn't know how yet.

Crowley went straight to his kitchen and started brewing a pot of strong coffee. At the moment he was running on pure adrenaline and anger, but he knew he would eventually crash from that and would need the caffeine to help him get through the work ahead.

He stormed into his office and powered up his desktop computer as well as his laptop. There were still a lot of puzzle pieces missing from Leah's story that Crowley would have to figure out on his own.

Crowley called Matt as he poured his first cup of coffee and asked for his help. Matt promised to get on it immediately and call Crowley back with any news. He sat at his desk and tried to shake off as much emotion as possible so he could focus on making things right for Leah.

Crowley had enough information gathered and had a flight booked to Washington by the time the first hints

of sunlight appeared. Matt had called a few of his connections, and his connections had called their connections, which led them to finding the lead investigator of
Brent and Gabriella Sadler's case. The investigator eagerly
agreed to meet Crowley at the airport.

With all the trip details settled, Crowley powered
down his laptop and placed it in his briefcase with the
other information. He pushed away from his desk and
headed upstairs to pack a carry-on bag and to shower.

After dressing in a button-down shirt, jeans, and a
pair of casual brown leather shoes, Crowley grabbed a
blue sports jacket and his bags and headed out. He made
a pit stop at the café to check on Leah before heading to
the airport. He found Lulu in Leah's normal spot behind
the counter. The café was still empty.

"You're up early," Lulu said as she eyed him closely.
"Or maybe it's time for bed."

"Where's Leah?"

"She hasn't come down yet." Lulu poured a cup of
coffee and placed it before him. "After yesterday's break-
down I told her to take the day off."

Crowley's eyes wandered toward the stairs.

"Just let her have some space, okay?"

With his gaze still glued in the direction of the stairs,
Crowley reluctantly agreed. "Yes, ma'am. I've got a flight
to catch anyway. Can I get some coffee and a sandwich
to go?"

"Where you heading?" Lulu asked as she began toast-
ing an English muffin.

"I'm heading to Washington. I don't intend on coming back until I fix this mess for Leah." He watched Lulu
assemble his sandwich. He softly placed his hand on top
of hers to still her. "Miss Lulu, I love you dearly and am
completely ashamed of myself for how I talked to you

yesterday. It was very disrespectful. I hope you can forgive me," he said sincerely.

Lulu placed her other hand over his massive one and stared into his somber eyes. "Honey, you were disrespectful, but if you ever had an excuse to act that way, it was definitely yesterday. I love you too. And you know I have already forgiven you." She squeezed his hand before releasing it to finish his breakfast.

Crowley bent down and inspected the partially eaten cake sitting in the display case.

Lulu shook her head. "Whatcha reckon I ought to do with that? It's pretty good. I sure hate to have to throw it away."

"Put it in a to-go box. I have a long few days ahead. I think I could use the extra sugar boost."

Lulu did as he asked, slicing it before sliding it into a container and handing it over to him.

Crowley gathered everything and placed a kiss on Lulu's cheek. He looked back at the staircase, hesitant about leaving without seeing Leah. "Tell her I'm going to take of things, and I'll be back in a few days."

Lulu nodded. "Be careful."

"Yes, ma'am." Crowley slipped out the door and set out on a mission.

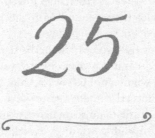

25

CROWLEY'S PLANE TOUCHED DOWN in Olympia, Washington, late Tuesday afternoon. As he made his way through the terminal's waiting area, he spotted a bald-headed man in a blue suit who fit the description of the investigator. He glanced up from a file in his hand and seemed to recognize Crowley as well.

"Crowley Mason?" he asked, his hand outstretched.

Crowley shook his hand. "That's me."

"I'm Detective Mitch Collins. I hear you've found our girl." He tapped the thick file he was holding.

"I *may* have. That's why I've flown out here." There was no way he was admitting anything to this man.

Mitch quietly chuckled. "Spoken like a true lawyer. Let's go get to work." He led Crowley out of the airport to a waiting late-model sedan and opened the trunk for the carry on bag.

As both men got situated in the car, Mitch told Crowley the plan. "I figured the best thing for us to do is head on over to the Sadlers' loft, and I can fill you in on the investigation from there."

Fifteen minutes later, they pulled up to the swanky loft. Mitch led Crowley through the garage, where a Range Rover and Mercedes sports coupe sat abandoned.

Mitch motioned to the Range Rover. "That is Mrs. Sadler's vehicle. It was found with the passenger and driver's doors open."

As Crowley followed Mitch up the stairs, he couldn't help but wonder if it was the same set of stairs that Leah had been thrown down. His gut told him yes.

Mitch unlocked the door to reveal a modern space that looked more like a museum than a home. He stopped in the foyer and shuffled through a stack of photographs he pulled from the file. "A cleaning crew came in and scrubbed the place clean, so I brought along the photos." He handed one over to Crowley. It was a picture of the foyer with a few drops of blood on the white floor. "A grocery delivery guy arrived at one o'clock that day with an order. He found the front door wide open, noticed some blood on the floor, and called the police." Mitch pointed to the blood. "Those were probably from some superficial wounds. We think a small scuffle between the spouses happened here and then moved to the bedroom."

Mitch led Crowley deeper into the loft to the master bedroom. The bedding and mattress had been removed. He motioned Crowley to join him in the large walk-in closet, where he handed over a few more pictures. Crowley looked each one over. One showed a full shot of a tousled mess with clothes pulled down and glass shattered all over the floor with bloody footprints leading out. Another photo was a close-up of one of the bloody footprints.

Mitch tapped the photo. "The footprint is the same size as Mrs. Sadler's foot."

"Where did the glass come from?" Crowley asked as he imagined Leah cornered in the space, frightened.

"A bourbon bottle. Rumor has it that Mr. Sadler was quite a fan of the stuff. The autopsy proved that he was pretty pickled." Mitch pointed out a bloody towel thrown on the floor in one of the photos. "This was still damp, so we think Mrs. Sadler tried to clean up before disappearing."

With that comment, Mitch directed Crowley to the master bath next and handed over more photos of the crime scene. These photos showed more bloody footprints as well as bloody streaks along the wall and floor. Crowley figured she'd been stumbling around, unsteady on her feet. Another shot showed the white shower floor spattered with blood and a few bloody towels scattered on the floor.

Mitch moved back into the bedroom and stood by the bed frame. He hesitated before handing Crowley the stack of photos. "These are of Brent Sadler's body."

Crowley nodded and held out his hand. "I've survived some pretty gruesome murder trials, Mr. Collins. I think I can handle it." He accepted the photos from Mitch.

Crowley studied the first photo. The man was older than he'd expected. Instead of seeing a dead man in his twenties, he saw one in his forties. The dead man stared blankly at the camera with empty eyes as he lay in an odd position on his side. Some more glass was shattered by the bed, and blood streaked the pillow beside Brent's head.

Crowley flipped through to another image in which the white cover had been moved to expose a puddle of blood in the center of the mattress.

"You want to know the wildest part about all of this?" Mitch asked.

Crowley continued to stare at the nightmare Leah had lived out, captured in the photos. "What's that?" he asked quietly.

"Of all this blood, not one drop belonged to Mr. Sadler."

Crowley looked up from the photo. "How's that possible if she killed him?"

"Who said she killed him?"

"What?" Crowley's eyebrows knit together in confusion.

"Mrs. Sadler didn't kill her husband. There was a blunt force blow to his head that probably knocked him out. The shattered glass in this photo was a crystal vase. The autopsy showed that he died of a massive heart attack." Mitch slid the autopsy report out of the file and handed it over to Crowley.

"The man was the epitome of health. He was known to be disciplined with diet and exercise. Hard to believe a heart attack took him out at only forty-five years of age."

Crowley handed the autopsy report and pictures back and shook his head. "I thought this was a murder investigation."

"No. This is a missing person's investigation. The grocery guy told the police he was delivering to Mrs. Sadler, which the store manager confirmed. Of course, she'd vanished into thin air. But there's more to it than that." Mitch gestured for Crowley to follow him. "Come on. There's something else you need to see." He led him into the guest bedroom and over to the closet door.

Crowley noted the two sets of locks on the door, one on the knob and another at the top of the door. It was all he could do to control his rage. The realization that he was standing at the door of her prison punched him hard in the stomach. Seeing it in person overwhelmed him. He was about to head out of the room, but Mitch motioned him to take a look inside.

"We found a coffee can that appeared to be used as a portable toilet. Food and bottles of juice and water were strewn around. It looks as though Mrs. Sadler may have spent a good bit of time locked in here." He fished a well-worn Bible out of a pillowcase and handed it to a shaken Crowley. Crowley tucked it under his arm as Mitch continued to explain his findings. "Baby wipes, a toothbrush, and toothpaste were found tucked in a shoe box. A flashlight and wristwatch were under a sleeping bag. We also found—"

"Dear God," Crowley said, voice quaking. His vision blurred as his pulse throbbed in his ears.

Mitch pointed at the unassembled light fixture. "Guess he didn't allow her to have a light."

"I need to get out of here," Crowley mumbled as he headed outside, still clutching the Bible. He thought he could tough it out like any other case, but with it being so personal he just couldn't bear it.

Mitch joined him by the car a few moments later after locking the loft up. "The children's home that Mrs. Sadler helped to build is only a few miles down the road. Would you like to go?" he asked.

"Leah. Her name is Leah Allen," Crowley corrected. "What do you mean she helped to build?" he asked as they reloaded the cramped car.

"Leah sponsored numerous charity events to raise funds to build the home and was there to assist in any way from the very beginning. It seemed to be the only thing the husband allowed her to do. The director actually reported her missing a few days after the grocery guy called the police." Mitch started the car and headed for the children's home.

Mitch pulled up to a cheery-yellow two-story home with a colorful sign in the front yard that said *New Hope Children's Home*. Small lettering underneath it read *Where Everyone Can Feel at Home*.

They walked in, and Mitch introduced Crowley to

the director, an older lady named Sue. She gladly gave him a tour after he explained who he was and his affiliation with Gabriella while Mitch waited outside.

She led him to a wall of framed pictures. He spotted a redheaded Leah in one right away. She stood in the midst of a bunch of kids, who all had grins lighting up their faces. The caption explained *First Day Home with Founder Mrs. Gabriella Sadler*. They moved farther down the hall until Crowley spotted another picture of Leah, a couple of years older and a bit heavier than in the first photo. She stood behind a group of kids on a large playground. She was smiling along with the children, but her eyes seemed lifeless. This caption read *Playground Completion Celebration*.

After Crowley inspected the pictures, Sue led him into a large game room, where a birthday party was under way. She pointed out a group of women standing by the cake table.

"Those women volunteered a good bit with Gabby, if you would like to ask them any questions. I have a few board members waiting in my office, but take your time." Sue reached over and placed her hand on Crowley's arm. "Please tell Gabby we miss her terribly and are so relieved she's okay."

He smiled and offered his hand. "It was nice meeting you, and I will definitely tell her. Hopefully she and I can make a trip back out this way soon."

"That would be wonderful. Please do so." She shook his hand before hurrying off.

Crowley turned back to the cheerful room with kids running around and playing party games. He studied the table of women. They looked like bored trophy wives needing something to do to fill their time.

An announcement for the kids to go outside to the

bouncy inflatables sent the little ones barreling toward the door. Crowley smiled at how quickly the room cleared.

He glanced back at the group of women, trying to decide whether to head out or speak with them. A leggy brunette caught him looking and turned to her friends and mouthed something. Before he could decide what to do, three of the women sashayed over to him.

"Are you *the* Crowley Mason?" the leggy brunette asked.

He ran his hand through his tousled hair. "I don't know about the *the* part, but yes, my name is Crowley. How might you have known that, ma'am?"

The brunette placed her perfectly manicured hand over her heart. "'Ma'am'? Oh, my, ladies. We have ourselves a real-life Southern gentleman." She looked over at her friends and then turned her attention back to Crowley. "You were featured in *Cosmo* magazine as being one of the top millionaire bachelors in the United States," the brunette cooed. "My name is Junie, and these are my friends Hannah and Sara. We volunteer here."

"Nice to meet you." Crowley shook each lady's hand. "I was wondering if you could tell me a little bit about—" it pained him to call her this—"Gabriella Sadler."

Sara adjusted the headband in her dark-blonde hair and waved her hand to dismiss the topic of Gabriella. "That woman was a hot mess. I have no idea what Brent ever saw in her. That man gave her the world, and she couldn't even keep herself up for him." She tried to wrinkle her forehead in disgust, but it looked like the Botox wouldn't allow it.

Her hatefulness toward Leah shocked Crowley, but he didn't let it show.

"Why? Did they finally find her?" Hannah asked.

"Yes, she's fine," Crowley said as he studied his watch.

He decided the women weren't anything but a bunch of hens clucking away and he was wasting his time with them.

"Please tell me that loser isn't coming back here," Junie said.

"Why would you call her a loser?" He glanced around the room.

"She had the best man in these parts, and she didn't even take good care of him. If Brent belonged to me, I would have made sure that fine heart of his was in tip-top shape." She rolled her hips slightly. Her friends snickered.

Crowley looked at the group before him. *These women were jealous.* He placed his hands in his pant pockets and took a deep breath. He'd had enough of the clucking. He eyed Junie and stated matter-of-factly, "Ma'am, that man was an alcoholic who tortured his wife by locking her up in a closet in their loft. He almost beat his wife to death before God took mercy on her and took him out with a heart attack." Crowley let that sink in. "If you ladies didn't spend your time resenting her and casting your judgment, you might have realized she was being abused. She sure could have used someone on her side."

He turned to walk off but stopped and glanced back at Junie. "You don't have to worry about me being on any silly bachelor list, ma'am. I'm in love with Gabriella and will be for the rest of my life." He walked away from the speechless women and headed to the car, where Mitch was waiting for him.

Mitch noticed the haggard look on Crowley's face. "You feel like grabbing the best cup of coffee and donut in town?"

"Sure. After that, do you think you could drop me off at a hotel? I've been up for one . . . two days straight now. It's catching up with me."

Mitch drove them over to a retro place called the Donut Diner.

"Cool place, man," Crowley commented as they walked through the door.

"They bring donuts twice a month to the children's home, so the director had the police contact them to see if they knew anything on Leah's whereabouts. Leah visited nearly every Thursday, according to the owner's daughter, who helps run the place." Mitch pointed over to a twenty-something strawberry blonde. "There she is now." Mitch gestured to Crowley. "Shayna, I'd like for you to meet a good friend of Gabby Sadler's."

Crowley nodded. "It's nice to meet you."

The young woman's face was full of anguish. "Please tell me Gabby is okay."

Crowley nodded again. "She's fine."

A slow smile washed over her face. "Thank goodness."

Crowley pulled up a picture on his phone from their last fishing trip and handed it to Shayna.

Shayna looked at a picture of a grinning Leah, who was holding up a good-size bass she had just wrangled in. "Wow. She looks awesome."

Mitch looked at the photo and let out a low whistle. "That's one beautiful woman."

"I absolutely agree," Crowley said proudly as he put his phone away.

Mitch cleared his throat. "Shayna, dear, can we have two coffees and half a dozen donuts?"

"Sure. Any ones in particular?" she asked as she headed behind the counter.

"Gabby's favorites," Crowley answered before sitting down wearily.

"That would be Bavarian cream filled with chocolate

ganache icing, lemon curd–filled powdered, and apple fritters," she said as she began filling a box.

Shayna served the donuts and coffees, and then she turned to speak to Crowley. "Please tell her I'm so glad she's okay and that man is dead."

"You knew about Brent abusing her?" Crowley asked.

"She never told me, but the signs were pretty clear. I tried to get her to open up, but she never did." She shook her head.

Crowley placed his hand on her arm before she strolled away. "Thank you for showing her kindness."

She smiled. "Gabby is a great woman. She deserves a world of kindness."

Crowley agreed completely and vowed to lavish kindness on Leah as soon as he returned home, hopefully for the rest of his life.

*   *   *

Mitch dropped Crowley off at a hotel. Before he left Crowley, he gave him the information for a hospital in Lincoln, Nebraska. "This was as far as we got to finding Leah. She was admitted and treated for close to a week. Her trail went cold after that."

Crowley took the information and then shook the investigator's hand. "Thank you, Mitch. You've been a great help. I'll give you a call as soon as I get back to South Carolina."

"You're welcome, my man. I'm glad this case ended on a positive note. Most of my missing persons don't."

As soon as Crowley was checked in and settled into his room, he looked over the hospital information and booked a flight to Nebraska for the following morning. Something was bothering him and he couldn't figure out what it was. Another puzzle piece was missing, and hopefully he would find it tomorrow.

After a quick shower, Crowley was desperate to hear Leah's voice, so he tried calling the apartment's number but got no answer. The café's number went unanswered as well. He powered on his computer and pulled up the security cameras at the plantation. He didn't want to spy on her, but he was truly worried. He hoped to see some indication that she was okay. He slumped in the chair and sighed when he found no signs that she'd been around the house in the past few days. He was about to close the window when a light in the distance from the pool camera caught his attention. It was coming from the river cabin.

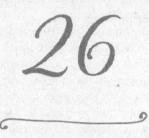

26

To Crowley's relief, the connections to Lincoln, Nebraska, went smoothly. As soon as he arrived, he took a cab straight to the hospital. He was more than anxious to get this behind him so he could head home to South Carolina. He had called Matt late last night and asked him to set up meetings with the doctor and main nurse who treated Leah.

He made his way to the reception desk in the lobby of the hospital and stated his name to the receptionist. From there, he was directed to a small conference room to wait for the doctor, who was delayed.

Thirty minutes later a casually dressed woman walked in the room. She smiled in greeting. "Mr. Crowley Mason?"

Crowley stood and offered his hand. "Yes, ma'am."

She shook it with some gusto. "My name is Mona. I was the head nurse for Gabriella Sadler. Sorry about the wait. I'm off today and just got the call you wanted to meet. If you can wait ten more minutes, I'll go grab her medical record. The legal department has cleared some information for release."

Crowley nodded. "Sure. Sorry about you having to come in on your day off."

"No, don't worry about that. I'm just so relieved that she is alive and well. I honestly wasn't so sure she would make it."

"I'm supposed to meet with a Dr. Daniels as well . . . ?"

"Sorry about that, too," Mona said as she was halfway out the door. "He had to perform an emergency cesarean." She closed the door.

Cesarean . . . Crowley turned the word over in his head as he ran his hands over his weary face. He took a seat as he processed what that one word brought to light. *The scar so deep down, she had screamed at Lulu about it. Pain so deep that sometimes she couldn't breathe.*

"Some scars don't ever heal. . . . They're just too deep." She had told him this as he held her in his arms in the pool only a few nights ago. His mouth went dry and his own stomach ached in raw pain.

Mona hustled back in within ten minutes, sat down beside Crowley, and unfolded the record's contents. "Where to begin . . ."

"From the very beginning. Please, just be straight with it."

Mona glanced from the file to him and then back to the file. "Mrs. Gabriella Sadler arrived here in late October with numerous wounds and in premature labor. She was hemorrhaging profusely, so our first order of business was to try to stop the bleeding, but it was too late. Dr. Daniels had no choice but to deliver. The baby girl was stillborn. She weighed only one pound and ten ounces."

Crowley cleared his throat. "How far along was she?"

"Our estimation was about twenty-five weeks. After she knew the baby didn't survive, Mrs. Sadler shut down and refused to give us any information. I guess she thought there was no point in it."

"She goes by her first name now as well as her maiden name. Please call her Leah Allen." Crowley couldn't stand Leah being attached to that man's name.

Mona nodded and made a note in the file before continuing. "I cleaned the baby up and tucked her in a blanket and let Leah hold her before we had to take her away. She held that baby tight for several hours while we tended to her wounds. Once Dr. Daniels stopped the bleeding and had completed a blood transfusion, he instructed one of the nurses to take the baby." Mona shook her head and lightly coughed.

"Ma'am?" Crowley asked in a low voice when she remained silent.

"Mr. Mason, in all my years of nursing, I have *never* before seen, nor will I *ever* forget the agony of that mother that night. I have nightmares about it. She screamed and wailed and refused to hand the baby over. I tried to talk to her, promising I would take care of her baby, but she would just hold her closer and sob harder."

Crowley swallowed hard. "What did you do?"

"Eventually we had to sedate her to get the baby away. I tell you, I have no idea how she remained conscious throughout the entire ordeal before the sedation. It was as if she knew once she closed her eyes, the baby would disappear forever."

Crowley rubbed his stubbly chin. "Was there permanent damage? Can she have—?"

"No permanent *physical* damage. She should be able to have more children with no complications. Dr. Daniels reassured her of this, but she had already shut him out."

Crowley nodded and watched her pull out some photos from the medical record.

"These are shots of Gab . . . Leah. We took them to file a police report, but she refused to cooperate. We took them without her permission after we sedated her. I also had to search her purse for her driver's license to get some information. She wouldn't even share her name with us. We really weren't sure she was going to pull through."

Crowley looked at the first photo. It was of a redhead with her face so distorted that Crowley would have never identified her as his Leah. Her left eye was purple and so swollen that there was no way she could see through it when she was awake. All of the wounds he had seen on her face when he first laid eyes on her, only two weeks after this night in the pictures, were now evident in their most raw form. The woman in the picture looked dead.

"She required stitches for the wound over her eye and the one on her bottom lip. The chin wound only needed a butterfly bandage."

The next was a close-up image of her neck. "Those bruises are handprints on her neck. She had been severely strangled. We braced her neck to help with the sprain." Mona pointed to a swollen shoulder image. "She sustained a fractured collarbone. I gave her a sling to wear, which was to also help with her broken wrist."

The nurse then spread out the last two gruesome photos. They were shots of Leah's abdomen. Her belly and left side were covered with swollen bruises that were so deep they looked painted on. "This was the obvious trauma that caused her to go into labor. She was either hit with a blunt object or punched. She also sustained two cracked ribs."

Crowley thought about the broken bourbon bottle. *If Brent weren't already dead . . . What kind of monster is allowed to do this to someone?* A quiet rage took over. This wasn't just anyone . . . but the woman he loved.

Mona put the photos away and momentarily closed

her eyes before speaking. "I dreamed of being a labor and delivery nurse ever since I was thirteen years old, Mr. Mason. It was the year I was blessed to witness my own mother give birth to my baby brother. Such a beautiful thing—to see life enter this world . . ." She shook her head. "I never imagined I would ever witness such a horrible beginning and ending to a mother's story of her firstborn child." Mona tapped the photo of Leah's battered face. "This woman's joy was stripped away from her body, and it sickens me that there was nothing I could do." She wiped away tears. "Sorry."

"You didn't let her die, did you?" Crowley gave his best attempt at a smile.

"I did my best, but I'm sure she lost part of her soul that night." She rose and Crowley followed. "Mr. Mason, do you have time to let me show you something I had promised Leah I would do for her? I'd like for you to be able to share it with her."

"Yes, and please call me Crowley."

The world had been one cruel place to Leah and had abused her in ways ungodly. He was so grateful this woman had been on Leah's side.

●　●　●

Twenty minutes later, Mona parked her minivan in front of her church. She led Crowley over to a well-kept cemetery just off from the front of the church. She stopped in front of a pink granite headstone.

"The next day when she regained consciousness, she went into hysterics. I tried to comfort her. Even climbed into the bed and held her while she sobbed." Mona brushed a few fallen leaves from the headstone. "She kept begging me not to let the hospital throw her baby away.

She had me take ten thousand dollars from her purse to take care of the expenses."

Crowley knelt by the small headstone and ran his fingers over the inscription—*Our Precious Angel Spread Her Wings and Flew Home to Heaven*. Delicate angel wings were engraved above it, and a date below—October 22. He took in all of the small gifts left for the baby. A wind chime with stained glass and scrolling metalwork sang lightly in the warm breeze. Off to the right side of the headstone dangled a glass butterfly suncatcher that sent sparkles cascading along the pink granite. Both lovely gifts dangled from silver stakes. A small bouquet of daisies sat in front of the headstone.

He stood and studied a small bench at the foot of the petite grave. It was also pink granite. "You've taken really good care of her baby. I know Leah will find comfort in that."

"The community was so moved by this tragedy that everyone came together to take care of the costs of the funeral. I had our little Angel dressed in a handmade white gown with ruffles upon ruffles. She truly looked like an angel. The funeral home provided a powder-pink baby casket and donated their services. The local florist donated lovely pink-and-white arrangements for the service. She still places small arrangements on the grave for the changing seasons. The church was packed that day with mourners. Please let her know that."

Crowley nodded, finding it too difficult to speak. Grief had overtaken him. He felt he had lost a loved one at the murderous hands of Brent Sadler, too. A little girl he could have loved . . .

"I couldn't find Gab . . . Leah to return the money. After much thought, my church began a charity with it in honor of Gabriella and Angel. It's called the Angel Fund, and it helps support local programs that fight against domestic violence and child abuse. I'll make sure the paperwork is revised to change her name to Leah."

"So you have information about the charity?" Crowley whispered hoarsely as he stared at the small grave.

"Yes. We have packets in the church that explain it all. Would you like one?"

Crowley nodded.

"Let me go grab it. I'll be right back." She quickly walked over to a side entrance of the church and dis-appeared inside.

Crowley sat down on the bench. He pulled his phone out and snapped several pictures of the grave site. By the time he whispered a prayer to God to help him and Leah get through this together, Mona had returned with the information.

Mona graciously dropped Crowley off at the airport afterward. He was desperately homesick for Leah and boarded the first available flight to start the trek home. On his first flight, the events of the past few days weighed on his mind to the point of sending him to the restroom to vomit up the only thing on his stomach—coffee and bile. Never had his grief for someone caused him physical sickness as it did for Leah.

A flight attendant served him ginger ale to help calm his stomach. After a while, he felt up to opening the packet on the Angel Fund and reviewing it. During his layover in Atlanta, Crowley phoned Jake and gave him the basic information of the fund.

"Will you take care of the required paperwork and donate a half-million dollars, anonymously, from my personal account?" he asked his friend who handled his finances.

"I'll take care of it, man," Jake said.

"Oh, and I have a problem I need you to take care of too. My name has been put on some stupid eligible millionaire bachelor list. How do you suppose that happened?"

"I'll see what I can find out." Jake laughed.

"It ain't funny. Make sure it gets removed." He hung up and began boarding for his last flight.

27

HOME, SWEET HOME. Crowley sighed when he pulled up to the café late that Wednesday evening. He had only been gone for two days but felt like he had aged years in that span of time.

A light was still on in the kitchen, so he unlocked the door and made his way inside. He was surprised to find Lulu and not Leah. He grabbed the little lady up in a fierce hug and lifted her off the floor.

"I've missed you, old lady," he said as he breathed in the comforting scent of spices that perfumed Lulu.

"Me too, my boy."

Crowley set Lulu down and looked around. "Where's Leah?"

Lulu turned the burner off under a pot of soup and turned back to stare up at him. "She's gone, Crowley. Has been since Monday night. Her Jeep is outside packed with all of her luggage, but she just abandoned it. I've been staying here in hopes she'll return for her belongings and I can talk some sense into her."

"Don't worry. I know where she's at," Crowley said as he grabbed an empty canvas bag Lulu kept on a hook. He began filling it with bottles of Gatorade, juice, a few wrapped sandwiches, and premade salads. "Can you get me a couple containers of that soup? I got a feeling she's not eaten since Sunday."

"It's actually her favorite vegetable soup," Lulu said as she pulled two containers from under the kitchen work-table and filled them with the steaming soup. "Where is she?"

"The river cabin. I checked the cameras while I was gone and saw the light on." He packed the soup and some wheat crackers in another canvas bag.

"Humph. I rode out there but didn't see any sign of her. How'd the trip go?"

Crowley gathered the bags and shook his head despairingly. "The monster died of a heart attack—not by Leah."

"That's such a relief." Lulu sighed.

"She lost a baby, Lulu," he whispered in anguish as he rubbed the back of his neck.

Lulu nodded.

"You knew?"

"I put the signs and symptoms together when she arrived last November."

"Why didn't you tell me?"

"Her story ain't mine to tell, my boy. You know that. Plus, would you really have wanted to know that then? No." Lulu placed her hand on his forearm. "Now go take care of our girl."

Crowley leaned down and placed a kiss on her cheek. He walked toward the door and said over his shoulder, "Leah's right. Ana is the only person in this town who believes in gossip."

●   ●   ●

Leah lay bundled under the covers in the same spot where she had been since late Monday night. Crowley hadn't come to find her, and she was thankful to have the seclusion. The pain she had been holding in since last fall had bubbled out with such intensity it had scared her.

The dark sky had just opened up outside and was mourning in a roaring downpour. Sheets of rain pricked the tin roof in a somber melody.

Leah was dozing when she felt a presence by the bed. Trembling, she peeked from the edge of the blanket. "What are you doing here?" she asked in a voice so rusty it sounded like it had been left out in the rain.

"It's my cabin. What are *you* doing here?"

"Hiding. Waiting on the cops to show up. Are they with you?"

"No. Just me." Crowley turned to leave the room. "I've brought food and Gatorade. I'll be in the kitchen when you're ready to join me." He stopped at the doorway. "Leah, Brent died of a massive heart attack. Not by anything you did." He left her alone, closing the door quietly behind him.

Shock and relief mixed about as well as oil and vinegar as Leah tried to grasp hold of it all. She didn't know quite how she felt in that moment. The nightmare of Brent's death was over, but it had come at a great cost. She now knew she wasn't responsible for his death, but she still felt the weight of guilt for losing her baby girl.

$$\bullet \quad \bullet \quad \bullet$$

Crowley sat at the dining room table, where he had eaten his container of soup, a salad, a sandwich, and half a dozen peanut butter cookies before he heard Leah stir in the guest bathroom. She shuffled into the kitchen moments later, squinting at the flood of light. Her red eyes were rimmed with dark circles. Her curly hair hung in a dull tangle, and she was still in the clothes he last saw her wearing on Monday. Crowley thought she looked pale and maybe a bit dehydrated.

Leah sat opposite of him and accepted a bottle of Gatorade he had waiting for her. She drank the entire bottle. He walked over to the microwave. "Lulu made your favorite vegetable soup. I was hoping for chili, but I guess we can see who her favorite really is," he said with a smile, but she didn't respond. He placed the warmed soup in front of her and handed her a spoon.

Leah only took a few bites and pushed the container away. She grabbed another bottle of sports drink and headed to the covered porch. She sat in a rocking chair and watched the rain dance off the top of the dark river.

Crowley joined her. He tucked a quilt over her before turning on a small lamp beside her rocking chair. He knelt in front of her and waited until she met his gaze. "I love you, Leah."

He watched as she shook her head in short jerks and a tear trickled down her face. He stood and took the rocking chair beside her, and he reached over to hold her shaky hand. They sat in silence, listening to the rhythm of the rain as it cried over the bank and river.

He reluctantly reached into his pocket to pull out his phone, knowing he had to break her even more before they could start to heal. He pulled up the photos and handed her the phone.

Leah gazed in confusion, then understanding, at the image on his phone.

"I went straight to Washington on Tuesday morning. Then I spent most of today in Nebraska with your nurse, Mona." He paused, waiting for a reaction. "She took good care of your baby, as she promised."

"Mona," Leah repeated. "I couldn't remember her

name." She dropped the phone in her lap as her body began to tremble and a gut-wrenching sob pushed past her lips. Her pain was so raw that it sliced right through him.

He couldn't take it any longer. He gathered her in his arms, tucked the quilt back around her, and rocked her in his lap. Feeling helpless, Crowley cried and mourned along with her. She quieted a bit at some point when the rain finally decided to subside. Crowley took that moment to explain the fund set up in honor of her and the baby, sending her into another wave of sobbing, soaking through the shoulder of his shirt.

Leah cried herself out and fell into a restless sleep around midnight. Crowley carried her to his bed but couldn't bring himself to let go, so he crawled in beside her and cradled her in his arms. As he brushed his fingers through her tangled hair, he thanked God for allowing Leah to weather the storm her life had served. Holding her protectively, he begged God to bless her with healing. As Crowley prayed, a calm washed over him, and he felt for the first time in days that he could breathe.

•   •   •

Leah awoke around four in the morning with her bladder screaming from the two bottles of Gatorade. She untwined her body from Crowley's and quietly made her way into his bathroom.

After taking care of business, she glimpsed her reflection and sighed. She had more business to take care of and couldn't put it off any longer. A thorough shower followed. She had found everything she needed under his cabinet, including a new disposable razor and an unopened toothbrush.

After about an hour of grooming, Leah stared down

at her only set of clothes, which had already been worn past clean. She tiptoed back into the bedroom and rummaged through a chest of drawers, relieved to find a fresh pair of soft cotton boxer shorts and a T-shirt. Standing in the dark room, Leah let the damp towel fall away and slipped the clothes on.

She tiptoed back to the bed, where Crowley was sprawled on his stomach with his face turned to the side. His bottom lip wasn't poking out as it did when he slept, so she knew he was awake before he even opened his eyes. She climbed onto the bed and planted a kiss in the middle of his bare shoulder blades, which produced a muffled groan from him.

Crowley smiled up at her. "I sure am glad this place has more than one bathroom. I was beginning to think I was going to have to go in there after you," he said in a husky voice full of sleep. He turned over, pulling Leah with him until she was snuggled against his chest. He ran his hand through her damp hair. "You have no idea how great my boxer shorts look on you."

Leah raised her head and pressed her lips to his as a thank-you but then delivered another out of pure love. She pulled away from his lips and whispered what she knew was absolute truth. "You're the first man I have ever loved, Crowley Mason." She pressed another kiss to his smiling lips and then repeated, "I love you."

He ran his hands along her sides and growled in aggravation.

Self-consciously, Leah froze as his hands cradled her sides. "What's wrong?"

"I can feel your ribs." He sat up and pulled her onto his lap. "I've got to feed you."

"I'm not hungry," Leah said, but her stomach betrayed her by letting out a noisy rumble.

Crowley laughed. "What was that you said?" He kissed her one last time before scooting her off his lap so he could get up.

"Where are you going?"

"To take a cold shower; then I'm going to go grab some breakfast for us," he said in a strained voice as he shut the bathroom door.

Later that morning, after the two had devoured a hearty breakfast, Crowley told Leah to go sit out on the cabin porch and keep her eyes closed.

"Are they closed?" he asked before joining her.

"Yes, but what am I waiting on?" She heard Crowley walk near her and then felt something slender leaning against her arm.

"Open your eyes."

Leah laughed at the wrapped gift, which was obviously a fishing pole. "Did you have this tucked away here just for me, or do you keep spare presents around for all your guests?"

Crowley grinned. "Nope, you're special. Actually, I had forgotten that I ordered it for you. The store gave me a reminder call while I was grabbing your suitcase out of your Jeep. I picked it up and swung by the town house to wrap it."

Leah giggled as she ran her hands along the gift wrapping that reminded her of the past Christmas. "Did I ever tell you someone snuck a Christmas tree into my apartment without me knowing?"

"That—" Crowley said between sips of coffee—"was no easy feat. Lulu told me to sneak the gifts in and put them under your tree, but when I got up there, you had no tree. I snuck back out and hauled my tree over from the town house and hid it behind the café. I waited until you headed to the park so I could drag it upstairs." He laughed. "I had a trail of tinsel and tree needles everywhere and had to hustle to get it cleaned up. I was nearly late for the caroling."

Overwhelmed, Leah laid the gift down and sat in his lap. She wrapped her arms around his neck and kissed him thoroughly. "You gave me my very first Christmas tree. I spent the night camped out under that tree, mesmerized by it." She kissed him again. "Thank you."

He rubbed her back tenderly. "I want to give you the world, Leah Allen."

Leah heard the determination in his voice and had no doubt that he would give that promise his all. She hopped up out of his lap and unwrapped the gift, revealing a glittery hot-pink and vibrant-turquoise rod and reel. "Can we go try it out?" she asked excitedly with Crowley agreeing just as enthusiastically.

The couple spent the afternoon lazing on the end of the dock, fishing as their feet dangled in the cool water.

Leah had just pulled in a hand-size fish as Crowley watched. She unhooked the fish and slowly released it back into the water. Then she placed another cricket on her hook and cast it out to tempt another fish.

Crowley nudged her with his foot. "That right there has got to be the hottest thing I've ever seen," he commented as his own pole came to life and he reeled in a fish double the size of the one Leah had just caught. He pulled his off the hook and let it go too.

Leah rolled her eyes. "Show-off."

He grinned and recast his line. "I toured the New Hope Children's Home on Tuesday. You did a remarkable job."

It amazed Leah that he had walked through her entire previous life in such a short amount of time.

"Everyone was relieved to find out you're okay." He smiled at her encouragingly.

"I bet I could name a handful who were probably a bit disappointed." She smirked as the hateful women's faces flashed through her head.

"You talking about that bunch of hens, aren't you?" Crowley asked.

"You met them?" Leah asked, and Crowley nodded his head yes. "I've always secretly referred to them as a bunch of hens clucking." They both laughed.

"I bet they fell head over their too-high heels when they saw your *GQ* self saunter in."

"I put them in their place." He looked sternly at the water.

Leah leaned over and kissed him on the cheek. "My hero."

"I met Shayna, and she served me all of your favorite donuts. Let me tell you, I ate every single delicious one of them. She says to tell you she's glad you survived and that Brent is finally dead."

It was surprising for only a split second that Shayna figured out the situation with Brent, because deep down Leah knew the young woman had noticed things were off from the comments Shayna made. Lost in those thoughts, she felt Crowley nudge her leg with his to get her attention.

"You have a small fortune waiting for you to claim in Washington too."

"I don't want any of it. Can you set it up to be donated to the children's home?" she asked as she gazed out over the river.

"I'll take care of it. I'll give Sue a call this week and start working out the legal part of it," Crowley said.

Leah looked down at her hands. "Did you meet any-one else I knew?"

"No. That was it."

"The only one you didn't meet was my doctor in Washington. I need to let her know that I'm okay," Leah whispered as she absentmindedly brushed her hand over her flat abdomen.

"We can do that tomorrow. What's her name?" Crowley rubbed her back.

"Dr. Clara Simmons."

The name reminded Crowley of something. Hopping up quickly, he hurried off to the cabin. "I'll be right back," he said over his shoulder.

Leah watched as he shuffled inside and back out in a flash, carrying her Bible.

"I thought you might want this, but the name inside threw me." He handed over the Bible and Leah flipped through the dog-eared pages.

She sniffed away tears as she smiled warmly down at the pages. "She gave me this the very day I met her. She said I needed to get to know God better. And she was absolutely right."

"Sounds like my kind of woman," Crowley said, smiling.

"You need to thank her for intoxicating me enough with her Georgia twang to the point I went in search of one for myself." Leah smiled at the memory of Dr. Simmons with her rich Southern roots.

"I'll send her a vanload of roses and chocolates for sending you to me."

"God sent me here. He just used her to point me in the right direction."

"Amen," Crowley stated proudly as he wrapped an arm around her shoulders. "I'm glad we're finally all on the same page about that."

28

It was just before dawn on Sunday morning; Leah lay snuggled under her chenille blanket in her bed. A quiet knock on the door sent a smile to her lips. She wrapped a light throw blanket over her shoulders and padded to the front door. Knowing who it was, she opened the door and met the gaze of those ocean-blue eyes.

Crowley wasted no time pulling her close. "You're taking the place of my addiction to sweets, Miss Leah. You make my mouth water," he whispered as he skimmed his nose along the sensitive skin of her neck.

"You say that a lot. Tell me, Mr. Crowley, when was the first time I made your mouth water?" she asked as he brushed kisses along her jaw.

He pulled back enough to meet her eyes before answering. "The first time my mouth watered over you, my fine lady, was during the ice storm. I came in after shooting fireworks and stole me a kiss right off that sweet cheek of yours." He smiled and placed his palm on the cheek in question.

"No way. I was getting over the flu." She looked at him doubtfully.

"Believe it. I knew right then and there."

"What did you know?" she asked.

He ignored the question. "Would you please accompany me on a walk?"

She let the question go and agreed. Crowley stole a quick kiss before agreeing to meet her downstairs.

Ten minutes later, she was dressed in a soft-yellow summer dress with her hair tamed as best she could. She found Crowley sitting on a bench outside the café. It was the very same bench he had been stretched out on the first time she met him.

She strolled up behind him and placed a kiss on the back of his neck. "Good morning."

"Yes, ma'am. That it is." He smiled appreciatively as he took her in from head to toe before meeting her eyes. "You look delicious."

Leah laughed. "Stop flirting with me and tell me where you're taking me, sir."

Crowley stood and took her hand in his massive one. "I'd like to show you the sunrise at the plantation. It's quite spectacular to see how the sun rays dance through the oak trees."

"I'd love to see that," she said as they continued walking hand in hand.

Crowley led her through the gate and stopped halfway up the drive. The sun was beginning to peek through the trees. Before long the couple was treated to the breathtaking sunrise. The rays partook in a magical dance with the ancient oak trees in such a way it made Leah gasp in awe.

He leaned close and whispered, "Welcome to a new day."

"Thank you for inviting me," she replied.

Crowley led her closer to the house and stopped near the front steps. "Leah, this plantation has been in my family for many generations. My name goes back to at least four of them. My ancestors believed in a strong family bond and values. I want to continue that legacy. I helped rebuild this house hoping God would bless me with a wife who would help me fill it up with family. I just never dreamt it would take him so long to send you to me. He made it clear to me during that ice storm you were finally home."

Crowley pulled a delicate silver and diamond ring out of his pocket. "This ring has been passed down in my family, just as this plantation has. It was my mother's." The muscles in his neck flexed as he met Leah's watery gaze. "Leah, will you do me the honor of becoming my wife for the rest of my life?"

She nodded. "Yes." She lifted a trembling hand to accept the ring while blinking back tears. Never did she think such a man as Crowley Mason existed, much less that he might one day be hers.

Crowley slid the antique ring on her finger. Then he pressed his lips to it. He gathered her in his arms before taking his lips to hers.

●　　●　　●

The wedding followed within one month of the proposal. Crowley said he had no patience when it came to starting his life with Leah, and honestly, he was tired of cold showers. The couple married right in the front yard of the plantation, with the groom wearing new leather flip-flops with his suit. The bride was in an antique lace gown and the highest of heels she could find.

It was a daylong event with the entire town showing up to celebrate. Intricate flower garlands of honeysuckle and peonies draped from the big oak trees and seemed to dance right along with the jovial guests. A scrumptious wedding cake prepared by Nate accompanied the Southern spread prepared by Lulu. The guests ate and danced in merriment throughout the day as they celebrated the new life beginning for the Masons.

Long after the guests left that evening, the new couple swung in the porch swing and reflected on the wonder of the wedding celebration. The crickets were beginning to welcome the night when the groom finally stood and swooped his bride up in his arms.

"Are you ready to go *home*, Mrs. Mason?" he asked his lovely wife as he walked her to the front door.

"Absolutely, Mr. Mason," Leah said as she placed lazy kisses along his neck.

With that, he carried his new bride over the threshold of their home.

Epilogue

TWELVE YEARS AND A WHOLE LOT OF HAPPINESS
LATER

Leah stood in the formal living room of the plantation home with a laundry basket planted on her hip, staring at the large portrait hanging over the fireplace mantel. A smiling couple sat in a vintage canoe with fishing poles in hand. It was from their wedding day. A photographer wanted to capture them on the river behind the plantation. Crowley had agreed to the whole photo shoot after the photographer promised to take some with their fishing poles.

Shouts brought Leah out of her reminiscing. "Momma! Momma!" the twins whined in unison.

Leah looked back to find her six-year-old girls rushing toward her. "Yes?"

"CJ won't play tea party with us!" Layla and Lola looked up at her with identical ocean eyes just like their father's.

Their eleven-year-old brother, Crowley J. Mason V, walked up behind them with a look of pure misery on his face. The look wasn't surprising since his little sisters tended to worry him to no end. At only eleven, the kid was nearly as tall as his momma. No doubt he would top out around the same height as his dad. This meek boy was the finest wedding gift ever received, arriving almost nine months exactly after his parents' wedding.

Leah restrained the laugh trying to escape her lips, for the sake of her son. "Girls, it's almost time for your daddy. Why don't you go make him a special snack?"

"Yay!" They scurried into the kitchen with the tea party instantly forgotten.

CJ walked up to his momma and placed a kiss on her cheek. "Thanks, Momma. Here, let me put the laundry away for you," he said as he pulled the basket into his arms.

"My sweet boy, thank you."

As she watched her oldest son head upstairs, Leah heard, before seeing, two race car drivers round the corner. Justin was pushing little Gabe in a wagon at record speed as the toddler held on to the handle while making wild car noises.

Justin was a nine-year-old bundle of energy who seemed to never give out. This was a great thing since he enjoyed running after his three-year-old brother, Gabriel Allen Mason, almost nonstop.

"Whoa there, sir!" Leah raised her hands to stop the speed demons. Justin came to an abrupt stop in front of her. Leah dug out a wipe she had tucked in her skirt pocket, ready to ambush when the time came. She quickly darted her hand out to clean today's lunch off her toddler's face before he could protest.

"No, Mommy. Gotta go!" Gabe squealed as he tried to maneuver out of her grasp. "We gotta dwive!" Leah released him, and the two boys took off again.

She turned her gaze back to the black-and-white portrait with a grin. Her life couldn't get any sweeter. As she thought this, warm hands worked their way under her blouse as she was pulled into a strong, broad chest.

"You make my mouth water, woman," Crowley said playfully into his wife's ear as his hands caressed her abdomen.

She pushed her rounding belly into his gentle hands. "Smooth talking like that, my husband, is the reason I stay in this shape." The baby kicked at that moment as if to emphasize her momma's point.

Lydia was scheduled to arrive in just a few short weeks, topping the Mason children's total at a whopping six.

"There's nothing sexier than my beautiful bride round with growing my family," he said as he nuzzled her ear.

The twins rushed in with their daddy's snack of homemade granola bars slathered in natural peanut butter and sprinkled with raisins. "Look what we made you, Daddy!" Lola said in delight.

Crowley released his bride and bent down to accept their offering. He crammed a huge bite in his mouth and started chewing playfully. "Yummy. Thanks, my two princesses." He winked, causing them to giggle.

The race car drivers also zoomed into the scene to celebrate their daddy's arrival. Crowley had been upstate for the past few days, stuck in a courtroom, and his family had missed him considerably.

Crowley shared a bite of the granola bar with his eagerly waiting toddler. Leah grimaced as little Gabe smeared peanut butter across his chubby cheeks. She swiped a stray raisin off the plate and popped it into her mouth, trying to ignore his mess.

"How'd it go?" she asked.

"We won, of course," he said with a smug grin. "We need to celebrate." He looked around, amused, as the kids cheered at his suggestion.

"How 'bout some fishing to celebrate?" CJ said as he descended the stairs.

"That's a great idea. Everyone needs to go get their fishing gear!" their dad said excitedly and watched as the children scattered to retrieve their hats and flip-flops. He turned toward the stairs to go change out of his suit when he noticed Leah on his heels. He stopped to look at her. "Where you going, ma'am?"

"To change into my fishing gear."

He wrapped his arms around her. "Why don't you just stay here and rest awhile?" She pouted, pushing out her bottom lip in protest, and he leaned forward to bite at it playfully. "Lydia is going to be here soon. You know you need to take breaks now while you still have the chance."

"Fine. I'll rest as long as you promise to catch me a river monster."

"I'll do my best." He gave her a kiss and began heading upstairs to change, with Leah still on his heels. He turned to give her a questioning look.

"Just going to go take in the view of my handsome lawyer changing into my charming fisherman," she whispered.

Crowley grinned. "Well, hurry up then before the troops get restless," he said as he hastily took two steps at a time.

A half hour later, Leah was propped up on a lounge chair in the shade, watching her crowd head out to the river with fishing poles in hand. Five children, with nearly white-blond hair that curled every which way as their momma's did, accompanied their gentle giant of a dad. Crowley was carrying little Gabe in one arm while holding one of the twins' hands in the other. Every so often he would lean down to say something to the other twin, sending her into a fit of giggles.

"Oh, how I love that man of mine," Leah declared quietly just as her phone vibrated in her pocket. She pulled it out and smiled at the name flashing on the screen before answering. "Hey, Momma."

"Hey, sweet girl. Has our boy made it home yet?" Lulu asked.

"Yes, ma'am. He's celebrating with our babies at the river," Leah said.

"That's good. How's the café?"

"Good. The new girl started today. I think she's gonna work out great. Jessup stopped by and fixed the back grill element."

"Starting Monday, I'm taking over your duties for a while. Our Lydia will be here soon and you need time to prepare."

"Okay." Leah grinned, remembering how she learned after a few baby rounds that there was no use in arguing.

"Supper will be ready by six. See y'all in a little while. Love you."

"Love you too, Momma," Leah said before hanging up.

Lulu had surprised her the following Christmas after the wedding by legally adopting Leah as her daughter. She also retired, saying she would need more time with her grandbabies. Leah gladly took over the café.

Smiling, Leah put the phone away and looked back at her family. They had stopped, and Crowley was crouched down, listening to a now-standing Gabe. They both looked back at Leah. Crowley nodded and the little boy raced back to his momma.

"What's the matter, baby?" Leah asked as he climbed into her lap.

"I wanted you."

"You did?" Leah asked as she brushed a sweaty white curl off his forehead. Lulu often liked to say that God used up so much color in them Mason young'uns' eyes that he didn't have any left over for their hair.

Gabe nodded as he gathered his momma's scarred palm in his chubby ones. "Mommy, why's everybody always kissing you here?" He pointed at the scar.

Crowley had kissed that palm so often that each child eventually asked the same question as her toddler now did.

"They are kissing my boo-boo away," she said.

He studied the scar for a moment before guiding it to his sticky little lips and placing his own kiss there. He looked up at his momma and smiled. "Aw better."

"Yes it is, my sweet boy." Leah's eyes filled with happy tears. The tenderness Crowley began on that night of her thirtieth birthday had trickled down with each one of their children. He had taken such an ugly scar with an ugly past and made it something exceptional. There was no way Leah could ever look down at that scar and not see the millions of precious kisses that had been placed there.

Leah was so thankful for the healing God had graciously granted her— taking her ugly past and blessing her with an exceptional life beyond those wounds.

With enough love, scars can completely heal.

"Heal me, LORD, and I will be healed;
    save me and I will be saved,
    for you are the one I praise."
JEREMIAH 17:14

TURN THE PAGE

FOR A PREVIEW OF

BEACH HAVEN,

BOOK ONE IN

T. I. LOWE'S CAROLINA

COAST SERIES.

In stores and online summer 2020

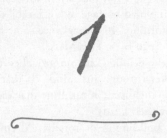

WEAVING THROUGH a jungle of the most outlandish antiques he'd ever come across, Lincoln Cole found himself dumbfounded and intrigued at the same time. Surrounded by unusually dressed pieces of furniture, he did a three sixty and scratched at the scruff on his cheek. The scruff indicated he was more than a few days past needing a shave, but the rebellion that had taken root in him since the injury he sustained in Syria had overruled grooming protocol that morning. Waking up from the recurring nightmare often left him too raw to focus on anything much. He had managed a shower and a fresh change of clothes before calling it good enough.

A whimsical feminine humming somehow found its way to him as he suppressed the limp trying to assert itself in his left leg and hobbled another few steps forward. Although it was a sunny day, his leg was telling him it wouldn't last for very long.

Nothing good ever lasts long. . . .

Lincoln huffed in frustration over his own thoughts and stood partially hidden in a section of old desks. Blinking a few times, he scrutinized the various tables and chairs suspended from the ceiling. A few had been converted into light fixtures, while the rest looked like they were being held hostage by thick cables.

"Good morning." A cheery voice came from behind him. "Welcome to Bless This Mess."

Eyes on the ceiling, Lincoln grouched out the first thing to flicker through his mind. "Is that even safe?" He pointed to the pieces of furniture that appeared to be floating above their heads.

"Oh yes. Building inspectors have deemed my mess safe." The woman's laughter-filled voice finally had Lincoln turning in her direction.

Peering at him from the other side of a wooden hutch that had been transformed into a bathroom vanity was a sprite of a woman with the wildest head of golden-red curls he'd ever seen. The tips were lighter, as if the sun had reached down and stolen their color. She closely resembled the mosaic fairy he'd seen on the outside of the building.

Clearing his throat, he offered a curt "Good."

A smile began to blossom across the woman's face as she smoothed her flowy blouse with a petite hand, causing a gaudy collection of bracelets to clang against one another.

Lincoln eyed her, assessing her as he'd been trained to do in the military. He measured her no bigger than a minute and figured he could apprehend her with one hand tied behind his back. But he cataloged those big green eyes of hers as her secret weapon. They sparkled, but that wasn't what set off the warning bells. No, those eyes were watching him way too closely and had already seen way more than they should.

Assessment complete, he began slowly to back away.

"I have the perfect piece for you." She held an index finger in the air, halting his attempted retreat. She skipped off in the opposite direction, sending the spirals of soft red and blonde hair into a dance around her head. "I'm Opal, by the way," she said over her shoulder.

He stood watching her until she disappeared from sight. "I didn't come here for furniture." He could hear banging and clattering from his two o'clock, giving away her location.

"Oh, that's okay. This piece was meant for you, nonetheless, so I insist on you taking it." She sounded like she was struggling with something.

Sighing, Lincoln looked at the craziness on the ceiling one last time before walking through the maze to find her. He stopped cold in his tracks when he found her sitting on a soldier's footlocker.

"I found this on a junking trip last year." Opal ran her hand over the thick gray cushion that had been fitted on the top. It reminded Lincoln of a military issue wool coat. "For some reason, I just knew it needed to be transformed into a bench seat. Possibly for an entry area, where someone can sit and put on their shoes. Or maybe at the foot of a bed." She swung her feet back and forth, looking like a little kid. Flip-flops peeked from the edges of her fraying bell-bottom jeans.

Ignoring for the moment the question of where she found such an odd pair of jeans, Lincoln crossed his arms and eyed the piece suspiciously. "Why'd you make it so tall?" His eyes dropped to the thick wooden spindles she'd used for legs, which were painted a neutral gray to coordinate with the creamy beige used on the trunk. It was tasteful and showed that she'd put a lot of thought into the piece, even re-stenciling the ID number along the front side in the same gray as the legs.

"I had a feeling the owner would need the extra leg

space. What are you, six-four?" She gave him a swift once-over.

Six-five. "Close enough."

She smiled. "If you're not here for furniture, then what are you here for?"

Lincoln moved his eyes away from the peculiar woman and swept them over the menagerie of furniture pieces while rubbing a hand through his hair. He was several months past due for a haircut, another ritual he'd allowed to die right along with his military career.

After giving her question some thought, he answered honestly, "I'm not sure." He turned and began moving away as quick as his aching leg would carry him.

"You forgot your bench," Opal called. "And you didn't even introduce yourself."

Her petitions did nothing to slow his already-sluggish getaway. He kept right on going until he was piled back into his Jeep and heading down the beachfront road.

"Smooth, Cole. Real smooth." He growled and released one tight-fisted pound against the steering wheel.

Between the throb in his knee and the unsettling encounter with the store's owner, all he wanted to do was go back to his beach cottage and hide. He'd had enough of feeling like he no longer fit in anywhere.

The doctors had done the best they could with his knee, putting in enough hardware to make him part cyborg, but no bolt or pin could reconstruct his destroyed life.

Discussion Questions

1. *Lulu's Café* is not only the book's title but a setting central to the novel. What role does the café play in the plot?

2. *Donuts . . . Donuts make everything better!* Leah turns to food for comfort and Jessup turns to alcohol. Leah was judged for her weight gain, but she herself turns around and judges Jessup. In what ways is this a common practice in our society? Why is that?

3. Leah feels trapped by her abusive husband, Brent, and believes she has no one to turn to. What advice would you have given her? How did reading this book give you a new or better understanding of domestic abuse?

4. Discuss the roles of the significant people Leah meets on her life's journey, such as Shayna, the young woman at the donut shop; Dr. Simmons, the obstetrician who gives her a Bible and promises to pray for her; Mona, the nurse in Lincoln; Gina, the hairdresser in Chattanooga; and of course Lulu. Have you ever encountered someone like this at a key point in your life?

5. What factors caused Leah to marry Brent Sadler? Years later, what draws her to Crowley Mason? Compare and contrast the two characters. What steps can you take to make wise relationship choices?

6. Food is a common theme throughout *Lulu's Café*. What were some of your favorite meals in the book?

7. The author paints vivid pictures throughout the book with her descriptive narratives. What was your favorite descriptive scene? Why?

8. What passages from the book especially stand out to you? Why did they make such an impression?

9. There's a fine line between sharing too much information in a book and allowing readers some freedom to fill in the blanks as they see fit. Was there a part of the story where you wish the author had shared more?

10. Everyone needs a Lulu, a generous and loving person who seeks out people to help. Do you know a Lulu? How can you try to be a Lulu?

A Note from
the Author

CHRISTMAS IS A TIME to celebrate the birth of our Savior, but Christmas 2011 is one I am ashamed to admit I did not celebrate. I began battling the most treacherous storm of my life during this season.

Sitting by my mom's side in an unfamiliar cancer center, I heard words so foreign to me I had to have the doctor repeat them and then spell them for me—"small cell carcinoma lung cancer." From the doctor's grim expression and cautious words, my mom and I knew she had been handed a death sentence.

I armed myself with research and set out to stand by my mom through rounds of radiation, chemotherapy, blood transfusions, and a barrage of tests and paperwork.

I prayed without ceasing, "Please, God. Please heal Momma."

While I begged God for a miracle, a story began to take root in my heart that became my creative outlet when the reality of losing my mom was too great a burden to bear.

During endless treatments, I shared some of the story with my mom. She made me promise to share it with the world. And I agreed that one day I would, but not right then. At that point, our focus had to be her and her healing.

In spring 2013, God answered my prayer, but not in the way I had envisioned. Rather than healing my mom's body, he healed her soul, freeing her from the abusive past and sinful life that had held her captive for far too long. That healing was the most precious gift I had received since the birth of my children, for my mom had suffered greatly long before the cancer invaded.

In May 2013, *Lulu's Café* was completed. I put the manuscript away for safekeeping and set out to help my mom get her affairs in order before the cancer robbed her of the ability to make decisions. Yes, the cruel disease had rebelled against treatments and had spread.

In summer 2013, I felt devastating pain and anguish I never knew could exist. I had to say good-bye to my mom, and selfishly, I was not ready. Watching her suffer and fade rendered me broken and defeated.

As I held her fragile body during the early evening of September 19, 2013, my mom took her last breath on earth, and I felt my own breath leave me in acute grief.

I fell into that grief for several months, not knowing how to resurface. Life kept going without me. My prayers were now for my own healing, for my heart was broken. The past three years had been all about fighting my mom's cancer, and now that the battle was over, I felt lost. I begged God to help me move on.

Finally in January 2014, God said it was time to share *Lulu's Café*. I was scared and didn't feel worthy to share it, but I had made my mom a promise. And I intended on keeping it. Through honoring the memory of my mom and through the strength of my heavenly Father, my broken heart slowly began to heal. I know it will not completely heal while I'm still on this earth, but one day . . .

Since sharing *Lulu's Café*, an abundance of stories have knocked on my heart's door and asked to be shared also. They are not perfect stories, for I am not a perfect woman. But as long as God keeps giving me these stories, I promise to share them.

Thank you for reading and helping me keep my promise to my mom.

Lulu's Café Playlist

"Fly Away" by Lenny Kravitz
"Better Man" by Pearl Jam
"Lightning Crashes" by Live
"The Joker" by the Steve Miller Band
"Magic Carpet Ride" by Steppenwolf
"Say Hey (I Love You)" by Michael Franti & Spearhead
"Her Diamonds" by Rob Thomas
"Born Again" by Third Day
"Home" by Phillip Phillips
"Walking On Water" by Needtobreathe

Acknowledgments

YEARS HAVE PASSED since *Lulu's Café* was first independently published, but I've felt in my heart for some time that there was so much more God had planned for this book. That feeling of his not being finished with Lulu was confirmed through email and phone correspondence with my agent, Danielle Egan Miller, from Browne & Miller Literary Associates, and Karen Watson and Jan Stob from Tyndale House Publishers. Thank you, ladies, for taking a chance on me and my stories. Hoping I make you proud.

To my friends and family for supporting me in this dream. Without you, it wouldn't have come true. Thank you for believing in me.

My Lowe Bunch—Bernie, Nate, and Lydia Lu—I love you to the moon and back plus one million! You not only supported this dream of mine, but you took it on as your own. Thank you for going on this writing journey with me.

To Christy Allen, for always having my back. You know I love you to the moon and back also.

In the beginning, when I wasn't sure about my ability to write, my stepmom, Brenda, my daddy, Jerry Stevens, and my in-laws, Kimber and Frank Healy, believed in me. Thank you.

Thanks to my church family at Bethlehem Baptist Church. Y'all lifted up many prayers on my behalf and for God's will to be done with this writing journey. We asked and he answered. Amen!

And to Teresa Moise, my mentor and running partner. Your enthusiasm about my dream gave me the courage to take that first leap! And your pep talks have made me continue to take those leaps even when they feel like mountains.

To Lynn and Kevin Edge for having me on your prayer mirror. Love y'all more than I can say.

Life isn't always sunshine and rainbows. Jennifer Strickland and Trina Cooke, thank you for showing up on the stormy days with a shoulder at the ready for me to cry on and for celebrating with me on the sunny ones. Good or bad, you are there, and that means the world to me.

My author-sister and writing partner in crime, Christina Coryell. Without your advice and messages of encouragement along the way, who knows where I'd be in this journey? Probably in a ditch, with little drive to get out of it. When moments of weakness crept up and I said I didn't want to do this anymore, you said to do it anyway.

A special thank-you to the Loris Library and my little hometown for always making me feel at home and for supporting my dream with encouraging words and by reading my stories.

Confession: I write even though I don't exactly know how. I do okay with spinning a tale, but it's the proper stuff I'm talking about. I've basically winged it up to this point, by reading lots and lots of books and studying blogs to figure out how to do this thing called writing. Yes, I have a long way to go, but the drive to share stories with y'all keeps me working at it. Now that I am partnering with Tyndale House, I have a superwoman on my side who is also known as my editor. Kathy Olson, you are a gift straight from God. Thank you for helping me polish *Lulu's Café*.

Above all, I want to thank my heavenly Father for the opportunities he blesses me with. Just hope I honor him in all I do.

About the Author

TONYA "T. I." LOWE is a native of coastal South Carolina. She attended Coastal Carolina University and the University of Tennessee at Chattanooga, where she majored in psychology but excelled in creative writing. Go figure. Writing was always a dream, and she finally took a leap of faith in 2014 and independently published her first novel, *Lulu's Café*, which quickly became a bestseller. Now the author of ten published novels with hundreds of thousands of copies sold, she knows she's just getting started and has many more stories to tell. A wife and mother who's active in her church community, she resides near Myrtle Beach, South Carolina, with her family.

TYNDALE HOUSE PUBLISHERS
IS CRAZY4FICTION!

Fiction that entertains and inspires

Get to know us! Become a member of the Crazy4Fiction
community. Whether you read our blog, like us on
Facebook, follow us on Twitter, or receive our e-newsletter,
you're sure to get the latest news on the best in Christian
fiction. You might even win something along the way!

JOIN IN THE FUN TODAY.

 www.crazy4fiction.com

 Crazy4Fiction

 @Crazy4Fiction